A WILFUL MISUNDERSTANDING

A PRIDE & PREJUDICE VARIATION

AMY D'ORAZIO

Quills & Quartos
PUBLISHING

Edited by Gail Warner and Julie Cooper

Cover Design by Cloudcat Design

ISBN 978-1-951033-54-5 (ebook) and 978-1-951033-55-2 (paperback)

For my darling husband

TABLE OF CONTENTS

PROLOGUE

1814, Park Street Books, Weymouth

THE SOUND OF HIS VOICE MADE HER STIFFEN WITH SHOCK. SHE had the book she intended to purchase in her hand, and she clutched it to her bosom, panic causing her heart to race.

He asked the proprietor for a book. *The History of Little Goody Two Shoes*—a children's book, what did he want with that?—but it did not signify, all she knew was that she needed to escape.

"This way, sir," said Mr Richie, the proprietor, and Elizabeth knew an immediate escape was paramount.

Elizabeth wound around the shelf on soundless feet, quietly passing the point where Darcy might have glanced up and seen her; thankfully, he had his head down examining the book in his hands and as a result, saw nothing.

Elizabeth scarcely breathed as she crossed the open section of floor, careful to avoid the board she knew had a tendency to squeak. Belatedly, she realised she still had the book in her hand and gingerly laid it upon the counter, resolving to purchase it some other day. Darcy's head remained in his book, his back to his fleeing wife.

For a brief moment, she ached, seeing that chestnut curl between his hat and collar, wishing he was purchasing a book for their son, wishing she could go to him and slip her hand in his arm. But a quick shake of her head dispelled that foolishness. *Get out now!* she ordered herself.

There was a bell on the door, but Elizabeth knew it would not jangle if she opened it slowly. Inch by excruciating inch, she pressed the door, her mind begging the bell to remain silent, until it opened just enough for her to slip through.

Then, just as a successful escape was nigh, Mr Richie turned, espying her. "Good day, Mrs Elizabeth!" he called out loudly.

Elizabeth jumped at his cry, inadvertently hitting the door, which flew the rest of the way open with a raucous jangle. She glanced over her shoulder where Darcy had looked up from the book. His gaze locked on hers immediately.

"Elizabeth!" He cried out, dropping the book to the floor with a loud crash.

As fast as she could, Elizabeth ran.

ONE

October 1811

THE MOMENT HE SAW HER AT THE ASSEMBLY IN MERYTON, HE knew he loved her.

Darcy had not wished to attend that night; in fact, he had been quite disgruntled to find himself at such an undistinguished gathering. His friend Bingley was delighted as usual, always apt to approve of everything and everyone he saw. Bingley had rapidly and expertly identified the most beautiful girl in the room and engaged her to dance, abandoning his two sisters, his brother, Hurst, and his friend as he immersed himself gleefully into Hertfordshire society. By the time Bingley came to him where he stood, trying to blend into the wall, and began to plague him to dance, Darcy was positively apoplectic with vexation.

However, just as he opened his mouth to deliver Bingley a pointed set down, Bingley said, "Miss Bennet is very beautiful, and I daresay her sisters are as well. Look over there; one of her sisters sits even now. You should ask her to dance!"

Darcy looked over at the lady, prepared to dislike her on sight, but then he met the lady's gaze.

At that instant, it was as though she had turned a key that opened some hitherto unknown vault in his heart, a vault that contained all his deepest thoughts, dreams, and emotions. A connexion formed instantly between them, a connexion formed of love and desire and the recognition of two souls that were counterpart, one to another. In her, and only her, lay his happiness; without her, he would be doomed to be a shell of a man, relegated to a life of misery and loneliness. Dance with her? No, he did not wish to dance with her; he wished to call her his own.

He settled for the dance, and he was not disappointed. Miss Elizabeth Bennet, she was called, the second eldest of five sisters, daughter of a country squire, with little but her charms to recommend her. He cared not a bit. She was perfection; she was poised on his arm, and he intended it to be that way forevermore.

When he invited her to dance a third set with him, Miss Elizabeth suggested they should instead partake of some refreshment. So they did, sipping at cups of sweet punch and talking about anything and everything that struck them. It felt as if he had spent the entirety of his prior seven-and-twenty years half asleep, just waiting to meet her so he could truly begin to live. She laughed when he told her he was usually regarded as sombre and reserved, even taciturn, protesting he was anything but those things.

He had never been the sort to be open in his affection towards a woman, particularly not when that woman was an acquaintance of mere hours, yet it seemed the most natural thing in the world to kiss her cheek later that evening on the terrace. Her cheek...and then, somehow, in some magical way, her lips. It was brief but glorious, and when she gave him a certain impish smile, he could not help but steal another and then another.

They had just resolved to return to the party when, from the doorway, the voice of her cousin, the young Mr Philips, came forth. "Elizabeth," said he, in tones that belied his tender years, "your mother is looking for you."

"Darcy, you had a very good evening," Bingley teased as the carriage began its journey back to Netherfield.

Darcy wished to greet his statement with impassive hauteur or perhaps even a scowl but instead found his face split in two by a lunatic grin. He turned quickly, hoping his friend would not see it.

But it was not to be. Bingley nudged his brother-in-law, seated on the other side of him, with his elbow. "See that, Hurst? Darcy has fallen in love!"

"In love?" Miss Caroline Bingley, across the carriage, sniffed and raised her nose yet higher. "Impossible. Not at such an unremarkable gathering as I have just been subjected to. I declare, the nothingness of these people! I saw nothing of beauty nor elegance, and there certainly was no fashion to be had! These Bennet ladies were described as the jewels of the county, and if such is the case, why then, I must say—"

"That is enough, Miss Bingley." Darcy's censure shocked even himself. A few moments too late, he added, "Miss Bennet and Miss Elizabeth are exceedingly beautiful."

Miss Bingley paused before continuing her protests. "But the younger sisters! And the mother! They would not be received in London, I assure you."

"I have no intention of marrying the younger ones." Darcy wondered what being possessed him—an angel? A demon?—and continued to toss such unguarded words from his mouth.

Hurst, half asleep in the corner, guffawed. "That wine must have been stronger than I thought. I could swear I just heard Darcy speak of marriage."

Darcy was saved from further comment by a jolt of the carriage, which had evidently hit a rut or something in the road. The occupants within were tossed about enough to make the ladies cry out, and some moments were spent listening to indignation about the state of roads in the country. From that, the ladies discussed the myriad other things they found to dislike in Hertfordshire, and Darcy's statement was forgot.

But Bingley had not put it aside so easily. Later that evening, as the two friends tired themselves out over Bingley's billiards table, he said, "Surely, no one will insist on marriage for the sake of a kiss."

"What did you hear?" Darcy asked sharply.

With a rueful smile, Bingley shrugged. "I was standing with Miss Bennet and her mother when Mrs Bennet sent Philips to go find Miss Elizabeth."

"Who else knew of it?"

"No one," Bingley said in tones meant to reassure. "Miss Elizabeth Bennet is unharmed, I assure you, and if anyone attempts to persuade you that honour demands—"

"What if I persuade myself?" Darcy asked quietly.

Bingley's expression was nearly comical. He stood dazed and astonished until Darcy said, "Close your mouth, Bingley."

Bingley did, with a chuckle and a shake of one finger at his friend. "You know, you are so infrequently a jolly joker that I nearly believed you."

"I do not jest." Darcy set his stick down, electrified by the words that came from his lips, words he could scarce seem to control. He slowly walked to the window, staring out at the darkened countryside. Was he staring in her direction? It felt as if he were.

Bingley was staring at him—Darcy could see his incredulity reflected in the glass. "Darcy? What is this? You surely do not mean to make an offer of marriage to a woman you have known mere hours."

Darcy turned, needing a confidante, someone to speak to about the perplexing feelings that had been coursing through him since the moment he had first laid eyes upon *her*. "I cannot explain how I feel right now. It is as if sense and reason have abandoned me. All I know is that in my heart, she is mine."

Bingley chuckled uncomfortably. "This is not like you."

"No," Darcy agreed. "It is not, yet somehow, in some way, it seems more right than anything I have ever known."

Bingley studied him for a discomfiting length of time, then carefully settled his cue into the rack and walked over to his friend. From the expression on his face, Darcy knew that what was to come would surely be unbearable.

"Bingley—"

Bingley laid a gentle hand on his arm. "Is this about Miss Harper?"

"Certainly not!"

Bingley continued to speak, his hand caressing Darcy's arm as if he were consoling a lover. "Your sensibilities are no doubt in a most precarious spot, particularly as it was scarcely a month ago that your pride was wounded—"

"My pride is perfectly well, thank you." With an impatient shake of his arm, Darcy was freed of Bingley's consolation. "It has been six weeks complete, and I assure you, I am not the bacon-brained, green lad you seem to think me."

"She used you ill and with an old friend—"

"She was his victim. I cannot despise her, but neither would I marry her."

"If you will only just bide your time—"

"If I bide my time, do not bide my time, bide half of my time, the result will be the same." Darcy felt the heat of frustration prickle beneath his cravat. "Why should I not enjoy my felicity sooner?"

"Because if it is not true felicity—"

"Who says it is not? You? The townsfolk? Mr Philips?"

"I am saying, do not compound one difficulty by adding onto it another," Bingley said patiently. "You kissed her, but it need not complicate—"

"There is precious little I have done since my father died to suit myself," Darcy snapped. "I have adhered rigorously to duty and gentlemanlike conduct, and if just this once, I should like to step outside of the ranks and do as I please, then I shall. Devil take the man who tries to stop me."

With that, he turned on his heel and quit the room.

7

DARCY PRESENTED HIMSELF AT LONGBOURN AT AN EARLY HOUR the morning after the ball. He found, in a decently-stocked book room, a kindly-looking, bespectacled gentleman in the attire of a country squire who did not much concern himself with London fashions. Mr Bennet offered him coffee and was in every way an amiable host.

When they had spoken for some moments about the weather, Mr Bennet enquired, "And did you enjoy the assembly last evening?"

Darcy put his coffee cup down immediately. "Ah...yes. About that... I wish to offer my apology, sir, if I offended your daughter in any way, and I assure you that I intend to make every possible reparation to her."

"Reparation?"

"Marriage." Never before had the word tasted so delightful falling from his lips. "I shall make an offer of marriage to Miss Elizabeth."

If he believed his words would be greeted with joy or relief, he was mistaken. Mr Bennet looked merely pensive, even a bit troubled, as he sat in silence. Little did he know that Darcy, too, was well versed in the techniques of reticence and could happily sit without speaking all day if needed.

At length, Mr Bennet ceded the battle. "Sir, I am not so much steeped in country manners that I would insist on an offer of marriage for the cause of a stolen kiss. That is not to say I am happy—"

"Sir, I am not a rake." Darcy felt a strange sense of panic within him. Surely this man did not intend to deny his suit? "I am not in the habit of going about kissing young ladies, and I should never have taken such a liberty last night were my actions not accompanied by ardent love—"

Mr Bennet stopped him with a raised hand and a quizzical

brow. "You do not mean to say you are in love with my daughter? On one night's acquaintance?"

Darcy flushed hotly. He pressed his lips together to quell his frustration before saying in careful tones, "I assure you, such a notion would have seemed preposterous to me even so recently as yesterday morning. But when I met your daughter, I felt a strength of attachment hitherto unknown to me."

Mr Bennet sighed and rubbed a hand over his forehead. "It is called lust, Mr Darcy, and although many men have married for it, I myself cannot recommend the practice."

Darcy shot to his feet in an instant. "I shall not sit idly by and hear such insults when—"

Mr Bennet rose, and although he was not a large man, he did manage to make Darcy feel smaller with a quiet but authoritative, "Sit down, Mr Darcy."

Slowly, with his eyes trained on the man who had become something of an adversary, Darcy did.

"I intend no disrespect to my own child, I assure you. If anything, Elizabeth is my…well, she is my treasure. I love all my daughters, but she has always been especially dear to my heart. That is why I could not bear to see her in an unequal situation or made unhappy by a husband whose burning love too soon turned to ash."

"That would never be the case, I assure you."

"And with equal vigour, I assure you that you cannot assure me. Sir, I do not deny you. I understand your consequence and that you are the sort of man who should not be denied anything once you have deigned to ask for it. But I ask you only this: if you do indeed feel as you say, take some time to get to know one another. A very little will suffice."

HE FOUND HER IN THE DRAWING ROOM WITH MISS BENNET AT her side.

As impossible as it seemed, she was even more beautiful than she had been the evening prior. Her hair was simple and her gown suited for a morning at home, but nothing could have enticed him more completely.

"Will you walk out with me?" He was pleased to see a modest blush in reply.

"Shall I join you?" Miss Bennet asked.

"Stay where you are," Miss Elizabeth told her sister. "We shall just wander about the garden for a bit."

There were some moments while she called for her pelisse and her bonnet, during which she did not look at him. The housekeeper assisted her, and when she was suitably attired, they exited by a side door into a fine autumn morning, the sun warm and the sky blue. He offered his arm to her, and she raised her eyes to his, smiling as she placed her hand upon him.

His breath caught. It was there again, that feeling, so strong, of the truth and the strength of the attachment between them. No, he did not know her, but did a lock need to know the life history of its key before the door could be flung wide?

"I hope my father was not too difficult," she said with an impish smile. "You must presume that at least half of what he said was designed to vex you, and the other half was to give himself a laugh."

"He was quite unreasonable," he said seriously, and the smile vanished from her face.

Appearing concerned, she said, "Oh no. I did tell him that it was nothing and no one saw anything, and he should not—"

"He seemed to think I must wait to marry you. I told him I simply could not."

He had surprised her, and she drew back, looking alarmed. After a few moments, she said carefully, "Sir, I do not perceive myself injured in any way—"

"Good. But you must know—except of course you cannot because you do not know me, not yet—that I could not have taken any such liberties unless true feeling lay behind them. I have never before kissed a woman at a party, and I would not have done so last night were it not for the strange, wonderful attachment I feel to you."

He stopped and stepped in front of her, taking her hands in his. "I want to marry you, Miss Elizabeth Bennet, and not because I kissed you last night, but rather, because we are meant to be together. Our happiness lies in each other. I cannot explain how I know that, but I do."

She was shocked into silence. She stared at him, her beautiful, intelligent eyes searching him, seeking to understand. "I...I do not know what to say."

"Say you will, at the very least, consider it?"

"Very well," she said. "I shall."

TWO

November 26, 1811

CAROLINE BINGLEY'S GUT ROILED WITH ANXIETY AS HER MAID fussed about, arranging her hair. "Not like that," she hissed at the girl. "With the curl coming down my shoulder."

As she watched her maid begin again, Caroline gritted her teeth, well aware that nothing, nothing at all, had gone as planned. Not her hair, not this wretched house, and not her plans with Mr Darcy.

Before they came to Hertfordshire, it had all been falling into place—all her schemes, all her arrangements—and *he* had been the one to ask Charles whether he might accompany them to Netherfield. *He* had been the one to murmur under his breath, with occasional glances in her direction, at Hurst's house that day —that blessed day—after which Charles announced Darcy would come with them. And had not her brother given her a significant look directly after? He had, and she did not misunderstand it. She had set off shopping immediately, arriving in Netherfield with her head held high and her trunks nearly bursting.

The first days had been promising. They had walked alone

12

together at least three times, he sat beside her at dinner, and he had even read to her from his book.

And then the wretched assembly, the assembly he had not even wished to attend but had been coerced into by her brother. *Stupid Charles!* If not for that, if he had never seen that dreadful chit, Eliza...ugh! She simply could not think of it without becoming enraged.

Tonight was it. Her last opportunity with him, her last chance to dispel this nonsense in his head about marriage to some ridiculous nobody from this dreadful, unimportant little place.

ELIZABETH ENTERED NETHERFIELD PARK WITH HER SISTER beside her and her nerves doing a merry jig in her stomach. The happy anticipation of the evening had been nearly too much to bear these last days, particularly as a succession of rain had kept them all indoors. To make matters worse, she had been wholly unable to see Mr Darcy.

What was this strange madness that seemed to have afflicted them both? She was most certainly not the sort of lady to be carried away by fancy, and by all accounts, he was not prone to excess sentimentality himself. Yet here they were, in the grip of mad love, sense and reason discarded.

The times they had spent together in the last weeks had been utterly rapturous. He was a sober-minded man, almost haughty in general demeanour—but *that* side of him was only for those around them. For her, he was quite different. Serious, yes, but with a sly humour that sometimes doubled her over with laughter. They spoke of everything and anything; she told him her life story—as dull as that was—and he told her his. Nothing was hidden between them. She felt wholly herself, wholly loved, and wholly accepted for the first time in her life.

"Oh! I beg your pardon!" She had nearly run into one of the soldiers, a tall man who had come to an abrupt halt while entering the ballroom.

The gentleman, a handsome, tall man, turned around. "Steady on! I hope I did not hurt you?"

"No, no. The fault was mine."

"Not at all," he said warmly.

"Lizzy!" Kitty was immediately at her sister's side. "What are you about, nearly knocking poor Mr Wickham to the ground?"

At that moment, the musicians began to rehearse their instruments, and Elizabeth missed some of what was said. Kitty spoke over them, performing some sort of introduction. "Whitman, did you say?" Elizabeth asked loudly.

Kitty repeated it, still to no avail, and Elizabeth gave up, mentally assigning him the name 'Whitman.'

Mr Whitman said something then, his words lost in a loud wailing from the musicians who were nearly ready to begin.

"Forgive me," said Elizabeth with another quick look around her. "I cannot hear you."

Mr Whitman leant into her. "I asked whether I might persuade you to do me the honour of dancing with me."

Disappointment cascaded through her. She had wanted to open the ball with Darcy, but he was nowhere to be found. With a sigh, she smiled at Mr Whitman. "Of course. The honour is mine."

Mr Whitman leant in again. "Excellent." With a few words to Kitty—no doubt securing a dance with her later—he led Elizabeth to the floor where other couples had begun to form a set.

She was pleased to see Jane standing up with Mr Bingley. Jane caught her eye and made an expressive look down the line —their younger sister Mary was standing up with Mr Collins, their cousin. Elizabeth smothered a smile.

As the dance began, she again took a look around. Mr Darcy remained absent, and she could not imagine what might have detained him. She would ask Mr Bingley. Surely he would know the whereabouts of his missing guest.

"Miss Bennet, I hope I am not so much a bore that you already seek your avenue of escape?"

Mortified, Elizabeth comprehended her rudeness. "How thoughtless of me, sir, I do apologise. Um…I had arranged to dance with someone who appears not to be in attendance this evening, and I was wondering what became of him."

"What is his name? Perhaps I saw him earlier."

"Mr Darcy. Are you acquainted with the gentleman?"

They were turning just then so Elizabeth had only a fraction of a moment to see Mr Whitman's brows shoot upwards. When he faced her again, his countenance showed only pleasure.

"I am very well acquainted with him, in fact. I grew up on his family's estate, Pemberley."

"Oh! Then you must know him very well indeed. He has not mentioned to me that so good a friend is quartered here in Meryton."

Mr Whitman's head lowered, and he looked momentarily abashed. "No, I should imagine he might not."

Elizabeth did not press his confidence, but after a brief moment, Mr Whitman offered it. "Darcy and I have had a bit of a falling out in our later days. A tale far too common I fear—our lives as adults become so complicated."

Uneasily, Elizabeth offered, "Perhaps Mr Darcy is simply unaware that you are here. After all, he likely has a large acquaintance that he has not yet mentioned to me."

With a gallant nod, Mr Whitman said, "Let us hope that is true."

With that, the awkward moment was left. Elizabeth went on to have an enjoyable and informative conversation with Whitman about Derbyshire and Pemberley. Mr Whitman had endless amusing stories of Darcy's boyhood, as well as enchanting recollections about his home.

It was a surprise when the dance ended. It was a further surprise to see Mr Darcy at the edge of the floor, glaring at both of them fiercely. Elizabeth felt a momentary pang beholding his darkened countenance and feared she had erred in being taken in by Mr Whitman's charm.

She exited the set on the soldier's arm. Mr Darcy's glare grew more fierce and more wholly centred on Mr Whitman with each step they took towards him. Mr Whitman appeared unconcerned, smiling genially. As soon as they were in earshot, he said, "Darcy, I have been getting acquainted with your friend—"

Darcy yanked her away from the man. "Elizabeth is not my friend," Darcy spat, and she startled at the use of her Christian name. "We are engaged, and as such, she is mine to defend. And defend her I shall. Should she come to even the least harm—"

"Harm?" Mr Whitman spread his hands wide. "How might I have harmed her? It was a dance, Darcy, and in case you had not noticed, this *is* a ball."

"See that it comes to no more. In fact, stay away from her and any of her sisters, else you will answer for it. Am I clear?"

People had begun to look at them curiously, and Elizabeth placed a gentle hand on Darcy's arm. "Mr Darcy, I assure you, I am well. Mr Whitman and I—"

"Whitman? The name is Wickham, my dear," Darcy said, turning to give her a tight-lipped smile. "George Wickham."

"My apologies then, Mr Wickham," said Elizabeth with a smile in his direction. "I could not hear very well when my sister introduced us and have been calling you the wrong name."

Mr Wickham bowed and murmured something while Elizabeth turned back to Darcy. "Mr Darcy, I find myself in great need of refreshment. Will you accompany me?"

Darcy agreed, and they nodded goodbye to Mr Wickham, Elizabeth mouthing her thanks to him as they went.

They retrieved glasses of punch, and Elizabeth was quiet, seeing that Darcy's carefully controlled anger had not abated. She wondered at his announcement of their engagement—it was not true, not formally, not yet—but was unsure how to begin the conversation of all that had transpired.

"Will you come with me to some place where we might

speak privately?" Darcy asked, having quickly drained his punch. He set the glass down on a nearby tray.

"Well…I…" Elizabeth looked around her, seeing her mother and the surrounding gaggle of gossips were well occupied. "Very well." She nodded, and together, they exited the ballroom.

CAROLINE BINGLEY WATCHED MR DARCY LEAD MISS ELIZABETH from the room, unsure whether to claim victory. Her plan to detain him, to keep him from dancing the first with Eliza, had been a success. All it took was a few tears with a bout of feigned anxiety, and his sense of honour had done the rest. She could not have arranged it better, to then find Miss Elizabeth dancing with Mr Wickham, who had treated Darcy so ill during the Season.

Darcy's rage had been unmistakable. But was it enough? Would he, at last, forswear his fascination with Miss Elizabeth Bennet and see that she was exactly like every other low-born chit whose head had nothing but red coats in it?

THEY FOUND A SMALL, UNOCCUPIED SITTING ROOM ON THE second floor. Darcy opened the door for her and, once they had entered, closed it behind them.

Elizabeth turned and looked at him. To another observer, he might have appeared calm, but she already knew him better than that. Seeing the tightness of his jaw and stiffness in his posture taught her of his dismay, and although she did not understand it, instinct propelled her forwards. She crossed the few steps between them in a trice, rising on her toes to take his face in her hands and kiss him firmly on the lips.

He wrapped his arms around her, and she could feel his tension ebbing away as they continued in their embrace. "I am sorry," she murmured when she could. "I had no idea—"

"Shhh," he said against her lips. "You did nothing wrong. You have no cause to apologise."

"But you were upset, and for that, I am infinitely regretful."

"Mr Wickham and I have a complicated and contentious history." Untangling himself from her, he took her hand and led her to a settee. "I cannot recall what I told you of my history with him, but we have known each other nearly our entire lives. Mr Wickham is the son of my father's former steward at Pemberley. He was my dearest boyhood companion. His father died when he was about thirteen, and my father cared for him until he came of age, even sent him to school with me.

"While we were at school, we began to grow apart. Rather than taking advantage of the opportunities afforded him, George rarely studied and instead spent his time gambling and drinking, engaging in dalliances with servant girls, and visiting brothels—things of that sort."

Elizabeth frowned.

"I disapproved of his behaviour and did not scruple in telling him so. We began to either argue or avoid one another, and many times, my affinity to him compelled me to pay his debts or otherwise cover for his actions. This naturally led to more dissension, and before I knew it, we were estranged.

"When my father died—"

"Five years ago?"

"Yes," Darcy affirmed. "My father left him a thousand pounds and the promise of a valuable family living at Kympton when it fell vacant, as he hoped Wickham would take orders. Wickham was sorely grieved with his inheritance; evidently, he had expected more."

"Indeed?"

"He wished to live as a gentleman. To that end, he requested that I grant him, instead of the living, a sum of three thousand pounds, which I did.

"Thus, Wickham was paid and, I thought, no longer my concern." Darcy sighed and looked away. "He came to me last spring when the old rector at Kympton died. He had decided he wished for the position after all—or at least the financial assurance that came with it. I denied him, and he became very angry with me, vowing that one day the tables should be turned, and it would be I who should depend upon *his* mercy."

"How foolish. Your father—and you—owed him nothing yet gave him a great deal. He should appreciate that which was given, not despise you for failing to give more."

"I agree, but such a man cannot be made to see reason. He has already made some attempt on a lady...a lady I once admired."

"Oh, really?" Elizabeth maintained a light tone. "Pray, tell me, Mr Darcy."

With great interest, she watched her serious suitor blush scarlet then look away and clear his throat uncomfortably. "Elizabeth, I...forgive me, I do not wish to bring you discomfort in any way. Let me assure you in the most violent of terms that the lady I shall tell you about is...she was a suitable match, that is all."

Suppressing a grin, she asked gently, "And you liked her?"

Darcy studied the carpet between his feet with great determination. "She...there was some slight connexion to my aunt, Lady Matlock's family. Miss Harper is a pretty girl, very kind-hearted, and we enjoyed one another's society. She came out a bit late, already one and twenty, due to an elder sister who proved resistant to marriage, but I liked that she was older and more serious, or so I believed."

Elizabeth watched Darcy struggle with what to say of the matter. "Did you offer for her?"

He shook his head. "It had not gone so far, but my attentions were...no one could have doubted my intentions, not her, not her family. I was invited to family supper twice. It all seemed as near to settled as it could be without my part in it."

He ceased speaking then, looking unhappy, and Elizabeth laid a hand on his arm. "I see that this pains you. I am sure I can guess the rest, should you wish to—"

"No, I am not pained. I did not love her—it is nothing at all to the violence of my affection for *you*. I might have married her, we would have been content enough...but to think I might have missed out on you..." He gave a slight shudder. "I cannot imagine it. No, my darling girl, I was angry at the time, but upon reflection, I must say Wickham did me a great favour."

"It was Wickham?"

"He seduced her," Darcy said with shocking bluntness. "Ruined her."

Elizabeth inhaled sharply. "You mean they—"

"He took her as his wife." Darcy shook his head. "She believed herself in love in a way she knew she did not love me. As I said, we were merely two people who recognised we might do well for one another. For Wickham, she evidently felt...well, the way I feel for you. And of course she thought he felt likewise. Little did she know he wanted nothing more than a bite of her fortune and revenge on me."

"She is wealthy, then?"

Darcy nodded. "Indeed. I daresay that the sum her father gave Wickham to keep silent on the matter did little to diminish it. Perhaps they withheld the money until she marries. In any case, she is off in the country now, and he is here, pretending at being a soldier. But it is you I worry for. He saw, plainly, my feelings for you, and I do not doubt—"

"You forget, sir," Elizabeth said with a smile. "I am too poor to tempt a blackguard like that."

The light in Darcy's eyes changed, softened. He leant in, placing a tender kiss on her neck. "But you are so beautiful," he murmured against her skin, "you make a man not care."

Elizabeth smiled as Darcy pushed her back against the arm of the settee, his kisses growing more fervid. "What if someone comes in?" she whispered.

"Then you will have to marry me."

"You told Mr Wickham we were engaged," she said shyly.

He stopped kissing her then, raising his head to gaze at her with eyes that burnt with his want of her. She thrilled at it even as it frightened her a little. "Forgive me," he said huskily. "I spoke from my heart's desire rather than my reason."

Her heart, already thrumming, began to pound almost painfully. Could he hear it too? "It is my heart's desire as well."

"Do you mean that?"

Unable to speak, she could only nod, inducing a low chuckle from him. "Come now, Miss Bennet. I know how much you love to talk. Can you not give your suitor the words he hungers for?"

She giggled a little, then said seriously, "I have fallen in love with you, Fitzwilliam Darcy, and I would be most honoured to become your wife."

With a sigh that became a moan, he began again to kiss her neck. "Thank God for answered prayers."

OUTSIDE OF THE SMALL SITTING ROOM ON THE SECOND FLOOR, Caroline Bingley's eyes filled with enraged tears. She shoved a fist against her mouth to keep from screaming. This...*this* could not be borne. How dare this low-born chit steal the most eligible bachelor of the ton!

What she could do about it, she knew not, but something must be done. Eliza Bennet *would* pay for her transgression.

THREE

December 1811

ELIZABETH LAY SLEEPING IN THE CROOK OF DARCY'S ARM AS they entered the lane to Pemberley. Looking at her, a wave of tender emotion assailed him. Astonishing, really. He loved her when he met her, but now, having stood at the altar with her, having pledged her his troth, there was so much more. She was everything to him, and he was at times almost terrified by how much he needed her. He had hoped marriage would alleviate his hunger, at least a little, but instead he found he needed her even more. Did she love him as he did her? Did anyone love someone else the way he loved her? He thought it impossible.

He rapped on the roof of the carriage when they reached a particular spot where the house might be seen to advantage. It had snowed the night prior, and Pemberley was a shimmering white paradise, perfect for introduction to his bride.

His knocking woke her. "Are we nearly there?" she asked sleepily.

"Come see." He opened the door and waved the coachman

away, helping her down himself. Then he offered his arm, and they stood side by side, gazing out over the delightful vista.

"Your new home, Mrs Darcy." He pulled her more tightly to his side. "I have waited such a long, long time for you to be here."

Giggling, she looked up, teasing him. "Such a long time? You have only known me two months complete."

He shook his head at her. "My heart has known you forever. It was only finding you that took so long."

THE DAYS PASSED QUICKLY AT PEMBERLEY. BEFORE SHE KNEW IT, Christmas had come and gone and it was winter, heavy snow turning Pemberley into a magical winter wonderland. There was a stark beauty to the denuded trees and frozen pond that somehow fit the bold terrain that was Derbyshire. Still, Elizabeth could not imagine how much more lovely it might be come spring and summer, as the meadows softened and became verdant and the gardens came alive with colour. Autumn would be beautiful as well, with the colours and odours of the harvest surrounding her.

Her life felt like a dream, a true paradise. She still could not believe she was mistress to such a place as Pemberley, that she lived there with her perfect husband and had such daily happiness and love surrounding her.

Her morning call had taken a bit longer than expected, but for good cause. Her host was entertaining other young ladies, and they had found much to speak of among themselves. As she entered Pemberley, the housekeeper, Mrs Reynolds, came forward to assist with her pelisse, informing her, "Mr Darcy wishes you to attend him immediately in his study, Mrs Darcy."

"Tell him I must briefly refresh myself and shall visit him shortly."

A deep voice answered, "That will not do, Mrs Darcy. I

believe Mr Darcy requires your presence right away. This very instant, in fact."

She turned, seeing Darcy had come into the hall and was leaning against a door frame, giving her a light-hearted grin that instantly warmed her. "Very well, Mr Darcy."

Holding out his arm to indicate she should precede him, he then followed her to his study. He was silent as they walked along the corridor and said nothing as they entered the room, pausing to close and lock the door behind them. She turned to look at him. "What…?"

"Hush." He pulled her into his embrace. "You were gone an excessively long time." He began to kiss her passionately, his need clearly expressed by his persistent mouth and hands laying urgent claim to her.

She giggled at his amorousness. "It has been but a few hours."

"You may never, ever leave me alone that long again." His fingers fumbled with the buttons on the back of her dress, opening it.

She protested weakly amid consenting laughter, her body already trembling with desire. "We cannot do this here."

"We can," he murmured. "I have thought about it all morning and have worked out just how it will be done." He gave her a naughty smile that nearly melted her. Picking her up, he carried her to his desk, then blindly shoved his papers to the floor, laying her in their place.

"Your papers!" She meant to say more, to make him realise he might have ruined his work, damaged something important, or lost something of value, but then she forgot it completely, her mind filled with her husband.

Not so long later, he asked, caressing her back gently, "How did I manage for seven-and-twenty years without you, when now, I cannot get through even a few hours without needing you desperately?"

She turned in his arms just enough to wrap her arms around him and kiss his face. "I feel just the same."

"No more calls," he declared. "Send word to the neighbours that the Darcys will enjoy only their own society for at least the next year, possibly two." She giggled at the prospect and kissed his cheek.

"Silly man," she said affectionately. "My silly man."

As the weeks of winter passed, Elizabeth found more to love in her husband almost daily. They had had such a brief courtship—nay, a brief acquaintance—that there was much of him she did not know, and it thrilled her to discover him. Both were avid readers and enjoyed many spirited discussions of the books they had read, sometimes agreeing and sometimes not. He could make her laugh as no one else did, and for the first time in her remembrance, she felt that displaying her wit was acceptable, even desirable.

More important than anything, though, was how very loved she felt by him. She knew not why he had fallen for her so quickly and so completely, but she felt the assurance of her power over him. It amazed her—she, who had been always the less pretty sister, the least admired by her mother—that she had obtained the ardent devotion of such a man as Darcy.

At the end of January, Elizabeth received a letter from her dearest sister telling her that Mr Bingley had proposed. She ran to find her husband, seeing him in his favourite chair in the library, his own letter in his hand.

"You tell me first," he said with a smile.

"Jane and Bingley are getting married!"

He chuckled, moving a bit so she could sit beside him. "You are happy for her?"

"Beyond everything! And happy for us as well—now we shall all be brothers and sisters, and our children will be cousins, and we shall...do you think there are any eligible properties to be had near Pemberley? Because three days is simply too long, and perhaps if they were closer, we could—"

Laughing, he silenced her with a kiss. "When we attend the wedding, let us bring a wagon with us, and we can begin removing their belongings immediately."

"Oh you!" She poked him. "I am simply so happy for her. She had begun to think it could not happen."

"Really? Why not?"

"Well…'tis no great secret that Miss Bingley and Mrs Hurst were not in favour of the match."

"Likely they believed she did not love him."

"Likely they believed she was not fine enough for him," Elizabeth replied. "Because I should think her attachment to him was quite plain."

"Perhaps." Darcy sounded dubious. "I myself had wondered at the strength of her feelings."

"You did?"

"Her heart did not seem easily touched, and I feared that she might marry him for practical advantage."

Her joy was immediately cast down, and she stared at her husband, smarting with indignation at such a response. "Jane is not mercenary," she said calmly, if a touch coolly.

Darcy was perusing his letter again. "No," he said absently. "But she does seem to wish to please your mother, and your mother's wishes were clear."

Yes, Mrs Bennet never had been circumspect about her goal of marrying her girls to wealthy men. Still, for Darcy to think ill of Jane for it! Elizabeth rose, feeling herself about to lose her grip on her irritation. "Excuse me."

"Darling, have I upset you in some way?"

"Upset me? Oh no!" Elizabeth gave a little, bitter laugh. "Why should I be upset that you think my sister would marry your friend for prudence only? Tell me—do you think it of me too?"

"In my darker hours, yes, I do."

A WILFUL MISUNDERSTANDING

Elizabeth gasped. After standing stupidly agape for a moment, she turned, intending to run off to who knew where. Before she could, he stopped her.

"Pray understand, I do not think it a mark on your character —it is only my own fears that make me think so."

"What cause have I given you to fear anything?" she cried, turning to face him. "What cause has Jane given you to doubt her attachment to your friend?"

"None," he said, soothingly. "I am not saying they are reasonable doubts, only those sorts of worries that come about late in the evening or when I have had too much port. I begin to ask myself whether you could really love me—and I fear my friend having the same dreadful moments."

"Jane loves Mr Bingley. Categorically and with nothing held back. Just as I love you."

"I am sorry, very sorry, for my doubt."

"But what is required for you to know I love you? What must happen for those doubts to be slain?"

He pulled her to his chest then. "I know not, but trust me when I say that it is nothing for you. You are the perfect wife, and I need only to accustom myself to my good fortune."

CAROLINE BINGLEY SIGHED AT THE CARD HANDED TO HER. IT was one thing to serve as Georgiana Darcy's confidante whilst attempting to secure the affections of her brother, it was quite enough to do it for no reason whatsoever.

Still, she would make of it what she could. The anger she felt towards Eliza Bennet had not abated. Standing there in the drawing room at Longbourn, part of a wedding breakfast that never should have been, she had seethed with resentment watching Eliza prance about, waving her left hand in the face of any and all. Her gown was an absolute crime, being the least fashionable thing Caroline had ever seen, and her hair was too curly, too simple, to even be termed a proper coiffure. The food

27

was good—she had to grant the Bennets that much—but who could eat in the face of such travesty?

Not that it mattered to Darcy. He stood there looking as though he was about to tear off his new wife's gown and take her right there on the dining room table. Caroline sniffed. Poor Darcy. Caught up in lust, and now his life was ruined.

Miss Darcy entered the room, and Caroline stood, cooing her greetings. The two ladies drank tea and chatted for some time, but Caroline could see there was something on Miss Darcy's mind. She hoped the girl would soon get to it.

"Miss Bingley?" Miss Darcy set her tea cup down on the table in front of the two ladies. "I…I wish to speak to you…that is, you will recall the…the man I told you about?"

"The servant boy?" Caroline asked, with a little smirk. "Yes. I do hope you have gotten rid of him."

"W-well…not a servant. Not exactly. He was educated as a gentleman."

"Hmm."

"And he is a lieutenant in the army. So…so he now has the status of a gentleman too."

Caroline thought it a rather useless distinction. A gentleman had an estate. If he did not have an estate, he was worthless, no matter what they called him. Was that not why she had so passionately urged her brother to purchase? Fat lot of good it had done her, but still, she had standards.

"Who is he?" she asked, implying that he had no family name. "Who are his people?"

"I suppose you could say his people are my people," Miss Darcy said hesitantly. "George Wickham—in truth, my father loved him like a son."

Almost too late, Caroline prevented herself from allowing her jaw to drop agape. George Wickham was Miss Darcy's beloved? She had not confided the whole of it, but Caroline knew that Miss Darcy had seen a great deal of the man, now revealed as Mr Wickham, over the summer in Ramsgate and was besotted with him. What was it with the Darcys and their inexplicable compulsion to marry beneath them?

"He is a…handsome man, I grant you that," said Caroline. "You spent time with him this summer in Ramsgate, I believe?"

"I did, but that horrid Mrs Elders, who Brother hired as my companion, behaved as if we were about to elope every time I so much as spoke to him! George is an honourable man. I cannot think why she behaved so to him."

As it was, Caroline did not think much of any man who would pay such attentions to a girl not yet out, but perhaps he simply made too much of the family connexion.

"Do you know him?" Georgiana asked.

"Know him? Heavens, no," Caroline said with a little sniff. "I am not in the habit of knowing soldiers. But I saw him in Meryton. You know he is quartered there for the winter?"

Miss Darcy nodded.

"But surely you must know nothing can come of it? My dear, you are Miss Darcy of Pemberley! You must marry well, particularly now that your brother—"

"Exactly!" the girl effused. "Do you not think that my brother's marriage shows he has changed his mind? He sees now that where there is love, other objections must fall aside!"

In a stroke of utter brilliance, Caroline saw how she might hit two targets with one arrow. Exact a bit of revenge on the nefarious Eliza Bennet and turn her young friend's thoughts around from her most unsuitable beau.

"Love? Miss Darcy," she said with as much gentleness as she could manage, "I am loath to tell you this but…"

"But what?"

Caroline turned her head, unaccustomed to playing the role of a compassionate friend. With a deep sigh, she looked at the girl and laid a hand on Miss Darcy's arm. "You must know…yet I see you do not…about…"

"About what?"

"About them. They are…well, they are in love. Have been

for some time, or so I was told. He took the commission there for her."

"Who?"

"Your new sister and George Wickham."

Injured humiliation rose on Miss Darcy's countenance, turning her face hotly red. "No, that is not possible. George loves—"

"I heard a story," said Caroline, "while I was in Meryton, that they intended to marry but her father forbid it. She has no fortune, as you know, and they would have been penniless."

"George loves *me*," said Miss Darcy stubbornly.

Her hand still on the girl's arm, Caroline squeezed gently. "My dear, such is our lot. A fortune is both a blessing and a curse —one never knows whether a man wants you or your money."

Tears sprung into Miss Darcy's eyes.

"And that is why these unequal alliances are never any good," Caroline continued. "Why, I would not be surprised in the least if Eliza married your brother intending to keep George Wickham on the side."

To her credit, Miss Darcy did not weep. Instead, she said again, more vehemently, "George told me he loves me."

"Then why," asked Caroline, leaning forward to portray earnestness, "did he while away his days in Meryton, going to card parties at Eliza's aunt's house, instead of staying here in London with you?"

"He thought that if he raised his prospects—"

"Indeed, he did raise his prospects." Caroline removed her hand from the girl and allowed a bit of harshness to seep into her tone. "Lover to a very wealthy woman, who will no doubt use her generous pin money to keep him in style."

Her face red and her eyes shining, Miss Darcy stared at Caroline for a long moment. Then with great hauteur, she rose, determinedly angling her nose towards the ceiling. "I must take my leave."

Caroline heard the anger rising in the girl's voice. "Of

course," she said soothingly. She stood and accompanied Miss Darcy to the front hall, watching silently while the girl donned her bonnet and cloak. When the housekeeper left them, Miss Darcy turned back.

"You must be wrong."

Caroline gave an elegant little shrug. "I speak as I find, my dear. I simply cannot do otherwise. You should have seen them at my brother's ball! Ask anyone—they will tell you how it was."

"How can I stand by and see my brother played for a fool in this insupportable manner?"

"He married her. It is done."

"I must do something!" Miss Darcy cried. "I have never known him to be this way, and to think it is all a humbug! To think she does not return his love! It is a sore humiliation. He does not deserve that!"

With these words, she swept from the room. Caroline watched the door close behind her, a small smirk playing on her lips. How she wished she might be a fly on the wall at Darcy House when all of this came home to roost! She imagined an enormous row, Mr Darcy in an arrogant, handsome fury, raining down his ire upon Eliza's head. Heaven knew she deserved that and much more besides.

But there was not much chance of that, was there? Eliza would say she had no idea what Miss Darcy was talking about, and in the absence of any tie between them, that would be that. No doubt Darcy would be too stupidly besotted to even care.

Caroline pondered over this. With the newly married Darcys at Pemberley, there was not really anything to be done, but when she could, it might be fun to throw a bit of kindling on the fire she had just lit.

FOUR

THE SNOW, WHICH HAD BEEN PREDICTED TO BE LIGHT AND barely cover the fields, came down in thick blankets. They had slipped and slid several times and were yet only about five miles from Pemberley, or so Elizabeth believed.

She wished to twist the handkerchief in her lap but did not. She had wanted to go to Longbourn last week, when an unseasonably warm spell should have made travel exceedingly comfortable. Darcy had insisted that it was impossible for him to leave then; however, what it was that made it so, she could not say. There had been little business accomplished save for the business of bedding her.

Do not be shrewish, Lizzy. She sighed. Her dear husband could not have predicted this weather, and she knew her ill humour was mostly because she feared they would not make it to Jane and Bingley's wedding, an event to be held in exactly four days hence.

That Darcy would not willingly spend an excess of time in her family's presence was not surprising. Mr Bennet had never given up being suspicious of him, Mrs Bennet crowed incessantly about his wealth, and the younger girls were silly and

32

brazen, constantly asking him when they could go to his London house. But still! This was Jane's wedding!

She bit her lip and looked out the window.

"You are frightened," he said from beside her. "You need not fear. The men driving are my best."

"I am sure they are. I cannot help but feel sorry for them though. Much as I want to see my sister's joy, I do not wish pneumonia on the coachman."

"Or worse."

Some minutes later, when another icy patch had nearly sent them off the road, she said, "Do you think we should turn back?"

It was not the first time she had asked the question. The others had been met with quick demurral, but this time, he hesitated. "If we can get as far as Derby, it will likely improve."

"Derby seems very far off at the moment."

"It is only about twenty-five miles, but in this weather"—he peered out the window—"it is very far indeed. We have likely gone no more than five or six."

Minutes later, the carriage stopped, and Elizabeth heard the coachman climbing down to knock. Darcy stepped out to speak to him and, a minute later, got back in with snow crusted around his face.

"The men are nearly frozen solid up there. We should return to Pemberley and perhaps try again tomorrow."

"If we travel tomorrow, we shall miss the wedding," Elizabeth cried. "Oh! But no, I know it is foolish to continue on, foolish and selfish."

"I am so very sorry," he said feelingly. "This is my fault. We should have gone days ago."

Elizabeth bit back her anger. It was useless to blame him for what was by no means his fault. "It does not signify. I shall see Jane soon enough."

Darcy sighed. "No. No, I fear Jane will be...Bingley intends to take her to Italy for a wedding trip."

33

In an instant her own despair was forgotten as Jane's delight was considered. "How lovely! Jane will be so very pleased."

"But perhaps London first? I am not certain of the plans. Let us do all we can do see them soon in London, shall we?"

"And what about Georgiana?" Elizabeth asked. Darcy's—and now her—younger sister made her home in London and had remained there with her companion while Elizabeth and Darcy enjoyed some solitude at Pemberley. "Forgive me for saying so, but in her last letter, she seemed rather lonely."

"She and Miss Bingley are good friends," Darcy said apathetically. "I do not doubt she has already contrived some scheme to go to the wedding and will enjoy herself there."

ALAS, IT WAS NEARLY MARCH WHEN DARCY AND ELIZABETH were at last able to travel to London. The snow had been fierce and unrelenting, trapping them in their own admittedly happy paradise in Derbyshire. Georgiana did attend the Bingleys' wedding as the particular guest of Miss Bingley, and she filled Elizabeth's ears with every detail, including, most importantly, the felicity of her dear Jane.

The demands of society were immediately upon them in London. Lady Matlock, Darcy's aunt, had done all she could to ensure Elizabeth's kind reception, introducing her to the right people and teaching her whom to avoid and why. Elizabeth rapidly formed a group of lady friends, including some who were powerful among the first circles, thus ensuring her widespread admittance. It was quite surprising to Darcy, and he could not fathom how she had managed it; for no matter the charm or personality of a lady, with that group, those who were from the outside remained on the outside and the wrong connexions were a death knell.

Yet she had formed alliances with some known to be pompous snobs, and what was more, they appeared to truly befriend her. Those who voiced dislike of her were discounted as suffering from sour grapes for having failed to attract Mr Darcy for themselves. The number of invitations the Darcys received appeared to increase daily, much to Darcy's dismay.

Elizabeth and Darcy enjoyed many evenings out together, as she loved the theatre and the opera as much as he did. Georgiana attended with them at times but, more often than not, left them to their own society. They perused art exhibits and attended dinners, and Elizabeth spent morning after morning making and receiving calls and attending teas. Indeed, on many a morning, with Darcy at loose ends in his study or whiling away his time at his club, he began to wish she were a bit less well regarded. But still, she appeared pleased by her reception, and so he could not complain.

When in her company, Darcy found that he did not mind mingling in society quite as much as he had previously. Although he would always prefer quiet evenings spent at home or with a small, select group of friends, he found society gatherings were much more tolerable now that he was married. The attentions of the unwed ladies and their mothers had turned to those gentlemen who remained eligible, and Darcy revelled in his reduction in desirability.

As much as Elizabeth was liked by the ladies, the gentlemen had more than a fair appreciation of her as well. It did not immediately bother Darcy that his wife was so admired. Although he was by nature a somewhat jealous and possessive man, he was reasonable enough to acknowledge that Elizabeth's light figure, enchanting eyes, and chestnut curls would be appreciated by more than just himself. In truth, there was a certain pride in knowing how other gentlemen could only wish for what was his, to see their envious stares as he entered the carriage with her at the end of the night. He had to admit, he did occasionally indulge himself with petty exhibitions such as standing too close to her, or caressing her shoulder as he helped her with her shawl, just because he could.

Still, more than once, he wished Elizabeth was just a little less comely and that he was not so often required to allow her to dance with a gentleman or be escorted into dinner by another. What foolishness was it that a man was not permitted to sit next to his wife at dinner? Many times, Darcy reflected on how extremely happy he would be to forget this social business altogether and take his lovely bride off to Pemberley once more, never to be seen nor heard from again.

But it could not be, and in any case, Elizabeth seemed to enjoy herself during their nights out, and thus he was resolved to try and enjoy them as well.

DESPITE HIS BEST INTENTIONS, DARCY WAS SOON WEARIED OF the social exertions. London was filled with people whose greatest desire was to separate him from his wife. He had scarcely known Elizabeth for six months by this time; surely, he was the one who most needed her society. He resolved that he must speak to his aunt quite soon, that she might teach Elizabeth how to appropriately limit the time she was required to spend calling on and receiving visitors.

Once again, he found himself on a fine April morning entering his club and handing his overcoat and hat to the servant. His cousins Colonel Fitzwilliam and his elder brother, Viscount Saye, were at a table with some other men, and Darcy made his way towards them.

"Darcy! What do you do here?" Mr Thomas Johns was dramatic in his portrayal of astonishment at the sight of him.

"Am I not a member?" Darcy took a seat next to Saye, signalling to the servant for a drink.

Mr Henry Macy responded, "If I had a lovely wife such as yours awaiting me at home, you would not see me here among this lot for a year!"

Johns snickered. "A man must come up for air at least once in a while, Macy!"

Unthinkingly, Darcy snapped, "Yes, and he must sometimes take care of his business."

The table erupted in gleeful hilarity, speculating on how often each night the lovely Mrs Darcy required him to 'take care of business', and whether any occasions of morning 'business' were permitted, and how often they, with a beautiful young wife—not even yet of age!—would tend to their 'business'. Darcy pretended to be amused by their teasing, understanding that if they knew how vexed he was by their crass behaviour, it would only become that much worse.

Saye at last spoke up for him. "Gentlemen! This has gone far enough. Let us show some respect for Darcy…"

It was not often that Saye was the voice of reason, but Darcy was glad to see this was one of the rare occasions.

"…after all, he is getting very little sleep these days! We would not wish to try his sensibilities!" Once again, the table erupted into loud laughter, leaving Darcy to force a tight smile through the haze of an incipient headache.

"Darcy, really," said Fitzwilliam as they left the club, "you must not let them get to you."

"Everyone wishes for a beautiful wife," Saye opined. "But, in truth, you are far better off with only a mildly handsome one. She will always be grateful you married her, and scarcely anyone else would look at her."

"The ideal wife," said Fitzwilliam, "is one who was ugly as a child."

"Yes!" Saye agreed enthusiastically. "An ugly child raised with a beautiful sister. Instils a deep-rooted sense of unworthy—"

"Do you two hear yourselves?" Darcy asked. "I am married to Elizabeth, quite in love with her, and if others see her beauty as I do…well, that it is a price I must pay."

"And of course you trust her," Fitzwilliam said.

"As much as you can trust anyone you have known a week," Saye added with a little snort. "I myself might not have taken my young bride who had been hidden in the country all her life and toss her right into the temptations of this den of sin we call London."

This gave Darcy some pause. He had not before considered how it might be for Elizabeth, who had scarcely been to London and certainly had not experienced the whirl of the *ton*, to suddenly became the belle of it all. The world of money and prestige had been laid at her feet. What did she make of it?

Saye and Fitzwilliam had entered into a debate about whether there was greater debauchery in the country or the city. It was Fitzwilliam who noticed Darcy's silence.

"Disregard us, Darcy. You love your wife, and that is all that matters."

"Who are we but two confirmed bachelors?" Saye added.

"I love her beyond my reason," Darcy said.

"Exactly!" Saye cried out.

"And having abandoned reason, I can only hope…"

His cousins studied him a moment, with Fitzwilliam at last saying, "It seems this might be a conversation better had indoors."

Within a quarter of an hour, the three men were seated in comfortable chairs in Lord Matlock's study. His lordship and Lady Matlock were away from home, and they were assured privacy.

"What is it Darcy?" Fitzwilliam asked.

Darcy absently swirled the drink he had been handed. "Nothing. It is silly really. But…"

"But what?"

He sighed deeply. "Georgiana came to me with a fantastical tale she heard from Miss Bingley."

"Miss Bingley?" Saye sniffed. "This tale has already lost credibility in my mind."

"I dismissed it immediately," Darcy assured him. "Miss Bingley tried to tell my sister that Elizabeth and Wickham…"

Fitzwilliam groaned.

"...were...lovers, for lack of a better word. And that he offered for her—"

"Offered for a poor woman?" Saye immediately protested. "No. This is lies."

"Except she is not a poor woman now, is she?" Darcy responded.

The gentlemen contemplated that for a moment until Fitzwilliam laughed a bit too heartily. "Come now! So in this scheme, Elizabeth and Wickham are lovers, hoping against all rational belief for you to come along and provide wealth for their schemes?"

"No," Darcy replied. "Evidently, the plan was for Elizabeth to marry some idiotic cousin who is heir to Longbourn, and he should provide funds for their schemes. I was an unlooked-for prize."

"This cannot be," said Saye. "It simply cannot."

"I thought as much myself except that..." Darcy stood abruptly, too many emotions in him to be still. To marry as he had was most unlike him. He had acted against his sense, his reason, even his character, and to imagine for even a moment that he had been deceived... It was difficult to bear. He wanted his cousins to reassure him, to call it all folderol, but could they?

He felt the weight of their stares upon his back. "Fields," he said, referring to his valet, "saw George Wickham leaving my house Thursday last. By the side entrance."

His cousins said nothing, no doubt digesting the implication of such news.

"I happened upon him yesterday, asked him whether he had been by, and he denied it. Asked what business he might have with anyone therein—certainly our association was finished, so why should he bother."

"Why indeed," Fitzwilliam echoed faintly. "But Fields is not a fool and knows Wickham well."

"Yes, he does. Has known Wickham for ten years, at least."

"So...?"

"I persuaded myself Fields was in error. But what if he were not?"

"Why would Wickham deny being there?" Saye asked.

"Wickham lies," Fitzwilliam interjected. "It is as natural to him as breathing. Even if he has no reason to, he lies."

"Unless he was meeting someone he did not wish me to know about," Darcy said softly, turning to face his cousins.

"This is foolishness," Saye burst out. "Darcy, you have no reason to mistrust your wife."

To this, Darcy made no reply.

OF ALL OF THE MANY SOCIAL EVENTS THAT THE DARCYS attended, none were so enjoyable to Elizabeth as attending plays. Having had but limited opportunities to see such productions in her life, she now found herself nearly rapacious in her desire to see them all. On this particular afternoon, she and Darcy had been engaged to see *The Virgin of the Sun* at Covent Garden, after which they planned to dine at the home of Sir Herbert and Lady Claremont.

Elizabeth had every expectation of a highly enjoyable evening. She had met Sir Herbert and Lady Claremont on several occasions thus far, and their society became more agreeable to her with each interaction. Lady Claremont was a young lady of two and twenty and married three years previous. Sir Herbert was a bit older, at eight and twenty, and had been at university with Darcy.

The couple had Captain Norman Bolton, elder brother of Lady Claremont, living with them. A gentleman of thirty, he had been at sea for most of the past seven years. He was not the heir to Lady Priscilla's family estate or fortune, but his exploits at sea had been rewarding, and he was thus in possession of a fine fortune in addition to being a fine figure of a man. He was widely regarded as one of the prime articles of that Season but seemed rather dismayed at the female attention he garnered in society.

The company at Claremont was friendly and easy, and dinner passed quickly. After the ladies had withdrawn, the gentlemen began to speak of some political concerns, and Sir Herbert at once recalled a certain matter of business he wished to discuss with Darcy. Darcy and Sir Herbert thus withdrew to his study after Darcy asked Captain Bolton to relate his location to his wife.

Captain Bolton approached Mrs Darcy just as soon as he and the remaining men entered the drawing room. "Madam, your husband has asked me to tell you that he and Sir Herbert have briefly retired to Sir Herbert's study."

Elizabeth thanked him with a smile and invited him to sit with her.

"I understand that you and Darcy are newly married?"

Elizabeth nodded. "Only since December."

Captain Bolton nodded. "Married life seems to agree with him. He is more easy in company than ever I have known him."

Elizabeth laughed. "You, more than anyone here, must imagine the relief a man feels when the female eyes of the *ton* turn elsewhere!"

With a mock groan of despair, the captain agreed. "I found it a great deal pleasanter to chase pirates and face down the French navy!"

"I have met a great many lovely and sweet-tempered young ladies in my brief time in London, and I imagine you would find them so as well—or at least better than pirates or the French."

"A moment if you will—I shall procure a sheet of paper and have you list their names for me!"

It was amid their laughter that Darcy arrived in the room. He appeared at Elizabeth's side in a moment. "My headache has returned, I fear," he announced, interrupting them. "I called for our carriage."

"Oh." Elizabeth stood hastily, wondering at his tone. "I am sorry to hear it. Yes, I am ready."

After a brief farewell around the room, they left. Darcy was silent and glum, scarcely speaking two words, and Elizabeth wondered whether his headache was the sole cause of his ill humour.

When they were nearly home, she asked softly, "Did you enjoy the evening?"

"I might have enjoyed it more had I not come into the drawing room to find you laughing with a rake in a secluded corner."

"I was doing no such thing!"

"The captain's reputation is poor; he has made much of his popularity with young ladies this Season."

"He appeared to be all that a gentleman should be," Elizabeth protested. "I liked him very well."

"A rake hardly walks up and announces himself, Elizabeth," Darcy said sharply.

Taking a breath to control her emotions before she spoke, Elizabeth replied, "We only spoke for a few minutes."

"Nevertheless, you seemed quite comfortable," Darcy retorted. His jaw clenched, and he stared out onto the street. The rest of the ride was spent in silence.

Elizabeth was quiet as her maid assisted her in her nightly ablutions, and she dismissed the girl as soon as she could. Tears stung her eyes as she wondered what she might have done differently. Should she have not spoken to the captain? Darcy had sent him to her himself— was she meant only to receive the message and say nothing more? It seemed ridiculous; she had always been friendly. Must that change? Was a married woman required to reserve all smiles and conversation for her husband?

FIVE

Fields was restrained the next morning, looking wary and unhappy as he shaved Darcy and set about helping him dress. Darcy had not slept at all after arguing with his wife and was in no mood for an ill-humoured valet.

"What is it, Fields?" he asked sharply.

"I beg your pardon, sir?"

"You are in quite the brown study this morning."

Fields sighed. "Forgive me."

"Of course, but if there is something that troubles you…"

Darcy watched as Fields's face displayed…well, next to nothing. A sure sign of trouble when one's loyal retainer was so stoic. "Fields?"

"Mr Wickham was again seen leaving right around dawn. Not by me, but by Robert," he said, indicating one of the younger footman.

Pique blossomed into something far more serious, and Darcy fought to remain calm. "And what did young Robert do for it?"

"He tried to stop him, naturally, but Wickham punched him,

breaking the poor fellow's nose, then took off running. Our boy did his best, but he was injured."

Wickham's sins were compounding rapidly. "And what was his purpose in being here?"

"Wickham's? He did not say, but I daresay we might assume it was nothing good."

Perhaps he did not say, but a sick feeling in Darcy's gut informed him of all he feared. Had she sent for him after they argued? If Darcy had gone to her chamber in the night, would he have discovered his worst fears tangled in her sheets?

Fearing he might vomit, he hastily sent Fields away, then stood against the mantel, shaking and furious. He could not imagine sitting across from her at the breakfast table and sent for a tray to be brought to him in his study.

He slipped into the servants' hall, hearing silence, and made his way to his study without anyone seeing him. Surely his countenance would have sent them all scurrying regardless, but he did not wish to speak for fear he might scream.

Alas, Georgiana had need of him and was already pacing the floors when he entered. "Brother—"

"Not now, Georgiana, please. Later." He sank into the large leather chair that had been his father's, wishing the man himself was there to advise him.

She paused, no doubt observing the sleeplessness on his countenance, the scarcely hidden emotion. "Is something wrong?"

He shook his head. "No. Just...did you sleep last night? Sleep well?"

She nodded. "I was asleep early. I think I walked too much yesterday with Miss Bingley."

"Oh, um...yes, Miss Bingley. Did she say...did she tell you any more about...?" He looked at her expectantly.

"About?"

With a sigh, he lowered his face into his hands. "Wickham and Elizabeth. My wife. Any rumours about any of that?"

"No. Only what she told me before." There was a pause. "Why?"

"He has been here to see her," he said solemnly, praying she was not so much a girl as to misunderstand him. A glance at her face—which had gone flame red—said she took his meaning perfectly.

He was spared further conversation by his butler, who told him Colonel Fitzwilliam needed to speak to him. Georgiana excused herself, and moments later, his cousin entered.

Fitzwilliam carried with him the air of a man on a mission—a grim one. "I have only a moment, but I wished to tell you something."

"What is it?"

"Wickham left the militia. Not sure exactly why, but he seems to have found himself in possession of a bit of money."

"How much money?"

Fitzwilliam shook his head. "I don't know, but he is back in town, ordering up all sorts of new suits, and somehow has managed to get himself invited to quite a few soirees over the next weeks. Not the first circles, of course—his currency does not extend so far as that—but certainly higher than his usual groups."

Darcy stared at his cousin a long time whilst he absorbed the news. Fitzwilliam's eyes were mostly inscrutable, containing only the slightest hint of what Darcy saw as pity. At last, Fitzwilliam came towards him, his boots thudding heavily against the floor. He clapped Darcy's shoulder.

"Forgive me, I must be off. Will I see you at Bickerdyke's ball?"

After a moment, Darcy said, "No."

THE YELLOW SILK GOWN ELIZABETH DONNED THAT EVENING WAS among the most beautiful she had ever worn. Although she had never imagined she would need nearly so many gowns as she had purchased for the Season, dressing was quite enjoyable with such an array of fine and fashionable gowns to choose from. Her maid had done wonders with her hair that day as well, managing to tame her profusion of curls by sweeping them up into an elegant style, adorned with sparkling jewels and small flowers. As she stared at her reflection, she allowed hope to creep into her heart.

Relations between her and her husband had grown strained. For over a fortnight, Darcy had been grave and silent, often watching her for reasons unknown.

But tonight, she looked pretty—she did not think it wrong to admit that to herself—and perhaps they would dance and regain some of the ardency of their earlier days. And that might induce him to confide whatever it was that troubled him. Likely it had nothing to do with her—perhaps trouble at Pemberley? She knew she ought not hope that was the case, but she did.

Walking into the sitting room that adjoined their chambers, she was surprised to see Darcy had not even begun to dress and was reading a book in a chair by the window. "Oh! You are not dressed?"

Darcy glanced up, a mask of hauteur on his face.

"Um…I mean, are you not going to dress for the Bick-erdyke's ball?"

"I sent our regrets."

"You did?" She felt stupid, exclaiming and remarking as she was, and schooled herself to speak more calmly. "I beg your pardon, I was not informed. Are you ill?"

He shook his head and kept his eyes on her. She met his gaze, remaining calm through the nerves that were making her stomach roll and her heart ache. What was this? Why had he not informed her? And why was he staring at her in an almost challenging way?

"Excuse me," she said at last. "I shall go change my gown to something more suited for an evening at home, then."

"Are you terribly disappointed?" he asked, though he did not much sound as though he cared.

She turned, forcing herself to smile at him. "No," she said. "No, this will be nice too. Perhaps I shall get my book and join you."

She left it at that and returned to her chambers to summon her maid. Her maid arrived in confusion and apologies that Elizabeth met with her own apology, assuring the girl it was she who had erred. All the while, a litany in the back of her head wondered what on earth was happening to the man she had married.

DARCY WAS MORE HIMSELF OVER THE NEXT FEW DAYS, AND SHE was relieved. Eventually, she persuaded herself that she had imagined much more to it than it was and resolved to forget about it. Part of marriage was learning how to form a life together from what had been two separate existences. She was finding that her husband was a complicated man and his controlled demeanour at times hid great emotion.

Some days later, she held in her hand an invitation to a ball hosted by Mr and Mrs Geoffrey Morton. In truth, she cared little for the Mortons; he was very nearly the haughtiest gentleman she had ever met, and the wife was silly and vain. However, Darcy had gone to school with Mr Morton, and they encountered them at many of the same dinner parties. Darcy always made an effort to be friendly with the gentleman, once explaining to Elizabeth that with an estate that was nearly as large as Pemberley in another part of Derbyshire, the Mortons were their equals in consequence and Darcy wished to maintain good relations with them. Thus, she knew Darcy would want to accept their invitation, and so she did without hesitation.

That evening after dinner, as they both enjoyed listening to Georgiana play the pianoforte, she remarked offhandedly, "The Mortons sent us an invitation to a small ball next week. I have sent our acceptance."

He stared at her, looking inexplicably tense. She could see a sudden hardness in his eyes and an almost angry set to his mouth as he replied in a tight voice, "I wish you had asked me first."

"But…you always wish to accept their invitations."

Rising abruptly, he strolled over to the window, staring out into the darkening evening for several minutes.

When he turned back to her, he seemed to have regained his composure. "Please do send regrets to them tomorrow, if you will."

She said little when he refused to attend the next two balls for which they had received invitations. When he at last decreed they would not attend any more balls, she spoke, mentioning advice she had received from Lady Matlock.

"Your aunt felt it important that I be seen amongst—"

"Is it such a hardship for you to forgo an evening spent in the arms of other gentlemen?"

"Of course not!" she exclaimed, stung. "You cannot think that is why I wish to—"

"No more balls. I do not enjoy them."

They sat for a moment, Elizabeth staring at the note in her hands that had prompted their disagreement. She startled when he rose and exited the room with nothing further said.

In the first months of their marriage, she had seen nothing to indicate that Darcy was capable of being so arrogant and high-handed as he now seemed. He appeared to have little concern for her thoughts on the matter—but as her husband, such was his prerogative. Had she embarrassed him? Was that why he wished to hide her away?

THERE WERE DAYS WHEN DARCY PERSUADED HIMSELF THAT HIS growing fears had no basis. Other days, he was certain he had fallen prey to what he had dreaded all his life—a fortune huntress.

No matter what dark currents swirled through his mind, Elizabeth appeared happy. She gadded about, ever more ebullient, making love to old dukes and young bucks alike, seeming to want nothing more than to be the talk of London. The more sober and grave he was, the more vivacious and charming she was. Even his decree that there should be no more balls—initially greeted with consternation—led to overwhelmingly good cheer.

Then again, who needed a ballroom when George Wickham continued to be seen lurking about Darcy House?

Fields had made it his business to follow the man—Darcy could not bear to involve anyone else in the house—and had seen him at least thrice more, slipping in or out a side door and seeming quite satisfied with himself for so doing.

Darcy had not visited Elizabeth's bed since Wickham's second appearance. He had come to understand it was his lust for her that had been his undoing. For a moment, his eyes closed, and his nose filled with the phantom scent of her, the feel of her skin, warm and silken beneath his hands. He felt himself growing weak as erotic recollections flooded his mind: her across his desk, him in her bathtub, them against the library wall...

Had George Wickham taught her that? Was it because of him that Elizabeth knew how well to please a man?

They had laughed together after their first joining, Elizabeth giggling as she said, "Mama told me to be enthusiastic, that it would help things along and bring the end more quickly."

Was her enthusiasm feigned?

He rubbed his hand roughly over his face, feeling the tears that had wet his skin. No, it was not merely lust that had afflicted him. She had seemed to be the answer to every question in his heart, the reward for all the love that life had taken from him. And now he knew it was all a falsehood, and it was a greater pain than any he had ever known.

Was this what a descent into madness felt like?

She had tried to speak of it—he could see that his silence weighed upon her—but he was not ready. He needed to confront her, to be sure, but the timing never seemed right to light the match that would burn one's own house down.

Elizabeth walked through Darcy House, wondering what the day might bring. Darcy left the house at an early hour, she knew, though she had no idea where he had gone.

Her head and her heart ached in equal measure. She had lain awake until pale grey dawn had begun to assert itself, wondering what she should do about her marriage. Could it be fixed? And if so, how? Happiness seemed impossible.

As she approached the breakfast room, she heard giggles within and opened to door to find Miss Bingley had joined Georgiana for breakfast. "How do you do, Miss Bingley?"

Miss Bingley smirked. "Very well, Eliza. How are you this fine morning?"

"You slept late," Georgiana remarked, sliding the basket of bread towards her. "I hope you are not unwell?"

"I was up late," Elizabeth said, forcing a smile. "My book caught my interest too well."

"Oh!" Miss Bingley rose hastily. "Miss Darcy…that book you mentioned. Shall I go get it?"

Georgiana looked confused for a moment. "It is on the table by my bed. I shall send a—"

"No need," Miss Bingley said quickly. "I need to refresh myself in any case. I shall be back shortly."

Alone in Eliza's dressing room, Caroline Bingley gritted her teeth, fingering the delicate items in the top drawer. Such finery! That low-born slattern was hardly worth half of the quality, to be sure! Rage still burned hot when Caroline thought of all Eliza Bennet had stolen from her, and it was rage that pushed the needle in and out of one of her brother's handkerchiefs, the initials 'GW' taking shape in moments.

As she stood, surveying her handiwork, Caroline sighed. What would it do, really? Eliza was married to him. It was done.

But no harm in causing her a little trouble, was there? The handkerchief would be found, hopefully by someone other than Eliza herself, and taken to Darcy, Georgiana would think Eliza had stolen her beloved and then hate her, or perhaps nothing at all would happen. Perhaps it would get tossed into the fire, who knew?

Tired of thinking of it, Caroline shoved it deep into the drawer. At the inopportune moment, a young housemaid entered. She gave Caroline a suspicious look. "May I help you, Miss?"

Though startled, Caroline refused to react in a guilty way. She slowly withdrew her hands, wiped them on her skirt, and smirked. "Not at all."

She then turned and walked calmly from the room.

MISS BINGLEY RETURNED TO THE BREAKFAST ROOM IN DUE course, and she and Georgiana exited together, off on a walk through the park.

Elizabeth received her mail while she nibbled at the dry toast she had selected for breakfast, seeing a letter from her mother included in the stack. She eyed it warily, knowing it was likely to contain something to distress her even more.

She could not deny that her mother was a silly, sometimes vulgar creature. She thought too little and spoke too much, and nearly all of her conversation centred on finding wealthy husbands for her daughters. She had naturally been delighted by Elizabeth's marriage, yet made no secret that she found it astonishing Darcy had not preferred Jane, who was so much more beautiful and charming than her younger sister.

This letter contained a scolding for Elizabeth for not having fallen with child as yet. Mrs Bennet was certain Elizabeth was neglecting her wifely duties and equally certain that Jane would return from her wedding trip pregnant. Elizabeth thought she would too. Jane did have a tendency to do everything to suit their mother.

Mrs Bennet's counsel of Elizabeth's wifely duties reminded her that her husband was eschewing both her bed and her. It was difficult to beget him an heir when he refused to even come to her room, and it was this, more even than her mother's words, that caused the tears to fall.

Darcy obviously was not pleased when he entered the breakfast room to find her weeping. "Mrs Darcy, I am certain that you cannot wish the household to think their mistress is discomposed in the dining room."

Elizabeth hastily wiped her eyes and straightened her shoulders. "Forgive me."

He glanced, frowning, at the letter in front go her. "I hope there was not bad news." He said it scornfully, as if possessing bad news was a character flaw.

"I…no. Um, my mother…" Elizabeth swallowed, gathering her courage. "She mentioned…children."

What she did not say, what she could not say, was that Mrs Bennet had bestirred the fears already plaguing her—that he had grown tired of her, that he would toss her aside for failing him. Instead, she quailed miserably under her husband's flatly dark scrutiny and tried to find some way to reach the man she had married.

"We are both young," he said at length. "There will be time for that later."

With not another syllable more, he left her, and she sagged back into her chair. She needed help, that much was clear. Her aunt would be the one, she decided. Mrs Martha Gardiner was always filled with good advice. She and Jane had sworn that before they wed, it was their aunt they would go to in order to learn how to be a good wife. Her aunt would surely know what she could do to fix her marriage.

An hour later, Elizabeth sat, silent and still, as her aunt finished telling her nursemaid that she would be much occupied in the next hours with her niece and should not be disturbed unless a grave emergency arose. The nurse nodded and took her charges, disappearing upstairs to the nursery. Pouring them both a cup of tea, Mrs Gardiner asked gently, "Have you quarrelled with Mr Darcy?"

Oh, that it could be that simple! Opening her mouth to speak, Elizabeth was suddenly overcome, and her words were lost in gasping, wracking sobs that threatened to tear her soul from her. She wept and wept and wept, managing only an occasional incoherent phrase to frighten her aunt, until she was quite on the verge of hysterics. Her sorrow seemed to come pouring out of her like a tidal wave, and it was very nearly as uncontrollable. Her aunt did the best she could to calm her, until finally, she called the housekeeper to administer a sleeping draught, then sent word to Mr Darcy that Elizabeth had become indisposed at her home and would need to remain for the night.

When Elizabeth awoke the next morning, she was at first confused to find herself in her uncle's home, until it all came back to her recollection. She wondered what her husband's response had been to the information that she was on Gracechurch Street, spending the night. He was probably horrified to imagine Mrs Darcy amongst the tradespeople, becoming unreservedly discomposed and overwrought.

She was just on time for breakfast, though she knew she would not have the appetite for anything. Her aunt was alone and smiled kindly as she entered. "How are you feeling this morning? I have always found a good night's sleep can make things look a good bit better."

Elizabeth offered Mrs Gardiner a wan smile, feeling a stab of a headache as she did so. "Oh, Aunt, I do wish it were so."

"I have willing ears should you wish to confide in me."

Elizabeth took a deep breath, willing herself to remain calm. As dispassionately as possible, she began to relate all that had occurred since she and Darcy had come to London. She offered her own thoughts and beliefs on the likely explanation for Darcy's behaviour. Intermittently, her aunt would offer some bit of protest, some attempt at reassurance, but these unfruitful efforts eventually waned as Elizabeth proved her sad case with example after example of how much her husband disdained her.

When it was done, Mrs Gardiner was pensive for a moment. "I hardly know what to say. I can only hope that you are not correct in what you are thinking, for if you are, it is an untenable situation. All I can say is that if you give him no cause for complaint, in time, the situation might improve. For better or for worse, you are married, and now it is up to you to make it work."

"What if I cannot? What if he is unwilling to allow me to improve things between us?"

Her aunt sighed heavily. "You have few choices, I am sad to say. Once you bear him an heir, he could send you away or possibly even petition for a divorce. That would be a mark on him as well, though, so it is very unlikely.

"In any case, you must do what you can to convince him that all will be well. Keep him happy. If he is willing to discuss this with you, do so and hear what he says, but do not do anything to aggravate him at this time. If he wishes to stay at home, then stay at home. Things will come around, I am sure of it. No one who knows you can resist loving you, Elizabeth. Perhaps once you return to Derbyshire, things will improve."

Elizabeth could say nothing in response, weeping quietly, her face covered by a handkerchief.

Mrs Gardiner leant in close. "Just remember, your uncle and I would do anything to help you, dearest, anything at all. You need only ask."

S I X

DARCY WAS A MAN POSSESSED IN GENTLEMAN JACKSON'S SALON, raining blows down upon his cousin, who returned them with equal, albeit confused, vigour. When they were done, the two men stood, sweat pouring from them and chests heaving with attempts to catch their breaths.

"Well," said Fitzwilliam at length, "the French seem like idle playfellows compared to that!"

"My apologies," Darcy muttered. It had helped a bit to immerse himself in the physical, to release his agony by punching and being punched. But it was not enough. The demon within him was temporarily resting, by no means vanquished.

They donned their discarded attire in silence, soon finding themselves back on the road, walking slowly towards Matlock House. "I need to do...something," Darcy said abruptly. "I cannot live in this way."

"Return to Pemberley, perhaps?"

"Imagining that dastard coming to defile my marriage bed at Pemberley is too much to bear," Darcy snapped. "It is bad enough to think it happens here in London."

"But you cannot be sure, Darcy. Unless you have spoken to her and she admitted it?"

Silently, Darcy reached into the pocket of his jacket, withdrawing a handkerchief. He handed it to Fitzwilliam, who opened it, nearly dropping the lock of hair folded within.

A short lock of hair, deep blond in colour, and matching that on George Wickham's head. Folded within a handkerchief that bore the initials 'GW'. Found in the drawer where Elizabeth's stays were kept. Darcy was unsure who exactly had found it and when, but Fields had been the unlucky man obliged to bring it to him.

Fitzwilliam cursed as only a soldier can. Darcy echoed him softly.

"Small wonder you wished to beat someone to death." Fitzwilliam gave him a wry smile. "Will you confront her with this?"

Darcy nodded. "I shall. I must. But there can be no denying this, and then...then what? I know not."

"What if she carries his child?"

"I cannot bear to think of that."

"But you must. For practicality's sake if none other. The *ton* would see it and know that she...well, it would force you to either recognise the child as your own or make her disgrace known."

His words brought an uneasy recollection to Darcy's mind: finding his wife crying in the breakfast room and mentioning children to him. Likely Elizabeth feared that if he did not visit her bed, he would know he was not the father of whatever bastard she might conceive. Did she cry because she suspected Wickham's son grew within her? Would he be subjected to this most painful of indignities?

"...house in North Yorkshire, excellent grouse moor. Quite out of the way of anyone. I daresay it is ten miles to the nearest village, certainly out of sight of the *ton*."

"What are you saying?" Darcy asked.

"I am saying that if you fear it has gone as far as that, perhaps the pair of you should go off for a bit. I would say abroad, but in these uncertain times…no, Yorkshire is nice enough, and you could fish and shoot until…well, until you know for certain. And Wickham would not know where to find her, and in any case, he cannot afford to travel so far."

"You are saying you think we should go away?"

"I do," Fitzwilliam said. "Until things can be worked upon. Get out of the chaos of London, remove her from her lover… I think it would be best, do you not?"

"And if she is with child? Then what?"

"Then…then perhaps my father will know what to do."

With a faint groan, Darcy rubbed his hand across his face and murmured, "God forbid."

ELIZABETH RETURNED TO DARCY HOUSE LATER THAT MORNING, only to learn that her husband had just departed with Colonel Fitzwilliam.

She still had not seen him by dinner time, and she learned from the housekeeper that he had returned some time previous and requested dinner on a tray in his chamber. She was nervous but decided she must try to speak to him, particularly as Mrs Hobbs had intimated that the master appeared upset in some way.

Tentatively, she went to his room and tapped on the door. There was silence for a moment until Darcy yanked it open.

"I wanted to make sure you were well. Mrs Hobbs said you wished to dine in your room."

Suddenly, she felt a need to touch him, at once certain that if they could only talk about things, she could reach the man she once knew, the man she had entrusted with her life. She reached out her hand, intending to lay it on his arm.

He stepped back quickly so that her arm fell into thin air. "Please do not—"

She entreated him, "We need to talk."

"Not…no." He was so stern, looking at her as though he had never loved her, never once cared for her even a bit. "I am not ready."

"Please?" Elizabeth heard the tremble in her voice and hated herself for it.

"You will excuse me." His voice was flat and without emotion.

"But perhaps—"

"Please leave me!" His face contorted as he said it, and he quickly closed his door.

She reeled back. Tears came as she ran to her own room, rousing only briefly later to inform Georgiana that she was ill with a headache and would not return downstairs that night.

She spent a desperate, sleepless night in her chamber, doing little more than weeping, feeling angry and betrayed, and trying to find a tenable solution to her problems. She could think of nothing but the possibility of returning to Hertfordshire. The very thought of it was utterly humiliating, but perhaps if she presented it to her family as nothing more than a visit, it would be less evident that her husband despised her.

When she entered the breakfast room the next morning, she found him standing at the window with a cup of coffee in his hand. He turned to look at her as she entered.

"Good morning." She nearly choked on her words. "I…I hope you slept well? I did not sleep well, but it gave me time to wonder whether…should I…"

Seeming to take some small pity on her distress, he went to the table, pulling a chair out for her and helping her sit. He then sat beside her.

"What is it?" he asked, not kindly, but not unkindly either, which was the best she could hope for these days.

With a fortifying breath, she said, "I thought it might be best to have a respite from this situation in which we find ourselves. Given time, we might find some solution to it."

He took a sip of his coffee and coldly enquired, "To what situation do you refer?"

She barely stopped herself from rolling her eyes. "You seem angry and upset, and I cannot force you to discuss it with me. Perhaps time apart—"

"Time apart?" He gave an unexpected and bitter laugh. "You have somewhere else you would rather be?"

"N-not…no, that is not what I meant."

"A wife's place is with her husband, regardless of what you might think."

"I did not mean that I wished to—"

Darcy stood abruptly and, in dire tones, informed her, "Be careful what you wish for, Elizabeth."

She had grown accustomed to eating dinner in her bedchamber from a tray, and it was both thrilling and frightening when Darcy summoned her that night to dine with him.

Elizabeth scarcely tasted a morsel through the tremblings and flutterings that afflicted her. She snuck surreptitious looks at him as they went through two full courses. Even after everything, she ached to realise how she loved him still and how much she hoped that something might be said to put things to right between them.

He might only wish to discuss ordinary matters. Things pertaining to the household, perhaps plans to return to Pemberley. It might be nothing at all. She did not know whether the thought was a comfort or a disappointment.

Darcy's countenance was unreadable as he asked her to join him in his study after they finished. Fear rose up within her as he gestured her towards a seat across from his large desk. She wished she had not eaten even the small amount she had, as it began immediately to roil about within her gut.

For a long moment, he was quiet. Then, at last, he reached slowly into his desk, producing a handkerchief and laying it before her. He said nothing but studied her carefully and dispassionately.

She looked at it, dumbfounded. It was a man's handkerchief, plain but elegant, looking to be one of Darcy's own. Did he think that what he was about to say might make her cry? Why would she need his handkerchief? "Wh-what is this for?"

Coolly he replied, "It was found in your bedchamber."

"N-no. It is not mine."

"I know it is not yours."

He reached across the desk and flipped the handkerchief over, revealing a monogram. 'GW' was embroidered simply and elegantly in one corner. With no immediate comprehension of who or what 'GW' might be, she looked at him questioningly, her heart pounding wildly, and her stomach clenched in nervous tension. She wished she could think clearly, to try and determine what was happening, but she simply could not. Fear and upset ruled her, and she could only focus on restraining her tears, understanding instinctively that they would only cause him to grow angrier with her.

With shaking fingers, she reached for the handkerchief, unfolding it to reveal a lock of hair. Light hair, hair that belonged to neither her nor her husband. In fact it looked like her brother Bingley's hair, down to the corkscrew curl of it. "B-Bingley's hair?"

"I will not hear your lies!" Darcy shouted, scaring her.

Elizabeth startled, tears pouring from her eyes as her hand jerked and knocked the handkerchief to the floor. She immediately bent, picking it up, enclosing the lock of hair, and returning it to the desk. When she stood again, Darcy was at the window.

Speaking very calmly, he said, "Your maid tells me you have not had your courses for two months. Is this true?"

Was that true? She could not make sense of his meaning. She understood the sentences well enough but not what he implied, particularly with such underlying anger.

"I…perhaps…I cannot say, but I would not make too much of…"

When he turned from the window, his voice was again cool and distant, and his entire being had become suffused with a deadly calm that was infinitely more frightening than his anger had been. "I believe it would be best for all of us if you would consent to spending some time at an estate I have let in North Yorkshire."

He was sending her away.

It was astonishing and devastating, yet part of her had known, had realised it would come to this from the very moment her aunt had mentioned it. He despised her and all that she was, and now he wished to be rid of her.

He continued to speak, telling her all the hateful details. She heard none of it save for the fact that she would go tomorrow. She was stunned, sitting motionless in shock, reminding herself to continue to breathe.

"For obvious reasons, I would much prefer no one know where you are, not even your family. Write them, assure them you are well, but have them send your letters to me. I shall ensure you receive them."

Then he escorted her from the room, depositing her outside his study and closing the door quietly but firmly behind her.

THE NIGHT WAS LONG AND PAINFUL. ELIZABETH WAS RESTLESS and numb, needing something to do but knowing not what.

In the end, she wrote a long letter to him, telling him that she loved him, needed him, and was willing to do absolutely anything at all if only he would allow her to stay with him. She told him of her fears that he had decided she was unsuitable and of her willingness to change and become everything his wife should truly be. Over and over again, she begged him to please, please not send her away and to give her and their marriage another chance. All pretence of pride and dignity was discarded;

she offered him the rawness of her soul and the desperation of her spirit, and she pleaded with him to offer her mercy in return.

When she had finished her letter, her head ached from the tears she had shed, and her stomach was in a painful knot. She sealed the note and handed it to a footman to give to her husband. She wondered what the servants thought of the matter, believing they were probably speculating as to all manner of scurrilous doings, but still they treated her with respect, a kindness for which she was very grateful.

She awaited Darcy's response on pins and needles, jumping every time she heard a footstep outside her door or a creak of the floor.

Darcy offered her no response whatsoever.

He did afford her the dignity of seeing her off in the morning, standing gravely beside the coach as the footmen finished strapping her trunks on. Georgiana was there as well, her eyes wide and unsure, looking as if she might cry.

Elizabeth knew she should depart with dignity and did her best, but at the last, she could not help but ask him, "Did you receive my letter?"

He nodded once, slowly. "Yes, I did." Then he stepped back to permit the footman to assist her into the coach.

Elizabeth numbly entered the conveyance, sat down, and stared at the floor, desperately trying to keep at bay the tears that flooded her eyes and threatened to break into stormy sobs. The door closed, and Darcy signalled to the drivers to depart.

She looked at him once more, standing so tall and silent and solemn, and then she was gone.

SEVEN

THE JOURNEY WAS LONG, EVEN IN THE COMFORT AFFORDED HER. She could not read, sleeping was impossible, and the hot metallic taste of nausea in her mouth made eating untenable. The trip required five days but felt like the journey to the other side of the world.

Whoever had told Darcy it was an estate had not been entirely truthful. It was actually a gentleman's hunting lodge, located in the midst of a vast acreage of a grouse moor. The nearest town, one about half of the size of Meryton, was more than ten miles away and appeared to be comprised of miners. "Lead," she was told when asked, the smelting of which evidently produced odiferous fumes that hung over the valley and made her gag and cough.

The house was clean, at least, and decently appointed. Entering her new home, she looked about for some servants, but there were none.

"Mrs Nelson'll come over from Muker," said the coachman. "Every day 'cept Sunday. She'll cook and clean for yer." The man disappeared up the stairs with her trunk, and Elizabeth followed him slowly, reluctant to settle into such a place and despising the need to lay claim to any part of this situation.

Her bedchamber was austerely furnished and smelt of the smoke of many generations of hunters, but it seemed clean enough and warm. She sat heavily on the bed, feeling much older than her twenty years. She could not help but allow her thoughts to wander as to how this had all happened, that he had sent her to this wretched place so far away from her family and friends. Finally succumbing to her despair, she lay back on the hard, musty-smelling bed, and wept until she fell asleep.

The next day—and many days thereafter—she awoke determined to somehow find a way to make the best of her situation, although bleak was the most generous word she could think of for this horrid place on a good day. She tried to find something to enjoy in walking the endless moors or in the people she met along the way, but things were rather grey, people and places alike. Would he make her remain until winter? She was loath to even consider how dreadful it might be when the days were short and the winds whipped across the fields.

Mrs Nelson was not an unkind woman, but neither did she have any interest in the curious lady who had come to stay. She would nod at Elizabeth briskly, then set about doing her duty to the house. She came on an irregular schedule that was far from the daily visit Elizabeth had expected—many days would pass with no sight of her.

It did not take much time for Elizabeth to realise her health was affected by her dreadful circumstances. The nausea that had beset her on the journey had not left her, and she soon required a nap of two or sometimes three hours each afternoon. It helped pass the time, so she did not worry about it too much. She would wake, go for the longest walk for which her legs could maintain strength, then return to her chambers and fall into a blessed oblivion, a place where Darcy still loved her and Pemberley was still her home. Was it any wonder her body did not wish to wake?

She wrote to her husband nearly every day, striving to sound accepting of the situation, yet at the same time acknowledging how bereft she felt without him, without their love. She promised, in letter after letter, to do whatever was needed to put things to rights. Some letters she sent, others she kept, deeming them too excruciating for the post. When five had been sent, she suspected he did not intend to reply. When ten had been sent, she was sure of it, and after that, she either kept her letters or burnt them.

Before long, she had given up trying to find good in her situation. She at last admitted defeat and acknowledged that she could not make this situation better, allowing herself the small indulgence of wallowing in self-pity.

Elizabeth prayed desperately for a breeze as she climbed Tan Hill one hot July afternoon, but none was granted. A succession of wet days had not granted any relief to the heat; rather, it was muggy and uncomfortable, but she persevered nevertheless, determined not to while her days away like some pining heroine.

As she stood gazing out over the land, a strange feeling arose in her stomach. A rumble of hunger? The flutter of nerves? Similar—yet she knew it was none of these. Her hand instinctively rose to gently touch her abdomen as her mind embraced the answer to the question she had been asking herself for several weeks now.

It had been Darcy's angry question—nay, his accusation—that first raised the possibility in her mind. *"Your maid tells me you have not had your courses for two months. Is this true?"* And it was true; she had not—not then and not since. "Four months complete," she murmured to herself, still cradling her hope in her hand.

Would it make him happy to know his heir might be within her? She hated the part of her that still yearned for him, for his love. She wished she could despise him more, but he had taught her to love him too well. There was an aching hole in her heart that could only be filled by his presence.

On returning to the house, she again took up her pen and

wrote to her husband. She hoped rather than believed she would receive a reply this time, and dutifully, one week later to the day, she asked Mrs Nelson. Although the lady had not given her any post, there was always the possibility she had forgot.

"Mrs Nelson?"

"Yes, ma'am?" As always, Mrs Nelson was careful not to look at her, as if Elizabeth's disgrace would turn her into a pillar of salt.

"Is there any post for me?"

"No, ma'am."

For some reason, the false deference in her reply struck a chord deep within Elizabeth. A scream—'I have done nothing wrong except fall in love!'—lodged in her throat, but Elizabeth would not allow its release. Instead, she turned on her heel, going directly to her bedchamber where she wrote a letter, allowing the full bitterness of her spirit to bleed onto the page.

Fitzwilliam,

Be not alarmed, sir, on receiving this letter, by the apprehension of its containing any repetition of those sentiments which have been, of late, so disgusting to you. I write without any intention of paining you, or humbling myself, or by dwelling on wishes, which, for the happiness of both, cannot be too soon forgotten...

WHEN SHE HAD FINISHED, SHE SAT BACK, CONSIDERED, THEN added one more line to the page.

She would leave; she could not be expected to raise a child in poisonous solitude. She knew how people here saw her—Mrs Nelson's Christian disapproval made it clear enough that everyone knew she had been set aside—and expected no help from anyone. The air smelt like poison all the time, fumes belched and darkened the air. She needed no more reasons than these to run.

No longer was her marriage her first concern. Their child —*her* child—was. And her child needed fresh air and sunlight and a mother who did not weep three times a day.

Her removal would be done in secrecy, she decided. Some day, Darcy might decide he wanted his child and take it from her. Even thinking of that caused a pain unlike any she could imagine, but she knew it was his right to do it. Furthermore, he might decide to divorce her. This caused a similar agony, but she could not consider it at present. Surely he could not divorce her if he could not find her?

Her letter to Darcy would not be sent. She would leave it here, to be found in the event he ever came, which she suspected he never would. In any case, it had served its immediate purpose —the poison within her was drained, and she could now think clearly and rationally and form a reasonable scheme for removal. One more letter was written and sent, a short missive to dear Jane. Dear, sweet Jane, whom she had no reasonable expectation to ever see again.

It was sixteen miles to Richmond, she had learnt, and she hoped she would be able to walk it. She did not fool herself that it would be easy, but there were no animals kept at the estate, and she knew not how to manage it otherwise. She worried it would be bad for her child but reasoned that if nomadic tribes could manage it, so could she.

She left before dawn, walking a good pace but not unduly exerting herself, and arrived in Richmond at about the time Darcy would have been served his breakfast in town. A post coach was due to arrive shortly after noon, and she would board it and go wherever it might take her.

The days from there jumbled as she boarded one coach and then another, hoping that she would feel 'at home' in one of the many towns she alit upon and wish to stay. Her choices were made haphazardly, and in retrospect, she knew she likely doubled forward and back many times over, though she cared nothing for that.

She stopped when she came to a sweet-looking port town, shocked to find herself in Weymouth. Her route had been determined by which coach left next at the various stations where she found herself, and the only destination she had wanted was 'away'. She knew not how she had travelled or where, being too much lost in her thoughts and fears to pay heed to what was outside her window.

But Weymouth had a good look about it. Elizabeth, after some enquiries, found an economical but clean inn operated by a kindly looking older woman and her husband, a Mr and Mrs Danforth. If Mrs Danforth was surprised to see an unaccompanied young lady ask about her rooms, she did not show it. Elizabeth summoned as much graciousness as she could muster and said, "I wish to let a room, but I know not how long I might stay. It could be one night or several."

Mrs Danforth nodded. "We have a place. Will you need some assistance with your bags?"

Elizabeth looked down at the bulging satchel into which she had crammed as many gowns as she could. "No, I do not think I shall, though if someone might help me press what I have, I would appreciate it."

She bit her lip and, after a moment of consideration, asked, "I...I wonder whether you might be able to help me? I am here to seek employment. Would you happen to know of any situations in the area?"

The last was said in a rush of breath and anxiety that Mrs Danforth appeared to sense. She looked up from her ledger, her eyes appraising Elizabeth. Elizabeth tried not to shrink from the woman's gaze, instead keeping as much serenity on her countenance as she could, as if being abandoned by one's husband and being made to seek employment was something that happened every day.

Slowly, Mrs Danforth asked, "Have you ever served as a lady's companion before?"

Elizabeth blushed deeply. "I have not been employed before."

"Mrs Macy, down the way, needs someone. I shall warn you, though, there have been others, none good enough for the old gal." Mrs Danforth gave Elizabeth a sly smile. "She's a tough one, but kind once you know her."

The next day found Elizabeth, clad in a gown that had been pressed to a respectable form by Mrs Danforth herself, off to see Mrs Macy. A carriage had been sent for her, causing Elizabeth's eyes to fill with tears. As she settled back into the comfort of the plush squabs, she scolded herself. "Really, Lizzy, have you grown so accustomed to being disregarded that decency makes you weep?"

But that was part of being with child, she had learnt. Her sensibilities lay close these days, always ready to spill over into tears.

Mrs Macy's estate, Upton Park, was nothing to Pemberley, but it was very grand. Elizabeth summoned her most ladylike demeanour as she followed the housekeeper to the sitting room where Mrs Macy awaited her. As she curtseyed, she furtively examined her potential employer, aware that at the same time, she was being scrutinised as well.

Mrs Macy was likely more than seventy years of age, but her hair was in an elegant style, and her sparkling blue eyes shone with intelligence and wit. Her dress and her jewels were done to perfection, and she sat with the straight posture of a much younger woman.

"Mrs Darcy," she said, "please sit and let us get to know one another. I once knew some Darcys—from Derbyshire, I think. Lady Anne was the daughter of the Earl of Matlock. They had a son, I believe. Is he your husband?"

Elizabeth froze as her dreams of employment in this home

shattered around her. *Stupid, stupid girl!* How had she not considered that a lady of means might know the Darcy family!

Frantically, she searched her mind for a reasonable explanation, a rational story, and briefly, she considered simply standing, apologising, and leaving. However, she could not, as she had arrived in this lady's conveyance and thus was quite fixed until the lady herself was done with her.

"I…I…hardly know how to explain myself, ma'am," Elizabeth stammered.

Mrs Macy's gaze was intent upon her, and Elizabeth realised, with little hope of a position to be gained, that she must have out with it.

"I should not have come here. I hope I do not importune you with the untenable position in which I find myself. As I have trespassed thus far, I feel I owe you a full recounting of the truth of the matter."

The lady nodded her head.

"Yes, as you suspected, I am the wife of Mr Darcy of Pemberley—the son of Lady Anne and Mr George Darcy. Mr Darcy and I met last autumn and were married quickly, within only two months of meeting one another. We spent some months at his estate in Derbyshire and then returned to London for the Season.

"Although I am a gentleman's daughter, I am not of Mr Darcy's sphere. I was raised on a modest estate in Hertfordshire, and our property is entailed on a distant cousin. My mother's people are in trade, and my four sisters and I have no fortune of our own, merely a portion the five thousand pounds my mother brought to her marriage."

"And how did you meet so illustrious a gentleman as Mr Darcy, then? In London?"

"No, ma'am. We met because his friend, a Mr Bingley, took a lease on an estate in Hertfordshire that borders my father's, and Mr Darcy went with him to see the place."

The lady said nothing and merely looked at Elizabeth thoughtfully.

"I know not exactly what happened once we were in London, but as the Season went on, it seemed my husband became regretful of the fact that he had married me. He grew distant and cold, was frequently angry, and refused to be seen in company with me. After about a month or two of such behaviour, he decided he would send me to North Yorkshire to live at the estate of some friend of his."

Mrs Macy inhaled audibly at this, and her chin raised; however, she still said nothing, and Elizabeth felt as if the old lady's sharp gaze could see right through to her soul. After briefly pausing to sip her tea and quell her emotions, Elizabeth continued her tale.

"He did not answer my letters, nor did he send any of his own. I soon realised I had been abandoned and, what is worse, in a delicate state."

Mrs Macy's gaze flicked to Elizabeth's abdomen.

"Once I had the interests of my child at heart, I realised I must not stay. I took what little pin money I had remaining and left. I feared having my child there as the smoke from the mines is constant, and it is a very remote place with few people around to help me."

"And is the child the rightful son or daughter of Mr Darcy?"

It was shocking to hear it said so boldly, and by a stranger no less. Elizabeth lowered her head, humiliated by the contemptible position in which she found herself. In tones as sedate as she could manage, she replied, "Absolutely, ma'am. I hold my vows sacred and always shall, no matter what he does."

To this defence, Mrs Macy offered no comment.

At length, Elizabeth said, "I do beg your forgiveness for any imposition on your hospitality or any discomfort I have caused you by requesting this meeting today. I find I am made very aware, suddenly, of the vulnerability of my present condition. Perhaps I ought to have done best to remain where he left me."

There was a dreadful, long silence. Elizabeth was about to request that Mrs Macy send her back to the inn when the lady spoke.

"Do you play, Mrs Darcy?"

"I do, and I sing a little." Elizabeth forced a faint smile. "My drawing, however, is dreadful."

"Can you speak French?"

"Yes, and Italian and some German too."

Mrs Macy rose and Elizabeth with her. "My carriage will return you to the inn for your things. We shall dine at six sharp and can then speak more about my expectations of you."

"You are hiring me on?"

Mrs Macy smiled thinly at this, saying only, "I think you will do."

As Elizabeth had scarcely unpacked, it took little time to return to Upton Park. She was shown to an elegant apartment in which a maid awaited to help her with her things.

Slightly before six, Elizabeth descended the stairs and was directed into the dining room by a footman. Mrs Macy was already there, at a table set for two, and motioned her to sit. The soup was served as soon as Elizabeth was in place. She could not help but note the fine china and newly polished silver.

After the soup was cleared and the next course had been served, Mrs Macy spoke. "Mrs Darcy, you have entrusted me with your secrets, and now I shall beg your leave to entrust you with mine."

Elizabeth nodded her understanding.

Mrs Macy dismissed the serving girl and began her tale. "I was raised Miss Amelia Carter, the only child of a very wealthy man who owned and operated a successful wool and textile business."

At the sight of Elizabeth's surprise, she nodded, smiling.

"That is right. My father was in trade. He worked very diligently that I might have the life I was privileged to lead.

"I was about your age, perhaps a little younger, when I caught the eye of Mr Arthur Macy, a handsome young gentleman just a few years older than myself. We met in a park. He was with his friends, and I was with mine. We fell in love just that quickly, and soon we were engaged.

"His family did not like the match. He had already inherited this estate; otherwise, I believe they would have cut him off. As it was, they would not associate with us, nor would they acknowledge the marriage.

"We cared not. We were in love and needed only each other, and that was how it was for nearly twenty years. Unfortunately, Arthur had a weak heart, and when he was only five and forty, it proved to be his end. I was left a widow of only one and forty. We had never been blessed with children, so I was then quite alone, and so have I been these last thirty years altogether. I have been without him now for far longer than I was with him, yet not a day goes by that I do not think of him and miss him dearly."

The lady took a sip of her wine. "Here is the bit where I shall need your secrecy. Despite my years, I am hearty and strong. My teeth are my own, I hear as well as I ever did, and I still enjoy a daily stroll around my gardens no matter what the weather. However, my doctor tells me I am suffering from a disease of the mind."

"Of the mind?"

"Yes." The lady pronounced it firmly with no feeling or emotion. "My wit is destined to leave me. It could take years, it could take months, but it will eventually kill me, and there is nothing to be done for it. Of course, the cousins who stand to inherit this estate are licking their chops. I have no doubt whatsoever that it has galled them to see me sitting here alone in this huge house all these years, but I do not care. They will receive their inheritance when I die and not a moment sooner.

"I have a nurse who cares for my bodily needs, and servants

to care for the house. What I realised I needed was someone to take care of me. Someone I can trust to ensure I am not shipped off to Bedlam by greedy relatives. A genteel person who will provide the sort of care I might have received from a daughter or granddaughter. My household, too, will need looking after, someone who can reassure them and provide for them when I am gone.

"I am likely presuming a great deal to put such a thing on a girl I met but this morning. However, I believe you need me just as much as I need you."

Suddenly it all made sense to Elizabeth, and she thanked Providence for leading her to this place.

THE NEXT DAY, ELIZABETH AWOKE BEFORE DAWN. SITTING UP, she looked around her, feeling, for the first time in many months, safety and comfort. Alas, with thoughts of survival abated, her other thoughts and griefs could assault her, and she bent over in her bed, pulling her knees up and resting her forehead against them that she might have some support while she wept.

She wept and wept and wept until she could weep no more. Sobs tore from her chest, and she shook with grief and agony. Her nose began to run, and her eyes swelled and turned red. The handkerchief she had pulled from her night table grew soaked with her tears, so she used the corner of the counterpane to deal with the rest. Finally, she ran out of tears and sat for a moment gasping for breath, winded by the exertion required for the release of her pain.

Then she rose, washed her face and hands, and sat down at the dressing table to have a talk with herself.

"You, Lizzy Bennet, are not the sort who is formed for ill humour. Yes, I could bemoan him and curse him and behave like a lady in a novel, but that is not me. I wish to be happy, and so shall I be, and if it is a different sort of happy from what I imagined, then so be it. He will be forgotten."

What had come before was now nothing but a dream, and she would create a new life in its place. She had much to be thankful for, she reminded herself. A beautiful place to live, a kindly lady to serve, a baby on the way: Bennet if a boy, Jane if a girl. Of those things alone, would she allow herself to think.

EIGHT

WHEN THE CARRIAGE WAS GONE TO YORKSHIRE, DARCY TURNED, striding towards the mistress's bedchamber. When he had arrived therein, he closed the door, locked it, and began his search.

Silently but quickly, he rifled through drawers, peered into reticules, and opened books that looked like journals. He found only one thing, a note begging her to meet him, signed 'GW'. It said nearly nothing, yet it destroyed him completely.

> *You know how I feel about you, how I burn for you. I spend my days longing for you, and my nights are filled with dreams too fervent to commit to paper—indeed they consume the paper into ash just as you have consumed me. Your words in your last letter assuring me that your feelings have not changed have given me hope…*
>
> *Come to me on Thursday, I beg you.*
> *GW*

What Thursday had it been? Had she met him as requested?

Likely she had; she was always out 'making calls', or so it was said. He sagged onto the bed, holding the note, and prayed for the release of tears. Instead, resentment afflicted him; angry, violent resentment that took his breath away and made him wish to destroy things.

It was this anger that greeted the letters she sent him over the next weeks, letters he consigned to the fire without so much as a glance.

For many days—he knew not how long, maybe days, a week, or even two—he stayed in his bedchamber. Sometimes he wept, sometimes he paced about angrily, but mostly he just sat and stared at the wall. It ended when Georgiana, timorously brave, sent word via Fields that she insisted on speaking to him. Fields helped him dress, at least combing his hair and donning a clean dressing gown that did not reek of brandy.

She was pale and fearful, awaiting him in her sitting room. "Brother, you look very well."

"Do not tell falsehoods, dearest, it does not suit you." He attempted a smile as he sat. "You wished to see me?"

She nodded. "I wished…I mean, I do not know what is happening right now. Are we going to Pemberley?"

"As you wish."

She stared at him a moment. "Not as I wish, but…to join Elizabeth?"

Hearing her name made him wince. "Elizabeth…um, Elizabeth did not go to Pemberley. We can go, however, if you would like. Let us go. I think a change of scene and society could help us both."

"But…where is she? Did she go to her family?"

"Um, no. Not her family."

Georgiana sat staring at him, clearly troubled, and he realised he must confide in her, loath as he was to do so.

He swallowed, and with no little difficulty, said plainly, "It would seem that the tales you heard about town were…not incorrect. Um…my wife, it seems, is not faithful."

Her hand flew to cover her mouth. "But I…surely my account—"

"No." Darcy shook his head firmly. "No, it was not your account alone that…that…"

Not sure how to say it, he reached into his pocket for the note, handing it to her. She took it gingerly, opening it, and she immediately gasped, dropping it.

Alas, the unhappy tale was not yet done. "Furthermore, I suspect…she may be with child."

"Your child?" Georgiana asked, brief delight immediately giving way to horrified comprehension. "Oh. Oh, I see."

"It could be my child, if even there is a child," he acknowledged reluctantly. "Though it is unlikely. My plan is that we should have this time apart to see…well, clearly it would be best if she were not with child. That is my hope. Where we go from there, I cannot say. She does not love me. She married me under a falsehood, and the question will be whether she will give him up, whether I want her to devote herself to me, whether I can trust—" His voice cracked under the strain of the dire possibilities. He wanted to be loved. He wanted her faithfulness to come from her delight in him, not to be forced upon her—but it was too late for that, was it not?

His emotion threatened to overwhelm him, so he asked his sister to leave, and she did at once, closing the door gently behind her.

GEORGIANA WALKED SLOWLY DOWN THE HALL TOWARDS HER bedchamber. Her gasp at seeing the letter in Darcy's hand had been sincere, though its cause was likely misunderstood by her brother. The note he had waved about, the request for a liaison, could very well have been her own, although it was her habit, at George's insistence, to always destroy any written word that passed between them.

Why had Elizabeth come to be in possession of a note from

George? Were they truly lovers? But no—she was nearly certain that was her note. But why? How had it come to be in Elizabeth's possession?

One thing was certain. She could not admit the truth to anyone.

June 1812

THE WORST PART OF ELIZABETH'S DEFECTION—AND DARCY HAD ample time in the first month she was gone to weigh it all carefully—was his return to the lesser Darcy he had been before her. He knew he was dull. He knew he was haughty. But with her, he had been different. He had been liked, welcomed even, and for more than his money and his status. She had made him feel livelier, more interesting, a better version of himself. Without her, he was back to being the old man he had been so happy to cast off.

Lady Matlock had put about a story, a stupid one, about Elizabeth falling with consumption and needing to be sent off to some place in Brussels. Or was it Berlin? Perhaps Boston. What did it signify, for it was all lies. Darcy thought for sure the truth would come out, but somehow it did not. Letters filled with well-wishes and earnest distress poured into Darcy House, much to his shock. How had she even known so many people? He had been among the *ton* since his earliest days, and even he did not know half so many.

An adulteress, he reminded himself grimly, tossing the notes into the fire. She is not worthy of any of them.

There was a chair in Darcy's study in which he slept very well, and it was in this chair that he often succumbed to the scant hours of restless slumber he could manage in this post-Elizabeth life. He knew not how long he lay there when, at once, he bolted upright, seeing the door to his study creak open very slowly.

Shaking the vestiges of sleep from his head, he sat up. "Who is there?" he called out, only to see a gentleman enter in a rush, pouncing upon him, clearly foxed and clearly his cousin.

"Darcy!" Saye crowed. "Get up, we have a present for you."

Darcy shoved him off. "What present?"

"Come, Darcy." Fitzwilliam entered, less drunk than his brother. "Wickham is down on Marylebone street."

"Wickham!" At once Darcy was fully alert. "Where is my pistol?"

"Easy, easy!" Saye crooned, wrapping his arm around Darcy's shoulder. "We need a plan is what we necd, and I say we go in there right when he's bare arsed and near completing and just pummel the truth—"

Disregarding Saye, Darcy asked Fitzwilliam, "Where has he been all this time?"

"Evidently, there is yet another story involving yet another heiress...a Miss King? Packed off to an uncle in Liverpool. Wickham went after her, trying to keep her interests, but the uncle was too smart for that, and now Wickham is back in town."

"Poor Wickham." Saye belched. "Being a rake is a tricky business when all the ladies keep disappearing."

Darcy was busily doing up his boots, which he had removed to sleep. "Forgive me if I do not feel sympathy for him."

Before long, the three men were in Saye's carriage, headed for the brothel where Wickham had been spotted. "Who spotted him?" Darcy asked. "I cannot think you two would stoop to such an establishment as Wickham could afford."

Fitzwilliam gave his brother a look, and Saye grimaced, clearly not wishing to speak the truth, but Darcy guessed it before either brother could speak. "I see… Wickham has fuller pockets of late, is that it?"

"He looks like he's eating well, I shall grant you that," said Fitzwilliam. "But perhaps the family of this Miss King has lined his purse."

"I have lined his purse." The now-familiar anger burned in

Darcy's gut. "Elizabeth's pin money bought Wickham a whore tonight."

"You do not know that," Saye said, consolingly. "Elizabeth has been away a month. Wickham likely gambled her pin money away weeks ago."

Darcy sighed.

"Did you ever examine her accounts?" The lamp from outside the carriage cast shadows over Fitzwilliam's face. "How much has she given him?"

"Well…yes, I did look at her account books."

"And?" Saye asked.

"I could not find anything missing," Darcy admitted. "The bills from the modistes came to me directly, and otherwise… otherwise she has scarcely spent a farthing. Books, that is all she has bought."

There was a short silence while they all considered that.

"Perhaps her own money—" Saye began, but his brother interrupted him.

"She had nothing,. Only a share of her mother's fortune after her mother's death."

"But Wickham would surely not bother with her if—"

"Speak of the devil himself," Fitzwilliam growled, his attention drawn outside the window.

They saw Wickham, his hair askew and countenance satisfied, strolling down the street. Darcy pounded the roof of the carriage, which was brought to an immediate halt.

He flung the door open, jumping down and running before he had any thought of what he was doing. Wickham turned at the sound of his steps, his face creasing into that ridiculous, genial smile just as Darcy set upon him, slamming into him with the full force of his weight and falling atop him as they tumbled to the ground. Raising his fist, he pounded Wickham in his face, his gut, his ribs. Wickham cried out, but passers-by were waved away by Saye and Fitzwilliam, who had exited the carriage after Darcy.

"Think that's enough?" Fitzwilliam asked his brother.

"A few more," Saye advised, while Darcy continued to punish his wife's seducer.

Wickham, fighting back, split Darcy's lip, at which time Saye nodded to Fitzwilliam, who leant in and pulled Darcy off. Saye, with a haughty sniff, offered Wickham a hand to assist him in standing, removing it as soon as Wickham was raised, and wiping it on his breeches. Darcy shook off his cousins' assistance, keeping his glare trained on his adversary while he righted his clothing and held his handkerchief to his bleeding lip.

"Get in the carriage, loser," said Saye. "We require a word with you."

Dawn had begun to lift the veil of night over London. "Mother and his lordship are gone from town," Saye informed them all. "Let us go down to Dunraven street."

With an air of resignation, Wickham obeyed, climbing in with only a moment to consider the ivory squabs.

"If you get dirt or blood on my seats, I shall take it out of your hide," Saye informed him.

"Who gets ivory seats?" Wickham asked.

"Ivory *silk* seats," Saye corrected him with a sniff. "I do. Beauty over prudence, just like me. Now hold your tongue and mind your dirt."

The other men settled themselves in the carriage, Darcy next to Saye and Fitzwilliam beside Wickham. The men were silent as the carriage moved through the streets. Darcy had too much and too little to say and tried his best to order himself. All would be laid bare now; all would be known. It was for the best.

"I must observe," said Saye at length, "that our old friend Wickham here does not seem surprised to find himself set upon by Darcy."

"I have some comprehension of what this is about," Wickham replied, dabbing his handkerchief on his face and examining the results.

"Do you deny it?" Darcy spat.

Wickham raised one brow and coolly replied, "I have no wish to deny it."

Darcy lunged at him, held off at the last moment by Fitzwilliam. "Steady on, Darcy. Let us hear what this vile excuse of a man has to say first."

They arrived at the Matlock town house minutes later. Fitzwilliam kept a tight hand on Wickham's arm, guiding him through the side door and down the hall to his father's book room. Entering, he nearly threw him into a chair while Saye went to the sideboard and began pouring brandy.

"Saye, it is morning."

"Morning is the time after you sleep," Saye acknowledged. "I have not yet been to bed; ergo, still night. Darcy, I daresay, you need it more than anyone."

Darcy stood in front of Wickham reflecting on the man that had once been a playfellow, then a mate, and now his foe. His thoughts were a jumble; the first question emerged as a hoarse croak.

"How long—" His voice broke, and he paused, clearing his throat. "How long has this been going on?"

Wickham's eyes darted to the side where Saye lounged and Fitzwilliam stood looking like he was ready to fight.

"I want only for the truth," said Darcy. "And I do not intend to stop until I have it, so pray, save us both time and speak in honesty."

"Last summer," said Wickham.

The words felt like a blow to Darcy's chest, such as they confirmed what rumours he had been told, but he remained outwardly composed.

"And it has been…continued? Throughout…? That is to say, until the present time?"

Wickham met his gaze and nodded. Darcy had to turn then, going to look out the window while he struggled to remain calm.

"Do you love her?" Fitzwilliam asked.

"'Course," said Wickham. "I mean, she is a lovely girl, is she not? You men need not worry on that score—I do intend to marry her."

Darcy whirled about, setting upon Wickham and yanking him into an upright position by his coat. His face inches from Wickham's, he hissed, "You will need to kill me first."

Wickham shook him off, pulling himself away. "If you keep assaulting me in this way, that should not be a trouble."

"And you have…you have…?" Darcy asked, unable to stop himself from knowing, and equally unable to finish the sentence.

Wickham's pitying look was all the answer he needed. "If it is any consolation, I know—I am quite certain—I was the first."

Darcy's hand shot out, hitting Wickham across the face and causing the man to stumble backwards over the chair he had so recently vacated. "Enough," Wickham howled while Fitzwilliam pulled Darcy away again, echoing Wickham's sentiment.

"We need answers not animal fury, Darcy," he scolded. "Challenge him later if you must."

"How is that a consolation?" Saye snapped while Darcy sank into a nearby chair. "You think Darcy wishes his marital rights appropriated by another man, most particularly you?"

"A duel," Darcy said hoarsely. "We shall settle this as it must be. Fight to the death. Get your pistols, Saye."

"Marital rights?" Wickham asked, disregarding the challenge he had just been issued. "How do you mean?"

"What do you think he means, you idiot?" Fitzwilliam shouted. "You have lain with his wife!"

"Mrs Darcy?" Wickham stood, looking around the room at the men. "What? I never—"

Darcy rose from his chair, crossing the room in a quick pace to stand in front of Wickham. "I shall not hear your lies!"

Wickham shoved him back, somewhat half-heartedly. "Enough, Darcy. I have never touched your wife."

"Then why did you think Darcy set upon you?" Fitzwilliam asked. "Your guilt is clear!"

"I have guilt enough," said Wickham slowly, "but none for Mrs Darcy. I thought we were speaking of Georgiana."

Mrs Jane Bingley, having recently returned to Netherfield after a three-month wedding trip to Italy, sat down to breakfast one morning in late July and was handed a letter. "It is from Lizzy," she said, smiling and showing it to her dear Charles. "Do you think we might prevail upon them to come to us?"

"It is Darcy's habit to go to Pemberley in July," her husband replied. "They are likely there now."

Jane peered curiously at the mark on the letter. "No, 'tis from Leeds. How strange! What could they have been doing in Leeds?"

"Perhaps Darcy had business there, and your sister attended him," Bingley suggested. "What does it say?"

Jane broke the sealing wax, opening the letter. She was immediately disappointed to see no more than a line or two written inside and read them with haste. Then she uttered a small gasp and raised her hand to her mouth.

"Charles? What can this mean?"

Bingley took the letter from her hand, reading the words aloud.

Dearest sister,

Please be assured that I am well. I love you, and I wish you every happiness. Do not fear for me when you learn the unhappy news—I am sure all will be well.

Yours &c,
Lizzy

HE LOOKED AROUND AS IF HE EXPECTED ADDITIONAL PAGES might have fallen from the table, but that was it. There was no more.

Jane bit her lip as she watched him, wishing he might reassure her but already suspecting he would have nothing of comfort to offer. He smiled at her but seemed unsure.

"Your mother, has she spoken of them?"

Jane shook her head. "She worried a bit that Lizzy was not yet increasing but said nothing besides that. Charles, what can it mean? Is Lizzy ill?"

"I shall write to Darcy directly," Bingley assured her. "Do not fret my love, we shall get to the bottom of this."

NINE

WITHIN LORD MATLOCK'S BOOK ROOM, CONFUSION REIGNED.

"Georgiana?" Darcy asked.

Fitzwilliam walked slowly towards Wickham. "What have you done to Georgiana?"

Wickham leered at Fitzwilliam. "Why, no more than what I taught her to do to me."

Fitzwilliam would have leapt upon the cur, but Darcy stopped him, his hand shaking with rage, fear, and any manner of emotion he knew not how to name. The thought of Georgiana sickened him, but for now, he must focus on this business of his wife. "What about Elizabeth?"

"Elizabeth who?"

Without a word further, Fitzwilliam slapped Wickham, and Wickham reeled back, cursing. "What the devil!"

"Answer the questions!" Fitzwilliam ordered. "Mrs Darcy! Mrs Elizabeth Darcy!"

Wickham's eyes narrowed to slits. "I am scarcely acquainted with Mrs Darcy! I danced with her only once, and she likely still does not know my name."

A tumult arose in Darcy—he knew not how to act. Turning

from the scene, he paced, a memory arising within him of the ball at Netherfield when Elizabeth referred to Wickham as Whitman. Had it been an act? Surely this deception was not so well founded.

Turning back, he closed the distance between himself and Wickham, who still held a hand to the cheek that Fitzwilliam had slapped. "You will answer me," he said. "Truthfully and solemnly on our fathers' graves, and damn you to hell if you try to deceive me."

Wickham made a little grunt of assent.

"When did you meet my wife?"

"Bingley's ball at Netherfield."

"November?"

Wickham nodded. "Is that when it was? Then, yes."

"Never before?"

"No."

"Have you met her since?"

Wickham finally dropped his hand from his bruised and swollen cheek and shook his head slowly.

"Why were you seen coming to and fro, sneaking from my house?"

With a mean sneer, Wickham replied, "Because your sister likes to dance the blanket hornpipe in her own comfort."

Fitzwilliam lunged again, but Darcy stopped him. His mind would not accept it, would not allow that Georgiana had willingly engaged in her own ruination with George Wickham, even as another part of his conscience whispered *yet you thought it of your wife.*

"Of Georgiana, I cannot speak, not now," he said. "But do not think you will not be called to reckon for that. This, however, you must confirm."

He reached into his pocket, removing the handkerchief, the lock of hair, and the note. At once, it all seemed quite silly. Even in the dim light of very early morning, he could see that Wickham's hair was darker, more fine, and less curled than the bit in the handkerchief. He held it up anyway, squinting at it while Wickham scoffed.

"I assure you, I never give any woman a lock of my hair, not even your sister, Darcy, and do believe me when I say she has asked for it."

The letter received more serious consideration, Wickham cursing when he saw it. "I always tell her to burn the notes."

"Elizabeth?"

"No! Darcy, pay attention. Your sister." Wickham sneered a bit. "When she is my wife, she will need to be more attentive to my orders."

"That day will not happen under my command," said Fitzwilliam. "I would see her married to my batman first."

"Unless she is with child."

"Please," Saye said with a chuckle. "You have been all about town with nary a by-blow to show of it. I daresay those tallywags of yours have more wag than tally in them."

Perversely, this was the first thing of the whole that Wickham seemed insulted by. "You do not know of what you speak."

"How many have you tupped since school? A hundred? Two?"

"Too many to count!" Wickham protested.

"Miss Harper, for all your reported effort, remains—"

"The art of the dry bob—"

"Face it, Georgie," said Saye with a mean grin. "Your flute is silent."

"Enough of this," Darcy roared. "Wickham, I must know for certain. Have you had relations with my wife?"

Wickham rolled his eyes, beseeching the heavens. "Can someone please get Darcy to stop with the questions of his wife? No! How many times must I say it? If you do not believe me, think of it this way—why should I waste my time on Mrs Darcy, who might give me only a bit of her pin money here and there, rather than apply my efforts—"

"And the waning strength of his doodle," Saye added, to receive only a glare from Darcy.

"—on Georgiana."

"On Georgiana's thirty thousand pounds, you mean," said Fitzwilliam.

Wickham, far from being insulted, nodded. "Never let it be said I am not prudent."

Darcy clutched the back of a nearby chair, needing something to keep him upright. His mind simply would not make sense of it all. Georgiana, ruined. His wife—good Lord, his poor wife! Was there someone else? Some other GW? Was it all a lie? He felt himself sag under the weight of his confusion.

"Get him out of here," he ordered, and Fitzwilliam did so, removing Wickham from the house.

Darcy ran his hands over his face, thinking of the tears she wept the day he told her that he intended to send her to Yorkshire, the times she had tried to speak to him, the hurt in her eyes. He had always said it was an act, a falsehood. Was it? From whence came the handkerchief? The hair? It had to belong to someone. Did it not?

GEORGIANA HAD JUST SAT DOWN TO HER BREAKFAST WHEN THE door was unceremoniously thrust open and her brother and cousins entered. She immediately set down the cup of chocolate she had just sipped, her hand flying to cover her mouth at the unkempt and wild appearance of the three of them.

"Where have you all—"

"Is it true?" her brother asked. "What have you done, Georgiana?"

"What do you mean?" she cried, while Saye ordered the footman to leave them and told Darcy to sit down. Darcy paid him no heed and walked to the window.

A pulse of fear went through her when Fitzwilliam sat beside her and pulled his chair very close.

"Georgiana, we three learnt something very disturbing tonight, and I wish, before anything else, to hear your version of the tale."

Her brother turned, but thankfully remained at the window. "Have you allowed George Wickham to ruin you?"

"Wha—? No! Of course not!"

Darcy sagged visibly. "I knew it was all lies."

"Lies?" Georgiana repeated.

"No? His account of it was quite different," Saye replied, leaning towards his young cousin. "He said that he intended to marry you and had already taken the liberties of marriage."

Georgiana felt herself turn pink, and she could not keep her cousin's gaze. "We are in love," she said softly. Hearing the groans and scoffs of the room, she raised her eyes again. "We are! George is not the reprobate you all think, and simply because of…of misbehaviour of his youth—"

"What was it then, Cousin?" Saye asked. "Has he fondled your bosom?"

Georgiana felt her pink cheeks turn to a more scarlet hue. "I cannot answer—"

"Answer him," Darcy said, his gaze hard.

What followed became painful, and she wept a little, humiliated as Saye forced her, with excruciating plainness of speech, to explain what she and George had shared in private moments. Saye had no regard for the sensibilities of a lady, insisting upon detail in the crudest possible language. It would have been shocking were she not so terrified. At her brother, she dared not look; indeed, she mostly just looked at her hands, twisting white and pale in her lap.

"At least I did not…" she said, and they hung on her words. "I had not yet allowed him…"

After a too-long pause, Saye asked, "Your maidenhead? From my calculations, it seems a slim distinction—but not wholly unimportant."

"That was…it was going to be on my birthday."

Saye cursed, and Fitzwilliam leant back and said, "Lord almighty," then shook his head with unmistakable disgust. "Splitting hairs, but nevertheless, it is something. At least we know Wickham was only bluffing when he mentioned the possibility of a child."

"No!" Georgiana cried. "No…I…of this we may be sure, I am not with child."

Then her brother extracted the note he had shown her before and waved it at her. "This, then, was to you?"

She nodded. Too much had been disclosed to dissemble about a note.

"And what about this?" Darcy walked towards her and laid a handkerchief in front of her.

"N-no," said Georgiana, relieved to finally be able to deny something. "I have never seen that before."

"We are surprised to see you in town," said Caroline Bingley as her brother joined her at the breakfast table. "I should have thought you and Mrs Bingley would be cosy and content at Netherfield for some time."

"And so we might have been," Bingley owned, "save for the strangest letter that Jane received from Lizzy."

The sound of *that* name spoken so familiarly by her own brother made Caroline's lip curl. "Oh?"

"Very peculiar indeed…almost a code. Something about an unhappy truth… We came straightaway to speak to Darcy about it and be assured all was well."

Caroline, filled with delight as she was, spoke unguardedly, "I assure you, Brother, all is very much unwell, if I am not mistaken."

Her brother paused in the act of stirring his coffee, looking at her curiously. "What have you heard?"

Caroline leant towards him. "It could not have escaped your notice how these Bennet girls were in Hertfordshire. Flirting and making a spectacle of themselves. Not Jane, no…" she hurried to add, seeing rare anger crease his brow. "But the younger girls? Quite unseemly. And there were quite a few rumours about Eliza and George Wickham."

Bingley was shaking his head, discounting her before she even got the words out. "No, I heard nothing of that."

"Perhaps you did not hear of it because you heard nothing but the sound of your wife's whisper in your ear," Caroline retorted. Realising she spoke too loudly, she lowered her voice. "A letter was found and Wickham's handkerchief with a lock of his hair—right in Eliza's bedchamber."

His coffee forgotten, Bingley leaned back in his chair, frowning. "That cannot be. Surely not."

"It surely is. After all rumours might mean nothing, but a lover's token is not so easily explained away now, is it?" Caroline smiled again, feeling that keen sense of triumph she always had when things worked out just as they should.

"I shall not believe it until I have had it from Darcy's mouth."

With a smile, Caroline dabbed delicately at her lips with her napkin, then tossed it on to the table. "Well, let us go speak to him, then, and hear the truth of the matter. It is early, but we are all such family, he will not mind."

WHEN THE FOOTMAN ENTERED TO ANNOUNCE THE ARRIVAL OF the Bingleys, Darcy had to sit down. At Georgiana, he could not look, but neither could he bear the rage on Fitzwilliam's face or the petulant scowl on Saye's. So he stared at the top of the fine mahogany table that had been in its place for over five decades and wished everyone away so he could make some sense of his life.

Miss Bingley immediately uttered a mewl of insincere sympathy on seeing her young friend sitting tear-stained and huddled over her untouched breakfast. Bingley entered behind her and, after greeting the others, sat next to Darcy, who had declined to stand upon their entrance.

"Darcy? Are you well?"

"No." Darcy rubbed his face. "It is a long story, but one in which you do have an interest."

"I daresay, I do," Bingley agreed. Taking a letter from his pocket, he said, "Jane received this at Netherfield."

Fitzwilliam leant in, reading the few brief words that Darcy could not. The words swam before his eyes, and all he could think of was her pale, delicate hand, the way she had touched him, the way he had touched her. Nothing made any sense right now, but one thing was certain—that light touch seemed very far away.

Fitzwilliam rose from his perusal without comment.

"Where is Lizzy?" Bingley pressed. "What is the meaning of this? I am sure I do not need to tell you how my dear Jane—"

"Yorkshire," Darcy choked. "She is in Yorkshire."

"Yorkshire? But what could she be doing in Yorkshire?" Bingley asked. Darcy was saved from replying by Georgiana, who had been speaking in low tones to Miss Bingley.

In a tremulous, high pitched voice, Georgiana said, "I did not tell you that. I did not know it myself until this morning."

There was a brief pause whilst the men in the room turned to look at the pair. Georgiana's colour was high, two fiercely red spots on her cheeks, as she insisted, "I did not, I could not have told you so, Miss Bingley."

"Of what are you speaking?" Darcy demanded, exhaustion rendering it impossible for him to defer to female sensibilities.

There was another pause, and Bingley then said sternly, "Caroline? What is this about?"

"Miss Bingley knows about the handkerchief," Georgiana interjected.

With a false, brittle laugh, Miss Bingley said, "Well, I had believed it was you who told me of it, but now that I think of it, it may have been—"

"There is no one outside of this room who knows of the handkerchief, and Georgiana was told only this morning," said Fitzwilliam, easily slipping into the role of interrogator. He moved towards the hapless lady, looking down upon her. "What do you know of this, Miss Bingley?"

Miss Bingley stared up, meeting his icy blue gaze and, for once, quailing under the scrutiny. "I…well, it is all about town that Mrs Darcy—"

"Is it?" Saye strolled forward, his insouciance masking a resolve that was just as firm as his brother's. "Because I do not think it is, and between us, I think my sources are better."

Miss Bingley licked her lips, then dropped her gaze. A shaft of sunlight pierced the room, illuminating the back of her neck and Saye's eyes narrowed as Darcy watched. Saye glanced at his brother and then at Darcy, returning his gaze to Miss Bingley before saying, "Will you hand me that handkerchief, Darcy?"

He understood immediately, even if part of his mind refused to comprehend it. Numbly, he reached into his pocket, handing the hated article to Saye, who unfolded it and then held the curl to Miss Bingley's head. It matched, precisely, the curls at the base of her neck.

Feebly, the lady said, "It was a prank, that is—"

"A prank!" Anger roared in Darcy's head as he fought the impulse to reach across the table, take Miss Bingley by the shoulders, and shake her.

"A row," she whimpered. "We thought you would have a row, that is all, and I wished to help my young friend…"

She glanced at Georgiana, who looked stricken and opened her mouth to say nothing. Darcy immediately looked at his sister.

"You knew about this?"

"No!" Georgiana cried.

"And this was your confidante?" Fitzwilliam asked. "Hearing all about your affairs with George Wickham?"

"I…well, I told her…"

Miss Bingley, eager to redeem herself, said, "I told her it was a bad idea!"

"And did you tell her to blame my wife?" Darcy demanded. "Did you spread rumours about the *ton* to the same effect?"

"No...no, I did not, I assure you."

"If you did," said Saye, "I shall find out. And I know people who know how to take care of loose tongues in the most dreadful, disfiguring way possible."

Miss Bingley looked shocked but only shook her head.

"Was it true when you told Georgiana you had heard rumours about Elizabeth?"

"No," said Miss Bingley. "No, it...I heard nothing. Everyone likes Mrs Darcy."

"They do. Must have eaten you up." Saye leant over her, taunting. "After all, *she* got your prize. All those years, all those gowns, and walking about to show your figure, and he never gave you a second glance. Then she just snatched him right up, did she not?"

With a haughty sniff, he straightened. "Bingley, get your sister out of my sight. If I have my way, she will never be received by anyone of consequence again."

TEN

COLD SHIVERS OF FEAR DESCENDED ON DARCY AS THE TRUTH emerged in excruciating plainness. Bingley struggled to discern what had happened in the brief months since his wedding, questioning and countering and insisting upon things in such a way Darcy could not have imagined.

"You have it plain, Bingley," he said at last, too exhausted to be frustrated. "I presumed to think my wife unfaithful on the testimony of some false gossip. That gossip was substantiated by some prank of your sister, and Elizabeth has gone to Yorkshire. Where I shall go now too."

Darcy announced the last abruptly, rising from his chair and stumbling immediately towards the door. Grief, fear, and sleeplessness combined to form a sort of stupor over him. "Yorkshire," he added.

"I shall accompany you," Fitzwilliam told him.

Darcy shook his head. "No. Going to ride fast."

"You cannot ride," Saye protested. "You will kill yourself and your horse for that distance."

Darcy chuckled darkly. "Would that not be ironic justice?"

"Darcy, go get some sleep," Fitzwilliam urged. "We shall go

at first light tomorrow. She is not going anywhere, and you will be better prepared to manage this…this…"

"Jumble? Catastrophe? Disaster?"

"You need rest to be able to think clearly," said Fitzwilliam. "Retrieving her will be the least of your concerns—you will need to find a good way to make it up to her."

THE TWO GENTLEMEN LEFT FOR YORKSHIRE THE NEXT MORNING, just as the first light of dawn began to seep over the horizon. Darcy cursed the tedium of the travel, wishing he could hasten the days and be by Elizabeth's side immediately. But the horses, fine as they were, seemed to crawl towards their destination.

"What are your thoughts, Darcy?"

"The enormity of my error," Darcy replied glumly. "And fears as to what this will mean for my marriage."

"You should have bought her a present," Fitzwilliam suggested. "Perhaps we should stop—"

"Present?" Darcy chuckled darkly. "I would have brought ten presents if I thought baubles and fripperies could have any meaning whatsoever to her. She is not that sort…I—"

A choking sob threatened to humiliate him, and he paused a moment. He ran a hand over his face, collecting himself.

"I am a fool." Darcy pressed the heels of his hands into his eyes, which burnt with exhaustion. "All I could think of was how quickly we married, and how little we really knew each other. It seemed…not surprising…when I was told she wished to have me only for my wealth. I could easily imagine George Wickham constructing such a scheme, and I could not bear to ask her and hear her tell me it was true, that she loved that scoundrel and not me."

"And so it was not," Fitzwilliam assured him in kindly tones, far more kind than was deserved. "She does love you and, let us hope, sufficient enough to forgive you."

Fitzwilliam had the foresight to send an express to the housekeeper of Gunnersdale, but nevertheless, she was not on hand when they arrived. No one was. It was a rather foreboding place, and Darcy shot his cousin a look. Fitzwilliam understood him immediately.

"It is a grouse moor, Darcy. I never promised Chatsworth. And I thought you intended to accompany her."

"Add this to my list of failures," said Darcy glumly. "Smelly, hideous place, no doubt she thought it an unjust punishment."

With no one to answer the door, eventually they admitted themselves. "Hallo there?" Fitzwilliam called out while Darcy called for his wife. There was no reply to either of them.

They made a quick tour of the sitting areas. Elizabeth was not in any of the common rooms, nor was she in the park closest to the house. Darcy supposed she might have either gone on a walk or was as yet unequal to seeing him. Of course, they had arrived a bit earlier than expected, and a walk was the most likely explanation—or so he hoped.

A quick tour of the grounds nearest the house yielded no clues. A queer sort of frantic feeling had entered into his gut as Darcy stood looking over the vast, inhospitable land. Where was his wife? Where was anyone?

Fitzwilliam seemed to hear his thoughts. "I have not the least notion what came of the housekeeper, but there is a little village to the west. Let us ask around there."

To call Muker a village was generous; it was something more on the order of a miners' encampment. However, it did yield up a Mrs Nelson who was meant to have charge of the house. Mrs Nelson was quick to aver that she had faithfully attended Mrs Darcy daily…except perhaps for the last day or so? Mayhap a week since she had seen her?

"She wanted for very little," Mrs Nelson insisted. "Hardly wished me to be hovering about her all the while."

"Mrs Nelson, my wife is gone!" Darcy roared causing Mr Nelson, who had just entered the small cottage, to step towards the men.

"'Scuse me, good sirs, but what're ye hollerin' at me missus fer?"

Darcy stepped back while Fitzwilliam took command of the situation. Terror had begun a fierce staccato in his breast, and he wanted to scream and shout and run madly about the countryside. Where was Elizabeth?

"It weren't too long but we knew what all this was about," Mr Nelson was saying to Fitzwilliam, rather sternly. "Only one sort of thing where the mister sends his lady off by herself and that be a fallen woman. Mrs Nelson is a decent church-going lady, and she did her duty, but we has our own reputations too. We dint wanna be too friendly."

"I beg your pardon," said Darcy icily, turning around with a glare that should have smote the man where he stood. But then he realised he could not. After all, he had believed it of her. Why should not this man—a miner by the looks of him—think the same? No doubt the entire neighbourhood would turn against her on just such a prejudice.

With her husband at her side, Mrs Nelson gained courage sufficient to be truthful, telling Fitzwilliam, "Begging your pardon, sir, but Mrs Darcy was often…well, more than a little upset. She ate barely nothing I cooked, and the bed was just as oft made as not. Then one day I realised it had been some days since I saw or heard from her and thought I had best attend her. When I went to her rooms, I saw she was not there."

Darcy began to pace, "It is very likely she had an accident while out walking. Was a search mounted?"

"No, sir."

"Why not?" Darcy demanded.

Mrs Nelson clasped her hands together to stop their trembling and looked up defiantly. "Because, sir, it appears she took her things."

"Took her things? Impossible," Darcy growled. And while he might have wished to say more, Fitzwilliam did not permit it, taking his arm and telling the two Nelsons that they would look into the matter back at Gunnersdale.

DARCY STRODE TO THE BEDCHAMBER IMMEDIATELY WHEN THEY returned to the house, intent on showing Fitzwilliam, the Nelsons, and any others who might concern themselves that Elizabeth had not left the house and her belongings were indeed in place. His cousin followed him, going directly to the armoire.

"First permit me…" Darcy's voice died as he realised that nearly everything was gone. He knew not precisely what she had brought with her, but of stockings, petticoats, corsets, and chemises, there were none. One gown remained in its place, a gown that had been a particular favourite of his. He wondered whether its abandonment was deliberate.

Her trunks were stowed in a corner of the dressing room, and the two gentlemen knelt next to them. The largest contained little more than a few house slippers, and Darcy reached in and pulled out a pair of half-boots.

Fitzwilliam observed, "Shoes require a good deal of space. It is likely she took only the pair she wore. A sturdier boot perhaps?"

"She had a different pair in Derbyshire, more suited for winter conditions or rockier terrain," Darcy said in a pensive tone. "She could not have walked to Richmond to get the stage. It is above 20 miles!"

"Sixteen, exactly," said Fitzwilliam. "I have walked that and a bit more in a day."

"You are a soldier. Elizabeth is a lady."

"A lady who often walks miles each day. Even the cold of Derbyshire did not stop her, correct?"

Darcy could not reply.

Fitzwilliam continued, "When I train new recruits, the first thing done is to strap a pack on their backs and hike a long distance—ten or fifteen miles or so. They survive."

"Men. Not ladies."

"The legs work the same. I would daresay, when motivated, a lady might accomplish what she needed to."

Darcy ran a hand over the small boot, then closed his eyes for a moment, unwilling to cede to the truth—not yet. Rather, Darcy responded to his fear in the way that was most familiar to him, that being to leap into action. They returned to the Nelsons' cottage and soon gathered a search party comprised of Mr Nelson's friends, and a survey of the grounds was begun but with little expectation of a good result.

It proved most fortunate that Colonel Fitzwilliam had accompanied him to Yorkshire, for if left to his own devices, Darcy might have proposed to walk every inch of the estate himself, seeking clues as to the location of his wife. The two gentlemen spoke to the local magistrate regarding Mrs Darcy, and he asked at the nearest post coach stops about any women of her description. Alas, there was no information forthcoming, and Darcy was reduced to spending hours on horseback, riding around the estate shouting Elizabeth's name.

After over a week of doing all they could to gain some clue as to Elizabeth's whereabouts, Fitzwilliam made a discovery—a letter behind the table in the bedchamber where Elizabeth had slept.

"Darcy, I found this," he said, entering the make-shift study Darcy had organised. It was furnished only with stacks of paper and two hard chairs, but it was all they had. "I believe it is your wife's hand, though I cannot know for certain. I read only the greeting and brought it to you immediately."

Darcy took the letter, unfolded it, and read:

Fitzwilliam,

Be not alarmed, sir, on receiving this letter, by the apprehension of its containing any repetition of those sentiments, which have been, of late, so disgusting to you. I write without any intention of paining you, or humbling myself, or by dwelling on wishes, which, for the happiness of both, cannot be too soon forgotten. You must pardon the freedom with which I demand your attention; your feelings, I know, will bestow it unwillingly, but I demand it of your justice.

I have been gravely offensive to you, though the nature of my offence, I know not. Was my father correct? Was your infatuation with me merely lust that reduced itself to ash in our months at Pemberley? Was my offence that I was not born high enough for you, a fact that became too obvious once we left the country for town? You grew to disdain and despise me—this much was made evident— but whether it was for what I am or what I failed to be, I shall never know.

What I do know is that you vowed before God to love me, and you have done poorly at that. I have loved you with all my heart, but now I shall stop. Indeed, I must stop before it kills me. I shall go on, somewhere in a place where no one has ever heard of Elizabeth Bennet and Fitzwilliam Darcy, and I shall not again intrude upon your notice, so help me God.

Just know that you were loved wholly and completely with a maiden heart that knew not love before, and you threw it away.

I shall only add, God bless you.
Elizabeth

He stumbled back, her words dealing a blow that he could not have imagined. Wordlessly, he handed the letter to his cousin, who paled a bit when he read it but tightened his jaw and merely said, "Perhaps we shall find her with her family."

Darcy nodded, already knowing it was not likely to be true but wanting to hope. "Let us return to London at first light. We shall stop in Hertfordshire."

THE GENTLEMEN TRAVELLED TO HERTFORDSHIRE, HOPING RATHER than believing that they would find Elizabeth at Netherfield or Longbourn. Bingley greeted them with a smile that suggested he had not told his wife any of what he knew; Jane Bingley looked as serenely delighted as ever. Darcy groaned internally, knowing he was minutes away from unleashing pain and agony upon her smiling face.

When they were settled in the drawing room and the servants had been sent away, Bingley asked carefully, "Is Lizzy in London then? I had hoped we would see her with you."

Sweet and guileless, Mrs Bingley exclaimed, "How I wish my dear sister had accompanied you. I simply long to see her!"

"I…I wish she was with me too." Darcy dropped his eyes and cleared his throat. "Bingley…um, has…does Mrs Bingley—"

"Jane," said Mrs Bingley warmly. "After all, are we not brother and sister now?"

"Jane," said Darcy with as much of a smile as he could muster, "have you…"

"The tale is yours to tell, Darcy," said Bingley. Jane glanced at him, finally seeming to perceive that all was not well. Her eyes turned from delight to curiosity as she looked to Darcy for answers.

He paused a moment to collect himself and then began, first, with the stories of their time in London, of the alleged rumours and the secret love affair of Elizabeth and George Wickham.

At this, Jane burst into laughter, raising her hand to cover her mouth. "What on earth! Who would say such ridiculous things of Lizzy?!"

Bingley patted her hand. "Loath as I am to admit it, it was our own sister Caroline."

"Caroline! But…no. Perhaps she misunderstood…"

Darcy explained Caroline's role in hiding the note and the handkerchief among Elizabeth's things. Jane's amusement turned to a flush of anger, sending her husband fierce looks of which Darcy could not have imagined her capable.

"She will never live under my roof again," she hissed quietly.

"I shall never argue with you on that score," Bingley promised, then took a moment to explain to Darcy that Caroline had been sent to Scarborough to stay at the home of their grandmother.

When Jane learnt that Lizzy had been sent to Yorkshire, it was worse yet. Tears came to her eyes, and she stared at Darcy with a cerulean gaze that pierced him. "Alone? You sent her off alone?"

"I…I did not wish Wickham to find her, and we thought she might… She is…with child. With…with my child."

At this, Jane let out a small gasping sob, turning her face into her husband's chest and weeping piteously.

"But as soon as they learnt the truth," Bingley said with optimism, "they went off to retrieve her. Full of apologies and promises, I am sure, eh, Darcy? And where is our Lizzy now?"

Darcy looked down, rubbing his hands together, dreading telling them more. Jane had stopped crying and was looking at him with frightened, tear-filled eyes. He finally said, "I do not know. I had hoped to find her here."

BINGLEY RETURNED TO HIS STUDY OVER AN HOUR LATER. JANE had become completely undone at the notion that her dearest friend and sister had gone missing. Bingley had carried his hysterical wife to her room and called her maid to give her something to help her sleep, and then he had held her in his arms as she sobbed herself into slumber.

Darcy looked at him as he entered. "Is Jane well?"

"I can take care of my own wife, thank you. I believe your

efforts would best be directed towards worrying about your own."

Darcy hung his head.

Fitzwilliam spoke. "Bingley, Darcy does realise the full extent of his error."

"Perhaps," Bingley said. "But what now? Can you imagine the manner of harm that might have befallen Lizzy by this time?"

At this, Colonel Fitzwilliam spoke, detailing for Bingley the various search efforts that were being undertaken, the planned activities of the professional men, as well as those of himself and Darcy. He then asked Bingley whether he had any other ideas or possibilities they had not yet considered. Bingley had none; Darcy and Fitzwilliam had laid out a thorough plan for the search. Despite this, the three gentlemen spent the next several hours reviewing the schemes to be executed post haste and the scant clues and theories they had about her flight.

When Bingley's curiosity was satisfied, there was a brief period of silence until he spoke. "It is difficult to comprehend you, Darcy. Did you ever love her?"

"How can you ask me that? You were here. You saw us falling in love."

"I saw her falling in love. I saw you losing your wits. I think she was a plaything that delighted you until she did not."

"How can you say so? We were…we were so happy until…until…"

"Do not think I forgive my sister her part. Indeed, I do not. But if someone played such a trick on me, if someone told me Jane was unfaithful, do you know what I would do? I would laugh. And then I would tell her of it, and we would laugh about it together. Jane is a beautiful woman, the most handsome I have ever known, and I do not doubt that every man we see longs to possess her. But she pledged herself to me, and I believe in the inherent goodness of her enough to trust that. You did not believe in Lizzy. You decided her character was false."

"The truth of it is," said Darcy, "I did not think much about her at all. I was too concerned with my fears and my past with Wickham. I was selfish. I was too quick to look upon her with disdain."

"Where could she have gone?" Bingley asked, as much to himself as the other men. "Why not come to her family?"

Fitzwilliam said, "In Yorkshire, we learnt that the house-keeper...well, she believed she had charge of a fallen woman. She was thus not friendly for fear of her own reputation. I have no doubt Elizabeth knew of that prejudice against her, and the last thing she would wish is to bring that into her home county, to see her old friends and relations turn against her."

A choked sound came from somewhere in the tight knot in Darcy's chest. The other two looked at him and then just as quickly looked away. "Forgive me," he said hoarsely, but he knew not whether he spoke to them or to Elizabeth, wherever she might be.

KNOWING ELIZABETH WAS NOT AT LONGBOURN BUT understanding the need to speak to Mr and Mrs Bennet, they called there next. It was a terrible meeting, with Darcy and Fitzwilliam gathered together in the sitting room with Mr and Mrs Bennet whilst the younger ones flitted about, talking of sons of earls and regimentals.

Darcy related the tale without any attempt to either defend himself or ameliorate his circumstances. Mrs Bennet, as would be expected, immediately began to scream and weep, crying for her salts and demanding as much attention as she could. As Hill bustled in to take her to her chambers, Mr Bennet said nothing.

Several minutes ticked by. Still, Mr Bennet said nothing, looking at Darcy with an unreadable expression in his eyes. At last he spoke, "Mr Darcy, when you asked for my daughter's hand, I told you that I felt you were both acting in haste. When you prevailed over my wishes, I tried to reassure myself that you were an honourable gentleman and would make her happy.

"How deeply regretful I am to see that I am both correct in the former and incorrect in the latter. How much I do rue the day that my daughter laid her eyes upon you. Please leave my home now and importune my family no further."

With that, he rose and exited the room. Darcy felt numb as Fitzwilliam led him from the house and back into the carriage.

When Darcy and Fitzwilliam returned to London, their immediate wish was to visit the Gardiners, with whom Elizabeth had been intimate. Darcy prayed the entire way back to London that he might find her with them, or at the very least, that she might have written to Mrs Gardiner telling of her plans to depart Gunnerside.

Although his acquaintance with the Gardiners was brief, they had impressed him with their genteel bearing and the elegance in their manners. It was an awful task to go to them now and tell them what he had done to their beloved niece.

After admitting him and his cousin, the group adjourned to the sitting room. Darcy knew Elizabeth had come to her aunt on at least one occasion for advice. He remembered one day when he received Mrs Gardiner's note informing him that Elizabeth had fallen ill and would stay in Cheapside for the night. He had believed it was a cover for an assignation with Wickham.

Mr and Mrs Gardiner looked more than a little wary as they greeted the men, though their manners, as always, were impeccable as they waited for Darcy to explain the purpose of his visit.

The entire scene was reminiscent of what had occurred at Netherfield. He informed them that she was gone, and they told him that they had no notion of her whereabouts. Mrs Gardiner wept; Mr Gardiner was angry and demanded answers and plans.

By far, however, the most painful part was when Mrs Gardiner attempted to blame herself. "I am so sorry... When she came to me, my advice was poor. I am ashamed when I think—"

"No, no," Darcy protested immediately. "None of this is anyone's fault but mine."

Mrs Gardiner was by now weeping earnestly. "If I had only come to you myself…"

It was her simple words that had the most effect of any he had heard thus far, as he realised in full how frightened and sad Elizabeth must have felt, blaming herself and not knowing what to do to make it right between them. Mrs Gardiner's anger he would have expected; anger, disdain, and disgust were all emotions anticipated by Darcy—and understood. However, to receive kindness and an attempt to assume some of the burden of shame he so richly deserved was unexpected and doubly more agonising than Mrs Gardiner's contempt could have been.

It was so painful that for a moment, it broke him. Ashamed and embarrassed, he attempted to explain to these people who were so dear to Elizabeth that he had never, not even for one second, stopped loving her, nor had he ever regretted having her as his wife. Over and over, he told them, "I cannot tell you how I regret my stupid pride. My cruelty! I have acted despicably and foolishly, and I am so, so sorry. Yet, although I own the error of my ways, it makes no difference. She is gone, and I do not know whether I shall ever see her again."

It was then that Mr Gardiner mercifully terminated the entire interview, rising and telling the gentlemen that he must attend to his weeping wife, and he asked them to leave.

ELEVEN

December 25, 1812

ALIGHTING FROM HIS CARRIAGE, DARCY STEPPED DIRECTLY INTO an icy puddle, the chill of the water instantly penetrating his boot. He sighed, caring nothing for his discomfort, but immediately wondering whether Elizabeth was warm, wherever she was.

Elizabeth had now been gone over six months. Somewhere in the world, she had come of age, and they had been married a year complete. Perhaps she had given birth to their child. Perhaps she had died in childbed. Darcy tried not to consider that.

He had spent countless sums of money and every spare moment searching for her. Hired men went all over England, and Darcy himself spent many days and weeks going into little towns and places that had any small connexion to her or to them in the hope someone might have seen her.

When he was not traveling about, Darcy spent every waking hour thinking of her, going over the various reports and notes that had been generated as part of his searches, as well as interrogating the men he hired to find her. In general, he slept little, he drank too much, and he accomplished nothing. His money, his influence, his friends in lofty circles meant nothing for the recovery of his wife. Elizabeth was gone.

In London, the rumours begun by Lady Matlock continued to circulate. Some said Elizabeth had consumption, others thought it was a miscarriage, and some believed it was a carriage accident. Some said she had died, a tale supported by Darcy's increasingly gaunt figure. Others took his frequent absences as proof that he had gone to see her. Saye proved ruthless for any who dared question the family lore; he had served the cut direct to one hapless maiden who had voiced her doubts, and the poor lady was not spoken to by any of her circle for a month complete. After that, Mrs Darcy's terrible sickness was not questioned, and her name was frequently raised in the prayer circles at St George's.

It being Christmas, he had been bidden to appear at Matlock House for dinner in a manner that suggested refusal was not a choice. Lady Matlock had made it plain that she expected his presence even if she had to drag him bodily from his study.

"Darcy!" Lord Matlock exclaimed from the doorway a bit too heartily, obviously trying to force the cheer in his voice. "I doubted that even my wife's relentless efforts would get you here!"

Tiredly, Darcy forced a grim smile to his countenance. "Happy Christmas, Uncle."

"To you too." Lord Matlock held out his arm, gesturing Darcy down the hall towards the salon. He entered the room to find only his aunt and Fitzwilliam awaited him. "Where is my sister?"

"Here I am," came a quiet voice from the doorway. Darcy turned to see his sister and tried not to gasp at the pale, wraith-like creature who greeted him with a wan smile.

Darcy was so busy traveling and seeking his wife, it had seemed best to leave her in the care of Lady Matlock. Georgiana sank into a deep depression following the events of the summer. Recognising that she had ruined her own prospects as well as contributed to the destruction of her brother's life, she could not bear to be in his presence.

He could not deny it—he was angry with her for what she had done. It was not his way to lay the burden of his errors on others, but neither could he hold her blameless. She had lied and schemed and all but lain with a man not her husband. He had failed, but so had she.

But now he would try to help her. He wanted to forgive her just as he wished to be forgiven—and when better, than at Christmas? He had hired a new companion for her, Mrs Annesley, a woman in her mid-forties who was the widow of a clergyman. He was frank with the lady when he employed her, explaining the situation with George Wickham, though not the truth of Elizabeth's whereabouts. He dearly hoped Mrs Annesley would help his sister heal from her past indiscretions and provide the needed remedy for his own failures with her.

After he embraced Georgiana and told her about her new companion, Fitzwilliam invited Darcy into his father's study. When the two men had closeted themselves, the colonel went immediately to the sideboard. "Drink?"

"Thank you," Darcy replied, as Fitzwilliam found his father's hidden store of French brandy and poured some for each.

"I hear Bingley's wife is with child," said his cousin. "They anticipate the birth in late February or early March."

A shock of commingled pleasure, pain, and envy went through Darcy. In general, he dared not think of his own child—if indeed the child existed. But it was close hitting, this notion of Bingley and his happy marriage turning into a happy young family. "Wonderful," was the only utterance he could make. "I congratulate him and wish them well."

"He has not written?"

Darcy smiled faintly. "Even if he had, whether the news was legible would have been questionable."

"True." Fitzwilliam chuckled lightly.

After a pause, Darcy prompted, "But you did not call me in here to speak of Bingley."

"No, no. I heard from Chester just a few days ago." Chester, a lead agent with the Bow Street Runners, was the principal man engaged in finding Elizabeth. A retired army man, he had formed a bond with Fitzwilliam, much preferring him to Darcy. Despite the fact that Darcy paid his bill, it was clear Chester did not respect a man who had lost his own wife.

He watched as his cousin took elaborate care in pouring a second drink for himself, offering another to Darcy as well. Then taking up a position by the fireplace, Fitzwilliam at last spoke, evidently choosing his words cautiously. "Chester and I reviewed the status of the various tracks they have followed in looking for Elizabeth. From a...practical perspective, it might be worthwhile to reduce the scale of things, or so he suggested."

"I do not understand," Darcy said.

"With no new information and few good possibilities, it makes no good sense to employ so many men to go into places where she is not likely to—"

"He wants to quit?" Darcy interrupted angrily. "I had not realised that I had engaged such a bootless group. Let us find someone with a bit more fortitude then, someone who—"

"You misunderstand me," Fitzwilliam hastened to say. "This is for your own interests. He does not wish to see you waste your money for vain efforts."

Darcy was not mollified. "Until Elizabeth is returned to her home, these efforts are not in vain! She is out there somewhere, and surely someone must have information on her whereabouts!"

"The most likely clues have been exhausted, and the possibilities for significant enquiry depleted. Yes, he can continue to search blindly, going into random towns in search of her and billing you accordingly if that is what you wish, to continue mounting expenses—"

"Twice as many men," Darcy ordered, "going into twice as many towns."

Fitzwilliam held up his hands. "No one is saying you should give up on her, but putting more men onto a haphazard effort will only drain your coffers with little chance of reward."

"What good is my money if my wife is…if she is…"

"She might have left England," Fitzwilliam added gently. "If so, the chance of finding her is quite slim."

"They would surely have found evidence of her passage on a ship, would they not? Somewhere in the manifest?"

"If she used the name Darcy," Fitzwilliam said. "Or Bennet or Gardiner or any of the other names we supposed she might have used. One thing is certain—your wife was canny about her disappearance. We are not merely seeking someone who is lost, but rather, someone who wishes not to be found."

"Her intelligence is one of the things I love about her," said Darcy softly.

"At this point, I do not think that Mrs Darcy will—"

"Do not say it." Darcy drained his drink in one aggressive motion, swallowing the fiery liquid and appreciating the pain in his throat. "Just…keep the men on. No changes. Find her—that is all I ask."

Fitzwilliam studied him carefully.

"Perhaps in…another few months, we shall revisit the need for their services with an eye towards possible retrenching. I just think that—"

"Enough," Darcy replied sharply. "It will have to do."

"Very well, then," his cousin said. "Shall we join the others?"

NOT SURPRISINGLY, DARCY COULD NOT ENJOY HIMSELF. EVEN before the conversation with his cousin, he had been irritable and anxious; now he was prodigiously uncivil, and he knew it. With his sister, he was gentler, but to the others, he was distinctly lacking in good cheer. He excused himself as early as was decent, and no one tried overmuch to stop him.

It was a relief to be at home in his own bedchamber, safe

within walls of familiar misery. For a time, he restrained himself, sitting by the fire and staring vacantly into the flames. At last, he rose and went to his desk, pulling open the drawer and selecting a parcel that lay inside. He refilled his brandy, then went to sit by the fire once more.

He stroked the parcel, a small, elongated box that contained an exquisite and expensive necklace of opals. He had spent hours selecting it at the jewellers, debating its merits against those of the other lovely pieces on display, but he had ultimately chosen it because its luminosity reminded him of Elizabeth's skin.

For a moment, looking at the opals made him think of one night they had spent at Pemberley in his bed. It had been a full moon, and he had not drawn the curtains around them. Elizabeth had fallen asleep after their intimacy, and she remained unclothed, touched by the moonlight and turned into a luminous, ethereal beauty. Her wild tumble of dark curls had only emphasised the effect. The vision was so enrapturing, it had stolen his breath away, and he had sworn that his heart stopped beating for several moments while he gazed on her that night.

He opened the box and ran his finger lightly over the jewels. "You pale in comparison, although you are quite lovely."

Closing the box, he leaned his head back, thinking of last year at this time. He had given her a beautiful fur-lined pelisse; she had given him a new set of books and a fine French brandy that her uncle had procured for her. He had urged her to taste it with him, which made her look at him in that wide-eyed, startled look that he loved, but he had insisted.

The first tentative sip had caused her to choke a bit, but he had encouraged her to persevere, and the second went down a bit better. A few more generous sips, and she was giggly and flushed and delightfully responsive to his amorous advances.

The recall to his current location and situation was devastating, and thus it was, with the drops that remained of his fifth brandy still drying in the glass, that he offered himself a bit of a

Christmas present in the form of a good prolonged period of quite unmanly weeping.

THE YEAR OF 1813 BEGAN AS WOULD BE EXPECTED IN JANUARY, with a sleety, snowy rain that kept most of the inhabitants of London indoors. Darcy stood on the first day of the New Year, restive and unsettled, though he knew not why.

His anxiety for Elizabeth's health had rapidly elevated in the days since Christmas, and he could not understand, in the absence of any new information, why it would be so. The depth of his concern for her was even greater than it had been in the initial days of her disappearance. He was now having nightly dreams of terrible fates befalling her, and even during the day, he could not push his concerns from his mind, experiencing a constant niggling fear that somehow she was not well, that wherever she was, she was ill or in grave danger. Impulse drove him to run to her—and he would have if he knew where to go. Instead, he stood at the window, frustrated and useless, wanting to scream out her name.

His butler entered the room. "Miss Caroline Bingley, sir."

"Miss Bingley?" Darcy's brows shot up. What on earth was Miss Bingley doing calling upon him? He agreed to allow her entry, irregular as it was.

He did not invite her into his study, rather choosing to meet her in the street-facing blue saloon. She was standing therein, gazing out the window to the street below. When Darcy entered, she turned, looking uncertain.

"Thank you for receiving me."

"What do you want?" he asked sharply.

She opened her mouth, then closed it again. After a moment's hesitation, she said, "I came to town hoping to see my brother's child…"

"A bit early for that, are you not?"

"Yes." She lowered her head. "Yes, I had hoped they would allow me to remain but...but I am needed in Scarborough."

"What is it you want from me?"

She disregarded his attempt to come to the point. "Louisa tells me they will name her Elizabeth if she is a girl. As if... almost as if..."

Darcy stared coldly.

"Well, as if they think she is dead. Do you think her dead?"

"We are finished now." Darcy walked towards her and extended his arm towards the door. "You will go. Thank you for calling, but do not trespass on my notice again."

"A moment!" she cried. "Forgive me, I did not mean...I mean, surely it has crossed your mind?"

"Do you understand," he said tightly, "that you played a substantial role in my wife being out on her own, yes, possibly dead, yes, possibly hurt? The blame is mine, but you do share it."

"Yes, and I wish to apologise to you and hope that you would allow me to"—she licked her lips—"make it up to you."

Darcy quickly backed away. "I do not know what you mean."

Her voice husky, Miss Bingley reached for his hand. "What is the harm in you and I resuming our...particular friendship?"

"I beg your pardon," said Darcy as icily as he could. "There is no particular friendship between us."

"You are a man with a man's needs, Darcy, and Eliza never could have filled them. The baser needs perhaps...but I think you will soon see that I can do it all." A tall woman, it required very little effort for her to press her lips against his, her hand reaching around to pull him to her.

"Stop it!" Darcy leapt backwards.

Miss Bingley smiled, her hand lightly tracing her bodice. "Come, Darcy. Why be faithful to a wife who is lost to you?"

"I do not know—"

"What woman could ever love a man who treated her so very infamously?"

"Get out," Darcy ordered, feeling his rage turning his face purple.

"You need me," she said, with a knowing smile. "And I am willing to fill that need."

She moved towards the door, pausing a moment to say, "We are not done here, Darcy. I shall tell everyone I know about our *affaire de coeur*, and how your country mouse simply could not abide it."

"Do not dare spread your filth," he hissed. "I shall see you ruined. Scarborough will be too good for you when I am done."

The last fell on deaf ears as she had already quit the room. Darcy sank into a chair, running his hand through his hair. "Hateful, stupid woman."

TWELVE

September 1812

ELIZABETH'S SITUATION WITH MRS MACY WAS EXCEEDINGLY pleasing, far better than she ever could have imagined when she ran away from Gunnersdale. Upton Park was beautiful, and she had plenty of places to walk and enjoy. Mrs Macy encouraged Elizabeth to be out of doors as much as possible, from a belief she held that it was good for ladies in a delicate condition to be exposed to fresh air.

The neighbourhood had the notion that she was a niece or a granddaughter, related to some Macy who had been killed...in the war? An accident? The story varied, but no matter, Elizabeth did nothing to discourage the tales. After all, she wished to keep some sort of dignity about her, and there was no hiding the fact that she was with child by now. It would not do to appear as some sort of fallen woman.

She found a great deal in common with Mrs Macy. The older lady was intelligent and well-read and had many interesting stories to tell of her life. Elizabeth could not help but wonder whether the doctor had mistaken her malady. Unfortunately, as the autumn began to gain on them, she started to see an increasing number of signs of Mrs Macy's illness. There were bad times interspersed with good, and the doctor who attended her told Elizabeth that she should expect an increasing number of bad times until the good, lucid days were but a rarity.

She came upon the good lady one day on a bench in the garden, weeping over the death of her spring flowers.

"Just look at what those gardeners have done! They killed all the bluebells. Just yesterday, these hills were covered with bluebells, and now the gardeners have gone and killed them all. Why would they do such a thing?"

"My dear, it is nearly autumn. I am sure we shall see the bluebells again in the spring."

"Autumn? That cannot be," Mrs Macy protested.

"Indeed, ma'am, it is the end of September," Elizabeth insisted gently. "We shall see the bluebells again in the spring."

Mrs Macy said nothing to this, merely nodding uncertainly and allowing Elizabeth to lead her back to the house.

Another time, as they sat in the drawing room after dinner, Mrs Macy announced, "My goodness, I am hungry. What shall we eat for dinner? I do hope for a roast duck."

"We have just had our dinner, roast beef. Shall I tell cook you would like a roast duck tomorrow?"

Querulously, Mrs Macy said, "I have not had my dinner. Would you starve me to death?"

"Of course not, but we have dined already. Let me see whether there are some biscuits for you to have with your sherry."

The older lady frowned severely, her jaw trembling. She paid no heed to the offer of a biscuit and instead picked up the sewing in her lap.

Less than a quarter hour later, she brightly announced, "Oh, I am so hungry this evening! What shall we dine on? Mutton? As hungry as I am, anything will do."

BENNET FITZWILLIAM DARCY WAS BORN ON THE SECOND DAY OF January 1813 after a remarkably easy delivery that left Elizabeth thinking she had expected there to be more to it than there was. Bennet proved an uncommonly easy baby as well, eating and sleeping as he was meant to right from the start. In both looks and temperament, he closely resembled his father, being a serious, thoughtful child with a burgeoning head of dark curls and a clear tendency towards above-average height. Even the styling of his hands and feet attested to the fact that he was Darcy's son.

The arrival of Bennet invigorated the household, which, with the exception of Elizabeth, was by and large older. The butler and housekeeper, Mr and Mrs Mercer, were only a few years younger than Mrs Macy, and even her nurse, Harriet, was in her fifties. Yet once Bennet appeared, nearly all seemed to shed decades. Mrs Mercer revealed a previously hidden talent for singing as she battled Nurse Harriet for the right to rock him to sleep in the nursery, and Mr Mercer seemed to wish for nothing more but the chance to tell him story after story with no recompense but the firm grip of her son's fist on his finger. Elizabeth wondered at times whether the old wives' tale was true that a child carried too much will never learn to walk, for if so, Bennet was doomed. He spent almost every moment, awake or asleep, in the arms of the many loving adults who lived with him.

For Mrs Macy, Bennet's arrival restored her senses in a way none of the tonics or elixirs she drank ever could. Throughout the spring and early summer of 1813, she was sharp witted and unconfused, and Elizabeth began to feel she might have recovered after all.

In September, Mrs Macy went to Elizabeth while she played with her son in the nursery. "Oh, Amelia, just watch! Look what he can do!" Elizabeth beamed proudly as she induced her son, who was crouched uncertainly on all fours in front of her, to make a few shuffling movements towards a small carved horse she held just beyond his grasp.

"Well done, Master Bennet," said Mrs Macy with a delighted sigh. "You will be chasing him all over the house soon enough, Elizabeth."

"Just when I think I have the knack of one thing, he comes up with something new!" Elizabeth said with a rueful laugh.

"Come and sit with me," said Mrs Macy. "I have something less pleasant than our dear boy to discuss."

With a nod, Elizabeth rose. They had hired a sweet young girl from Wales named Meredith (who preferred to be called Merry) to help care for Bennet—Nurse Harriet had not liked it, but there were many days her hands were too full with Mrs Macy to see to the child—as Mrs Macy thought it unseemly that Elizabeth should have the care of her own child. Merry went to Bennet immediately, and Elizabeth left them to go sit with Mrs Macy in the parlour.

The old lady situated herself in a swirl of ochre silk and the scent of gardenia. She had taken of late to wearing ball gowns during the day. Elizabeth said nothing of it, unsure whether it was her disease or mere eccentricity. "You must prepare yourself, Lizzy, for I feel very certain I shall not last the winter."

"But no! You have been feeling so much better, and I think with the new tonic—"

"New tonic," Mrs Macy scoffed. "Sugar water and laudanum. Does nothing for me but make me sleep through the pain. No, my dear, do not protest. I feel it spreading, this disease, eating away at my bones, and it is gaining on us. I shall not see spring, to be sure. One comes to know these things. But much as I know my own fate, yours weighs heavily on my mind."

"Do not think of me," Elizabeth replied immediately.

"But of course I think of you. My dear girl, you have become the child of my heart, the daughter I never had. I treasure the comforts of these last months more than you will ever know."

Tears sprung into Elizabeth's eyes, but Mrs Macy was not finished.

"Will you go back to him?"

"To...to Darcy?"

Mrs Macy nodded.

"No," Elizabeth said immediately. Then, with more thought, "Who is to say he would not take Bennet and divorce me? I have lately read of a case where a woman was sent to the gallows for stealing her husband's property—that property being his child."

Mrs Macy nodded. "I presumed as much. I should hope someone from such a family as the Darcys would not stoop to such evil, but you know him, and I do not."

"I wonder whether I ever knew him myself."

"In any case," Mrs Macy continued briskly, "upon my death, Upton Park reverts back to my husband's family. Try as I might, there is nothing to stop those dreadful jackals he was related to from taking it. But I have my own property, a house in Johnstone Row, that has been let for some time. The tenants are giving it up, and I intend to leave it to you, along with sufficient funds to maintain it."

"A house?" Elizabeth gaped and then laughed. "Oh no. You are too generous, and I simply could not—"

"You must. Please do not insist that I waste my dwindling breath persuading you. You have nothing, and I wish to provide for you and Bennet. Do an old lady the favour of graciously accepting the offer."

It was too much in return for the slight service she had given Mrs Macy, but the older lady held firm. "One day, you will be old, God willing, and when you are, you will find there is nothing quite as important as feeling loved and cared for. For whatever personal misfortune brought you to me, I am simultaneously grieved and blessed."

Mrs Macy passed on January 6, 1814. They had come to expect it—she had lain unresponsive in her bed since before Christmas—but it was a shock nevertheless. Elizabeth sent

Bennet off on a walk with Merry and wept hard, long, and loud for the loss of the woman who had become mother, grandmother, and best friend. "Please stay," she said in a choked, futile whisper, using the backs of her fingers to caress the wrinkled, papery cheek. "Please."

But it was not to be. Elizabeth did all she could to honour the lady in death, caring for her household just as she would have wished. After the good lady was buried, her more primal grief subsided into numb acceptance, though one refrain would not leave her. It was a phrase used by her mother, and Elizabeth now felt she understood the powerlessness behind her mother's oft-repeated lament: what will become of us all?

As a household, they moved to the house on Johnstone Row in February. It was a double-terraced house of stucco with bowed windows and a mansard roof, boasting a view of both the sea and the statue of old King George. Mrs Macy had purchased it in 1810, newly built, with the intention of letting it out for income.

Elizabeth was pleased by the situation, it placing her near several of the acquaintances she had made: Miss Lillian Goddard, Miss Olivia Lacey, and Miss Jenny Haverhill. Her secrets prohibited true intimacy with the young ladies—it was easier to remain distant than explain her complicated past and why she was not Mrs Elizabeth, as they called her, but in fact, Mrs Darcy—but they were all pleasant ladies, and one could easily while away an afternoon here or there with them.

She missed her family desperately. She wondered often about Jane, thinking it likely that she was an aunt now and Bennet probably had cousins. She thought of her younger sisters, hoping that they were well and had matured beyond the stage of trying silliness and youthful over-exuberance. It was possible one of them might be married as well. She thought often of writing to them but reasoned they had likely grieved her and moved on with their lives. A letter from her would only reopen wounds best left closed.

Sometimes her mind wandered to thinking about her

husband, though she did all she could to avoid those unhappy times. It could do her no good to dwell on what was past or what might have been. Oftentimes, she wondered at her curious lack of anger with him. Other than her first day at Upton Park, she had never really spent much time crying over her situation nor regretting him. She had done such an excellent job of maintaining an appearance of happiness that it had become her reality. She conceded that it was likely best to simply move past that which could not be changed.

In March, she was required to go to London briefly for some last dealings with Mrs Macy's solicitors. It was the first time she was in town since she had been sent off, and it roused in her no small amount of anxiety. Fortunately, the location of the solicitors' office was in an unfamiliar part of town, though she knew she must remain firm in her resolution not to go anywhere near Gracechurch Street or Darcy's home.

Alarmingly, she soon learnt that she had met Mrs Macy's heir previously. Mr Henry Macy was a gentleman of her husband's acquaintance, though not of his intimate circle. Fortunately, she had the foresight to introduce herself as Mrs Bennet. Thinking she was his aunt's paid companion, he dismissed her immediately from his notice.

To soothe her nerves and stretch her legs, she decided to take a short stroll in Hyde Park before returning to her carriage for the journey back to Weymouth. She restricted herself to the quieter, lesser-populated paths to avoid seeing any whom she knew. It was early enough in the morning that none of the *ton* could be stirring, although the park was rife with governesses and children.

Just as she entered the park, she passed a pair of small boys being forcefully led away by their governess, who was delivering them a fierce scolding.

"...such horseplay is not fitting to young gentlemen! Why you nearly knocked down that fine gentleman, and if you had, I would not have been a bit surprised if he had switched you right there! You can be sure your mother will hear of this…" Her voice faded away as she pulled her small charges by their hands out of the park.

Elizabeth felt a bit wistful watching them go. Bennet would never have a brother to engage in horseplay with, and it was unlikely he would ever even see Hyde Park, not as a child anyway.

THIRTEEN

London, 1813

DARCY, FEELING HOW MUCH HE HAD FAILED, EMBARKED ON A scheme to improve himself. In his first efforts in that regard, he had penned long letters to each of Elizabeth's family members, apologising to them for what he had done. He was painfully honest, owning to all the defects in his character that had led to his present circumstance.

I have been a selfish being all my life, in practice, though not in principle. As a child I was taught what was right, but I was not taught to correct my temper. I was given good principles, but left to follow them in pride and conceit. Unfortunately an only son (for many years an only child), I was spoilt by my parents, who though good themselves (my father particularly, all that was benevolent and amiable), allowed, encouraged, almost taught me to be selfish and overbearing, to care for none beyond my own family circle, to think meanly of all the rest of the world, to wish at least to think meanly of their sense and worth compared with my own. It is this that has led to my downfall, but I assure you, it will be no more. I shall change, and I shall become a husband worthy of Elizabeth when she returns.

Mr Gardiner called on him soon after receiving his letter, and the two men shook hands. From the Bennets, however, he heard nothing until the spring of 1813 when Mr Bennet sent him a letter shortly after Easter.

Mr Darcy,

I write to you not because I wish it but on behalf of my wife. She has gladly seen Mary settled into matrimony, and that done, she is anxious to complete the business with our two youngest. Your friend Bingley, as I am sure you are aware, is greatly occupied with expanding his nursery. As your own is, and will likely remain, empty, I should think you can spare a place for your mother-in-law and her daughters, perhaps even secure them some introductions to likely suitors.

Try not to lose any of them. Silly and ignorant though they are, I am fond of them.

T. Bennet

Darcy learnt from Bingley that the former Miss Mary Bennet was now the second Mrs Collins. Mrs Charlotte Collins had died in childbed, and Mr Collins had wasted very little time in setting his sights on a second wife. Unseemly? Perhaps, but a man who had sent his wife away could scarce have an opinion.

As for the proposal that he take on the younger Miss Bennets, Darcy had but one thought: *culpae poenae par esto. Let the punishment fit the crime.* But would he ever be forgiven? Did he deserve forgiveness from this man? Likely not, but Mr Bennet did deserve the respite it would afford him, and thus Darcy agreed.

Kitty and Lydia Bennet, now ages nineteen and seventeen respectively, were still silly and nonsensical. Both girls were delighted to be in London and wasted little of the opportunity afforded them. After a short period of time spent depleting their clothing allowance, they attended any event to which Darcy could secure them an invitation. They were more determined flirts than ever, each focused on the goal of finding a husband, preferably before the other did. Mrs Bennet did little to check them, no matter how wild they were. Because they were also pretty, more was forgiven them than Darcy might have imagined. Nevertheless, the Season began to draw to a close without a single offer made for either of them, the gentleman of the *ton* being ever mindful of fortune.

BY THE MIDDLE OF JULY, WHEN TOWN BEGAN TO EMPTY OF everyone and everything of interest, Lydia Bennet thought that life among the *ton* was not nearly as interesting as she had hoped it would be. She walked with Kitty in Hyde Park one dreadfully hot day, dreaming of something or someone to take her mind off the tedium.

"Kitty, look over there! Is that not Mr George Wickham? You know, the very handsome one who used to be with Colonel Forster's regiment?"

"Aye, Lydia. And more handsome than ever! See there—a man can look as well without his regimentals as with!"

"Kitty! Who have you been seeing without their regimentals?" With a loud laugh at her own wit, Lydia called out to Mr Wickham, causing their mother, who was fanning herself on a bench nearby, to chastise her for brazenness. Lydia disregarded her.

A beaming grin breaking over his face, Mr Wickham strolled over to them, offering an exaggerated bow. "Miss Kitty Bennet and Miss Lydia Bennet. I daresay this is the finest thing that has happened to me all week, to see you both here."

"And ours too!" Lydia said with a smile. The three broke into easy chatter. Mr Wickham seemed most interested to learn they were living with Darcy but said little of it.

Though scarcely seventeen, Lydia fancied she knew as well as any how to entice a man. She made sure to jiggle her bosom when she laughed, and she touched her finger to her lips whenever she could, giving Mr Wickham longing glances as she did it.

Too soon, Mrs Bennet rose. "Girls! I shall melt in this heat! Let us get back to Darcy House now."

They obeyed her reluctantly. As they began to stroll away, Mr Wickham tugged Lydia's arm slightly, whispering, "Same time tomorrow... Come alone."

Thus began a pattern that persisted over the next fortnight of clandestine meetings and whispered sweet nothings. By the end of the first week, Lydia Bennet was clay in Wickham's hands. At the end of the second, she was quite convinced they were in love, and as was natural for people in love, she permitted him a few liberties: kisses, some caresses, and even a brief peek at her bare bosom.

In short time, Lydia believed they had made a plan to elope. She left Darcy House one morning, prepared to meet Wickham at the place she had learned he was staying, so that they could depart for Gretna Green immediately. She left behind a note that declared she had fallen in love and intended to marry Mr Wickham, which fortunately was found only an hour after she departed.

Darcy went at once to Wickham's lodgings, a small room above a tavern on Little St Andrew's Street, a place that stank of too much sweat, smoke, and despair. For his life, he could not comprehend why Wickham was adept at fooling young girls who had lives ahead of them, better lives than this; but so it was.

It was Lydia who flung wide the door, thinking it was Wickham who was evidently away. Her delight turned quickly to vexation. "Get out, Darcy," she hissed. "George will return in moments, and we are going to—"

Darcy said patiently, "Wickham is not going to marry you, and if he did, your life would be one I would not wish on anyone. Now come home with me, and let us forget all about this."

"Home? Home?" Lydia was suddenly and thoroughly enraged. "I do not live with you."

"For now, yes, you do, and I do not think your father—"

"My father hates you for what you did!"

"I do too, but it does not mean I shall surrender you to George Wickham. I intend to see that you do not come to harm."

"Oh? Like you kept Lizzy from harm?" she retorted immediately. "You are so selfish, always thinking about yourself and what *you* want to do. What about what *I* want to do?"

Darcy began to move slowly around the room, gathering a reticule he assumed was Lydia's, a shawl, and some small parcel. "Wickham thinks only of his own wants and needs. Money is spent on gambling or drink before even he feeds himself. Is that the sort of life you want?"

Lydia looked as though she was considering that. "George is owed money by—"

"I have known George nearly my entire life, and never, in nearly three decades, have I heard of anyone owing him anything. It is generally the opposite. What I do think likely is that Wickham wished to harm your reputation in some manner that would cause me to pay him off to save you. I believe we can think of better ways to spend my money, do you not agree?"

Lydia seemed to be considering the offer. Finally she asked, "Why?"

"Are we not family?" He extended his arm, and she took it almost absently, allowing him to remove her from Wickham's rooms.

She shrugged. "Maybe, but Lizzy is probably dead, so likely we are not any more family than any other man she ever knew."

The careless way she spoke hurt more than anything else she

might have said. His voice was hoarse as he replied, "Pray, do not speak so."

He handed her into the carriage, and once he entered and was seated across from her, she spoke almost gently, "If she were alive, do you not think she would have returned to you by now?"

He shook his head. "No, I treated her quite abhorrently. I cannot think anything but sheer desperation would induce her to come back to me."

"I always thought she might come to Longbourn, if she were able. But perhaps she was too ashamed. Mama would not have looked kindly upon her. I do miss her. She was a wonderful sister and always took good care of me."

Such simple words made Darcy unspeakably sad. He looked at Lydia with compassion, hoping he had not taken her sister from her forever. Silently, he offered the girl yet another of his many worthless apologies. How he wished he had considered what his selfishness, his resentful temper, could have wrought before he did any of what he did in 1812!

"I hope you know...I hope everyone knows, Elizabeth did nothing wrong. All of this was my fault."

Lydia, with some measure of her usual impertinence returned to her, tossed back, "Yes, I believe we all think this was entirely your fault."

There was silence in the carriage for several minutes before she spoke again, "May I ask you a question?"

"Certainly."

"Do you want her back because you love her? Or because she belongs to you?"

"Because I love her," he said immediately. "Deeply and ardently, and I...I simply cannot abide the notion of living without her."

"What will you do if you find her, only to realise she does not wish to return to you?"

"W-well..." Darcy stammered a bit. "A woman's place—"

"I mean, after all, you have just removed me from Wickham

because you say his selfishness makes him unable to care for a wife. Cannot Lizzy say the same of you?" She tossed herself back into the seat with a little flounce, pleased by her devastating logic.

He could not deny her charge. Whereas Wickham was ruled by vice, he had been ruled by temper and pride. In both cases, the outcome was ruination.

"If ever I find her," he said, "I hope she will allow me to show her that I have changed. My heart is, and always was, hers, but the fault in my temper that disallowed it has been remedied."

Lydia studied him for a moment, the movement of the carriage causing the massive bonnet on her head to dip and sway about. At length she said, more gently this time, "I think it very likely she died, but if she did not and merely hides from you? I daresay you have little chance of finding her. Lizzy has always been very good at hiding, always in a place you would never imagine to look."

HAVING RETURNED LYDIA TO THE HOUSE, DARCY WENT BACK TO the place he had found her, entering the tavern beneath Wickham's rooms. Wickham was at a gaming table in the back, no doubt losing money he did not have, and Darcy sat at a table to await him.

After nearly an hour, Wickham strolled over and sat down, leaning back and affecting a posture of great nonchalance and ease. With a bored sigh, he said, "Will you challenge me? As you will, but she proved quite the disappointment. For all her education and supposed refinements, Georgiana was much more responsive. I guess all these jokes you hear about country girls have little basis in fact. I must say, I feel quite dissatisfied."

Darcy disregarded the last and said, "Whether there is a challenge is up to you. I come here with an offer: passage to the colonies, Australia, the Indies, wherever you wish, and funds to get you settled into business once you are there."

Wickham looked sceptical, so Darcy added, "I want you gone, but I would prefer not to kill you."

"No?" Wickham raised one eyebrow. "That surprises me."

"Consider this my final effort to see you as something but a schemer and a spendthrift."

"How will you know? If I am in Jamaica…"

"You wish to go to Jamaica?"

"Sounds as well as anywhere else. Or perhaps Boston? I have heard lovely things about Boston."

"Just inform me of your decision that I may arrange your passage. In any case, I shall not know how you behave. I can only hope."

Darcy summoned the publican and settled Wickham's bill, much to the man's astonishment. Rising, he turned to Wickham. "Pray, do me this much, if you will. If, on your way, you should happen to see her…"

"Who?"

"My wife." Darcy paused, clearing his throat.

"If I see her? Where? In Jamaica?"

"In the course of your travels," Darcy replied impatiently. "Jamaica, America, Van Diemans Land. Should you see her, send word to me and me only, lest you forget our arrangement."

Wickham stood, looking surprisingly sympathetic. "I can scarce recall what Mrs Darcy even looks like. I met her only once. Unless she was introduced to me again, I would have no idea who she was."

Darcy could think of nothing but to nod in reply, and then he left.

BY THE FESTIVE SEASON OF 1813, DARCY, IN THE CURIOUS WAY of the bereaved, began to doubt that he remembered Elizabeth exactly. Was her hair a chestnut brown? Or were there traces of auburn in it? Her eyes, he could never forget, but how exactly was the sound of her voice? Did she eat ragout? Were her feet small or large? These and other things tormented him; he could not abide beginning to forget who she was, all the small intricacies of her.

But one thing he did remember: how he loved her. He remembered them laughing, talking all night, even their arguments—such precious, dear moments. Some days, the agony of missing her had numbed, but other days, it screamed within him. Oh, what his pride, his resentful temper, had cost him!

It was one such day when his cousin had the misfortune to meet him in his club. "Happy Christmas!" he cried, seeming a bit drunk despite the fact it was a Monday morning.

"What have you been into already?" Darcy asked suspiciously.

"Nothing at all," Saye replied. "Cannot a man be happy for the season?"

"The season?"

"The festive season? Christmas, Boxing Day, making merry under the mistletoe, and pretty girls drinking egg nog?"

"Oh. That."

"Yes, that." Saye reached over and chucked Darcy under the chin, a habit that had vexed Darcy as a child and did even more so now. He batted his cousin's hand away.

"Be nice, Darcy, for I have exciting news to tell you."

"More news?" Darcy groaned. "I have already had it from Bingley that he will have another child soon."

"Another one? Was not the first just whelped?"

"A girl. Elizabeth, but they call her Liza. She is six months old, I believe."

"Well I know what I shall give Bingley for Christmas," Saye said. "A packet of condoms. For his wife's sake, if none other."

"Elizabeth's aunt, Mrs Gardiner, is expecting a child as well. As is her younger sister, Mrs Collins."

"Of course, in the manner of all things from France, the sheaths can be rather inconstant in their utility."

"The whole world is moving on," said Darcy wistfully, "without Elizabeth to be here for it."

"Which brings me to my brother's news."

Darcy jerked immediately from his gloom. "What?"

Saye chuckled gleefully, then leaned forward and spoke in hushed tones. "Miss Marianne Thorpe…"

"Merchant's daughter?"

"*Wealthy* merchant's daughter. Her fortune is fifty thousand."

Darcy raised his brows with surprise but said nothing more.

"She seems to be in a state, and my dear brother is reportedly the cause. So Father is off to the archbishop, and we shall have a wedding just after the New Year."

"Good lord! I am all astonishment," said Darcy. "Fitzwilliam did not drop a word of this to me."

"It has all happened rather quickly," Saye acknowledged. "But quickness is needful in such cases as these."

"And his lordship? Is he enraged?"

Saye shrugged. "He might have wished for someone with better connexions, but Miss Thorpe's father is very wealthy and well-placed. And you know he is ever mindful that if the jig has been danced, the piper must be paid."

"And Richard?"

"What about him?" Colonel Fitzwilliam had arrived at the table unseen by his cousin and brother, and he tossed himself into a chair. "I gather you have told Darcy my news?"

"He has," said Darcy. "I must congratulate you."

"She is a sweet girl—"

"And very pretty," said Saye. "I feel she might have done better than a gnarled old soldier."

Fitzwilliam offered a half-hearted, obscene gesture to his brother before saying to Darcy, "I daresay we shall be very happy together. At my age, no sense wasting time. Unlike my brother, who will be forty and still haunting Almack's."

"God forbid," said Saye with a noisy slurp of his drink. "It is not my fault the ladies of London are so dull. The sameness of them all! Darcy, once this one is done being shackled, I shall insist you and I go off adventuring. We shall find me a bride in the back country, or by the sea perhaps."

FITZWILLIAM MARRIED MISS MARIANNE THORPE IN A MODEST and rapid ceremony just after Twelfth Night. Anyone who looked askance at the rapidity of the matter was told firmly that there had been an understanding in place for some time.

In February, in a decidedly less modest fashion, a ball was given to introduce the new Mrs Fitzwilliam to the Matlocks' circle, a group comprising several hundred or so. It was at this ball that Miss Lydia Bennet met Mr Wallace 'Jolly' Rollings, a gentleman from Dorset who had been at school with Darcy. Jolly was a large, oafish sort of fellow who somehow always contrived to look unkempt despite having fortune enough for both an excellent tailor and valet. Lydia proclaimed that she found him unattractive and silly and red hair was her least favourite on a man.

Yet somehow her heart was captured. "I cannot stop laughing when I am with him," she told them all at the breakfast table one morning. "He is ever so much fun, and everyone likes him. I daresay that we would never want for diversion."

Jolly came upon Darcy one early spring day as he walked in the park with Georgiana and Saye during the fashionable hour. Kitty and Lydia, being less inclined towards exercise, had not wished to accompany them.

"Ho, Darcy!" called Jolly when he saw them. "I was just on my way to call at your home."

"Were you?" Darcy asked drily. "How unfortunate. Only the young ladies arc at home right now."

"It was you I wished to speak to," Jolly said. "You simply must bring Miss Lydia to Oakdale Park after Easter."

Oakdale Park was the seat of the Rollings family. Although Lydia had initially dismissed it as being near to 'dreary Dorset', as she had deemed it, learning it was quite near the fashionable Weymouth soon made her more interested in seeing it.

Darcy's immediate notion had been to refuse, but Lydia, it would seem, had accepted for them all. In any case, it had been some time since he had been in that county, and while he doubted he would find Elizabeth anywhere near there, neither could he rule it out. Moreover, he was certain Kitty would also wish for the visit. If there was one thing he had learnt about Elizabeth's youngest sisters, it was, when their interests were roused, there was scarce that could stop them.

They paused a moment; two young boys went tearing by, the smallest of them careering directly into Darcy, then bouncing back onto his bottom. He was too shocked to cry, and Darcy bent, helping him back to his feet. A red-faced, angry governess was upon them in a moment, full of apologies for Darcy and promises of the switch for the boy. There was something about the whole scene that made Darcy feel rather wistful.

"Darcy? Will you come then?" Jolly pressed, returning him to the present.

"Very well," said Darcy. "Consider it done."

FOURTEEN

Park Street Books, Weymouth, 1814

MERRY HAD HERSELF A SUITOR, AND ELIZABETH COULD NOT have been happier for her.

Señor Esparza was a Spaniard from the Basque region who had fought at Badajoz. He had come to England seeking relief from the turmoil that was post-Napoleonic Spain and instead found love. Of course, it was difficult not to love Merry—she was pretty and sweet and played the pianoforte with the hands of angels. It was how they had met; one evening, as Merry played, Señor Esparza, passing by, heard her through the window and vowed that he should one day meet her.

He did, and Señor Esparza had captured Merry's heart, and they made a handsome pair. Elizabeth had not the least doubt that she would soon lose her friend and Bennet's nurse to the bonds of matrimony.

The three of them sat at the beach with Bennet happily playing in the sand beside them, and Elizabeth felt herself decidedly *de trop*. She had asked Señor Esparza—Pedro, as she now heard Merry calling him—a few questions about Spain and

Badajoz, but it was clear that he was far less interested in speaking to her of his homeland than he was of lovemaking to Merry. With a smile, Elizabeth turned away, deciding to visit the bookstore that was mere steps away on the esplanade.

"Bennet, would you like to come to the bookstore with Mama?"

"No!" Bennet cried enthusiastically. "Dig!"

"Leave him with us," Merry urged. "He is full of sand, and I am sure Mr Richie would much prefer he stay here."

"That is true." Elizabeth bent and kissed her son's sandy cheek. He would need a bath after this, to be sure. "I shall not be very long."

DARCY ENTERED THE BOOKSHOP IN WEYMOUTH, SEEKING nothing more than respite from all the talk of fripperies and lace. Even Georgiana had succumbed to it, but then again, it was enjoyable to see her behaving as any other lady of eighteen would. There was a book he wanted for Bingley's children—heaven knew, Bingley's library was as sparse as it ever was, yet somehow Bingley's daughter, like her namesake, was already voracious in her appetite for the written word.

He was perusing the book when he heard the shopkeeper call out, "Good day, Mrs Elizabeth." Hearing that name caused him to look up, and there she was. For a moment, he could do no more than doubt. His heart dropped into his stomach, and he froze, unable to do anything but cry out her name. By the time Darcy had recovered his wits sufficiently to act, she was gone, having flung wide the door with a raucous jangle. He ran after her immediately.

The street was clogged with passers-by, and he halted, looking left and right. His eyes frantically roved over the crowd —groups of ladies, a gentleman with an odd green-coloured hat, a bearded soldier carrying a small sandy boy, who was protesting violently, off the beach—none of them were Elizabeth.

She had been too fast and had had a clear advantage being close to the door. Had it really been her? Had his eyes, his mind, his heart deceived him? Frustrated, he called, "Elizabeth!" into the crowd, causing some of those on the esplanade to give him strange looks—but none of them were her.

Breathing quickly, he turned, running towards he knew not where, acting on pure instinct, but the next corner showed no dark-haired beauty with enchanting eyes. Turning, he ran back the other way, his eyes always seeking but finding nothing.

How could she have disappeared so quickly? The area held no alley ways; she must have had to run up some length of pavement. But she always had been light-footed, and he supposed she must have some knowledge of the place. He glanced into some nearby stores and walked the length of the shops—there was no sight of her.

At length, Darcy went back to the bookshop. "Sir? The woman who was just in here—"

Mr Richie looked up from his counter with a smile. "Mrs Elizabeth?"

"Mrs Darcy. Mrs Elizabeth Darcy."

Mr Richie appeared suddenly wary. "I do not know anything about a Mrs Darcy."

"Mrs Elizabeth, then. She is known to you?"

"She is a good customer."

"How long have you known her?"

Mr Richie's eyes slid over Darcy. It was clear he was no fool; his shop was prosperous, and men like Darcy were likely the reason for it. Still, he was slow to reply.

"About two years, I think, since she came to live with her aunt, Mrs Macy. The aunt just passed, some disease in her brain. Very sad. May I ask your interest in the matter, sir?"

Darcy disregarded the question. "My intentions are honourable, I assure you. What is her direction?"

"Forgive me, sir, I cannot give that information away, not without the young lady's permission."

"But she does live here? In town?"

With a frown, Mr Richie lowered his eyes.

"Sir, I believe...I think Mrs Elizabeth might be a...a relation of mine. A long-lost relation. If I should give you a letter for her —perhaps I can add it in with this book she wished to buy— would you deliver it to her?"

Mr Richie considered that, his grey brows contracted as he folded a piece of paper on his counter carefully.

After watching him for several expanded minutes, Darcy reached into the pocket of his coat and withdrew some money, all the money he had on his person. He laid the notes on the counter and slid them towards the man. "For your time, Mr...?"

"Richie," the man said, glaring at the money and sliding it back towards Darcy. "And I do not need to be paid to do what's right. I just need to know that it is, indeed, right."

"It is," Darcy said urgently. "I assure you, it is the right thing."

"Bring me your letter," said Mr Richie. "And I shall see that she gets it."

BENNET WAS HOWLING WITH DISMAY AS HE CAME INTO THE HOUSE with Merry and Señor Esparza, but Elizabeth could not even go to him. She heard Merry sending for water to bathe him, but she could not move from where she was curled into a chair, her legs tucked under her, and shaking and shivering like nothing she had ever known. Her mind would not form rational thought, and her lips could not form words—she could only tremble.

Merry found her there some minutes later. "Elizabeth? Why, my dear, you are as white as a ghost!"

Merry went to her at once, and she found she scarcely had the strength to turn towards her friend. Merry laid her hand on Elizabeth's head. "No fever," she pronounced. "But you are clammy and cold, which might be just as bad. Let me help you into bed."

"I am not ill," she whispered.

"But of course you are! I never saw you in such a state."

"A fright," Elizabeth managed. "I…something frightened me. Is Bennet…is he…?"

"Perfectly well, but his skin was turning pink. It was time to leave the beach, and he felt otherwise." Merry smiled as she said it. "Gave Señor Esparza quite a kick when he picked him up."

Elizabeth smiled faintly. "Poor Señor Esparza. Do extend my apologies on my son's behalf."

"Bennet does love the beach." Merry was moving around as she spoke, picking up the reticule, the shawl, and the shoes that Elizabeth had tossed away when she entered the room.

"He does," Elizabeth agreed, "though…though maybe it is time to leave here."

Merry stopped what she was doing, staring in shock at Elizabeth. "Leave?"

"Some other place." At once, the chair was too small; indeed, the room itself felt too small, and her corset seemed to be preventing all breath. She rose, pressing her hand to her chest. "Spain? Señor Esparza speaks so very eloquently on the beauty of Spain, I daresay I should—"

"Señor Esparza fled Spain," Merry reminded her gently. "Too much political unrest. What is this about? What has you so unsettled?"

Elizabeth felt the doors closing as surely as if they had slammed her on the nose. She was no longer a woman alone in Yorkshire. There was a house, servants, a child, a nurse, all of whom depended upon her. She could not set out with a satchel in the night any more. A sob escaped her.

Merry left the room, returning a moment later bearing a glass of sherry. She handed it to Elizabeth, who sipped at it. *He did not want me,* she reminded herself. *He sent me away. Likely he wishes to see me as little as I wish to see him.*

She smiled at Merry. "I…I think I need only lie down a little. I think I have also had too much sun today."

Elizabeth could see that Merry did not believe her. There

were clear questions in her eyes as she nodded and left, promising to keep Bennet occupied while his mother rested.

ELIZABETH COULD NOT REST, NOT THE WHOLE OF THE DAY OR THE night. She sat at breakfast the next morning, jumping out of her skin every time a carriage slowed or any sound resembling a knock was heard. *He cannot find me,* she assured herself over and over. *He barely saw me. He does not wish to see me.*

She did not dare venture out of the house, and poor Bennet was forced to stay in his nursery even though the day was sunny and bright. Rarely did her child know a day without being outdoors, but this day would be the exception. She wondered where Darcy stayed and for how long. Was he passing through? Had he taken a house?

A note was given to her on the next morning at her breakfast. She knew the handwriting immediately and her heart sank.

Elizabeth,
Pray do me the honour of meeting me Thursday. I shall come to you, wherever you stay, or meet at some place convenient to you.

With hope,
FD

She was out of breath when she finished reading it. To see her husband seemed a ridiculous fancy, yet here it was, a meeting arranged by a note in his own hand. For a moment, she wished to weep, but she did not. Her first inclination was to refuse him, to toss away the note and pretend it was never seen; but could she?

Curiosity won out. Curiosity as well as the surety that her husband, in wanting an audience, would have his audience. Refusal was not possible for such a man as Darcy; what he wanted, he got. It was necessary to plan carefully for this meeting. She could not reveal the presence of Bennet nor did she wish him to know where they lived.

She wrote back, instructing him to meet her at the esplanade in front of Gloucester House. It was a very short walk, but she hired a chaise to take her, wanting to give the notion that she had travelled a distance.

She got there ahead of the prescribed time and was unsurprised to see he was already awaiting her. He stood with his back to her, staring out at the sea, and she approached him quietly, paying no mind to the small voice within that urged her to turn and walk away.

When she was near enough to touch him, she cleared her throat. He startled and then whirled about. She was glad she had surprised him.

But she was surprised too—surprised by the depth of emotion that arose in her heart. Tears sprung to her eyes and were blinked back furiously. Her breath came quickly, much too quickly for the short walk she had undertaken, and she paused a moment, trying to calm her jangling nerves. She held a parasol to shield her from the sun, and it shook violently.

"Elizabeth," he said, in a hoarse, reverential whisper. "It is you."

"It is," she said, pleased with the strength in her voice.

And before she could stop him, before she could do or say anything, he bowed, low and servile, over her hand, placing a gentle, scarcely felt kiss on the back of it that seared through her glove. She did not yank her hand away as she might have wished —she was too amazed by his actions and, even worse, by her feelings.

He was so handsome, and she was struck by how much she still loved him. She had tried so strenuously to avoid thinking of her husband these two years past, and when she did, she had struggled determinedly not to acknowledge the feelings that still remained in her. Although she had garnered some measure of success, being in his presence completely undid her efforts, and the sudden great force of her love and her want for him threatened to knock her off of her feet.

"Is there someplace where we could go to talk privately?" he asked. "Are you staying nearby?"

She disregarded his question and gestured towards a nearby bench. He gave it a dubious look but did not argue.

When they were seated, Elizabeth stared at her lap, feeling Darcy's eyes intent upon her. There was too much to be said to begin; evidently, he felt likewise for he was silent.

At length, she decided to ask that which she wished to know. "Do you intend to divorce me?"

"No," he said immediately, sounding shocked at the very notion. "No."

She nodded.

After another painful pause, he asked, "Why are you known as Mrs Elizabeth?"

"People presumed I was Mrs Macy's relation, and I did not correct them. To prevent the confusion of two Mrs Macys, I became Mrs Elizabeth."

"I see." A slight breeze ruffled his hair as he looked down at the pavement beneath his feet. When he raised his head, naked agony was in his eyes. It both entreated and repulsed her. "Come back to Pemberley with me," he whispered.

She was shaking her head before the words had been fully said. "I am sorry, but I cannot. I shall not."

"I know I have made a horrible, dreadful mistake that has cost us—"

"Everything," she said sharply. "It cost us everything. For whatever it was, it is not there now. We have nothing between us."

"There cannot be nothing," he argued, traces of his customary hauteur returning to him. "We are married, we—"

"Married? This is your notion of marriage?" Sudden, intense rage filled her.

"Of course not, no, I—"

"I was cast out, unprotected and alone, and I…I…"

Too much emotion filled her. She was nearly crying, almost screaming, and feeling an unaccountable impulse to vomit. Above all was the desire to flee, to run away from him and the contrariety of feeling that he excited.

"I need to go," she gasped, rising.

"Elizabeth, wait—"

"No! I…I am sorry. Please, just…just forget me." She had turned and was nearly running back to the hack chaise she had hired for the trip.

"But where can I find you again?" He ran behind her, grabbing her arm to stop her. "Elizabeth, please…you cannot know how I have searched for you, how I have missed you."

She pulled her arm away from him. "People are staring."

"Let them stare."

"People here think my husband is dead. No doubt people think Mrs Darcy died as well."

They stood for a moment, staring at one another until finally Elizabeth said, "Forgive me, but I cannot." She then turned, entered the waiting hack chaise, and left him.

GEORGIANA DARCY AND KITTY BENNET WALKED BY THE SEA, Mrs Annesley strolling behind them. The day was fine and warm, and the walk was filled with people enjoying the sun. "I think I could live by the sea, could you?"

Kitty giggled. "I could indeed, though not if it meant I would marry Jolly Rollings!"

Georgiana chuckled at that but admonished, "He is a very eligible match for your sister!"

"That he is, though I do hope she finds him a valet who can tidy him up a bit."

Georgiana's eye was drawn by a small boy, a toddler playing in the sand, while a dark-haired, petite young woman watched over him. He was a sweet little boy with a full head of dark, curly hair. He seemed quite serious and intent on his task of digging a hole. She tapped Kitty's arm. "A handsome little boy, is he not?"

"Aye," Kitty replied. "I saw him the other day with the same lady."

They greeted the lady with a nod. She returned their greeting just as the boy dug a bit too vigorously, tossing a shovelful of sand onto her lap. The woman laughed and said, "Master Bennet, please do not bury me in the sand!"

The child looked up at the woman and giggled at seeing the sand he had tossed at her.

"Did she call him Bennet?" Georgiana asked Kitty.

"Surely not. Probably Benjamin. It is hard to hear when the breeze blows."

Georgiana agreed but turned her head to look back. The toddler had gone to the lady and was trying to brush the sand out from her skirts, but his hands were so sandy, they only served to put on more. The woman laughed, then pulled the boy to her and kissed his head, whispering something in his ear.

Absorbed as she was in the little scene, Georgiana startled when she heard Kitty suddenly screech, "Lizzy!" She turned just as Kitty began to run towards a hack chaise that had recently let out a passenger, a lovely young lady who stood stock-still while her sister went careering towards her.

FIFTEEN

ALTHOUGH HER MEETING POINT WITH DARCY WAS MERE STEPS from her home, Elizabeth had taken a hack chaise for the sole purpose of deception. She did not wish him to realise she was so near; she wanted him to think she might have come from Poole or Bournemouth or wherever. She did not want him to know about Bennet. She did not want him to have any comprehension of her situation.

Yet she could not have imagined nor planned for a scene such as this. Kitty was walking with Georgiana while her son was mere feet away with Merry. And then Kitty was shrieking and calling her name, and Bennet was shouting, "Mama," and running towards her, and Merry was smiling, and Georgiana was confused, then Bennet fell and tore his gown, and blood appeared on his knees, which caused more screaming and confusion as Merry tried to retrieve him, but in the obstinate way of a toddler, he wanted only for his Mama.

And she ran over to him because a mother's instinct could permit no less, and she took him from Merry, heedless of the blood on her muslin, just allowing him to sob into her neck while she kissed his agony away. Kitty hugged both of them, also crying, and laughing, and Elizabeth alternated kisses to her son and her sister.

And when Elizabeth raised her head, there stood Darcy, staring at them all.

HAVING LEFT THE CARRIAGE, DARCY WALKED TO HIS MEETING with Elizabeth. Following that, when he was again master of himself, he had gone to retrieve the ladies from their walk on the esplanade, only to be greeted by a scene such as he could not have imagined.

A small boy, one long, knobby-kneed leg having been cut on some sharp object in the sand, was howling his dismay into his mother's bosom—his mother being Elizabeth, who held him tightly, kissing his head as Kitty hugged them both. A dark-haired, young lady consoled the boy from the side, and Georgiana stared in wonder, Mrs Annesley by her side.

He walked to them slowly, comprehending that Elizabeth would have likely desired his absence. "Is the child well?" he asked.

"Lizzy! Is he my nephew?" Kitty asked eagerly.

Elizabeth glanced at Darcy, still holding the boy to her chest. "This is Bennet," she said, not directly answering Kitty.

Having heard his name, Bennet paused mid-sob and looked around interestedly. Darcy's breath caught upon seeing him, feeling an instant tug at his heart. Although he was a baby, it was clear he had the Darcy nose and chin, much like Darcy himself had. In a trice, he saw the boy walking the halls at Pemberley, its future secured, and the thought made him weak in the knees with humility.

The petite, dark-haired woman to Elizabeth's side stepped forward. She was plainly curious about the scene occurring before her but said only, "Let me take him and get him cleaned."

But Bennet immediately resumed shrieking at the very notion of being removed from his mother's arms, so Elizabeth hurriedly said, "Let us all…we shall go…into the house, I suppose." With another glance at Darcy, she added, "Just across the way."

Elizabeth set off then, walking down the pavement holding her precious bundle, with the young lady on one side and Kitty on the other, who was chattering away, seemingly insensible of the undercurrent of turbulence around her. Georgiana took Darcy's arm as they followed behind, casting him the occasional anxious glance but saying little. Mrs Annesley chose to wait by the sea on a bench that allowed a delightful view.

The house they arrived at was very fine, large and well situated. Elizabeth walked in the front door to be greeted by an elderly man who knew his business but could not help some grandfatherly clucks in Bennet's direction.

"Shall I send for the apothecary, Mrs Elizabeth?" he asked.

"No, no," said Elizabeth with a fond smile. "It is merely a skinned knee, but he likes the attention he is receiving over it."

Bennet at last agreed to be relinquished into the care of his young nurse—Merry, she was called—and Elizabeth said she would retire above stairs to refresh herself. "May I come?" Georgiana asked.

With a forced smile, Elizabeth said, "Perhaps both of my sisters will join me? I daresay we have much to talk of."

Darcy stepped towards her, "May I—"

"The sitting room is that way," she said with a quick thrust of her chin towards a closed door to the left. "Wait there."

ELIZABETH'S MAID WAS A WOMAN NAMED BLAKE, WHO HAD BEEN in the service of Mrs Macy for the decade prior. Blake came now to Elizabeth's bedchamber, chuckling over the state of her gown. "I am become quite the expert in the removal of such stains, ma'am."

"It will be a sad day for me when he no longer runs into my arms with skinned knees," Elizabeth said with a smile, "but not as much, perhaps, for you."

"There you are wrong, ma'am, for the laundry is well worth the hugs and kisses we all get along with the skinned knees."

Still smiling, Elizabeth directed her two sisters to a settee by her table, where they watched while Blake put her back to rights.

"So," Elizabeth asked with feigned cheer, "how is it that you are in Weymouth?"

"There is a friend of Darcy's nearby," said Kitty. "A Mr Rollings. He is taken with Lydia and invited us all down to visit."

"With Lydia? Do you think they will make a match of it?"

"He is ever so wealthy, but our sister does still like a man in regimentals, and Jolly does want for those." Kitty giggled. "Oh, Lizzy, how much we have to tell each other!"

Elizabeth smiled at her young sister. "Are our parents here too?"

"No," Kitty said. "Mama's nerves could not bear the travel. In fact, Lydia and I have been with Darcy for some time now."

"It is very agreeable for me," said Georgiana, her first timid foray into the conversation. "I have learnt what it is to have sisters, which has long been my wish."

Elizabeth did not speak her thoughts—that Georgiana did have a sister, and that sister had been sent away. But such things could not be said in front of Blake, so Elizabeth merely asked, "And what is your opinion of the match, Georgiana? Will it work?"

"She likes him very well. I do think he will offer for her. He is mostly in town, which I think Lydia will prefer."

"I see." Elizabeth nodded and thanked Blake who had, expediently as usual, set her to rights again. Blake curtseyed and left them, and Elizabeth turned to her sisters. Before she could speak, however, Georgiana stopped her.

"Lizzy...I mean, Elizabeth, that is to say I...did my brother...what..."

She had become distressed, and Elizabeth wondered at the meaning of it. "What is it Georgiana?"

"I wonder whether I might speak...to tell you some things

my brother…did my brother tell you much about why…?" She shrugged helplessly.

"Why he sent me off and abandoned me?" Elizabeth smiled. "No, our conversation ended before that."

"Then perhaps you would like me—"

Elizabeth held up her hand. "It is not necessary, I am sure."

Georgiana began to weep, and Kitty took her hand. "You should hear her, Lizzy. After all, you are married to the man. You cannot un-marry him."

"He does not want me," Elizabeth said calmly but firmly. "And I no longer want him either."

Georgiana's tears had begun to flow in earnest. "But no! Please! You must hear why my brother…what made him do as he did. I do not wish to defend him. Indeed, he despises himself for his own errors, but let me explain. Please."

Elizabeth rose from her dressing table and brought Georgiana a moistened handkerchief. "My dear, do not pain yourself so. I shall hear whatever it is you wish to say, but please, do not think you can fix what he, himself, has broken."

Georgiana nodded, dabbing at her face and attempting to gather her equanimity. Elizabeth took her seat again, this time facing the two younger ladies.

With a fortifying breath, Georgiana began, "Back in '12…no, it began in '11…I fancied myself in love with George Wickham."

She seemed to think the name might have some significance to Elizabeth, but Elizabeth had no recollection of any such person. She looked over at Kitty who said, "Mr Wickham was in Hertfordshire in '11, Lizzy, part of that regiment with Colonel Forster."

"Did I meet him?"

"I think so. He was fearful handsome. We were all in love with him—well, all except you. Your head was too full of Mr Darcy to look at the poor soldiers."

Her jest, given in the usual way of sisters, was ill timed. It made Elizabeth frown before she forced a wan smile, "That must be true, for I do not remember him or any of the other soldiers very well at all."

"He was a poor soldier," Georgiana agreed. "But he was raised at Pemberley, a playmate to my brother and given a gentleman's education. When my father died, he was left a sum of one thousand pounds."

"Oh, I do remember this now. He believed he was owed more?"

"The living at Kympton," Georgiana corrected. "My brother had paid him a sum, but George wanted more. He formed a design to get to me, but stupid as I was…"

Here she paused, additional tears forming in her eyes. "Stupid as I was, I thought he really loved me."

Kitty put her arm around Georgiana, and Elizabeth, moved to compassion, reached for her hand. "These are painful recollections for you, my dear. Pray, do not feel—"

"There is more," Georgiana blurted. She went on to explain how her friend and confidante had advised her in the matter and told her that Elizabeth and Wickham were lovers of long standing, co-conspirators in a scheme to cuckold some wealthy man who would keep them in fashion and turn a blind eye.

At this, Elizabeth burst out laughing. "Good heavens! What an imagination your friend may boast!"

"And…and the truth was, I was angry about that. Because of what she said, I came to think of you as a rival and, worse, a fortune huntress, someone who had come to take advantage of my dear brother with your nefarious schemes."

Elizabeth sobered, suddenly understanding what she was being told. "So you told him these tales?" It was all rather fantastical and her mind struggled to connect this to herself. Surely Darcy would not believe such lies told by a young girl? He had never breathed a word of any of this to her, just began treating her as though all of it were true. It was laughable, at least until one considered how deeply it had affected her and her son.

"I told him," Georgiana confirmed, unable to look Elizabeth in the eye. "And at other times, it was the unspoken truth that persuaded him."

"But...he believed you? How could he believe such absurd stories?"

"He did," Georgiana said, a deep, scarlet hue spreading over her chest and face. "Particularly as...well, Mr Wickham had been caught by the servants on several occasions sneaking in and out of the house."

It took Elizabeth a moment to understand. "To see you?"

Fresh tears flowed as Georgiana nodded. "A note was found as well...one of mine, but my brother thought it was for you, particularly as it was placed in your bedchamber with..."

She was crying harder, and Elizabeth looked to Kitty for further clarity.

"A handkerchief embroidered with the initials 'GW' was found in your bedchamber. It had a lock of hair wrapped in it and the note asking for an assignation."

"But...but how?"

"Georgiana's friend had put them there. She had made the handkerchief herself and used a lock of her own hair. Her hair was similar in colour to Mr Wickham's so it made for good proof."

Elizabeth found herself fighting strange and contradictory impulses. Should she laugh? Should she cry? It was like a bizarre novel gone awry, and she could not make sense of any of it. Behind it all was rage, rage that her husband had believed all of this silliness with never a word to her. "Who is this supposed friend that caused such problems?"

"Miss Bingley," said Kitty. "Miss Caroline Bingley."

WHEN DARCY HEARD FOOTSTEPS DESCENDING THE STAIRS, HE rose hopefully, but it was only Kitty and Georgiana who appeared. Georgiana was pale and had clearly cried, and Darcy went to her immediately. "Are you ill?"

Georgiana shook her head. "No, but...I spoke to Elizabeth and told her what I did, and Miss Bingley as well."

"I see. And what did she say to it all?"

"Nothing really," Kitty said. "She laughed at first, thinking it all quite fantastic. But then she was quite sad by the end of it all."

"Where is she now?" Darcy asked.

"I think she would like us to leave," said Georgiana. "She seemed very tired."

"I cannot leave, Georgiana. I need to speak to her."

Georgiana pursed her lips for a moment, then glanced at Kitty. "We shall collect Mrs Annesley and go to the carriage. Elizabeth was in her bedchamber. At the top of the stairs and to the right."

"Very good."

ELIZABETH HAD MOVED TO THE CHAIR IN HER ROOM. IT LOOKED out towards the shore, and she often would gaze at the water to calm her nerves. Alas, with the state her nerves were in presently, it was not having its usual calming effect.

The first knock was so quiet that she barely heard it. When it was repeated more strongly, she said, "Come in."

The door opened very slowly, and Darcy entered cautiously and looked around the room. Elizabeth had decorated it in pale, airy colours that matched the seaside—aqua and blue and indigo —and Darcy appeared to like it.

"I should have thought you had left by now."

"I could not, not until we had spoken." He went to her chair and knelt. "Elizabeth...the boy..."

"Bennet."

"Yes, Bennet. He is your son?"

Elizabeth caught her breath. This was what she had feared all this time, these many months. Would Darcy want to take him away from her? "He is our son," she said slowly.

"Mine?" Darcy asked.

She glared at him. "Yes, yours. Or did you think he belonged to George Wickham, since you evidently believed that of me."

"No, no. I did not mean to question—"

"I am well aware that you do not ask questions, you merely pass judgments, but in this case, I shall tell you beyond a shadow of a doubt that Bennet is your son." She rose and turned to the window, wrapping her arms around herself and rubbing the skin of her upper arms, desperately trying to calm her nerves, but to no avail.

He rose as well and came behind her, standing very close. "Elizabeth, I do not doubt he is mine, nor do I doubt your good character."

"You mean you do not doubt it *now*."

"I have made gross errors in judgment against you, for which I am so deeply sorry. It is my only wish that you will permit me to beg your forgiveness, to show you how I have changed... Rather, it *was* my only wish, but now I must also wish to meet my son."

Elizabeth rolled her eyes, unseen by Darcy as she still faced the window. How she longed to deny him this! She was shocked at the resentment that burnt in her and by how badly she wanted to make him suffer, to make him hurt as she had hurt these past two years.

However, she reminded herself sternly, she needed to think of her son and place his best interests first. Bennet deserved a father, even if that father did not deserve him. In any case, it was Darcy's right. She could not deny it to him any more than she could banish him from Pemberley.

"He is napping now. Come back tomorrow. You may meet him then."

SIXTEEN

Darcy arrived far too early the next morning, but in truth, he had scarcely slept—scarcely slept, barely ate, and did nothing but walk about in agitation since seeing his wife and son.

When he left Elizabeth, he had gone straightaway to a shop where he purchased tin soldiers, books, a ball, and alphabet blocks. Then he went to a jewellers and purchased pearl hair clips and earbobs for Elizabeth, though he knew not whether he would have the courage to give them to her.

And now, he stood on the pavement outside her door, wondering whether he had the courage to knock.

The decision was taken from him by the butler, who opened the door and said, "If you please, sir, Mrs Elizabeth is in the sitting room."

With a nod, he followed him.

It took no more than a glance to see that Elizabeth appeared to have slept as poorly as he. She was pale with shadows beneath her eyes and distress in her countenance. "Thank you, Mercer," she said as the butler showed Darcy in.

Mercer allowed himself a mistrustful look at Darcy before he left them. When he had gone, Darcy turned to her. "Are you well?"

"Yes," she said briskly. "Now about Bennet. He is rather shy and does not do well with strangers. It is likely he will not speak to you and may be too timid to even look at you directly."

"I understand."

"What do you want to be called?"

"Called?"

"Papa, Father, Mr Darcy, Sir...?" She raised one perfect brow, managing to look simultaneously imperious and beautiful beyond compare.

Papa! Such a sweet word, yet how unworthy he was of the appellation! With trepidation, he asked, "Would you mind if he called me Papa?"

Elizabeth retorted sharply, "Why should I care what he calls you? You are his father, and it will not defy custom for him to call you Papa."

"Thank you."

Elizabeth pulled the bell cord that would summon the nurse, then returned to her previous seat. Darcy took a seat as well, and they silently awaited the appearance of their son.

The nurse from the day prior entered in a few minutes, holding Bennet by the hand. When he saw his mother, Bennet immediately yanked away from her and ran to Elizabeth. "Mama!"

Suddenly, he saw Darcy and skidded to a stop, his eyes widening. Fearfully, keeping one eye on the strange gentleman, Bennet hesitantly tiptoed towards his mother's arms, pressing his face into her legs once he had arrived.

Elizabeth leaned over to speak to him in a low voice, albeit one Darcy could hear. "Bennet, this is your Papa."

"No," said Bennet.

Elizabeth smiled. "His new favourite word. I am told he will give it up soon."

"No!" Bennet said.

"Yes," said Elizabeth gently. "This is Papa, and like Mama, he loves you very much."

Thoughtfully, Bennet reached out, winding a curl of Elizabeth's hair into his fist. He played with her hair a few moments before saying, "Pop."

"Papa," Elizabeth insisted gently.

With a smile, Bennet said, "Pop. Pop. Pop." Then he leant into her and whispered into her ear.

"Snack?" Elizabeth's eyes went immediately to the nurse. "Merry, has not this young man had his breakfast?"

"Indeed he has," said Merry. "Nearly the whole bowl of porridge today."

Bennet continued to whisper into his mother's ear, and Elizabeth laughed and sighed. "Well, he insists he is in need of a snack."

Merry went to Elizabeth, leaning in to take the boy. "Master Bennet, I must spend at least half of my day feeding you!"

"Snack," said Bennet as she picked him up. "A-day Pop."

"Good day," Elizabeth clarified, looking at Darcy. "He is saying good day to you."

"And a good day to you, Bennet," Darcy said softly. The contrariety of emotion in him was hard to define. He was sorrowful to see the boy leave, yet he knew he needed, above all, to make some progress with Elizabeth.

Elizabeth watched Bennet leave, then turned to Darcy and remarked lightly, "Being raised in a home with all sisters, I believe I had no notion of what constancy was required to keep ahead of the appetite of a growing boy."

Darcy smiled faintly. "Most of my childhood memories involve Mrs Reynolds chasing me out of the kitchens at Pemberley."

Elizabeth looked down with a light chuckle that became a sob. She squeezed her eyes closed and pressed her fist tightly to her mouth, but it seemed she could not stop herself. "Please do not take him from me," she choked. "I do not think I could bear it."

"Take him from you?"

"By law, he is yours."

"By faith, he is yours," Darcy replied. A moment later, he knelt beside her. "What I want, more than anything, is to have you back, to bring you home, both of you."

"I am home."

He tried to take her hands, but she kept them tightly balled, one in her lap and the other still pressed to her face. "Elizabeth, darling...I know there are no words I can say that will take back what I have done—"

"Yes," she said, "and forgive me, but...I just do not think I can forgive you for it."

"I know how badly I have hurt you, and—"

"Do you?" She raised her head, her tears suddenly dry. "How can you? How could you possibly know what it is to be a female, alone and with child, cast off to a poisoned wilderness, afraid, unsure, despised, fearing for your life...tell me, Fitzwilliam, what about that can you possibly comprehend?"

He swallowed hard. "Very little. No, nothing at all. You are correct. I only meant to say that—"

"Just say nothing, because there is nothing you can say."

A painful silence fell. Two roses of fury had blossomed on her cheeks, but she did not release further resentment. In many ways, he wished she would.

"You said yesterday that there was nothing left between us," he began softly, "but there is. There is something very important between us—our son. Bennet is my heir, and he deserves to be raised at Pemberley. He has a legacy to fulfil and a heritage to enjoy. All that is mine will be his one day. You surely would not wish him to be deprived of that."

Elizabeth closed her eyes, seeming pained by the mention of Bennet. With an enormous sigh, she said, "Yes, I...you are correct. I would deny him nothing that was in his best interests."

"And would not it be in his best interests to have his parents reconciled? Home, in the place they belong?"

With a cool glance, Elizabeth replied, "I belong right here, with those who cared for me when you did not."

"It is true, I put my own feelings, my own pride and selfishness, above you for that horrible, disastrous time, and it has cost me, and you, dearly. But never did I stop caring about you. Never did I stop loving you."

He reached out, taking her hand, and was pleased to see that she did not pull away, though she did not look at him.

"Please come home. Nothing more. Just return home with me so that we can work through these things. I may not comprehend the extent of what I did, but I do know I have hurt you. I shall never deserve your forgiveness, but I shall forever try to earn it. I vow to do anything that you wish to fix this."

"And what if it cannot be fixed? What if it is too wholly broken?"

The thought opened a painful hollow in his chest, and he could not answer her.

SHE WAS A RIDICULOUS, SILLY FOOL, AN IDIOT. THIS MAN HAD tossed her aside like yesterday's soiled napkin; yet, here she was, accepting him into her home, showing him the very son she had wished to protect—*idiot!*

But what choice did she have? To deny Bennet his heritage and raise him alone in Weymouth, forever living a lie? Always looking over her shoulder to see whether her truth had caught up to her? Bennet, the son of a scorned woman rather than the Darcy heir? It was absurd to even think it.

Darcy had wished to stay—she could see in his eyes a desire to spend time with them—but she would not allow it. Telling him she had a great deal to think on, she sent him away, but invited him to call again the next day with her sisters.

After he left, she sat in the sitting room, first indulging in a good cry and then worrying and fretting, thinking of all the reasons why she could not fathom becoming, once again, Darcy's wife.

Would his friends and relatives whisper gossip about her? Would the servants scorn her? What did people think of a wife who had gone missing for two years? Surely London gossip had long since tried and convicted her.

Could she and Darcy ever have a marriage that went beyond cold civility? What if she could not resist loving him, and he did this to her again? Could she face his tendency to be cold and arrogant if he grew displeased? Could she resist him if he were tender and caring?

By the time dinner was announced, she had worried herself into such a state that she could not eat even a bite. She apologised to the housekeeper and retired to the sitting room with some tea, where she spent the evening staring into space until she could retire to her room. Then she spent a nearly sleepless night staring at the ceiling.

She had to go, of course. She had no option. Darcy had appeared perfectly amiable, even a bit contrite and penitent, but who was to know what he might do if she refused him? He still had every right to take her son; she must not forget it.

Many people, particularly those of their station, were quite content in loveless marriages of cordiality. Could not she and Darcy have the same?

People of their station. What was that exactly? She scarcely knew who she was, much less which station to assign herself to. Was she a great lady, married to a wealthy gentleman of the first circles? Or a servant, companion to an elderly lady? She supposed, in truth, she was neither.

She most certainly was not Mrs Darcy, but neither was she Mrs Elizabeth, as people in the household were wont to call her.

She certainly could not claim to be the mistress of Pemberley. She had only been at that estate for a very brief time several years ago. No, she was no more its mistress than she was its head housekeeper. She really could not even recall very well what it looked like, though she supposed it would be familiar when she saw it again.

Although the servants of this household—and even those in Upton Park—treated her as mistress, in verity, she was not that either. Because Mrs Macy had treated her as a treasured family member more than a paid companion, they had done likewise. When Mrs Macy died, they had naturally begun treating her as their mistress, though they should not have. She was in nowise their superior, but rather, she was indebted to them for caring for her when she could not go to her family and had no friends to fall back on. Tears rose to her eyes anew as she thought of the kindness she had received from all of them, from Mrs Macy herself down to the scullery maids at Upton Park.

The ambiguous reality of her present existence swirled through her exhausted mind as she sought to make sense of her life. She was neither wife nor daughter, not servant, not mistress. She belonged to nothing and no one.

Then, with a brief shot of clarity, she realised that was untrue. She did belong to someone: Bennet. She was the mother of Bennet, and that was all she was. Yet it was more than enough.

Bennet would be master of Pemberley one day, and for that cause, she must reunite with his father. She simply had to do it; Bennet must be allowed the proper upbringing, the rights and privileges he deserved as Darcy's son. Her selfish wish to avoid being Darcy's wife could not take precedence over what was Bennet's entitlement. Bennet needed Darcy to be his father; ergo, she would have to be Darcy's wife.

Loving Darcy was not the issue. She still loved him very, very deeply, which put her, she knew, in grave danger. Truthfully, she longed to hate him, wished for it with every breath she took; yet, even on her worst days, she failed miserably. Even just seeing him again—infuriated though she was, and hurt, betrayed, and destroyed—she had to admit that a small piece of her wished for nothing more than to forget about the past and rush straight into his arms.

Yes, she loved him, but her capacity to show him love had been damaged, likely beyond repair. When a person had been so grievously wounded as she was, there was a wall erected—a thick, immovable wall through which nothing could get in and nothing could go out. It was necessary for survival.

A civil union; that was the most she could give to him. He surely could not expect more.

SEVENTEEN

ELIZABETH ROSE EARLY THE NEXT MORNING. WHEN BLAKE CAME in to dress her, she said, "Blake, I need the household to gather downstairs later. Perhaps in an hour?"

"Everyone, ma'am?"

"You, the Mercers, Merry... The younger ones need not trouble themselves. Anyone who served under Mrs Macy should be there though."

Blake nodded. "I shall arrange it, ma'am."

They were all waiting for her an hour later, sitting at the long walnut table where they had their meals. She smiled at the sight of them all.

"No doubt all of you have wondered about the strange goings-on in the house of late. My...friends who have been coming and going."

"Ain't none of our business, it an't," said Mr Mercer, and Elizabeth smiled at him.

"You are too good, sir. But in this case, I do not blame you for being curious, and I am only regretful to tell you...to admit to you that I..." She lowered her face, staring at her folded hands on the dark table. "I have lied to you these two years that I have known you."

Silence greeted her admission.

With a deep inhale, she said, "I am not any relation of Mrs Macy. Mrs Macy took me in when I had nowhere to go. In truth, I know not why she did it, but I was desperate. You see, the man who has been here these last days...he is my husband. Mr Fitzwilliam Darcy of Pemberley in Derbyshire is my lawful husband, and I...I ran away from him. That is to say he...there was a misunderstanding, and he sent me to Yorkshire, and I did not remain. I left and came here. Well, not here. Upton Park."

After a short pause, Mrs Mercer said gently, "We knew, dear."

"Yes, we did," Mr Mercer echoed softly.

"Yes, didn't we all?" said Blake. "Ma'am, you need hold out nothing for us. So he found you now?"

"He had believed me..." Elizabeth could not speak the word, but they understood her, and they all nodded. "In any case, I shall...we shall reconcile. For Bennet's sake. He is Mr Darcy's heir, of course, and he should have all the benefit of that. But I would not have any of you worried for what comes. I swore to Mrs Macy that I would take care of all of you, and so I shall, just as you have cared for me these two years."

Tears sprung into her eyes. "To know that you did so even while in possession of my shameful secret...well, it is too much. Truly, you are all too good."

Merry followed her as she left the servants' hall, quietly requesting a private audience. "Come to my sitting room," Elizabeth said.

"I have some news myself," said Merry. "I have been looking for the right time to tell you, but too much has been happening."

"Well?" Elizabeth smiled, already having some idea what the news might be. "Do not make me wait in agony!"

Merry blushed, her bright eyes lit with a glow. "Señor Esparza has asked me to marry him."

"Oh Merry!" Elizabeth leant forward to hug her. "You cannot know how happy that makes me."

"Truly?"

"Oh, yes. There is something in you, a sweetness of temper perhaps, which has always reminded me of my elder sister, Jane. Likewise, Señor Esparza is much like her husband, my brother Bingley. I just pray you will be as happy together as they are."

"I think we shall," said Merry with a giggle. Becoming more sober, she added, "There is more though. Señor Esparza has some small fortune, and he wishes to establish himself in London as a music master."

"Indeed?"

Merry nodded happily. "He is quite brilliant on the bass clarinet and with the dulcian. He plays flute and the serpent and has just helped a friend of his with a new instrument called the ophicleide. And I shall give pianoforte and harp lessons to young ladies. I daresay we shall be very happy doing what we love…"

"And with people you love." Elizabeth smiled indulgently. "I shall miss you sorely. You cannot know how it has pained me to deceive you. You have been the nearest thing to a friend of the heart I have had these years past."

"Perhaps we shall know one another in London?" Merry asked tentatively.

Elizabeth knew what she meant. "I shall know you everywhere," she promised earnestly, then leant over to kiss her friend's cheek.

SOME TIME LATER, ELIZABETH WAS AT HER DESK WRITING letters to her family when she heard Mercer opening the door. *Darcy*, she thought with a sinking feeling. But a moment later, she heard a loud, boisterous cry—"Lizzy!"—that could only be Lydia.

Moments later, Lydia and Kitty burst into the room, full of chatter and nonsense. Elizabeth embraced them both, kissing their cheeks with all the feeling of a sister. Soon enough, Lydia was done with it.

"Well, this is a pretty place. Have you had any balls here?"

"Here? In this house?"

"Oh! Jolly says he will have a ball! Lizzy, you must help me for I have already spent the money Papa gave me—"

"Do not dare help her, Lizzy, for Mr Darcy is too generous with her by half, and Georgiana gave her a very beautiful gown that she had scarcely worn—"

"You speak of the blue silk? The very blue silk that you greedily wore yourself in London? I can hardly make Jolly propose in someone else's cast-off gown, now can I?"

"Tell me about Mr Rollings," said Elizabeth, all the old techniques for managing her younger sisters coming immediately to the fore. From the corner of her eye, she noticed Georgiana and Darcy were shown into the room.

Lydia immediately set off abusing the poor man, decrying his lack of fashion sense, his red hair, and his dreadful habit of slurping his soup. But at the end of it all, Kitty teased, "Yet she is violently in love with him," and Lydia did not deny it.

Bennet was brought down from the nursery by Merry; he was eager to be off to the beach, ready to spend some time with his small shovel and a bucket. He offered Darcy a shy greeting of 'Pop', after which he hid behind Elizabeth's skirts, peeping occasionally at his aunts. Lydia had no interest in him whatsoever, so she was naturally his first object of admiration. He eventually screwed up the courage to approach her, holding up his shovel for her to admire. "I do not want that," she said with a sneer, but Georgiana rhapsodised about it to Bennet's satisfaction.

When she was done, Georgiana asked nervously, "Elizabeth, I wondered whether I might speak to you for a moment?"

"Of course," said Elizabeth. The outing was thus commenced without them. Merry took Bennet along with Lydia and Kitty and agreed to meet the other three in a short time.

Elizabeth could see Georgiana was very nervous about what

she needed to say, her hands shaking and her eyes already tearing. "Georgiana, what is it?"

Georgiana inhaled deeply and straightened her back, clearly gathering her composure, with a last glance at Darcy to fortify her. "I spoke to my brother last evening. He says you are reluctant to come home."

Elizabeth forbore replying.

"I understand that my error in this matter...when Mr Wickham and I...and naturally, it is unlikely I should marry..." The girl gave Elizabeth a helpless look, tears beginning to fall. "And the lies, of course... You must be disgusted by the very sight of me. In any case, I shall do as you wish."

"What I wish? I do not understand." Elizabeth glanced at Darcy for clarity.

"I contributed very significantly to the demise of your marriage to my brother. We thought that perhaps if I went away somewhere, then you would not—"

"Georgiana," Elizabeth spoke in a low, angry tone, "do you mean to tell me that you think I might wish to send you away?"

Georgiana nodded. "If you would like."

Darcy added, "She will do as you wish, Elizabeth, to make it easier—"

There was a loud clatter as Elizabeth rose so rapidly that her chair fell back and hit a table. Her breath came quickly as rage rose up in her, and she struggled for control. She strode to the window, gripping the sill as she attempted to calm herself.

At length, she turned and spoke, biting off each word. "Let me be perfectly clear, Georgiana. I cannot approve nor excuse the part you have played in this. However, you will not be sent away by me, and I am grievously offended that you or your brother would even think I could do such a thing to you."

"It is no more than I deserve!" Georgiana cried.

With deadly calm, Elizabeth said, her eyes fixed on Darcy, "No one deserves that."

Georgiana bowed her head low, her mouth opening and closing with no audible reply.

"No, I shall not send you away," Elizabeth said tightly. "Not permanently anyway. But for now, I would like you to go to my bedchamber. Pray, refresh yourself and wait in the sitting room upstairs.

Georgiana, understanding her dismissal, hurriedly left the room.

Darcy also rose and went towards Elizabeth. "I thought perhaps you might—"

"I have never been more offended in my life," Elizabeth hissed at him. "*You* might be the sort of person that casts people aside if they anger or embarrass you, but I am not and never shall I be."

"I meant only that I wished to make it more easy—"

"Easy?" Elizabeth shrieked. She stopped herself for a moment, seeking control and some semblance of calm. This would not do, not at all. She refused to allow Darcy to make her into a screeching madwoman.

Although earlier that morning, she had felt resolved to this path, at once, it all seemed far too daunting. The problems were too numerous, the emotions too raw. How could they possibly all live together? There was too much anguish and pain on all sides to be overcome. Surely it would not benefit her son to leave his peaceful life in Weymouth for a home where people shrieked and cried and argued all the time. It was unacceptable to her to become her mother, acting increasingly ill-behaved to gain the notice of a man who disdained her.

Quietly, she said, "This is a mistake. I cannot do this." She turned her back on Darcy and again walked away, back to the window, where she leaned her forehead against the glass.

Darcy approached on silent feet. She felt the warmth of him against her back and his hesitation as he raised a hand, laying his fingers lightly on her. "I love you...so much. I have spent two years yearning for your return and regretting my mistakes. I do not know what to do now. I only know that I want to fix this."

She turned around to glare fiercely at him. "Allow me be very clear on this point. I do not hold Miss Bingley or Georgiana —or anyone else at all—responsible for the destruction of our marriage. For whatever stories you were told, whatever pranks or handkerchiefs or whatever you were given, you *chose* to banish me. You chose to remove me without ever even asking me about any of it. It was you who did this, not anyone else, and yours is the blame."

"I know," he whispered. "I know I ruined us, and I am so very thankful that you have agreed to permit our marriage a second chance."

"Have I any choice?"

The instant she said it, she wished she had not. Darcy went pale, and his eyes betrayed his anguish. Elizabeth could not prevent unwanted compassion from arising, and for a moment, she reflected on how difficult it was to despise those whom you loved so deeply, no matter what they had done to you.

Reaching out, she took his hand and pressed it to her lips. She closed her eyes, savouring the feel of his skin but pained by the slight trembling she could detect. "Elizabeth," he murmured.

She dropped his hand abruptly, cursing herself. Already, the feel of him had weakened her substantially, and she resolved that she must not allow herself this sort of touch in the future—it was far too dangerous to her equanimity. "We should go meet the others."

CRAVING A WOMAN THE WAY HE HUNGERED FOR HIS WIFE WAS difficult. He longed for her touch; even the brief touch of her hand on his had awakened his yearning for her, but from the look she gave him, he dared not offer his arm as they walked towards the shore.

"What do people think happened to me?"

"Um…" He had to think for a moment what she meant.

"The reason why I have disappeared for two years. After all, I cannot simply appear in London with a son in tow and expect that people will not have questions."

"Ah." He cleared his throat. "Yes, well…Lady Matlock, in the early days, foresaw such a stumbling-block and put out some story about…consumption, I think, and time in the country, that sort of thing."

"And people believed this?"

"I was very rarely in town, so I am not entirely sure, but judging from the number of letters I have received wishing you better health, it seems they did."

"Rarely in town?" Elizabeth turned to see him around her bonnet. "Why? Where were you?"

He looked down into her dear countenance and said simply, "I was looking. Everywhere and anywhere I thought you might be—save for Weymouth. I did not imagine you should come to Weymouth."

He would have liked to hear what led her to Weymouth. He might also have liked to smooth away the curl of hair that escaped her bonnet…or take her hand…or lay his hand against the small of her back. But he did none of these. They had reached the ladies and Bennet.

Bennet had a great enthusiasm for digging, it seemed, and he had brought with him the small soldiers that Darcy had given him. He was determined to bury them all until Darcy, kneeling in the sand, showed him how to build trenches and hills for his soldiers to fight from. It was surprising how engaging it was, spending time with his son thus occupied; indeed, for some moments altogether, he entirely forgot his troubles with his wife.

When the others were suitably diverted, he quietly asked her, "How long have you let the house here?"

Elizabeth's eyes were on the sea. "I do not let the house. It is mine…ours, I guess I should say."

"You own it?"

"Mrs Macy left it to me when she died."

"That is extraordinary."

Elizabeth's gaze moved to her lap. "She was far too generous to me for the small service I rendered her."

He rose from where he had knelt beside Bennet and joined his wife on her bench. "You will need time, no doubt, to close the house?"

He watched as she pressed her lips together and took a deep breath, her eyes never leaving their son. "A little," she said at length, not looking at him.

For some moments, they reviewed the various members of the household and what each of them might wish to do. Of utmost concern to Elizabeth were Mr and Mrs Mercer. "At their ages, it is not likely they could find another place."

"Shall we come here? In the summer, perhaps? They could remain in the house."

Elizabeth disregarded the question. "They should have someone to look after them. I promised Mrs Macy I would see to them, not simply leave them here while I gallivant off to Derbyshire."

He could hear in the strained tone of her voice that she was becoming upset, so quickly he offered, "There is a cottage at Pemberley, quite near the main house in fact. They would see us often, and Mrs Reynolds, I think, should be glad of the company."

At last, she turned her face towards him. "How generous that you should wish to care for the servants of another house."

"I could not do less for the people who cared so well for you and my son."

To that, she would only nod, but her face seemed a bit less unhappy. He was glad that, for this moment at least, he was not the dastardly villain who had disappointed her.

EIGHTEEN

ALTHOUGH ELIZABETH HAD BEEN LOATH TO IMAGINE LEAVING Weymouth, as the days leading up to her departure for Pemberley passed, she began to wish she could leave sooner. Darcy was in near-constant attendance at the house on Johnstone Row. She found her heart sinking at the very sound of his footsteps, though she scolded herself for feeling thus. *You will soon need to see him every day!*

However, it was good for Bennet to have his father spend time with him, and indeed, Darcy did, laughing and playing with him, even attending Merry while she fed him. Elizabeth found herself much more inclined towards spending time with her sisters, though Lydia was too busy trying to secure Mr Rollings to do much else.

Elizabeth invited them all to a family dinner—it was odd to see Darcy at the head of her table, but propriety dictated it. She sat to his right with Kitty, and Georgiana was across from her.

"Lizzy, did Darcy tell you that Mary has a son?" Kitty said, giggling wildly. "She named him Fordyce, can you even imagine that?"

"Who is Mary's husband?" Elizabeth asked.

Kitty stopped giggling immediately and cast Darcy a look. Beneath the table, Elizabeth felt Darcy reaching towards her. She moved her hand to where he could not find it.

"Mary has married Mr Collins," said Darcy gravely.

"Mr Collins? Oh." Elizabeth lowered her eyes to her plate. "So Charlotte…?"

"She died in childbirth. In September, it will be two years that she is gone."

Tears immediately filled Elizabeth's eyes. After a few minutes, she rose, saying politely, "Excuse me for just a moment."

She hurriedly walked down the hall, hastening up the steps and entering into her bedchamber. Once there, she threw herself face down on her bed and screamed into her pillow as loudly as she could before dissolving into tears. Memories jumbled and crowded her mind: Charlotte playing games with her as a child, whispered secrets in the tree outside Lucas Lodge, stifled giggles in church, and a multitude of morning-after tittle-tattles following assemblies. Ah, but she had always imagined they would be old ladies together, clucking and gossiping just like their mothers.

Evidently, none of that was to be. Charlotte was long gone, and Elizabeth had not even the chance to say farewell.

Then again, such was life, was it not? Whether she had been in Derbyshire, Weymouth, London, or Meryton, death was sudden and complete. She would not have been there.

She composed herself as quickly as she could, then descended to the dining room. The others were just as she had left them—it seemed no one had eaten much or even spoken in her absence. "Elizabeth, I am sorry—" Darcy began.

She interrupted, a bright, false smile on her face, saying to Kitty, "Our mother must be delighted that one of her daughters will take her place as mistress of Longbourn."

Then to Darcy, she asked, "Is Lady Catherine happy to have my sister at Hunsford?"

Elizabeth still remembered Lady Catherine's thoughts on her marriage to Darcy. The lady, having long harboured wishes of acquiring her nephew as her son, was incensed that he had dared to marry, in the face of her disapproval and anger, a country nobody. In a letter to her new niece, she had denounced Elizabeth and all her sisters as common harlots, wise in the ways of luring a man into marriage through the use of lusty temptations. It had been a letter Elizabeth had thought on often during the dark days in London when Darcy rejected her.

Darcy cleared his throat uncomfortably. "For whatever Lady Catherine thought of the new Mrs Collins, hard on the heels of that announcement, our cousin Anne made her own announcement that she intended to wed one of Mr Collins's friends."

"Really?" Elizabeth did not know which part of this statement was more amazing—that Mr Collins had a friend or that Miss Anne de Bourgh had wished to marry him.

Darcy smiled faintly. "Yes, Mr Reece went to Hunsford to condole with Mr Collins after the death of his first wife. Reece has a small daughter, as he, too, had lost his wife in childbirth, though in his case, the babe had survived. Anne was immediately taken with the baby and had no objections to Mr Reece, and before anyone knew it, they were betrothed. Lady Catherine did not think it a suitable marriage as Mr Reece has neither title nor fortune, but it seems Anne did not much care about any of that."

Elizabeth permitted herself a brief laugh that the other two ladies echoed.

Georgiana continued the tale, "Lady Catherine was so angry, she suffered apoplexy."

"We do not know it was brought on by anger," Darcy interjected.

"In any case, she was very ill for some time but did recover in all capacity except speech." Georgiana hid her smile. "She cannot speak, and writing is somewhat difficult for her too."

Elizabeth had many uncharitable thoughts running through

her mind regarding the poetic justice of such a fate, but she merely said, "How unfortunate."

"But seen in a providential light, it is fortunate as well," said Darcy with a sly look. "Likely, had she not lost her speech, Anne and Reece would have moved her into the dowager's cottage at Rosings, but with such an affliction, they allow her to remain. Mary and Anne have become intimate friends, and I believe it is a happy situation for all."

Elizabeth smiled at the thought of that. "How do Jane and Bingley get on? Have they a child yet?"

Kitty snorted, and Georgiana lowered her eyes. "They have two," said Darcy. "A daughter and a son. They are but a year apart."

"I long to see my dear Jane and her family. I can scarcely believe she is a mother, but then she will likely feel the same of me." Elizabeth smiled a bit wistfully, looking down onto her plate.

"She is no less eager to see you, I am sure," said Georgiana. "Perhaps they will visit us at Pemberley?"

"Are their children as amiable as Jane and Bingley? I picture two smiling little cherubs."

"Baby Elizabeth is all that is smiling and amiable, as you might guess," said Georgiana. "Their son—"

"Thomas Archibald Bingley," Kitty interjected. "Which turned out to be an unfortunate name because he was, and remains, rather bald."

"You were bald too," Elizabeth informed her. "Mama despaired of you. So do not tease, else it should be inflicted on your own children."

"Thomas is very sweet," said Georgiana. "But much more serious and sober-minded than Baby Liza."

"Oh Lizzy!" Kitty interrupted. "Our aunt Gardiner has had another baby too! Also Elizabeth, but they call her Beth!"

"So many Elizabeths!" Elizabeth said with a little laugh. "Like they all thought me dead!"

She recognised her error immediately. Indeed, most people probably did think her dead, and her chuckle turned into a frown at that thought. So much hurt and grief surrounded her! Friends and family lost and mourned, people she would never see again, people who believed they would never see her again. As so often happened in these past few days, she felt the enormity of the task ahead of her. Could she ever be who she once was? Would that life ever feel like 'her' again?

She would not think on it now. With a nod to Mercer, she rose. "Let us have coffee in the drawing room, shall we?"

WHEN ALL OF THE STORIES HAD BEEN TOLD, THE TIME IN Weymouth with Darcy grew difficult. There were many times Darcy would try to apologise or speak of them and their marriage, but Elizabeth saw no point to that. Nor did she think it needful that he know what she had done these two years past. It was done, why discuss it? She was in Weymouth because of happenstance; there was no more to say of it than that.

Conversation thus languished, and their interactions became painfully polite. They could not be anything but awkward as Darcy attempted to further a reconciliation, and Elizabeth tried—politely, but with utmost certainty—to keep her distance from him.

Her feelings for her husband were conflicted. She loved him, but she hated him. She missed him, but she wished he would go away. She yearned to be held by him, yet his touch made her skin crawl. Her thoughts and feelings were in such a tumult that she could hardly make sense of it. She felt as though she was accosted by a new and unexpected emotion every five minutes, and in reality, it was sometimes all she could do to simply survive the day.

More than once, she would resolve in her mind that she could not go forward with this plan of reconciliation. She would decide it very firmly, prepare herself to inform him…and then she would get stuck. She would see Bennet and realise she had to move forward, or she would see Darcy and feel unable to disappoint him.

It was during one particularly difficult afternoon with him that she proposed a recently conceived notion.

They had spent their time in near silence, the discomfort between them nearly palpable. Elizabeth found herself unnerved by nearly everything Darcy did. His habit of twisting his signet ring made her tense, his tendency to gaze at her made her want to scream, even the sound of his breathing seemed like it was rubbing her raw. Had he always breathed so...so oddly?

She invited him to walk with her along the shore, and he agreed, because all he ever did was agree to whatever she said. Perversely, it vexed her.

"I do not think I can manage it."

"Manage what?"

She swallowed heavily as her eyes roamed the shore. Such familiar, dear sights were before her: the sea bathing machines, the esplanade, the gulls, all of it! It was impossible to think of leaving. "I had an idea," she began slowly, "that we might live at Pemberley for the autumn, town for the Season—or some of it— and then I could remain here with Bennet for the rest."

Darcy was quiet for a few moments. "I do not see any impediment to that. I should have to rely on my steward to manage things in my absence, but—"

"Oh." She uttered it inadvertently, but it caused him to stop and look at her. "Well, I just meant...you would...Weymouth is not really your home, after all, and it might be easier for us both if..."

She stopped, having turned to look at his face. He was impassive, but his eyes clearly showed his thoughts of her idea.

"It is too hard," she said, and tears, vexing, silly tears, began to leak from her eyes. "This is hard."

Darcy pulled his handkerchief from his pocket and handed it to her. She pressed it to her face, enjoying the warmth and scent of him that lingered on it and wishing she could permit him to hold her. She trembled slightly, feeling his gaze upon her and seeing in her mind's eye the worried and sad expression he no doubt wore. For just a brief moment, she indulged herself, utterly incapable of stopping herself from turning and pressing her face to his chest.

Hesitantly, he laid his hand on her back. In but a moment, her wall crumbled, and she felt every bit of the painful yearning she had for him, the ache of his betrayal, and the full force of her love for him. It poured from within her in the form of agonising sobs with terrifying fervency.

As quickly as it came, she pushed it back, swallowing her agony, putting aside her despair, and forcing good cheer to her countenance. She dabbed the handkerchief on her face, looking around and praying no one had seen her unseemly display.

"Let us walk," she said. Guilt compelled her to slide her hand into his arm.

They walked in outward silence as Elizabeth raged at her own foolishness. *Never again, Lizzy. You must not do this again.*

At length, Darcy said, "You wish to live apart."

"Forget what I said," she replied quickly. "Truly. I was feeling cross and tired and I just…please, pay me no heed. 'Twas silliness. Are you hungry? Let us go in for tea."

DARCY FOUND HIMSELF NEARLY OVERWHELMED WITH HAPPINESS at having his family with him in the carriage en route to Pemberley. He could only wish that Elizabeth did not look so resigned, but she had every reason to be wary.

She had proven quite resolute in her determination that they should not speak of the past. There had been surprisingly few moments of recrimination or emotion, though he knew that more was to come. He could only suppose that she wished to let all of them adjust to being together once again before such things could truly be discussed. He believed that many unpleasant discussions, tears, and arguments lay ahead, but for now, it seemed she wished to remain in a sedate humour.

However, despite the outward appearance that Elizabeth seemed determined to uphold, he could see she obviously and rightly harboured quite a bit of anger and hatred towards him. Occasionally, these would surpass her determined complaisance, and tears or harsh words would erupt. He did not shy away from them however; in fact, he wished for them, for he gladly accepted whatever would be required to relieve the heavy burden of anguish she carried, and he knew that false cheer and disingenuous optimism would not do that.

Briefly, he closed his eyes as a remembrance from last evening assailed him.

Elizabeth had entered the drawing room, her eyes red and watery in her wan countenance. Merely seeing her thus pained him, so he tried to offer apologies and comfort as he could. She had simply looked at him, motionless and wordless, and stupidly, he had decided then to gather her into his arms and tell her how much he loved her.

She went stiff until he dropped his arms. "I beg you would not say such things to me—nay, I insist upon it."

"Not tell you I love you?"

She shook her head firmly. "If you insist on doing so, then I…then I cannot go back with you. I shall not."

After a pause, he said, "Then I shall keep these unwelcome sentiments to myself."

"Thank you."

Even remembering it made him ashamed. Unwisely, unadvisedly, he had then pressed her. "Elizabeth, am I meant to behave as though I do not love you? Should you prefer I am cold and unfeeling?"

She tilted her head, studying him for a moment, before saying, "I should think it easy enough. After all, you had a great deal of practice our last months in London. Do now as you did then."

With a swish of skirts, she had left him then, and it was Mrs Mercer who came to tell him that Mrs Elizabeth had a headache and would see him on the morrow. So it was, that the next time he saw her was when she emerged from the house ready to enter the carriage to take them to Pemberley.

Pemberley. He prayed it would be a place of healing for them both.

THEY MADE THE JOURNEY TO PEMBERLEY IN FOUR DAYS DESPITE travelling with the many carriages required to convey their group. Elizabeth had Mrs Macy's carriage with Bennet and Nurse Harriet, who had agreed to stay on when Merry left them to marry. Darcy had brought two carriages to Weymouth for the conveyance of his party. One for himself, Lydia, Kitty, and Georgiana, and the other for his man Fields, Mrs Annesley, and the girls' maids. The Mercers and Blake joined that carriage, and a cart came behind with all their many things.

Regardless of how they had departed Weymouth, somehow, by the time they arrived at Pemberley, Elizabeth found herself alone with her husband and son. As their carriage came over the rise that would first allow them to view the house, Elizabeth prayed fervently that Darcy would not stop the carriage as had once been his custom. Her stomach was knotted in anxiety, and in truth, she thought if she stood, she might very well collapse from her nerves. She wondered how much time would be required to spend greeting the servants before she could run to the bedchamber and enjoy a bit of solitude.

She could not summon even the least bit of wherewithal required to console her son, who pressed against her, noting her anxiety. She could feel his eyes intent upon her face and tried her best to smile at him reassuringly.

Elizabeth felt as if she moved within a dream as she alit from the carriage, smiling and greeting the servants (who were all quite kind and respectful to her), giving instructions to the footmen for her belongings in a very natural manner, and then agreeing to Nurse Harriet's offer to accompany Bennet and Mrs Reynolds to the nursery. Everyone dispersed to their various duties with an almost eerie alacrity, and Elizabeth gratefully hastened to her bedchamber, praying Darcy would go to his study, to his own bedchamber, or off on a horse somewhere—anywhere, just so long as he did not follow her and further test her equanimity by his presence.

He did not. He kept hard on her heels, so much so that when she stopped in her tracks at the door to her bedchamber, he very nearly ran into her.

"Do you not need to attend to…things?"

He nodded, seeming as if he understood her none-too-veiled hint. "I do, indeed. I shall be in…my study I believe."

She nodded and gave him a tense smile before opening her bedchamber door. She paused at the threshold for a moment to look around. How different it was, looking on this room now and remembering being the wide-eyed bride, wondering whether she would be able to be mistress of such a place. For a moment, that same uncertainty assailed her, that same sense that she had wagered mightily on a horse that proved lame.

Nonsense. You are no lame horse. You saw an old woman to her last days in comfort. You birthed a child. You found yourself a comfortable position in place of being an outcast and alone, you can surely manage being wife to a man like Darcy.

She walked into the dressing room. Blake was not yet there with her things, and thus it was nearly empty save for the few trunks stored therein. One trunk in particular drew her interest, though she could not immediately understand why it was there.

It had a tricky latch, but her hands knew the way, and she slid it open with relative ease. Inside, Elizabeth found everything she had not taken when she left Yorkshire: a gown she hated, a few pairs of shoes, and a book. She reached for the walking boots, turning them to see the dirt that remained on their soles.

It gave her a strange, hollow feeling to remember that Elizabeth, the girl who had wandered the moors, afraid, alone...a heroine in her own dreadful gothic tale, a tale no one ever wished to be a part of. Her finger rubbed at the dirt, remembering how she was abandoned. "All those walks," she murmured.

"What?"

The noise from behind her made her jump, and she tossed the shoes back into the trunk like a child found snooping. She felt like she might cry but forced herself to look calm. "N-nothing."

"It sounded like you said something?"

She pushed past him, going back out to the bedchamber. She heard him follow her and busied herself moving the jars around on her table. "I did not say anything. Rather, I was talking to myself."

"You said, 'All those walks'. Did you walk a great deal in those shoes you were looking at?"

Elizabeth refused to reply, forcing herself to appear uninterested despite the flush rising up her neck.

"We, Fitzwilliam and I, brought that trunk back to Pemberley. I did not know whether you intended to discard those boots—"

"I do not want to speak of those boots!" She stopped and inhaled deeply for a moment. "I...yes, they are quite worn. They should have been discarded, I suppose." *Just like you discarded me. Toss them right out without another thought.*

"Please, pardon me, I really must see to Bennet." Before anything else could be said, she was gone.

JUST MINUTES LATER, SHE WAS STANDING IN THE DOORWAY TO THE nursery, viewing a scene that filled her with delight.

Evidently, in the time they were in Weymouth, Darcy set Mrs Reynolds to work purchasing every toy she could find that might be of interest to a small boy, as well as new linens and other items suitable for a nursery. Bennet had never seen so many toys and books in his life, and he looked around in wonder while busily stacking blocks in the middle of the room. It was wonderful to see him so happy and well settled, particularly given his usual tendency to be unhappy in new situations.

It is on things such as this that I must keep my mind, Elizabeth counselled herself. *He is a good man, he means well, and he is capable of doing lovely things such as this for his son.* She inhaled deeply; Bennet was happy. Was that not why she was here? Bennet was content, and thus she would be satisfied.

Mrs Reynolds had been nearly overcome with happiness at having a small child to care for. She had become teary-eyed when Elizabeth and Bennet alit from the carriage and almost instinctively reached for the boy before recalling her position and assuming a more rigid, proper posture. Elizabeth had laughed and was about to tell her that Bennet was too shy to go to her until he knew her better, when Bennet had other ideas. He reached for Mrs Reynolds, which Elizabeth could see was an overwhelming temptation for the housekeeper. Elizabeth nodded to her, saying, "Mrs Reynolds, I would be very well pleased to have you hold him."

Mrs Reynolds had quickly scooped him up, beaming and exclaiming, "Oh, my dear, are you not just the image of your father? We shall have such a good time, you and I." Bennet smiled happily at her.

Mrs Reynolds, although ostensibly occupied with helping Nurse Harriet settle into her accommodations, could not take her eyes off of him. Suddenly noticing Elizabeth, she exclaimed, "Oh, Mrs Darcy, please excuse me." She shook her head, remarking, "It is just so long since we have had someone in these rooms, and it brings such joy to my heart."

Elizabeth smiled hesitantly. "I am glad he already appears to be so easy. He is not usually this way."

Mrs Reynolds sighed happily. "What joy for all of Pemberley to know there is a Darcy heir. I daresay there was some worry in Kympton, but all that is better now."

"How do you mean?"

"So many in these parts depend upon Pemberley! The health

and well-being of the master and mistress of Pemberley directly affects all of those people. It has been of great concern that you have been gone all these years. Folks will be much comforted that you have recovered so well from your illness and gladdened to see the next generation of Darcys playing on the lawns."

Elizabeth nodded. "I can certainly understand that."

The two ladies then paused, their eyes on Bennet, who was deeply engaged in his blocks. Elizabeth wondered what Mrs Reynolds knew about why she had been gone for two years.

As if she had read her mind, Mrs Reynolds spoke, "Ma'am, forgive me if I speak too familiarly, but the master was…well, he was honest with me about what happened."

Heat rose in Elizabeth's face. "I see."

"I…I congratulate you, Mrs Darcy for your courage to return. Please know that if anyone in the household questions or gossips or—"

"What do they think happened?"

"They think you had to care for your relation," said Mrs Reynolds firmly. "And any who think they need to know more than that will answer to me. Do not worry about anything, my dear—we will make sure your reputation and character have no stain here."

NINETEEN

THE FIRST MORNING AT PEMBERLEY. DARCY WAS SHAVED AND dressed, all the while thinking of the task ahead of him.

Surprisingly, Elizabeth had been unfailingly cheerful and kind to him. Four days in the carriage to Pemberley, and she had said not a word against him. They spoke pleasantly of their time in Weymouth. They discussed some books she had read recently, as well as a few items in the newspapers. They spent a good deal of time talking of their son. What they had not discussed was anything pertaining to their separation.

He had not expected her cheerful demeanour, and in some ways, he wished for the necessary arguments to ensue. Awaiting them was dreadful, but it was his due. He would wait patiently until she was ready to speak, and then he would hear anything she wished to say. He only hoped that she somehow would be able to see how very different he was now! He had changed from the cruel man who had perpetrated such a heinous act upon her.

He hoped that she kept to her habit of an early morning walk; indeed, he had awoken with the anticipation of asking to join her. Once dressed, he went to the door of her bedchamber, tapping gently. He received no response.

He tried several more times but heard nothing within, no sounds of her stirring in her chambers. *Too early. She is likely tired from travelling.* Gently, he pressed open the door and peered in, surprised to find that Elizabeth was not in her chamber. Her bed was made, and the room had an air of vacancy. Where was she? A bit of panic began to beat within him as an irrational voice in his head whispered: *gone.*

No, he argued with himself. *No, you simply missed her. Likely she is walking now.* To be sure, he decided to investigate. She was not in the breakfast room nor in the mistress's study. The salon that she had so long ago enjoyed in the winter mornings was empty.

Darcy tried not to succumb to panic, but it was too reminiscent of his time vainly seeking her in Yorkshire for rational thought. Suppressing his desire to run, he immediately went to see whether she was in the gardens.

His heart now in his throat, he walked briskly along the main paths for twenty minutes before turning around, having not seen her. His hands shook and his heart pounded; he knew he was likely being witless, but still, where was she? Where could she have gone at such an hour of the morning?

Re-entering the house, he forced himself to calm down. It would not do for the servants to witness him charging maniacally around the house looking for Mrs Darcy, although what he wished to do was stand in the entrance hall and shout her name until she appeared. Fortunately, he saw Mrs Reynolds just as he walked in the door.

She smiled pleasantly. "Sir, Mrs Darcy asked me to inform you that she would be with Bennet in the nursery this morning."

For a moment, his knees went weak, and he knew his face must display a comical degree of relief. "Th-thank you."

"I must apologise; I should have given you the message sooner. I lingered in the nursery a bit too long making sure Master Bennet had his breakfast."

"Is that not Nurse Harriet's duty?" Darcy then saw a sight he had never before witnessed: Mrs Reynolds was blushing.

"She did not require my assistance," she said, "but I offered it nevertheless."

Mrs Reynolds had wished to sit with his son. Between his relief at knowing where Elizabeth was and his amusement at seeing Mrs Reynolds blush, Darcy chuckled before he could stop himself. His laugh made Mrs Reynolds flush still more deeply, but she gathered herself admirably and said in a respectful but firm tone, "It has been a dreadfully long time in this house without children. I am perhaps enjoying it a bit more than I should."

Remorse made Darcy stop chuckling and smile kindly. "You should enjoy it as much as you like, Mrs Reynolds. I believe I shall go and join them. Will you have a tray with breakfast sent to the nursery for me?"

He felt her staring at his back as he walked away and did not wonder that she was shocked. After all, the thought of his own father dining in the nursery was impossible to imagine. But the present master of Pemberley cared little for any of that. He would do as he liked for the happiness of his family.

Elizabeth smiled pleasantly when Darcy entered the nursery, which he found encouraging. Bennet said, "Pop," and attempted to rise to go to him. Darcy positively delighted in that.

"Elizabeth, I presumed to think you would keep your custom of a morning walk," he said. "I had hoped to join you."

Elizabeth's smile turned to an awkward frown. "A mother's customs change to suit her children. I take afternoon walks now while he naps. I like to sit with him when he eats."

At that moment, a servant entered with a tray of breakfast. Darcy motioned for it to be set at the small table where Bennet had been eating. He smiled at his wife hopefully. "Have you eaten? I have quite a lot here."

"So I see," Elizabeth said, seeming shocked. "Were you…did you intend to eat here?"

"I do indeed." Darcy nodded at his son. "With my family."

His cheer dimmed a bit when he saw a brief flash of something—was it irritation?—in her eyes, only to be quickly subsumed by complaisance. "Of course," she replied. "We are glad to see you."

In a serious tone, he responded, "I have been apart from both of you long enough, and I wish to spend as much time with you as possible."

"Very well, then," she said with a little nod. "Pray, sit. Next time, we shall not be surprised to see you."

THEY WERE NOT MANY DAYS AT PEMBERLEY BEFORE Elizabeth's intentions for them became clear—a civil union. When they were together, she behaved like a stranger at a party making polite and amiable conversation with a bore. She varied her schedule such that he often had no idea where she was, or whether she was even in the house. He always saw her in the nursery for breakfast but sometimes not again until dinner. At least twice a week, she claimed a headache or indisposition of some sort and took dinner in her bedchamber.

He supposed it was to their credit that anyone outside of their home would not likely realise anything was amiss. She treated him in a manner that was just short of loving when Bennet or their sisters or the servants were about. If Georgiana, Kitty, or Lydia were with them, she often fell silent, allowing the younger ladies to carry the conversation. He had learned to stop trying to press her to speak to prevent her running from him. She permitted him to walk with her at times, and she would sometimes read with him in their private sitting room in the evenings, but it was rare.

It was a most civil union—the sort of cold and sterile but cordial marriage that many of elevated society had. He hated it.

He would have far rather faced her ire in hopes of regaining her passion and love than to settle for this forced politeness.

It was frustration that induced him to try again one night after dinner when they had set out on a walk together. "I want to show you the lavender we planted for you."

"Lavender? For me?"

"Over on the east side of the paddock. We planted it last spring—1813, I mean. Jane was of great help. She had the gardeners at Longbourn send us some seeds of those variety as well as some other, newer varieties."

When Elizabeth did not immediately reply, he added, "I recall you saying how Hill always scented your bed linens and towels with lavender, so I had hoped it might be something you would enjoy having done here as well."

"Very kind of you."

They soon found themselves at the field, and Elizabeth made all the obligatory sounds of delight that he might have expected. But, as was the new custom, he saw that her replies were forced and dutiful rather than genuine.

"I suppose I can only hope you truly like it."

"I said I do. I like it very well."

"But if you were dissembling, I should never know." He shrugged, frustration getting the better of reason. "If you care about me or care about my lavender…no one will know."

She shot him a strange look and began to walk away, saying, "I do not comprehend your meaning, sir. Pray do not speak in riddles."

"I have anticipated that at some time we would discuss…us. Our problems. To confront the problems, and heal the breach. Alas, you seem determined to pretend nothing ever happened."

She laughed nervously. "We have. I am here, you are here, we have our son. What more is there to talk about?"

"How can you say that?"

She paused a moment, looking around as if for guidance from the fields themselves. "Upon my word, I am baffled by your need to argue with me. We do not need to have some vicious row or a dramatic outpouring of emotion to reconcile. A terrible thing happened, but you have done all you could do to set things aright. Let us just continue on with our life together now."

He regarded her carefully. "I am not saying that I wish to have terrible arguments or would enjoy your anger; however, I know how I have hurt you. I only want you to do and say whatever is necessary in hopes that you might feel less pain and I might one day earn your forgiveness." *And regain your love too, I hope.* But he was not bold enough to say so.

She smiled and quickly said, "I do forgive you, and it is not necessary for me to revisit the pain of the past two years in order to do so. Do you approve?"

Frustrated, he insisted, "It matters not whether I approve or disapprove. I only thought we might discuss it at some point."

"If it is all the same to you, I do not see any value in reviewing events that are painful to us. Remember the past only as its remembrance gives you pleasure—that is my philosophy, and I think it a good one. At any rate, our life is agreeable, and I do not think anything more could be expected.

He wondered at her choice of words. "What do you mean that nothing more can be expected?"

She would not look his direction, and he cursed her bonnet, so capably shielding her from his view. "Our marriage is as would be expected."

"Do you mean expected for now or expected for always?"

She would not answer him.

Quietly, he said, "I know I have no right to wish for more, but I must tell you that I have expectations that exceed amiability and commonplace civilities for our marriage. I am a fool perhaps, but I am fool who loves you still more than ever he did, and thus I cannot surrender my wish, not until you tell me I must."

He saw her sigh deeply. Eventually, she said, "My first object is a happy home for Bennet."

"I agree completely. I wish him to be happy and feel loved every day of his life. I also wish that for you." Elizabeth gave no sign that she had heard his words.

He stopped their progress, reaching to take her hands in his. She permitted it, yet she did not look at him.

In a very low voice, he said, "I shall do anything in this world to make you happy once again. I know how I have hurt you, and I have thought of little else for the last two years. Please allow me to make amends for my errors."

"Is it not the common way with adulterous wives? Punish them by sending them off to the outer reaches of civilisation to stitch handkerchiefs? One cannot blame you for wishing me away from a man you thought was my lover."

"I did think so," he admitted. "But I was incorrect and stupid and selfish and—"

"But it's over now, and you have changed, as have I. Why scream and shout at one another? It was all a misunderstanding, was it not?" She turned, gesturing towards the lavender field. "Even such as this—I do not need to know this was planted in 1813. I scarcely remember Pemberley, and it was winter when last I was here. Whether this field has been here since 1713 or you planted it yesterday, I should not know the difference. What matters is today. Here and now."

After a long pause, he said, "Very well. We shall not speak of any of it, if you please."

"Some might think arguments and fighting are best, to get all the grievances aired, so to speak. But no one really knows, do they? Has anyone ever succeeded in doing what we are trying to do?"

"In repairing a marriage that has been so affected?" He considered it for a moment, then admitted, "I do not know of anyone."

"No," she agreed. "Nor do I."

"Do you think it a hopeless case, then?" He turned to look at her fully.

She crossed her arms over her chest. The breeze blew through lightly, tumbling about the curls at her cheeks as she stared off, away from him. "We can never recapture the early days or the opportunity to build on the fresh, energetic sort of love that we once had."

It broke his heart when she said so, though he knew she was correct. "But perhaps there is something better," he suggested. "We are parents and—"

"Precisely," she said quickly. "Bennet must be considered above all. That is my first thought, and I am glad to hear he is yours, also."

She began to walk away, and he followed her. It seemed as though she wilfully misunderstood him but he would not try to further his point.

As the house came into view, Darcy was reminded of a request he had of her. He stopped her with the lightest touch of his hand on her arm. "May I ask you something?"

Her smile was impatient. "Of course."

"I wondered whether I might read to Bennet before he sleeps at night. He seems to be very fond of books."

"You do not require my permission to do anything you would wish with Bennet. He is as much your son as mine."

"Thank you, but I would not wish to do anything that might distress him—or you—or alter whatever patterns or schedules to which he is accustomed."

"I think it fair to say he is unaccustomed to any of this," Elizabeth said with a faint smile. "But he is still a baby, and babies are remarkably adaptable. I daresay he would much enjoy having you read to him."

"Is there a certain way it should be done?"

"Reading?"

"Yes. That is…I want to ensure I do it as well as you would."

"Nurse Harriet generally readies him for slumber and tucks him in his bed, so after that would be the ideal time. He will let you know which books he prefers."

"And I have noticed that when you read to him, you sit next to him on the bed. Shall I do likewise?"

With teasing gravity, she replied, "That would seem wise. Otherwise, one of you will not be able to view the book."

He chuckled. "True. Thank you."

DARCY WENT TO HIS SON THAT VERY NIGHT, HOPING THE LAD WAS not already asleep. Fortune smiled upon him; Bennet was just being settled into his bed by Nurse Harriet. "May I read to the boy?"

"Will that do, Master Bennet?" the nurse asked. "Can Papa do the honours tonight?"

With a smile, she handed him a book titled *The Butterfly's Ball*. Darcy settled in, taking it and holding it open to read. When he finished, his son, whose eyes were only slightly tired-looking, said, "Again, please."

By his third reading, he thought he might be able to simply recite it from memory. Blessedly, by the fourth reading (*Do all children wish to hear the same book read over and over again?*), Bennet had begun to grow sleepy and agreed to the extinguishing of his light.

Leaning down, Darcy kissed his head gently and bid him good night. He watched from the doorway as his son slowly turned over, pulling his arms and legs beneath him such that he was in a strange, uncomfortable-looking ball. He went back to him, moving the boy's limbs gently and carefully, but with a sudden, unintelligible grunt, Bennet yanked himself away and formed the ball again. Darcy laughed quietly. "So it is then. Sweet dreams, my darling."

TWENTY

THE LADIES OF THE NEIGHBOURHOOD, HAVING RECEIVED Elizabeth's cards, were delighted to find her in their midst once again and hastened to wait upon her. Elizabeth was pleased to find that her former acquaintances Mrs Dodsworth and Mrs Sinclair were as amiable as they had been previously. Miss Montgomery, she was told, was now Mrs Robert Bradwell and lived in Leicestershire but was close enough to visit often. There were many others who waited upon her, and from her reception, Elizabeth could only conclude that they had been genuinely concerned about her health. Bennet was brought out and exclaimed over, and she was certain that one and all looked to him as the probable cause of her long disappearance from their society. She received innumerable well wishes for her continued good health with poise and grace and became adept at turning the conversation as needed.

As Mrs Sinclair rose to leave, she paused. "I hope, Mrs Darcy, that you should be recovered enough for parties, for we shall have a ball at Southwynde and very much want you and Mr Darcy to join us."

Although the very thought made Elizabeth's stomach clench, she smiled sweetly. "How lovely! I hope we can attend."

Balls had last been discussed in that fateful spring of 1812 when they had then been the source of misery and conflict—though at the time, it had all been a mystery to Elizabeth. Now she knew that Darcy had been jealous seeing her dance with other gentlemen, and although she knew he was wrong—and he did as well—she still did not wish to test their understanding. She could scarce even imagine herself at a ball and believed it unlikely they would attend in any case.

Darcy mentioned it to his family members later that evening as they gathered in the drawing room after dinner. "Elizabeth, you have received an invitation to the Sinclair's ball, I believe."

Cries of rapture went up among the younger ladies, but Elizabeth only nodded. "I thought we would ask Mrs Annesley to escort the girls."

Darcy shot her a look but said nothing. Kitty, Lydia, and Georgiana formed their own tête-à-tête and began an immediate discussion about shoe roses and fans, but Elizabeth remained silent.

Darcy awaited his moment, and when the other ladies were no longer paying attention to them, he moved close and spoke to her in a low voice. "You do not wish to attend?"

"Do you?"

"I know there are many who wish to see you, and they will likely all be at this ball."

Elizabeth averted her eyes. "I am not sure I have a gown, and it might be difficult to have something suitable done up in time."

He took her hand, and she allowed it. "It is a country ball. Perhaps one of your finer day dresses could be made over by Blake? I do miss dancing with you."

She looked at him, thinking it would indeed be nice to see him in his finer clothes—he always did look particularly handsome in evening dress.

With a hesitant smile, she said, "I shall send our acceptance."

BY THE TIME THE SINCLAIRS' BALL CAME AROUND, ELIZABETH had worked herself into a bit of a state and wished ardently that they had sent regrets. She sat at her dressing table, thinking that no matter how hard she tried, she simply could not imagine being at a ball. She knew the waltz had gained in popularity in the two years she had been gone, and although she had learnt it back then, she had neither practiced nor performed it since. What if she looked silly?

She decided she would simply not dance. That would be for the best because it would also solve the problem of worrying what Darcy might think or feel if he witnessed her dancing with another gentleman. So resolved, she retired to her chamber to begin bathing and dressing.

How grateful she was that Georgiana, at some time in the last two years, had brought two of her ball gowns from London. That was at least one worry she might lay aside. Her maid pressed and laid out both that she might decide which to wear. Elizabeth rose from her dressing table and went to look at the two gowns.

She gasped when she saw it, her heart sinking.

It lay on her bed, jonquil and cheerful and pretty, and it made her pulse race. It had been a favourite. She remembered trying it on during fittings at the modiste and feeling for the very first time in her life like an elegant, beautiful lady. She remembered hoping her husband would like it.

Then she remembered how she had exited her room to Darcy's coldness, informing her he had sent his regrets to their hosts—was it the Bickerdykes? It had been the night she realised how much was wrong with them, with their marriage, and she remembered with painful clarity standing before him in abject terror, wondering what would come.

At once, a sharp pain clenched her stomach, and for a moment, she feared she might be sick. She sank to the floor, feeling the waves of nausea roll through her as her hands began to tremble and a sour, metallic feeling invaded her mouth. She raised a shaking hand to her forehead; it felt clammy. She laid her forehead against the side of her bed, feeling her breath coming rapidly as her stomach churned.

Blake entered the room. "Mrs Darcy, do you think you will want the bracelet that... Madam! Are you well?"

Elizabeth felt Blake take hold of her, trying to help her up, but Elizabeth could not stand. In a faint whisper, she begged, "No, I...just let me rest. I...my stomach..."

She heard Blake hurry away, only to return moments later with a cold, damp cloth to put on her face. Elizabeth murmured her thanks and heard Blake exit.

Moments later, Darcy arrived, the heavy oak door thudding against the wall as he entered with haste. He paused a moment, no doubt beholding her, and then—more gently than she could have imagined—he bent and lifted her.

It nearly made her cry to contrast the cold, unfeeling Darcy in her recollections with the man who gently laid her against her coverlet, then went to refresh the cold cloth on her brow, bending to kiss her cheek before he knelt beside her. "You are ill."

She gave him a tremulous smile. "Merely a little nausea. I only need a moment."

"I shall send word to the Sinclairs."

"No need." With a deep breath, she raised herself to a seated position. "See? I am already better."

He reached down to help her rise and, as he did, glanced over at the gowns. "That yellow is lovely. I seem to recall you were particularly beautiful in it."

Elizabeth froze, distressed, pained, and feeling the onslaught of every agonising emotion she had so long suppressed within her. She began to cry, not a ladylike weeping, but heaving, gasping sobs that curled her body into a tight ball atop the bed. She felt her husband sit next to her and pull her hesitantly into his embrace, but she was too weak to push him off. After a few moments, she realised she did not truly want to.

Finally, her sobs subsided and she spoke. "The last...I had planned to wear that gown...it was the Bickerdyke's ball, I believe...you did not wish... I was already dressed. It was so... so very humiliating."

"Forgive me...I...I cannot recall..."

Elizabeth enjoyed being in her husband's arms very well, but felt all the danger therein. With a deep breath, she pulled back, using the need to get a handkerchief as reason to move. After she had retrieved one and dabbed at her face, she sat on the bed. Darcy sat next to her, silently questioning.

She looked down and explained herself as shortly and simply as she could. "I love that gown. When last I wore it, we were meant to attend the Bickerdykes' ball, but you had sent our regrets without telling me. I was dressed before I realised you meant to stay home. It was that night when I first began to really fear what was happening between us. Seeing the gown gave me all that feeling again—that dread and uncertainty."

She looked at him then, really looked at him, not as her adversary nor her tormentor, but as her partner. "This is why I cannot speak of these things. There is too much, and it hurts far too much to release it."

Darcy closed his eyes briefly. "I never shall cease trying to redress the things I have done to wrong you."

"Thank you," she said quietly. Her stomach felt better, she noticed. Glancing at the clock on the mantel, she realised she needed to make haste to dress. She inhaled deeply one last time, dispensing with the clouds of sadness that threatened and summoning a more cheerful humour.

"I believe I must summon Blake. I would not wish to make us late."

"Let us not go," he said quickly. Then, just as quickly, "But...no, I mean, I want to go. If you do. I want to do as you want. Wear the gown if you like, or perhaps the other one?"

For some reason, his verbal stumbling made her laugh. "We shall go and enjoy ourselves. I am all anticipation to have a waltz with you! How shocking it is that such a dance has gained such favour and in only a few years. I hear it has been danced at Almack's!"

AFTER THIS INAUSPICIOUS BEGINNING, ELIZABETH WAS SURPRISED to find she had a wonderful time at the Sinclairs' ball. All who had not yet seen Mrs Darcy were kind and welcoming, and none seemed so inclined to enquire too deeply into the happenings of the two years past, which was a relief. She was congratulated on her son and forced to hear several birthing room horror stories, but on the whole, it was quite benign.

Elizabeth was pleased to dance the first with her husband, followed by dances with various gentlemen, none of whom were particularly handsome or even very clever. Silently, she mused that there was no possible means by which anyone could think she flirted with any among the lot of them, then rebuked herself for such an uncharitable (albeit truthful) sentiments.

The supper was served at midnight, and Elizabeth joined her husband at a table with other young, married couples. Spirits were high, and for a time, she and Darcy forgot their troubles.

She recalled how she enjoyed Darcy's humour, and she appreciated the intelligence with which he defended his opinions on various matters while still being respectful to the notions that others held forth. She could not help but feel flattered when he sought out her opinion on a recently published book that he believed she might have enjoyed. As it was, she had not read it, but from the description, she believed he was quite right that she would find it pleasing. She blushed a bit when he declared that he would send for the book at once.

He sounded even a bit boastful of her as he proclaimed around the table, "My wife is a great reader, you know. I have not the least doubt that once she has read it, there will be much to find within that has completely escaped my notice!"

"I am not a great reader," Elizabeth demurred, still blushing, but she could not deny she was flattered by her husband's compliment.

The waltz was called after supper. How strange to find herself feeling nervous and shy around a gentleman to whom she had been married for nearly three years! And still more odd that her body should betray her with a thrill from his touch. As he took her in his arms, she inhaled deeply. Darcy had always smelled delightful, and tonight was no exception. It made a strange and wonderful feeling come into the pit of her stomach.

"Mrs Darcy, I believe we must have some conversation." Darcy smiled down at her as the dance began.

She laughed. "It would look quite strange for us to be together in this manner yet silent for above half an hour. However, I am afraid witty conversation is quite beyond me while I try to avoid making a fool of myself with this dance!"

Darcy pulled her infinitesimally closer to him and leaned his head down to murmur, "I shall then observe that you are in nowise making a fool of yourself, and furthermore, that you are the most handsome woman at the ball tonight."

Elizabeth blushed with his compliment, and after a brief, shy look at the floor, looked up into his eyes. "Then it is only fitting that I am with the most handsome gentleman."

He smiled, clearly pleased by the compliment, and she realised then what danger she was in. Drawn to him again, her heart emerging from its shell, ready to bleed for him. *Oh no, oh no, oh no.*

Their dance was entirely too brief, and the night ended shortly thereafter. Soon, they were returned to the carriage for the journey home. The younger girls sat across from them, all tittering and laughing and recounting the triumphs of the evening while their chaperons remained silent.

In the darkness, Elizabeth felt Darcy's hand graze hers, then move away. A few moments later, it again came to rest immediately adjacent. She allowed her hand to drift towards his, her fingers sliding beneath his hand. A few seconds later, he joined his hands to hers, and it remained thus until they were home.

SHE AWOKE IN LONDON. STRANGE, BECAUSE SHE COULD SWEAR she had been in her bed at Pemberley. The room was unfamiliar, yet she knew it was London. Was Bennet here? Was Darcy?

She left the room to find her son, but she could not, and the ghostly, faceless servants she passed would not look at her, would not help her. Her walk turned into a run as she travelled passage after passage, twisting and turning in a maze, never able to find her son.

Panic welled up within her. At last, her breathing heavy and her pulse racing, she found her husband standing with his back to her in a room that looked very much like the hateful bedchamber in Yorkshire.

"I cannot find Bennet," she cried, as tears ran down her face.

He turned to look at her. His face was a cold, haughty mask of disdain, and he frowned disapprovingly when he saw her weeping. Reaching into his pocket, he pulled out a handkerchief with 'GW' on it, thrusting it towards her. "Take this," he ordered. "This is all you get."

She shook her head vehemently and folded her hands behind her back, not wishing to make contact with the item. "No, no, I just want Bennet. Where is he?"

"You should not be here. You do not belong here," Darcy said coldly, advancing on her angrily and holding the handkerchief towards her. She reeled backwards, not wishing it to touch her.

"No, I need to find Bennet!"

Still, Darcy shoved the handkerchief at her. "You will never have Bennet, so you must take this."

"No!" she shouted, and he grabbed her, shaking her shoulders, but she was quick, and she fought him, slapping at him until his voice penetrated her conscious.

"Hush, Elizabeth, darling. It is only a dream."

With a start, she woke, finding herself in her bed at Pemberley, her husband bending over her, holding her close even as she fought him off, her breath yet coming fast.

"Just a dream," Darcy murmured in her ear. "Only a dream."

She swallowed hard, willing herself into equanimity.

"Do you want to talk about it?"

She shook her head.

With a final hug, he released her. "Are you well?" he asked.

She was not well. Indeed, she was terrified.

The ball had been a huge mistake. She had all too readily fallen under Darcy's spell. She had revelled in his solicitude, become dizzy with the sight of him and the feel of being in his arms, and been thoroughly charmed by his manners, just as she had been back in Hertfordshire so many years ago. All sense had fled her, and she had succumbed to his flattery, tossing herself at him like a fool. As she held his hand in the carriage just hours earlier, she had longed for him to kiss her like a lover. She was his for the asking just as she had always been—*foolish girl.*

And no matter how much she loved him, she knew she could not trust him. The man who mistrusted her, who sent her away, was still in him.

"I am well," she said finally. "What are you doing here?"

"I heard you from my chamber. I thought you had perhaps fallen ill again."

"No, it was only a bad dream," she murmured.

"Will you be able to sleep now?"

"I shall. Thank you."

TWENTY ONE

THE MORNING AFTER THE BALL, ELIZABETH SLEPT LATE, HER exhaustion compounded by the dream that had awoken her and prohibited easy rest thereafter. She arrived in the nursery to see Georgiana there before her, with Bennet clearly dressed for the outdoors and eagerly tugging on his aunt's hand.

"Forgive me, Elizabeth, I ought to have asked—do you mind if I take Bennet to the garden? We thought a walk might be nice."

Elizabeth looked down into her son's happy face. "Of course not. You are his aunt, and you should spend time with him however you please."

"Will you join us?"

"I would love to." After a brief delay for Elizabeth to gather her things and put on walking boots, they were off.

They spoke of inconsequential matters as they walked, their conversation interrupted frequently by Bennet, who wished to show them something or asked what another thing was or required consolation for the various bumps and bruises he obtained while charging ahead recklessly.

"Do you miss Weymouth?" Georgiana asked.

"A little," Elizabeth replied. "I enjoyed the sea very well. Did you like it?"

"Very much indeed," Georgiana said with enthusiasm. "The sea air was so invigorating! Do you think you will keep your house there?"

"I...I am not sure. No matter how much I enjoy the beach or the sea air, it is still a place where...well, you know."

Georgiana had been gathering some good rocks for skipping that she planned to take to the pond with Bennet and was looking for more as she remarked absently, "My aunt Lady Matlock is very fond of sea air, and when I was living with her, she spoke often of how much she liked Weymouth."

"When did you live with her?"

"Mostly when my brother was looking for you in the time before Kitty and Lydia came to stay. He was never sure how long he would be gone and did not like me alone so much."

"He mentioned that he went looking for me, but I had not thought it so exhausting a process."

"Oh, it was." Georgiana turned to look at her, her face the picture of earnestness. "He went everywhere."

"Everywhere?"

"All sorts of places, big and small, like Nottingham, Ely, York, Hull, Lichfield, Plymouth. There were many more too. I simply cannot remember them all. If there was any connexion to you or any hint you might have been in a place, there he went."

All over England! Elizabeth was astonished. "I believed he had hired people to search for me."

"Well, yes, he did that too, and at first, he and Fitzwilliam, and sometimes Saye, mostly went about following up on the information the investigators provided. But then..."

"Then what?"

Georgiana gave a nervous-sounding laugh. "Well, it seemed you had done quite a thorough job of disappearing, and the investigators ran out of places to look. There were weeks and weeks when Mr Chester would come with a blank report.

'Nothing new' is all he would say, and my brother would get so angry. Or even worse, he would become sorrowful.

"It is a very hard thing, I think," she continued, "when a loved one is gone, and you do not know what has happened. When someone dies, one can at least begin to grieve, but when they are missing, one is stuck in a place that is mostly despair with just a tiny bit of hope. I believe in such a circumstance, the hope becomes one's enemy."

Georgiana chanced a look at Elizabeth. "But perhaps you do not wish to speak of this."

"No, no. Please go on."

"Some people thought you had died," she said gently. "The investigators certainly did, especially once they learnt it was possible you were increasing. A gently bred woman out on her own like that... My brother felt the investigators had reached their conclusion and were not trying their hardest, so he doubled his own efforts. By the end, he was simply travelling randomly into various towns and cities, hoping that one day he might come across you or hear word of you somewhere. I do not know how much hope he placed in such a plan devoid of reason or forethought, but I do think he wished to be doing something, not just sitting in his study and waiting for a report from a hired man."

"I just cannot understand why he went to such lengths," Elizabeth said softly, as much to herself as any other. "Was it for me? Or for his son?"

"He did not really know about Bennet. Suspicions are not the same as knowing something," Georgiana reminded her gently. "It was for you, because he loves you. He recognised early on what a dreadful error he had made in believing me and Miss Bingley as he did. I do not think his regret ever left his mind."

"Mama!" Bennet ran up to them. "My stomach growled at me!"

Elizabeth smiled with both pleasure and relief at the opportunity to leave behind this painful discussion. "Shall we go in and see what Mrs Reynolds will find for you?"

ELIZABETH WENT TO HER BEDCHAMBER AS QUICKLY AS SHE could, leaving Georgiana and Bennet to seek the snack. Once she had gained her room, she locked the door, sat in her chair, and thought about her husband.

She had purposely, in these months past, avoided the very thought of what Darcy had experienced in the years she was gone, and she had even decried him for suggesting he had suffered when he mentioned it during one of their very rare arguments when they first were reunited. Of course, that was when she thought he still wished her gone.

However, in the words of her sister, she was suddenly made aware of a different perspective on the matter. Darcy did love her —she knew and accepted that fact—and he had spent two years alone and unsure, searching and seeking, wanting what they once had while not knowing whether he would ever find it. In some ways, it must have felt as she had in London when he behaved so inexplicably, and she knew not what was happening but wished to find some way to have her husband returned to her.

She thought of his search process—first methodical and careful, following logical clues and investigators' reports, then disintegrating into a chaotic, random, and hopeless system, which followed neither reason nor rationality. It seemed so very desperate and futile, yet he had kept it up for two years together.

In some ways, she had had the advantage in these two years past. She had been busy with Bennet and then Mrs Macy's illness. She had gone on to a new life in a new county and home, which made it easier to put aside any thoughts or regrets. No recollections would intrude, or if they did, they were easily pushed away. He had not had that. From the sounds of it, he had very much lived in the constant presence of his sorrow and remorse.

I hate this. I despise thinking of all of those sad months. She felt as though she wanted to weep for him, and a large part of her wished to go to him that very moment and wrap him in her embrace.

She could not bring herself to do that, of course, but later that day when he joined the ladies in the drawing room, she found herself a bit more kindly disposed towards him. He looked over at her as he entered the room, and she smiled and gestured for him to join her on the settee.

His look of pleasure as he sat was so genuine, it made her feel quite ashamed that she simply could not give him more.

THE NEXT MORNING, DARCY HAD TO TEND TO QUITE A BIT OF correspondence. When at last he could take a break, he immediately set out in search of Elizabeth. The day prior had been encouraging; Elizabeth had seemed easier in his company, and he hoped for more of the same today. He wondered where she was and whether she would be inclined to take a walk.

As he headed towards their rooms, he thought he heard a little sound: a brief sniffle and a stifled cry. He looked around but saw no one and continued forth slowly. *There!* Again, a stifled sob, coming from somewhere close.

"Elizabeth?" he asked, but there was no reply save for another sniffle. Then he saw him—Bennet, hiding under a hall table, evidently terrified and crying with his face to the wall.

Darcy knelt beside the table. "Bennet? Are you hurt, Son?"

The boy looked at him with large terrified eyes but did not speak for several moments. Darcy very awkwardly reached in and patted the boy's arm. "Tell Papa what is wrong."

"Mama?"

"I…I do not… Shall we find Nurse Harriet?"

This made Bennet sob again, repeating, "Mama, Mama" over and over as he did so.

Darcy clumsily attempted to reach in to the boy and draw him closer, "Mama will be back soon, I am sure. Would you like Papa to read you a book?"

"No! Mama!"

"Let us play blocks," Darcy suggested, feeling an inordinate desire to be the solution to his son's dismay. "Or soldiers. Shall we play with your soldiers?"

Bennet said nothing, still crying and turning his face resolutely towards the wall.

"Are you hungry? How about a snack?"

Nothing worked. Darcy despaired of his stupidity where his child was concerned but then inspiration struck. "Would you like to go see the horses?"

Now he had his son's interest. Bennet stopped crying and looked at him hopefully.

"Pemberley has lots of horses, Bennet, and Papa has a big black horse named Orion. Would you like to visit Orion and the other horses?"

Bennet studied him soberly, then broke into a large grin and scrambled from his hiding place. Mama was all but forgotten as he shouted, "Horses!"

With triumph in his step, Darcy took his son to the stables after a brief stop in the kitchen for old apples and carrots. He soon faced a second issue, though, as he quickly learned the inherent difficulty of walking anywhere with a young child. Bennet walked slowly and stopped frequently as rocks, beguiling blades of grass, and the occasional insect caught his interest. Darcy slowed his pace to a near stop to indulge his son's curiosity but soon realised that if they were to ever arrive at the stables, he would need to carry him.

As they entered the stables, Darcy could feel Bennet's heart begin to beat rapidly and hoped fervently the boy would not become afraid or distraught. He need not have worried, however, for as soon as Bennet saw his father's horses, his eyes lit with pure pleasure and excitement.

Darcy took him from stall to stall, telling him briefly about each horse and occasionally feeding them an apple or carrot. On the second or third feeding, Bennet reached out his small hand

and joined it underneath Darcy's, wanting to participate. After they had visited all the horses in the stables, Darcy took Bennet outside where one of the grooms was exercising some horses in the rings. The horses were galloping, and Bennet inhaled sharply. Darcy saw his son's fascination with the animals as they ran and jumped, and he smiled, recognising his own love of horses reflected in his son's eyes.

It was then that it happened. Watching his son experiencing the beauty of the horses brought to Darcy's mind a powerful, agonisingly sweet recollection of himself with his father, riding Pemberley's horses at an age that was not much older than Bennet. Darcy was flooded with the sudden understanding of the bond of father and son, the bond that he had shared with his own father and now shared with the small boy in his arms. At once, Darcy realised that there was nothing he would not do for this child—happily give up his life if necessary. Anything to ensure that he had a long life of felicity and contentment. The love Darcy felt for his son was overpowering and precious, and like nothing he had ever felt before, even for Elizabeth.

His throat closed, filled with a restrained sob, and tears sprung to his eyes as he looked upon Bennet, who was still happily entranced by watching the horses run. Swallowing hard, he inhaled deeply to restore his composure, and then asked the boy, "How would you like to ride a horse today?"

The look of wide-eyed delight that spread over his son's countenance easily answered the question.

WITHIN A SHORT TIME, ONE OF THE OLDER, MORE DOCILE HORSES was saddled, and Darcy was in the seat with his son firmly between his legs and grasping the horse's mane. They walked slowly around the ring at a snail's pace, Bennet laughing in delight and Darcy smiling ridiculously at his son's happiness. They spent the next hour slowly walking a series of older horses and ended the afternoon watching as the animals were brushed and fed by the grooms.

Darcy asked Bennet several times whether he would like to go back to the house to find Mama, but each time Bennet responded with, "More horses?" so they remained at the stables. In time, Bennet began to rest his head on Darcy's shoulder and grew heavy and warm in his arms. Darcy realised the excitement of the day combined with a missed nap had led to Bennet's falling asleep.

He walked back to the house at a gentle pace after nudging his son into a more secure position on his shoulder. He felt the boy's breath on his neck and slowly rubbed his back with his free arm. The arm he was using to support Bennet had grown painful, having been contracted in one position for some time, but Darcy would not have surrendered his treasured burden for all the world. His son was asleep in his arms, safe and secure. It was altogether the happiest thing Darcy had ever experienced.

ELIZABETH WAS IN HER BEDCHAMBER AND HEARD DARCY GO INTO his rooms. She knocked lightly and entered as he bid her. "I hope Bennet was no trouble. I understand you have had him for some hours."

Darcy had a strange, pensive air about him and said only, "No, he was no trouble at all."

"Evidently, Nurse Harriet fell asleep. She was quite mortified to learn he had slipped away."

"We had a very nice time down at the stables with the horses. He seemed to like them quite a bit."

Elizabeth laughed although she was still unsure of his manner. "Another thing he must get from you, then, as we know horses are no great love of mine."

Darcy gave her an odd, vacant sort of smile. "Quite true. Now I must allow Fields to attend me. He is not going to be happy to see that I spent my afternoon at the stables in this coat."

Elizabeth started to leave but turned back almost immediately. "Is something wrong?"

"Not at all."

"Because…you are…this conversation is reminiscent of times that I would prefer to not remember." Drawing up her courage, she added, "Need I remind you that if you had spoken to me of things that upset you before, we would not now be as we are."

"Very well." Darcy sat down in a chair by the fire. "Bennet is…he is truly wonderful. I love him more than I ever could have imagined."

Elizabeth nodded, still wary. "Yes, it is a rare and wonderful thing, is it not?"

"It is." Darcy nodded. "And I cannot help but think that I might have missed out on it entirely. Indeed, I have already missed things: his birth, his early days, when he walked, his first tooth, his first word. How much more would I have missed had I not met you by chance at Weymouth? What if I had not looked up from the book that afternoon in the bookstore?"

Elizabeth could not reply.

"Would it have been Georgiana's sons that learned of Bennet when I died and they searched for Pemberley's heir? I know I have no right to be angry, certainly not at anyone but myself, but…it rankles. I cannot lie."

Elizabeth thought carefully before replying. "I think what matters is that he is here now, so what could have happened hardly signifies."

"But what was your plan? If I might ask."

"My plan?"

"Yes. Did you intend to come to me? Would you have told me I had a son? Did you intend to stay away from me forever?"

"My *plan*," said Elizabeth carefully, "was to survive. And to keep my son happy and healthy. That plan was all I had within me."

"So you would have stayed away forever? Kept Bennet from his heritage?"

Resentment, always a short distance away, arrived quickly. "Do bear in mind," said Elizabeth coolly, "that I had no idea you wanted me—or your son. If you will recall, you sent me away. You disregarded my letters. How could I think anything but that you wanted me permanently gone?"

"So I might have gone my entire life and never known what happened to either of you." He shook his head, looking sad and disgusted, and Elizabeth had no reply. She had assiduously avoided thinking of her future in those days, choosing instead the task of day-by-day existence. Would she have written to him at some point? She truly had no idea.

"Is there any part of you, no matter how small, that is glad to be returned?"

"I am glad Bennet will have his due as your heir."

"I did not ask about Bennet, I asked about you." He made a close study of her face.

She stared at the floor beneath her feet for a long time. In truth, she did not know the answer. Did she wish she still lived in Weymouth? Not exactly. Did she want to be here, at Pemberley? Not really. What did she want? Where did she wish to be?

At length, she looked at her husband still patiently awaiting her answer.

"Sometimes," was all she could say.

TWENTY TWO

SOMETIMES.

It was a word he considered often over the next days, twisting and turning it to see whether he could rightly find hope in it. It was not never, and he decided that was something to be glad about.

"Darcy, did you receive a letter from Jolly?" Lydia came into his study as she always did—not often but occasionally—without knocking, without ceremony, loudly, and brazenly. Still, he had come to enjoy it in some ways. It made him feel truly her brother.

"I did. Your father is not cooperative?"

Lydia sighed and tossed herself into a chair. "My father has likely not yet read his letter."

"I cannot give permission for your engagement. I am not your guardian and have no legal claim for you even though you have lived with me these many months."

"Pray, say you will go to Hertfordshire," Lydia urged. "We shall all go to persuade my father to accept Jolly's suit. When Mama hears that Papa has disregarded the request of a wealthy gentleman…"

"It is an excellent notion," said Darcy, although he did not much anticipate a meeting with his in-laws. "Elizabeth should see them, and Jane and Bingley are nearly mad to reunite with her. I have had many letters urging a visit, as Jane is not yet able to travel."

He and Elizabeth had decided together to spend time at Pemberley prior to seeing the rest of the Bennets, though in retrospect, Darcy was unsure it had been the best idea. Perhaps Elizabeth might have been happier had she spent time with her beloved Jane. With two such small children, it was difficult for the Bingleys to come to them, but he knew it weighed heavily on both of their hearts that they had not yet seen Elizabeth. In any case, it seemed the time was upon them.

"Speak to your sister," said Darcy. "But I should think it would suit her well."

IT DID SUIT ELIZABETH VERY WELL INDEED; SO WELL THAT SHE made haste that their travel could commence within the week. Georgiana did not accompany them, electing to remain at Pemberley with Mrs Annesley.

When the Darcy carriage entered the drive to Netherfield, Elizabeth could immediately see her sister and Bingley awaiting them.

Jane was already crying as the carriage door was opened and very nearly pulled Elizabeth out of the conveyance. Elizabeth also began to cry, happy tears of reunion and thanksgiving, as the two sisters embraced with Bennet squeezed between them. He looked with terror upon his newfound aunt, who was alternately kissing his and his mother's cheeks. Bingley stood by awkwardly, greeting the others as he awaited his opportunity to greet Elizabeth.

When it was his turn, he bowed over her hand. "You look very well, Lizzy," he said kindly but with concern in his eyes. "I greatly anticipate renewing our acquaintance."

After much joyful expression and weeping and the children had been exclaimed and cooed over, the happy party went into the house. Darcy and Elizabeth went to their chambers to quickly refresh themselves, then returned to the drawing room to join Jane and Bingley.

After about an hour, Bingley asked Darcy into his study as he wished to show him something. Darcy followed him, suspecting correctly that Bingley wished to give the ladies time alone.

Bingley gestured for Darcy to have a seat in his most comfortable chair, then went to the sideboard and retrieved a particular bottle. He handed it to Darcy, smiling sheepishly. "The brandy we drank the night you finally had permission to marry Elizabeth. You particularly enjoyed it, though whether it was the taste of it or your happiness that made it so enjoyable, I do not know. Uncle Gardiner assisted me in finding another bottle. I wanted to give you something to mark this occasion of all of us reunited again."

"Bingley, that is not necessary. You and Jane have been very good to me already."

"I am in eager anticipation for our future together." Bingley smiled enigmatically—or rather, enigmatically for him. "I do have happy news…"

Darcy raised his eyebrows. "Another child? Are you attempting some sort of record?"

Bingley laughed. "No, no, my dear Jane is busy enough with the two we already have! My news concerns Netherfield. We have given it up."

"Given it up?" Darcy exclaimed in surprise. "I thought you were settled here."

"At first, yes, it was good to be here, particularly with Lizzy gone and the Bennets facing such difficulty… I was glad to be here to keep Jane among her family circle." Bingley swirled the liquid in his glass. "But then…well, Mrs Bennet does require a great deal of attention from us. We dine there or they are here three or four times a week, and if we should seek to entertain other families without inviting them as well, then everyone is angry with us. She gives Jane quite a lot of advice about the children, and she even dismissed the nurse."

"Dismissed your nurse! What did you do?" Darcy was astonished.

"Well…Nicholls had already recommended her termination, and we had planned to do it ourselves anyway." Bingley shrugged with helpless amiability. "Jane was increasing with Thomas at the time and felt quite ill, so I am sure Mrs Bennet thought she was helping her. Jane only felt that she wished to manage her own household."

Darcy rolled his eyes at Bingley's astonishing ability to explain away such an affront. "I assumed you had purchased Netherfield."

"No, I merely extended the lease for an additional year after the first had ended. By then, we knew we intended to leave, but the timing was poor as Jane was then increasing. We were fortunate that the owners would extend the lease again, though we did tell them that should a purchaser be found, we would give way. Well, a purchaser has been found, and he would like to take possession by Christmas."

"So will you look for another estate?"

Bingley's face split open into a wide grin that immediately brought Darcy back to earlier, happier times. "I already have. I signed the documents just yesterday."

"Another lease?"

"No, indeed—purchased. I am at last a landed gentleman."

"My heartiest congratulations. So, where is your estate located?"

"Ohh…" Bingley drew out the word tauntingly. "Derbyshire, in fact."

"Derbyshire! Splendid!" Darcy felt a spring of hope burst within him. Jane and Bingley would be close by. Surely that would add to Elizabeth's joy. "How far from Pemberley?"

"About fifteen miles." Bingley could not stop his beaming grin. "It is called Hopton Hall."

"I know it well! A very easy distance! Nothing at all!"

Bingley became serious. "It has long been my dream, Darcy, to see our young ones playing on the lawns together and enjoy time with you and Lizzy. When I received your express saying Lizzy was found, it seemed fated. I am eager to start living my dream, as is Jane."

"Will Jane tell Elizabeth?"

"Yes, she will. We shall take possession in November once all the arrangements are made. We want to be settled before the bad weather arrives."

Darcy offered, "Stay at Pemberley if you need, and of course, if you require my assistance in any way, say the word."

"I believe the only assistance I might require is for you to tell Mrs Bennet for me. I cannot think that conversation will be happy."

"Perhaps they will be satisfied to know of the felicity Jane and Elizabeth will have to be in such proximity."

Bingley rolled his eyes. "Let us hope for it, though I think it unlikely."

BACK IN THE DRAWING ROOM, JANE RANG FOR TEA. ELIZABETH'S eyes drank her in, this new Jane who was her sister yet now a wife and a mother. There was a more mature air to her that Elizabeth thought becoming. Her gown, though only for morning, was very fine and flattering. Elizabeth mentioned how much she admired it.

"Yes, it is cut very well—it has to be to hide all the lumps and bumps that come with birthing two children in such quick succession."

"Oh Jane, you are as lovely as ever, and if a few lumps and bumps are the price of such beautiful children, then so be it."

With a smile, Elizabeth accepted her tea. "I cannot tell you how much I have missed you."

Jane's eyes filled with tears. "You cannot imagine how I have missed you. Oh, your letters have kept me from madness, but it was not enough, not nearly enough. I needed to see you to believe you were truly home and well."

Elizabeth looked down, her smile fading.

"And you and Darcy...you have forgiven him? Is everything well?"

Elizabeth was silent for a moment. "The matter is not so easy as that. I am determined, though, to have a happy home for Bennet."

Jane said knowingly, "As well as anyone else who might come along."

Elizabeth could say nothing to that, and after a moment, Jane moved on to news of the neighbourhood and their family. She had already related most of it in her letters, but it was such a pleasure to hear her voice and see her face that Elizabeth hardly cared. The happiest news of all, however, was to hear of the Bingley's impending move to Derbyshire. Elizabeth and her sister were yet embracing with delight when their menfolk joined them.

"What is this?" Bingley cried. "Still? I should have thought you would be finished by now."

"Silly man," Jane said. "No, I just told Lizzy our news."

"You will not mind having us for neighbours?" Bingley asked. "I shall warn you now, I expect a ball to be held in my honour."

"Gladly," said Darcy. "We shall hold ten balls if you wish."

THEY HAD BEEN SUMMONED TO A FAMILY DINNER AT LONGBOURN. Bennet accompanied them although the Bingley children remained at home—his grandparents had been too long ignorant of the boy and wished to see him.

It was not precisely an enjoyable evening. Mrs Bennet greeted Darcy coldly then paid him no heed for the rest of the evening. Mr Bennet disregarded him completely, turning his face when Darcy attempted to greet him. They were delighted with their daughter though, and even Mr Bennet got a tear in his eye as he embraced her.

Mrs Bennet focused on apprising Elizabeth of all the latest Meryton gossip, followed by a quick appraisal of Elizabeth's gown, which she thought was quite fine. She showed relatively little curiosity in Elizabeth's past circumstances, a concession for which Elizabeth was grateful. She had only a brief bit of interest in Bennet, but pulled Elizabeth aside to hiss into her ear, "Well done, my girl, you have given him his heir, now you do not need to do anything for him that you do not wish." Elizabeth sighed in response.

Thereafter, Mrs Bennet had only one thing to discuss—Jane. She effused about the neighbourhood's delight in Jane as mistress of Netherfield and the prettiness of Jane's children. From her conversation, Elizabeth had to conclude that her mother did not yet know of the Bingleys' planned move to Derbyshire. She gave her sister a look, but Jane only blushed and looked away sheepishly.

The discomfort continued at the dinner table. Laden with delicious food, it was not, however, overburdened with an excess of good manners. Elizabeth glanced at her husband uneasily several times, as he would attempt to join the conversation only to be disregarded or spoken over. He bore it graciously but eventually fell silent. Elizabeth would have liked for her family to treat him a bit kindlier; to witness them treating him badly raised her sympathy for him, and she did not wish for that.

It was Lydia who eventually came to the rescue. "Papa, Mr Rollings has written you several times."

"Rollings? I cannot say I know the fellow."

"He is a friend of Darcy's, and he wants to marry me!" Over

Mrs Bennet's squeals, Lydia began a recitation of Jolly's fortune and connexions, along with a description of his house in Dorset.

Mr Bennet bore it calmly, saying only, "Friend of Darcy's, is he? Not much of a recommendation for me."

"Papa," Elizabeth said, turning to him in exasperation. "Please."

Mr Bennet only sniffed and turned back to Lydia. "Well, if this Mr Rollings has a fondness for silly girls, who am I to stop him? Lydia, tell your young fellow I shall not be any impediment."

WHEN THE LADIES WITHDREW AFTER DINNER, MR BENNET STOOD also, motioning Darcy to accompany him to his study. Darcy followed but not without some trepidation. Mr Bennet shut the door behind them and offered Darcy some port, which he accepted, thinking he would likely need it for whatever Elizabeth's father wished to say. The two men settled into club chairs located by the bookshelves.

Mr Bennet was silent for a moment, thoughtfully regarding his port. Darcy waited patiently for him to begin.

"I am very happy that you have brought Elizabeth back here, Mr Darcy. I cannot tell you how I have longed to see her and how many bleak hours I have passed believing she was lost to me forever." Mr Bennet took a sip of the port. "Tell me, sir, what are your plans?"

"My plans?"

"Yes, your plans. Will you return to your estate and avoid London? Will you return to town and pretend nothing ever happened? Do you intend to send her off again? I only wish to understand what happens now." Mr Bennet sounded impatient and slightly vexed.

"My hopes are to regain my wife's forgiveness and trust, and my plans are to do whatever I can towards that purpose."

Mr Bennet snorted quietly. "You cannot think it will be so easy, Mr Darcy."

"I already know the difficulties I face, sir."

Mr Bennet studied Darcy closely. When he spoke, his tone was without malice, but the words were harsh enough without it. "As you are well aware, I was not in favour of this marriage. I was very concerned by the haste with which you insisted on marrying her and utterly destroyed by the speed with which you sent her away and lost her. Nothing has happened in the intervening years to make me think you are in any way a young man worthy of my daughter."

Darcy spoke quietly and without challenge. "Whether I am worthy or not, Elizabeth is my wife and the mother of my son and heir. I know I have erred greatly, but I do still love her ardently and hope to one day regain her love in return."

Mr Bennet leant across his desk. "A woman, any woman, yields up a great deal when she marries. Everything is entrusted into the care of a man—her heart, her soul, her everything. You, sir, broke the trust, and in my estimation, this must be your primary object now. You might earn her love, but if you do not have her trust, it will be for naught."

He stood, clearly intending to quit the room, and Darcy rose with him. However, Mr Bennet was not finished and delivered one parting blow. "I know my daughter, and her feelings are clear to me. Although legally she is yours—and she knows, as much as I, that there is little she can do about that—her heart in no way belongs to you. It did once, but it is there no more. I hope you can reclaim it, but I doubt that very strongly."

With that, he walked from the room, not caring to see whether Darcy followed him.

THE NIGHT ENDED SOON THEREAFTER. ELIZABETH WAS TIRED from their travels, and despite the two-year absence, spending the night immersed in her mother's silliness was wearing. She herself was to blame; she was no longer able to tolerate the utter foolishness and noise of Longbourn like she once had. It was hard to give significance to conversation of gowns, ribbons, and lace and tales of Lady Lucas and Mrs Long, not when she had such weighty concerns in her head.

Furthermore, her parents' behaviour towards her husband deeply embarrassed her. Mrs Bennet sat in the corner with Lydia, criticising every syllable from Darcy's lips, until Lydia said, with discomfort, "Mama, he will hear you."

"I do not care if he does hear me!" Mrs Bennet proclaimed stridently, and Lydia kindly and adeptly turned the conversation to some fabric she saw at the modiste's in Meryton. Elizabeth reflected on what an odd turn of events it was to rely on Lydia to maintain a standard of good manners and decorum. Did her parents not realise that their loyalty, while admirable, did not help her?

As they said goodnight later that evening, Elizabeth said to her husband, "My parents were very rude to you tonight. I am sorry for that."

"I am surprised they received me, if you must know," he said. "It was far less than I deserved."

"I do not agree with that."

"Elizabeth, I took you from them. They did not know whether they would ever see you again. I have only known Bennet a very short time, yet if someone took him from me, I do not think I could be held responsible for all I did to that person."

I did take him from you. She did not speak it aloud.

BINGLEY MET UP WITH ELIZABETH THE NEXT MORNING AS SHE walked out early. It was not his habit to rise early—neither his nor Jane's—so she was quite startled when he suddenly appeared wearing his hat and looking as if it were already mid-day. "May I join you?"

"Of course."

They set out along the path towards the maze, quietly talking about nothing in particular. "Will it upset Kitty that her younger sister will marry first?" Bingley asked.

"Kitty cannot long bear to be outdone by Lydia in any circumstance. The next man who seems good enough will do for her."

Bingley chuckled. "So speaking of sisters…"

Elizabeth laughed lightly. "Which? We have a great many of them between us."

"Caroline," said Bingley.

Oh yes. Her.

"It grieves me, what she has done to you and Darcy."

"What she did could have been of no consequence had not Mr Darcy made it so."

"While I do own that is true," Bingley said, his blue eyes bright with earnestness, "nevertheless, it was cruel and unfeeling."

"Far be it from me to shock you," replied Elizabeth with a smile, "but Caroline is not known for sweet temper nor her charitable nature."

"This is true. But I wished to assure you that our fealty is to you. Caroline's home is in Scarborough now, with our aunt."

"You sent her away?"

"Not exactly. But she was offered the chance to make amends and…well, she scarcely did right by it. So she was told she could not live with either Louisa or me until she did."

"I see." It was curious to Elizabeth, this lack of antipathy she had towards a woman who had wished her ill, whose actions had played a significant role in her estrangement from her husband. But the fact of it was, she scarcely cared about Miss Bingley. Let her rot in Scarborough or London or wherever else she might fall, it really did not signify.

Bingley said, "I just wanted to assure you, and also to beg your vow in one matter."

"What is that?"

He stopped walking then and turned towards her, taking both of her hands in his. "Darcy has changed quite a bit, and I daresay he has learnt his lesson in this. However, should you ever find yourself in difficulty again…"

"Oh!" Elizabeth gave a weak chuckle of dismay at the very notion.

"Any sort of problem, you will come to me. Do you promise? I shall not release you until you do!" He gave her a fond brotherly look but underneath it was the kindest of intentions. He was serious, and it made her realise there was far more to this Bingley than she had previously known.

She nodded. "I promise. And I thank you."

TWENTY THREE

AUTUMN HAD BEGUN TO LEAVE ITS MARK ON HERTFORDSHIRE, and the days shortened with sharp splendour, cerulean skies and scarlet-hued leaves all about. It beckoned everyone outdoors to enjoy the air before winter came upon them. Elizabeth was no exception, leaving every afternoon while Bennet napped for long rambles through all her old haunts.

Early in their marriage, Darcy would have felt free to join her; now, unless she would specifically ask him, he did not dare presume. On one particularly fine afternoon, however, espying her from the window at Netherfield, he decided to chance following after her in hopes she would invite him to accompany her. She did not follow the path he had thought she might, and it took him some time to find her. He had almost given up when a flash of colour in the trees drew his attention.

She was sitting on the bank of a small stream, a group of trees shielding her from the path. She would have been impossible to see were he not looking for her, and soon he knew why.

Elizabeth was crying.

She had pulled up her legs so that she could rest her face on her knees. She seemed to be staring at the stream, but with a small movement, Darcy could see that she mostly had her eyes closed, occasionally raising her hand to wipe the tears from her cheek.

He immediately stepped towards her—every instinct urging him to wrap his arms around her—but knew she would not like it. Instead, he stood helpless and useless, watching her sorrow. He laid his hand on a nearby tree, imagining it was resting against her back in a consoling fashion. His mind raced, conceiving and rejecting a thousand possibilities of what he might do to relieve her agony, but nothing would satisfy except the sure knowledge that what she would want most was to see him gone.

It seemed to Darcy as though she wept for a very long time. As she began to stop, opening her eyes and looking at the stream while sighing and wiping her tears, Darcy realised he should walk away. Quickly, he retreated back down the path and returned to his study.

It was above thirty minutes later when Elizabeth entered the house. From her face and demeanour, one would think she had not a sorrow in the world.

"Did you enjoy your walk?" he asked.

"Oh yes!" she exclaimed. "I think the colour of an autumn sky is the most beautiful thing in the world."

The next day was a repeat of the first. Having seen her leave, he lingered in the house an additional quarter of an hour. Then he quietly walked down the path where he believed he would find her again. She was there, exactly as she had been the day prior. Again, when she returned, she looked for all the world as though nothing could possibly be amiss. Darcy found her apparent good cheer terrifying, and he wondered how long these crying spells had been going on.

The third time, he did not leave her. He stayed, silent and sombre, until she stood, dusted herself off, and went to leave her spot. Her eyes fell upon him almost immediately, and she flushed red. For a moment, they stood still with eyes on each other.

Driven by instinct, he extended an arm to her. She moved slowly towards him, then quickly dashed into his chest, her face pressing into his neck as her hand wound its way under his cravat. He said nothing and neither did she, nor did she weep.

At length, she turned her face to the side. "When I was young," she began, "my favourite thing was to watch the sparks that shoot up from a knot in the wood as it burns, crackling and hissing. 'Tis magic, or so I thought. I always wanted to grab those sparks. They seemed so very special to me."

Elizabeth's hair brushed his cheek as she shook her head slowly. "I always burnt myself. Always in pain because I could not resist what was not good for me."

"That is a metaphor for me, I daresay," he replied. "Though I hope it is less faithful a picture than you currently believe."

There was a short silence until she admitted, "I do not know what I believe. I have, here in Hertfordshire, become reacquainted with the man I knew before. A man among friends and equals, who can laugh and tell stories, who can make me laugh. A man who is tender and kind to me, who is every bit my lover."

"That is the man I am," he said fervently, pulling away and waiting until she met his eyes. "I assure you, on my life, there is no other. There was a more loathsome creature within, but he has been banished forever. I promise you that."

She said nothing for a moment, but her hand rose to brush against his cheek. When it dropped again, she said only, "I must get back to the house."

THE NEXT DAYS IN HERTFORDSHIRE PASSED QUICKLY, FULL OF visits and calls, dinners and evenings with the neighbours… It was alternately delightful and exhausting.

It was strange seeing Darcy with his friend Bingley—it was a side of him Elizabeth had forgotten, the charming man who spoke well and laughed and teased. And he watched her often— she had forgotten how it felt to have his gaze upon her, to feel his desire and know her power over him. It confused her and sent her more than once to her secret girlhood spot to cry and relieve her feelings. She could not permit herself to desire Darcy, she simply could not. She refused, flatly, to love him again.

Mr Rollings was soon in Hertfordshire, making his application to Mr Bennet. He was granted his heart's desire to the delight of all, and a wedding in London was planned for a little more than a month hence.

"It would be more reasonable," said Darcy, "for us to remain in London for your sister's nuptials. We might hold a dinner for them, and you can help her shop."

"London…" Elizabeth echoed faintly.

She had no fond memories of London—or at least not of Mayfair and the house on Grosvenor Square, the brief glimpse she had had of life amongst the *ton*. She could not even contemplate it without shaking, but she supposed she must face it sometime. The longer she remained away, the harder it would be to go.

With a deep breath, she said, "Very well, then. To London we shall go."

THE DAY BEFORE THEIR REMOVAL TO LONDON WAS BUSY WITH packing and calls. Elizabeth scarcely afforded a moment for her son until later in the day when a mother's guilt drove her to the nursery to take him out. She was surprised to find Darcy had preceded her.

"The master came to collect him earlier. I believe their intention was to go to the stream to fish." Nurse Harriet smiled sheepishly. "He left me to my duties here, I hope you do not mind. 'Tis quicker without the young ones underneath my feet."

"Of course! And no, I do not mind," Elizabeth hastened to reassure her. "I did not realise Mr Darcy was spending time with him, that is all."

"Mr Darcy spends a great deal of time with Master Bennet—

does my heart good to see it. Would not be nearly so many rakes roaming about London if their fathers did what was right. A boy needs his father's touch." Nurse Harriet chuckled indulgently. "Why, I have returned to the nursery on several occasions to see him playing with soldiers, building with blocks, reading books, and he takes him outside whenever he can. No, the master is an excellent father, there can be no two opinions on the matter."

Elizabeth left the nursery lost in her thoughts. Evidently, Darcy was spending his mornings with Bennet. She had known nothing of it, but from the sound of things, it had been going on for some time. She walked outside slowly, deciding to join the pair of them.

Not more than ten minutes later, she discovered them. They had chosen to fish at a location relatively close to the house, and as she approached, she could hear them talk.

"…frogs eat the bugs?"

"They do. Flies and moths, snails, slugs, and worms." Darcy reached down to take Bennet's hand and place it on the fishing pole. "Do you remember how we did it last time? See, you will hold onto the pole just like that, and then we shall make a sort of throwing motion into the stream. It is called casting."

As Bennet held the rod, Darcy flicked it into the stream.

"Does the moths taste good?"

Darcy chuckled. "When you are a big boy and can gallop on your horse, you will learn that at some time you will have an insect in your mouth. It does not taste good, but neither is it too dreadful."

Bennet looked up at his father in astonishment, his eyes wide with surprise. However, any further discussion of insect eating was forestalled by the appearance of Elizabeth. "Mama!" The pole was dropped, and Bennet ran to greet her.

"I hope you gentlemen would not be averse to some company." Elizabeth smiled at Bennet but also glanced at Darcy.

"We are well pleased to have you join us." Darcy said, smiling back at her.

Bennet wished to be picked up, so Elizabeth pulled him into her arms while settling herself on the bank next to the tackle box. The discussion had halted with her appearance, so she decided to continue it.

"I heard only the last bit of your discussion, but if I might add my own experience, I once ate a cricket on a dare. I do not recommend it."

Darcy and Bennet both laughed and conversation resumed once more. The Darcys spent several hours by the stream, with Elizabeth departing at one point to request a snack be brought out to them. After they had finished their repast, Bennet became sleepy, so Elizabeth laid her shawl beside her on the ground for him to curl up on and nap. He was in deep slumber almost instantly.

Elizabeth and Darcy were both silent for several minutes. Darcy continued to fish, and Elizabeth, behind him on the bank, could not but help admire his form. *Seeing Darcy with Bennet is very attractive. Of course, Darcy is handsome in almost any situation.*

With a slight shake of her head to dispel her thoughts, Elizabeth ventured to say, "You have been spending quite a bit of time entertaining Bennet these days."

Darcy nodded, then paused in his fishing to set down the rod and sit next to her on the bank. "It is he who entertains me. I must say, he is very different from most children. Much more interesting and engaging. Quite witty, in fact, but funny too."

Elizabeth laughed. "I think most parents think their own children far beyond the common way."

"But Bennet truly is," Darcy insisted. "You have done an amazing, extraordinary thing, Elizabeth. Truly, I am...humbled and amazed."

Looking over at her husband, she felt it was almost painful how handsome he was. He was not looking at her directly, but rather, had his gaze fixed on the grass where he was plucking pieces, methodically separating the blades into strips and then plaiting them. Darcy's hair had fallen over his eyes, which she found particularly attractive. She allowed her gaze to trace his features and, for just a moment, to feel her love for him come into her heart.

Elizabeth reached over and gently brushed back the curl falling over his eyes, a pointless manoeuvre as it immediately fell right back down. "Thank you," she whispered.

It felt very natural to reach back over into that curl, gently smoothing it back, and then to wind her fingers deep in Darcy's hair. Then, with their faces so near she could feel his breath, Elizabeth closed her eyes and gently kissed his lips.

For as long as they had been without each other, the kiss ignited quickly. Darcy pulled her tightly against his chest, his arms encircling her back and his mouth devouring her hungrily. She was no less ravenous for him, winding her hand even more firmly into his hair while the other dove underneath his waistcoat to feel the warmth of his chest and the beating of his heart.

Relief washed through her, as her loneliness and sadness melted away, banished by the touch of her husband's lips on hers. A small voice in her mind urged caution and tried to warn her of the danger, but it was disregarded in favour of the rest of her that needed to touch her husband and to feel him touching her.

Then Bennet stirred in his sleep, making some small sigh of a sound, insignificant, but it brought his parents sharply back to their senses. Elizabeth jerked away, pulling her hands from underneath her husband's coat as Darcy slowly removed his hands from her. For a moment, they could only stare at one other in shock.

Elizabeth leapt to her feet. "We must take him back to the nursery. Nurse Harriet must be wondering what came of him." She busied herself in brushing the grass from her skirt and smoothing back her hair, anything that did not require looking at Darcy.

Darcy cleared his throat and also stood. "Allow me."

Reaching down, he picked Bennet up, and the three headed

back to the house. As they entered, Elizabeth reached for Bennet, saying, "I shall take him to Nurse Harriet."

Wordlessly, Darcy handed their son to her, and she walked away as quickly as she could.

THEY DID NOT SPEAK OF THEIR KISS, NOR DID ELIZABETH WISH to. It was a temporary madness, that was all. The small family departed Hertfordshire the next day, Bennet on her lap and Darcy across from her. The rest of the family would travel closer to the time of the wedding, but nevertheless, Jane sobbed and Elizabeth felt her throat tighten. But it was a good, relieving feeling to have reunited with them all, and it made her feel, if not happy, as much like happy as she had been in some time.

Twenty Four

ELIZABETH'S KNEES SHOOK MERCILESSLY AS SHE ENTERED THE place she never thought she would see again—the Darcy town house. Strangely, it looked exactly the same, despite what felt like aeons had passed since she last saw it.

She had made no mark when last she was there—it was Darcy House, and Darcy House it did remain, nothing of Elizabeth upon it. She went through it, thinking those curtains quite ugly and that chair so very dated, but to Darcy, she said nothing. She avoided his study, the scene of her deepest pain, and hoped the occasion would not arise where she would need to enter it.

Darcy had made jests that his aunt had spies within his household. Such a notion could only be confirmed when, within two hours of their arrival, Lady Matlock appeared on her eldest son's arm. "You do not mind, do you?" she asked, sweeping into the room. "Ah! And there she is!"

Elizabeth curtseyed. "Lady Matlock."

It was true that Lady Matlock, while not outright objecting to her nephew's marriage, had been reserved on her first meeting with the then-new Mrs Darcy. Their relationship had improved from cordial to friendly by the time Elizabeth was sent away, but evidently in the time since, Lady Matlock had grown fonder of her. She first embraced Elizabeth, then leant back and kissed her on her cheek. Tears shone in her eyes as she said, "My dear, dear girl. I did not think I should ever have this chance again." She said it with such tenderness it nearly made Elizabeth cry.

Saye was fortunately far less sentimental, offering only a bored, "How-do," and asking whether she intended to feed them. Elizabeth sent for tea, and they all sat, getting reacquainted.

"Firstly," said Saye, "I wish to hear all the ghastly ways you are punishing my cousin. Nothing too easy now! Are you spending his money? Forcing him to hear nightly scoldings? Or perhaps you have succumbed to beating him?"

Elizabeth laughed; it was a strange feeling to laugh so unreservedly and with true feeling.

It was Darcy who replied to his cousin, saying, "My wife has done nothing of the sort."

"Come now!" Saye gave Elizabeth a stare of elaborate astonishment. "What manner of wife are you? I had always thought a woman was keen to punish a husband for misbehaviour."

She laughed again, less comfortably this time. "I daresay you have known the wrong sort of wife, sir."

Saye leant back comfortably in his chair. "Well, perhaps I have, but pray tell me you have at least shopped? Jewels—a woman never has enough of those?"

"I am sorry to disappoint you."

"Darcy!" Saye exclaimed. "You, sir, have some penitential purchasing to endure. No less than three footmen to carry it all, and I am bringing Florizel."

"Who is Florizel?" Elizabeth asked while Lady Matlock protested, "You cannot possibly bring that animal to the modiste."

"If you are spending enough money, they let you bring anything," Saye retorted. Then quietly to Elizabeth, he said, "I have trained him to relieve himself on Darcy's shoes. That ought to begin the day properly."

"We are not shopping with a dog," Darcy said.

"I like dogs," Elizabeth countered. "In fact, I might like Florizel so much that I want one just like him."

"Ha! And I would get one for you," Saye replied. "Tuesday? Will that do?"

"In truth, it is not a bad idea," said Lady Matlock. "The *ton* should see you together. Most have believed you suffered an illness that kept you in the country…but tongues do wag, even with much less provocation than this. Let them see you out and about and in love."

"I understand I must thank you for preserving my reputation," Elizabeth said with a strained smile at her ladyship. "You thought quickly."

"I did indeed." Lady Matlock smiled graciously at her and then extended her look to both her son and nephew. A wordless signal was sent and evidently received, for both Saye and Darcy rose. "A few minutes, gentlemen," she promised.

When the men had closed the door behind them, Lady Matlock rose and joined Elizabeth on her settee. Though her manner was kind, Elizabeth felt her defences rise.

"My dear, how are you really?"

"Very well," Elizabeth replied tightly.

"That cannot be true, nor do I think it should be. You will need time to heal, but in the meanwhile, you must think of your position—yours and that of your child and any future children."

Elizabeth nodded. "That is my only thought, if you must know. I am here for Bennet's sake."

"Darcy did a stupid thing that is nearly unforgivable—nearly. But I think in time you will forgive him, and perhaps even forget, for your own sake if not his."

"My sake?" Elizabeth asked.

Lady Matlock reached out, her hand touching Elizabeth's. "Anger is a disease, my child, and it will eat away at you, turn you into a person you scarcely know. When you forgive someone for what they have done to you, it allows you to heal as well. The slight no longer holds you."

"This is quite a bit more than a mere slight."

"It is," her ladyship agreed. "Much more. Yet the remedy is the same."

She took a long drink from her tea cup. "Regardless, until that day when you can love him as you will, you must simply pretend. Stop the gossip right where it starts. Some doubt you could have been ill for so long, but Darcy was not much in town, and most people believed he was with you. It passed, but barely. But now, people will look at you to see how you are acting. Be in love, Elizabeth, passionately, ardently in love."

Act passionately, ardently in love with Darcy? When merely looking at him aroused feelings of hurt, betrayal, love, sorrow, and attraction? When sometimes simply enduring his presence made her nauseated with loathing and desire commingled?

"You do not know what you ask, Lady Matlock," said Elizabeth quietly.

"You are right, I cannot know. No one can. But, Elizabeth, do know this—we are your family. I shall help you however I can."

DURING ONE OF THEIR FIRST NIGHTS IN LONDON, BENNET HAD A bad dream, so bad that Nurse Harriet was unable to console him and sent for Elizabeth. She immediately went to her son, soothed and cosseted him and dried his tears.

Alas, he was wide awake afterwards and eager to play and begin his day. "My sweet boy, it is still night-time, which means it is time to sleep not time to play. Mama will read you a story to help you go back to sleep. Will that do?"

Bennet agreed happily and settled himself back into his bed to hear a story. After the first story, he remained wide awake. Nurse Harriet offered to stay and read to him, but Elizabeth dismissed the woman, telling her she needed her rest as she would likely have a cranky child to mind on the morrow. The good lady laughed and retired to her own bed in the room adjoining the nursery.

A second story likewise had little effect on Bennet's wakefulness. In the middle of the third story, he released a large, encouraging yawn. His eyelids grew heavy during the fourth story, and it was with great happiness that Elizabeth saw him finally surrender to sleep towards the end of the fifth. She blew out the candles, saving one to guide her back to her room, and tucked her son into his bed.

Elizabeth was startled on her return to her room to see it ablaze with light. As she entered, her eyes instantly went to Darcy who stood at her window, fully dressed excepting a cravat and boots. She looked to the mantel clock. It was not yet three in the morning.

"Why are you here?" she asked. "And why are you dressed?"

Darcy turned from the window, his countenance an inscrutable mask. He looked at her without emotion for one long moment, then, crossing the room, he grabbed her in his arms, crushing her to his chest. She could feel his heart beating rapidly and sensed great turbulence within him, but she could not understand why. After a brief hesitation, she encircled her arms around him, squeezing him gently. She felt his lips kiss her hair.

How long they stood thus, she did not know. Eventually, he loosened his hold, though he did not release her completely, and he tilted her head towards his. She thought he might kiss her, but he did not, rather choosing to rest his forehead on hers.

Finally, he spoke, his voice a low grumble, "I thought you left."

"Left? What do you...oh." Elizabeth suddenly understood what he meant. "Bennet had a bad dream, and it took quite a while to get him back to sleep."

Darcy said nothing, merely nodding his head.

"I am sorry you were worried," she said gently.

Still, Darcy did not speak and simply held her. Finally, he stepped back from their embrace, shaking his head, and running his hands through his hair. "It is I who should be sorry. I have allowed my anxieties to get the better of me tonight. I should have thought Bennet might need you. This is a strange place to him."

Elizabeth tried to reassure him with a squeeze of his hand, which seemed to bring him back to himself.

"I shall leave you now."

"Do not," she said quickly. "I can see you are troubled and perhaps…perhaps we could speak of it."

He turned his head away from her gaze to look out the window. Then he began to speak in a very low voice, "When I realised what had happened—when I knew I had been completely wrong and had injured you so grievously—all I could think was to get to you as quickly as possible and hope to God you would allow me to make amends for what I had done. Fitzwilliam and I were on the road to Gunnersdale by dawn the very next day, but when we got to the estate, you were gone. I had no idea where you were or how to find you. No one we spoke to, including Mrs Nelson, had any notion where, or even when, you might have gone.

"I had not before known such fear. I rode all over the estate… I can recall one day in particular, staring down into a ravine and wondering whether I should see your body at the bottom of it. Never mind all the highwaymen I thought might have stolen you. All I ever thought was that I was perhaps one day too late. I would retire each night wondering whether that day might have been your last, and, but for a bit more effort, I might have found you.

"Then Fitzwilliam found the letter you left for me, and I knew you were no longer in Yorkshire…and my terror could only increase. You were gone, out there, God knows where, and I could not find you." He sighed. "Of the child, I dared not think. As it was, I have spent these years on the brink of madness. Had I any comprehension of him, of Bennet, out there… I just cannot think I would have borne it. I should be at Bedlam now."

Elizabeth cleared her throat lightly. "I have sometimes thought that…that perhaps I had the better lot. I had Mrs Macy and Bennet to occupy my thoughts, and in any case, I knew where you were."

He gave her a wan smile. "I frequently have dreams where you are gone, and I am trying to find you. Sometimes I hear you or see you just out of reach, or I try to grab you but you slip away. After such times, I must…well, I look in on you."

"Look in on me?"

He flushed slightly, lowering his face. "I open the door to hear you breathing. Sometimes, I come into the room to see whether you are here."

"How often does this happen?"

"A couple of times a week. If it is a very bad night, then… then sometimes multiple times in the night."

She could not deny that it moved her, this new understanding of him. She went to him at the window and, after a short hesitation, wrapped her arms around him from the back. Her cheek rested on the fine lawn of his shirt. "I do wonder at times how it might have been had I remained just a little while longer."

With exquisite care, he pulled her underneath his arm, managing to bring her to his front without ever losing her embrace. "I do not blame you for leaving," he said. "Not when I saw how it was. Not when I knew all that you had endured there."

She raised her face, resting her chin on his chest, and looked into his eyes. She had always felt she could drown in his eyes although, in truth, they were rather unremarkable. Just ordinary eyes in the face of an extraordinary gentleman. "Should you like to stay with me?" she asked. "In my bed. For sleep, I mean. No more."

From the look on his face, one would have thought she had given him a great deal more. "You are certain?"

She nodded even though she really was vastly uncertain.

"Thank you. Yes, I would like that."

She climbed into bed as, with much hesitation, Darcy began removing his trousers and vest. His shirt, as it turned out, was merely his nightshirt that had been shoved into his trousers, so it was short work to be ready for sleep. He blew out the lamp while she climbed into bed and then slid in next to her. She had a large bed, and he stayed on his side of it, and she stayed on hers. But it was comforting to hear his breath and know he was over there.

He was obviously tired; his transition from wakefulness to sleep was rapid, and she studied his profile, such as was afforded to her by the pale sliver of moonlight that entered the room. Her eyes traced over the features of his face, which was softened by sleep. How well she remembered his looks on the day they married, the first time he asked her to dance, and when he asked her for her hand in marriage. And how he could not disguise the tenderness and pride that came into his eyes whenever he looked at Bennet.

A thought entered her mind as she watched him sleep, and that was simply that he did love her. He did, she knew that; moreover, she loved him too. Yet it was so very complicated between them, so muddled by painful memories and hurtful actions. How she wished it was not so. How she wished she might just be unafraid of him.

But he is changed, her heart whispered. *He has altered, and to love—ardent love—it must be attributed.*

HE WAS GONE IN THE MORNING WHEN SHE AWOKE, THE PILLOW cold beside her. She ran her hand over it and then rose, dressing and preparing for her day.

As she ate and then played with her son, there was one point of curiosity that niggled: the matter of Darcy's search for her. Georgiana had indicated something of reports and travels and so forth, and for some odd reason, Elizabeth had a strange impulse to know more. Had Darcy had kept any of the articles and, if so, would he be disturbed should she ask to see them? It seemed likely that whatever reports he might have kept would be in his London study, and so she hoped to be able to view them.

She went to him in the late morning, leaning against the study door. She could never forget her last time there and the scene between them as he sent her away, so she merely stood at the entryway rather than enter.

"Will you come in?" he asked.

"I just had a question for you." She smiled, feeling a bit nervous. "Georgiana mentioned something about the investigators you employed sending reports to you? And your own travels? You probably did not keep those, but if you did, I wonder whether I might see them."

"I kept all of it," he said, sounding a little surprised. "You wish to see one of the investigator reports? Something in particular, or any?"

Elizabeth shrugged. "No, nothing in particular, just something to indulge my curiosity. Whatever you think might be interesting to see—I am sure I do not know."

He nodded slowly, then bent and opened a drawer from which he removed six bulging files. "Where shall I put them?"

"May I carry them to my study, perhaps?"

"I shall carry them for you," he said. So they took the files, Darcy holding five to Elizabeth's one, to the small desk in the green saloon where Elizabeth sometimes wrote letters. The desk, a spindly, feminine-looking thing, seemed as though it might collapse under the weight, but it did not. From one portfolio, Darcy removed a journal.

"This is the complete record of where things are and what items of information are contained." He opened the book and pointed to a small numeral. "You see here? That indicates which portfolio the original report would be in. The first two numbers are the year, and the last three are the order. So the number 13-001 would be the first report received in 1813." He went on to explain further how items on the map were designated and linked to a certain report, and where other sundry items might be located.

When he finished, he looked up, seeing Elizabeth's surprise. With a chuckle, he admitted, "This is undoubtedly more than what you wished to see."

"Not at all. I am simply amazed by this system you have contrived," she teased. "The military has lost out by not having you in command. You no doubt would have put Napoleon to rest long ago."

Darcy flushed a bit. "Truthfully, the lead investigator that I hired was a military man, and he had a somewhat similar system that I noted on the first occasions when I visited his offices. I really only adapted it to fit my needs here."

"I am quite impressed by your thoroughness."

That earned her a small smile. "At any rate, it is all there. You may study it as you wish."

Elizabeth was shocked by the first report she saw. The pages had obviously been read so many times that they were dog-eared and tattered. She found that once she began reading the reports, she could not put them down. Interspersed with the investigators' reports were Darcy's own travels, painstakingly documented with a synopsis of each and every interview. He had used excruciating detail in his summaries, even making sketches where useful.

At first, she was merely riveted, but she soon became sad. So much time and energy wasted! And none of them, not the dark-haired woman in Bath nor the lady who was to serve as governess to a child in India, had anything to do with Mrs Elizabeth in Weymouth.

Darcy had made little notes in the margins of the various reports about his own activities, and in those, she could read his hope. Misplaced hopes, but he had hoped nevertheless.

The back part of the journal held the investigators' invoices for work provided. Elizabeth gasped at the amount on the first one and quickly leafed through them, arriving at a figure that astonished her. She would not have imagined half such a sum.

At long last, she began to replace the pages within their portfolios and closed the journal. She sat for but a moment in contemplation of what she had seen. No one who did not genuinely wish to find something would expend such effort, to say nothing of the cost, in searching for it.

After contemplating her findings for some minutes, she rose and went to find him. He was again in his study, this time reading, and she stood in the doorway to speak to him.

"Will you come in?" he asked, and she nodded.

She crossed the floor as if the carpet were made of poisonous eels and found a chair that did not immediately offend her. He watched as she settled herself into it.

"Did you find what you were looking for?"

"I was not looking for anything in particular," she admitted. "Just curious, that is all. I should not have imagined such an effort nor so much expense."

"Did you not? I would have done twice as much, but none of it led anywhere."

"No," she said, with an uncomfortable laugh. "I could see none of it was leading to me."

"Lydia once told me that if you did not wish to be found, you would not be. I daresay she was correct."

"It was a close thing, was it not? We might never have come upon one another. What would you have done had you not? When should the searches be complete?"

He raised his head, meeting her gaze with hollow-eyed fervency. "I would have looked for you until the day I died."

TWENTY FIVE

ELIZABETH COULD NOT DENY THAT SHE NEEDED GOWNS—MRS Macy had been exceedingly generous, but Elizabeth had needed very little in Weymouth—but it surprised her that Darcy and Saye would shop for them with her. Saye was quite eager for the task, as he evidently considered himself a first authority on the fashionable world, but she could not imagine how Darcy would divert himself. "It is quite tedious to shop for gowns, all the fittings and fabrics."

"Then it shall be my task to entertain you while they fit you."

"What will people think of a husband accompanying his wife to the modiste?"

Darcy smiled at her. "That he loves his wife so much he cannot bear to be parted from her?"

Elizabeth blushed and looked away.

As had been predicted, Saye's dog, a Pomeranian whiter than Saye's own starched cravat, immediately relieved himself on Darcy's boot. Darcy, having fallen victim to such mischief before, only scowled at his cousin and cleaned his Hessians with a handkerchief. Before he could speak a syllable however, Bennet appeared. Bennet, who was usually quite timid around dogs, was enraptured by Florizel and immediately fell to his knees to play with the pup. Florizel was likewise enthralled by Bennet, and this forestalled any complaint on Darcy's part.

They spent a good bit of time shopping over the next days. Darcy insisted if Elizabeth saw something she liked, it would be purchased, and he was unyielding in the matter. Left to her own devices, she would not have bought half as much, but she suspected that was why he wished to accompany her. He seemed to derive some pleasure to see that she was, despite her protests, enjoying selecting new clothes and all the trimmings.

She was ever mindful of Lady Matlock's encouragement to appear as though all were well with her marriage. She took Darcy's arm whenever possible, smiled, flirted—she hoped it was a convincing show. Darcy appeared to be taken in by it and took some liberties—including kissing her on the street!—that she bore with a feigned smile. She hated such pretence but understood the need for it.

Saye was, as promised, actively engaged in the process as well. Although his tastes were more showy than Elizabeth might have tended towards, she could not deny that he had an eye for what suited her. There was one gown in particular that was purchased on his direction—a deep indigo velvet with golden trim. She thought it a bit overdone for a woman not being presented at court, but Saye assured her it was just the thing. He then sent Darcy to the jewellers for sapphires, admonishing him not to purchase a ready-made piece but rather to order something.

Elizabeth felt awkward, knowing the costs involved and feeling rather uselessly fine, but Saye was not to be gainsaid and neither, it seemed, was her husband. She would be spoiled, and there was nothing to be done for it.

"Elizabeth?"

She turned, seeing a sweet, flaxen-haired beauty had entered the shop. "Miss Goddard!" True pleasure bolted through her along with a little alarm. Miss Goddard had been a friend in

Weymouth, but what would she think now, seeing the husband so many had believed was dead? She went to greet her friend, her mind trying desperately to recall what she had told the lady about her circumstances.

The ladies curtseyed to one another and then, after a small giggle, embraced. "How wonderful to see you. So far from Weymouth!" Elizabeth exclaimed.

"I am here with my aunt. I think she is to be stuck with me until I find a husband."

"You are new," Saye announced, sweeping in from nowhere, Florizel barking madly alongside him. "Who is your aunt? Anyone?"

"Saye," Elizabeth admonished. "Miss Goddard, allow me to present my cousin Viscount Saye. Saye, Miss Lillian Goddard."

"Goddard?" Saye looked as if he were in deep thought. "Charlescoate Park. So that means your aunt must be…?"

"My mother's sister," Miss Goddard retorted. "I was not expecting to see you, Elizabeth, but I do hope—"

"So where do you stay in town? May I call?"

"I am sorry, sir, but I am simply not interested in someone who advances with all the dignity of a cheetah killing a zebra." Miss Goddard turned to Elizabeth. "Good heavens, what relations you boast!"

"Indeed," Elizabeth said with a weak smile. "In fact, I should like to speak more about that to you. Will you call on me? I shall make sure there are no rogues lurking about the place when you come."

She spoke the direction quickly, and Miss Goddard promised to send a note. She left with a scowl in Saye's direction. When the door closed behind her, Elizabeth turned to scold her cousin but stopped when she saw the expression on his face.

"Saye? If I did not know better, I would say you looked…" She glanced at her husband who had come to join them.

"Lovesick," Darcy finished.

"I have met my wife." Saye heaved an enormous sigh.

"Really, Elizabeth, where have you been hiding such an enchanting creature?"

"You have offended her grievously," Elizabeth admonished.

"Oh la, I did not." Saye went to a nearby glass and examined himself critically. "Still as handsome as ever, yet she did not fall into me! Vixen! But it worked, I am in her thrall."

"Her aunt is the Countess of Albion."

"Really?" Saye stopped admiring his good looks and said, "Well, that is a connexion I would not mind having."

"I do not think she liked you, Saye," Darcy opined. "I was only here a minute or so but—"

"But nothing," Saye replied smugly. "See if I am not engaged to her by the end of the month."

It being September, the shops were busy, as the ladies of the *ton* visited town in autumn for new things for the festive season and to place orders for the forthcoming Season. None, however, purchased nearly so much as Mr Darcy bought for his wife, and soon much of society was all in a twitter with rumours and speculation of the amount of money he had spent on her.

Miss Caroline Bingley, returned to town to visit her sister, heard more of it than she ever wanted to within the first day of her stay. She had funds sufficient for one gown—two if she chose her fabrics prudently—and her need for economy further increased her pique.

There was no question that Eliza Bennet had ruined her life. A harmless prank! Nothing worse than what they had all done to one another at school, but now here she was, nearly a pariah in the society where she should reign as queen. Her brother and his Miss Bennet gave her no money, and stupid Hurst drank all of his, so she was living off her own interest. Ridiculous. She needed to marry, but how could she when she was stuck off in Scarborough all the time? The only eligible gentlemen who came to Scarborough were in their sixth decade, minimum.

She entered the shops just after the Darcys and Saye had departed, and sat meanly listening to the effusions of the shop girls over Mrs Darcy's selections, which were evidently the finest materials made into the most fashionable gowns. The shop girls also had much to say of Mrs Darcy's loveliness, mentioning her light figure specifically. It was utterly intolerable!

The unlucky girl who earned the task of assisting her was questioned mercilessly.

"I would imagine Mrs Darcy needs a new wardrobe as she can no longer fit into her other?"

"I am sure I do not take your meaning, ma'am"

"It can be so difficult for ladies to regain their figures after childbirth. You are young, but you will see one day."

"Lord willing," the girl agreed. "Raise your arms, please."

"Is she much altered? I have heard her face is painfully thin and her complexion lacks brilliancy. I am sure I should hardly know her."

"Her complexion seemed quite fine to me, ma'am."

"She has never been very stylish, you know. It comes from being raised in the country with but few trips to town. I am sure you must have all struggled to entice her to choose the more fashionable items."

"Not at all, I assure you. In fact, her selections were very elegant, first to last."

"Well, it would certainly surprise me." Caroline was quiet for a few moments.

"Her hair is always so-o-o extraordinarily untidy. I declare, I cannot think why—Oh!" Caroline shrieked as a pin poked into the sensitive skin under her arm. "Will you please have a care!"

The girl looked up, her face blank. "I do apologise. Perhaps I should work quietly to avoid further mishap."

Caroline scowled and spent the rest of the fitting musing hatefully on how very much she despised Eliza Bennet and the fact that she was living the life that she, Caroline, was meant to have. It should be *she* visiting the exclusive modiste for an untold number of fine gowns, richly decorated, and *she* who deserved the adoration of Darcy for having given him his heir.

Stupid Eliza Bennet. If only she had just died in the country.

THAT NIGHT, AS DARCY'S VALET READIED HIM FOR SLEEP, HIS heart pounded furiously. It had been a source of great astonishment that Elizabeth's invitation to sleep in her bed was to be extended. He had not thought it so, but when she casually had asked him whether he would be joining her as they retired, he was quick to agree.

He was embarrassingly eager to sleep in his wife's bed again, even though he knew it was no more than sleep. What he longed for, more than anything, was the comfort they had once shared together in the sanctuary of their bed. There was an inevitable intimacy involved in lying in the dark with your wife. The sharing of confidences, the revealing of secrets, and the outpouring of emotion seemed quite natural, in a way it could not be in another circumstance. He hoped very much that this additional time together would be beneficial for them. Although Elizabeth continued to be resistant to conversation about their separation, perhaps under the cover of darkness, she would feel more able to confide in him.

He knocked softly on her door and entered when bidden. She was already in bed, the covers drawn up, with a book on her lap. It felt awkward to slide in beside her—it was not something he had expected to ever be able to do again. "Thank you for allowing me to be here with you."

After a long moment, she said, "I do not know why, but it never really occurred to me before that you had suffered too. I am sorry for that."

He did not know what to say. "You are generous to worry about that. In truth, I am simply bearing the consequences of my own action."

"Things are no less painful when you have brought them on

yourself," she said, then hurriedly added, "But no need to speak of all that, not when it is bed time."

It was never the right time to speak of these things, but he did not say that. He was grateful for what he had and would not ask for more. He blew out the lamp and settled into the pillows. "Good night."

There was a pregnant pause, and then he heard the rustle of bedclothes as she moved towards him. She was motionless for just a moment and then he felt a slight, brief pressure as her lips touched his cheek. He fought against his instinct, which was to grab her and crush her body against his while greedily kissing her passionately. He instead remained frozen as she did it once again, then rolled away. "Good night," she whispered.

Quietly, he released the breath he had been holding.

An erotic memory of one of the last times they had been in this bed together came to his mind. He had been doing a bit of work in the library downstairs just before they retired. The lamp must have been smoking, or something of the sort, for he had developed a headache the likes of which he had never had before. His valet had given him some powders, but they provided him little relief. When he had at last come to her and told her of his woes, she was sympathetic and told him to lie back and allow her to rub his head. Needless to say, his aching head was soon forgotten for the joys of his wife.

Now, such things were but a memory. He wondered whether she ever thought of such things, if she ever longed for not only the physical comforts of marital intimacy, but also the attachment of the heart and mind that came with it. They had been good together from the start. She was…adventurous, for lack of a better word…and trusting, and together—

Well, it did not bear consideration. She had loved and trusted him in a way that she likely never could again, and he would be fortunate if they ever again shared that sort of intimacy. He had his heir, and he would never wish her to do anything from a sense of duty. He would much prefer to remain celibate.

Some time later, he woke to hear her saying quietly, "Please, no. Please?" She said it several times, tossing and turning as he sat up to look on her. She had been crying, he noted with dismay, and fervently hoped it was not he of whom she dreamed. But he knew it likely was.

He reached out to wake her, but surprisingly, as soon as he touched her arm, she grew more agitated. He tried to shake her a bit, and she began to struggle violently. Her distress alarmed him, and he leaned in to speak her name, and as he did, she reacted even more aggressively, shoving him violently while simultaneously bringing her knee directly into contact with his groin. Darcy reeled back, exclaiming loudly with the sudden and unexpected pain.

Elizabeth woke immediately and sat upright. "What happened? Are you ill?"

"No, no," he gasped. "Quite well."

"Did I...maybe my knee...accidentally...?"

"Uh...yes."

"Oh, I am so, so sorry! I was having a dream where...well, never mind that."

"I gathered as much." The pain was slowly subsiding, and Darcy inhaled deeply. "Do you want to tell me about it?"

He could almost feel her stiffen. "I cannot recall it. You know how that is."

He knew immediately that she did not speak the truth. After a few moments of silence, he offered, "In any case, I am sorry."

"For my dream?" She forced a laugh. "Really, I hardly expect an apology for things that happen in my sleep."

Quietly, Darcy said, "I apologise for the anxieties and fears you have had to face that led to your dreams. Those actions were very much my own."

Elizabeth did not respond, but in the darkness, he thought he saw her wipe her cheek.

LYDIA SWEPT INTO TOWN WITH AN AIR OF ROYALTY, FULL OF elaborate plans and schemes that her mother unequivocally supported. Kitty followed unhappily behind them wherever they went, glad to be reunited with Georgiana, who had also come to town for the wedding, but dissatisfied to be the remaining unmarried Bennet sister.

"You are full young," Elizabeth scolded. "No need to hurry into things."

"Lydia is so vexing! All the talk has been of dear Rollings and what dear Rollings has bought her and how much dear Rollings is enamoured of her... I declare, if this goes on any longer, I should run mad into the Thames."

Elizabeth laughed. "No need for that. Your time will come, my darling."

It had been decided that after Lydia's wedding, Kitty would accompany them on a wedding trip to Bath. Thinking it sounded very dull, she wheedled and pleaded until Georgiana was also invited to be one of the party.

As it was, the Darcys scarcely saw Georgiana even though they were all under one roof. She kept to herself many days, practising the pianoforte, reading, or taking walks with Mrs Annesley. Elizabeth felt rather guilty about it; their home was not wholly a happy one, and Georgiana felt the burden of her misdeeds even more now than she ever had.

"She had few friends before," Darcy told Elizabeth, and she understood that 'before' meant before her unfortunate affair with George Wickham. "She has always preferred more solitary pursuits but now is ashamed and untrusting as well."

My return has made things worse for everyone. Elizabeth knew it was not wholly true although some days it felt undeniable. She was not happy—she scarcely ate, her sleep was troubled, and her smiles were infrequent.

She had always believed a mother was the heart of any home. Whatever mood had lit upon her mother had always dictated the general air of Longbourn. Likewise, the Gardiner's home was friendly and easy, kindly and engaging, as Mrs Gardiner was. And Darcy's home? Well she knew not how it had ever been, but under her command, it was nothing to boast of. Silent, subdued, and melancholy. Unquestionably, her mood affected everyone.

With a sinking realisation, she knew it meant she must change things, and soon.

THE BENNETS HAD COME TO AN UNEASY TRUCE WITH DARCY—IN other words, they mostly disregarded him. They stayed at the Rollings's house in town for the wedding, but Elizabeth hosted a family dinner for them all, including the Gardiners, in honour of the couple. She was pleased to see that Darcy and Uncle Gardiner had grown close in the time since their marriage and remarked on it to her aunt in a private moment after the ladies withdrew. Lydia was holding court with tales of her dress fittings, and Elizabeth drew to the side with her aunt.

"He is friends with my uncle," said Elizabeth. "Quite extraordinary for a man whose family still thinks trade is quite beneath them."

"He sought out your uncle's advice many times over the years. He still does in fact. He was to see us only a few days ago."

"A few days ago?" Elizabeth exclaimed. "For what?"

Mrs Gardiner, lovely that evening in a gown of ochre silk, looked ill-at-ease. "You did not know? He comes often."

"I did not know anything of it."

"Perhaps you should ask him directly, then. I would not like to betray his confidence."

Elizabeth laughed at this. "Betray his confidence? Aunt, whose side are you on?"

She meant it in good humour, but her aunt frowned. "He is my nephew, and you are my niece. I am on the side of both of you being happy—and do not attempt to tell me you are happy, because I can plainly see you are not."

Elizabeth nodded, looking down at the bracelet she wore. Darcy's jewels—it seemed he was everywhere.

"It took a great deal of courage," Mrs Gardiner continued, "to marry a man you scarcely knew. It took even more courage to do what you did and do it so very well. I cannot imagine it myself, but you did it. And it took still more courage to come back to him for Bennet's sake and the future of Pemberley."

Tears threatened upon hearing her aunt acknowledge it all so succinctly, yet so truthfully!

"But if you want to be happy, and I mean truly happy, then you must perform the most courageous act of all—forgive him. Forgive him and trust him with your heart and soul once more."

"I have been thinking along a very similar line," Elizabeth agreed slowly. "I simply do not know whether I am equal to it."

"If you want your joy returned, the essence of good humour that once defined you, then you will do as you must."

Elizabeth smiled weakly, and her aunt leant over and kissed her cheek.

TWENTY SIX

THE NIGHT BEFORE LYDIA'S WEDDING, ELIZABETH FOUND IT impossible to sleep. "Silly thing," she murmured to herself. "It is the bride who is supposed to have nerves, not the bride's sister." She was not nervous for Lydia, not really. She thought it nothing short of a miracle that Lydia would soon be settled into domesticity and into a fine family as well.

Nevertheless, she did not sleep.

It was moments such as this that the true measure of her loss was made apparent to her. In the beginning of their marriage, she and Darcy would talk all night sometimes, and she had felt she might tell him anything. She missed having him as a confidante.

She looked over at his slumbering form. A pillow was between them; a pillow she had put in place. She removed it now to see him better. He was on his side, his face towards her, but with the curtains drawn, she could scarcely make him out. A fire had been lit in her room because the night was cold for September, but it was burnt low already and provided little light.

He was asleep, but perhaps if she just reached over and rubbed his arm...

Nothing. He was truly in a deep sleep. It would likely be kindest to simply allow the man his rest.

After a moment's pause, she reached over and pushed him, just a little.

He rolled a small bit, more onto his back, but remained completely asleep.

I must go to sleep. I shall clear my mind, and then sleep may claim me. She sought a more comfortable position for herself and closed her eyes, willing herself to fall into slumber.

It did not work, and a few minutes later she was again staring at Darcy's sleeping form. She nudged him a bit with her foot—not hard, but enough for him to pull his leg aside and make a sort of muffled grunt.

"Oh, sorry! Are you awake?" she whispered. However, her whispers remained unheard, and he seemed to be as asleep as ever. "Did I wake you?"

He snored, so she did it again, perhaps just the slightest bit harder.

Darcy sat bolt upright, looking about him in panic and confusion. "Elizabeth? What is it? Are you well?" He sounded drowsy at first, but became more alert as he spoke. She saw his shadowy shape move to rub his hands roughly through his hair, his usual attempt to wake himself.

"Um, sorry, I thought you were awake. Sorry. Go back to sleep."

"Is something wrong?"

"I should not have woken you," she whispered sheepishly.

"Think nothing of it. Are you well?"

Elizabeth felt herself blushing and almost laughed aloud at her silliness. "I am…in truth, I am just a little lonely."

He said nothing to that but settled himself back into his pillows.

"I have been thinking of those first months we were married. Do you remember the time we stayed up all night talking?"

He chuckled. "One time? I can think of several."

"True." She laughed softly. "Several times, for certain."

"Well, I am awake now. What shall we talk about?" Darcy asked, clear notes of anxiety in his voice.

She found herself moving just a little bit closer to him. "Anything, really. Do you have any secrets?"

He laughed loudly. "Um…no, actually, I do not believe I do. I have, perhaps, things I have never told you, but not because they are secret, just because…I guess we never had the time."

"Very well." She moved a fraction of an inch closer. "Tell me some of those. Something a wife should know that perhaps I do not. Perhaps something of your mother and father. I confess, I know very little of them."

"Yes, well, obviously, they are both deceased, my father most recently in 1806, about six months after I had finished at university…" From there, he went on to tell her about his father, the sort of man that he was: good, honourable, and generally kind, but very reserved, even cold. "He showed little affection to me or my mother. I never heard him say he loved anyone, though I presume he said so to my mother in private."

"You say it often, both to me and to Bennet."

"I was always determined that my children and my wife would never doubt my love for them for an instant."

"Did you doubt he loved you?"

"Oh, um…" Darcy paused a moment. "My father…well, we were never easy together, and he was never finished with raising me. There was forever a lesson to be learnt or an instruction to be given. If we had gotten older together, a friendship might have formed. I see it with Saye and the earl; they are much alike and have many interests in common. I should have liked that with my father."

"What about your mother?"

"She was a loving parent. Nothing like her sister, I assure you. But she was often sad and kept to her rooms for what felt like my entire boyhood. I am sure it was not truly so. She did not neglect me by any means."

"Why was she in her rooms so often? Was she ill?"

Elizabeth's small movements had brought her into contact with him, and it felt very natural to rest a hand on his chest and rest her chin on that hand. She could not see him, for the room was too dark, but she felt his breathing and heard the beating of his heart.

"The advantage of age has taught me that she must have had many miscarriages. At the time, I was simply told she was unwell."

"Poor lady."

"I would often find her crying on the rare occasions that I went in to visit her."

"How frightening." Elizabeth considered how she felt for her baby since the moment she first suspected his presence. To have lost that would have been very painful indeed. She had been fortunate that her pregnancy had gone so smoothly, she supposed, particularly given the adverse conditions she had faced. "How did she die? Was it related to Georgiana's birth?"

"She developed childbed fever shortly after and died when Georgiana was about two weeks old."

They went on to speak of family members for over an hour. Darcy told her everything he could remember of his mother, and they spent some time talking of Georgiana, mostly due to Elizabeth's observation that Georgiana had had little female influence in her life.

"I cannot suppose it was to her advantage. It was my selfishness that kept her here, for my aunts dearly wished to take her in, but I would not let them. Perhaps I should have."

Elizabeth knew to where his thoughts tended. "You and Fitzwilliam did the best you could, I am sure."

She remained resting on his chest, his arm having curled around her ever so slightly. One leg rested on his, her toes lightly touching his ankle.

"I am not certain two young men could ever truly know what

was best for a young girl. I should have allowed my aunt more influence. My pride did not permit it."

"Less your pride, I think, than your desire to keep her close."

"Maybe," he murmured, "though there is one thing I have learned: the moments when I am most sure of myself are the moments when I know nothing at all."

They both fell silent for several long minutes, hearing and feeling each other breathe, until the clock in the hall chimed twice.

"Oh my!" Elizabeth sighed quietly. "We should get some sleep."

"Are you able?"

"Yes, I believe I can. You need not fear a kick if you should drop off."

"Well, good night then." He paused for a moment and then added, "I love you."

Her breath caught…these were the times that were so, so difficult! She flattened her hand over the thin lawn of his night-shirt, smoothing it over his chest. "I still love you too," she whispered hoarsely. "But this is all…it is so very hard. But it is not because…I have not lost that."

She wished she could see his face to understand his reaction to this confession, which felt rather enormous for her. She felt his lips come to rest in her hair for a moment, and then she rolled away, returning to her own pillow.

THE WEDDING OF MISS LYDIA BENNET TO JOLLY ROLLINGS WAS not something Saye customarily would have attended. Miss Lydia had neither title nor fortune. Jolly had fortune but lacked fashion. Together, they were likely to produce a pack of raga-muffins who would run about London presuming upon his acquaintance, and he always believed it was best to put a quick and definitive stop to any such doings.

But then he overheard Elizabeth say *she* would be there. And sure enough, there she was.

The Rollings's town house was elegant but certainly too small for the vast number of people who were invited to the breakfast. Not a terrible shock, for people liked Jolly and wanted to get a look at his young bride. Miss Goddard stood in the midst of an enormous crush of people, fairly locked at the hip with the Countess of Albion. Saye did not care; he had played football in school and knew well how to push through a crowd to obtain a desired object.

Once he reached her, he disregarded her completely, bowing low over her aunt's hand. "And who might this enchantress be?"

It worked. The lady laughed before deciding to purse her lips and say, "Introduce me, Lilly."

She did, with plainly evident reluctance. The countess was appropriately cool, but he saw her eyes widen just a touch when mention was made of his title and position.

"Oh, none of that scraping," he said, affecting an air of modesty. "Future earl or dust man, we all put our trousers on the same way, do we not?"

"No," said Miss Goddard. "The dust man does not have his valet tug his excruciatingly tight breeches onto his body as some do. I cannot even think how you breathe, sir."

"Lilly," her aunt admonished whilst Saye tried not to look too gleeful. She had noticed his breeches, which meant it was likely she had surreptitiously examined his…

"Think nothing of it, madam," he said to Miss Goddard. "If I cannot bear a joke, then I am no man at all. However, I shall insist upon a penance for this grave offence."

Lady Albion looked concerned while Miss Goddard looked, for the first time, mildly interested. "Sir, I do not mean to offend you, but—"

"A penance," he said. "I insist you walk with me. With your charming aunt as our chaperon of course."

Miss Goddard heaved an enormous sigh, while her aunt

accepted the invitation for them both. The countess's attention then moved to a conversation on her other side, and Miss Goddard leant in to speak quietly to him.

"You are wasting your time with me, you know. I do not intend to marry, so I scarcely give two figs whether you have a title or two or six."

"Not marry?" Saye tilted his head. "Why ever not?"

"Because I want to do things that no man would likely wish his wife to do," she replied earnestly.

"Do you mean sexually?" Saye asked, matching her whisper. "Because I must tell you, I am up for nearly anything—you need have no fears there."

This made her laugh, and Saye found he was uncommonly pleased with himself. To see her pink-cheeked and smiling added to her beauty.

"No, and I shall thank you not to try your sort of shocking charm with me. It will not do, sir. I have fortune enough to do as I like."

"And what exactly is it that you like?"

She considered him for a moment, seeming unwilling to give up her secret.

"Come now, you must tell me, or I shall be forced to tell everyone you were giving undue notice to my breeches."

She rolled her eyes before admitting, "I like to draw. I do the illustrations for *Ackermann's* and *La Belle Assembleé*. They scarcely pay me a thing, but I like it very well, much more than endless landscapes anyway. I do not wish to give it up."

"Oh the scandal," he said.

She nodded. "I am afraid so."

"Well, you are correct. The future Lady Matlock can hardly be some magazine artist."

"Would not do at all," she agreed.

"Best that it ends here, then."

"Absolutely. So our outing…"

He gave her a charming grin. "We cannot disappoint the countess. I daresay she was looking at my breeches too."

This made Miss Goddard smile. "Oh, she did not. She is forty-six, well past the age to be examining young men's breeches."

"Horrid speech!" Saye exclaimed. "I shall have you know that among the licentious widows in town, the ones in their forties and fifties are the worst! It is the ennui, you know; they have nothing else to think of."

Miss Goddard laughed again. "Dreadful thought!"

"So Tuesday next? I find Tuesdays to be the days I am most agreeable to wasting my own time."

"Tuesday it is."

DARCY HAD COME TO BE VERY FOND OF MISS LYDIA BENNET, fond enough that seeing her married—albeit to one of his oldest and dearest friends—made him a bit sentimental. Jolly would soon get a child on her, they would retire to the country, and the mad giggling and running about his houses shrieking about bonnets would be no more.

He could not help but worry a little. Miss Lydia Bennet, at only eighteen, sometimes seemed so very young to him! Then again, so did Georgiana, who having just turned twenty, was the age Elizabeth had been when he married her.

It struck him suddenly how full of optimism this business of marrying was. Young ladies yearned for it, did all they could to secure a man, but was a man ever really worthy of such trust? He looked at Jolly, better known for his ability to drink ale than anything else—would he be a dependable husband?

Then again, who was Darcy to ask?

It struck him suddenly how much he had asked from Elizabeth. She had placed an enormous trust in him, and he had failed her. He recalled her words to him when they were first reunited: 'How could you possibly know what it is to be a female, alone and with child, cast off to a poisoned wilderness, afraid, unsure, despised, fearing for your life...? Tell me Fitzwilliam, what about that can you possibly comprehend?'

Grief pricked at him and drew forth an onslaught of more memories, playing in his mind just as fresh as if they were new. The yellow gown...how did he forget *that* night? She had been so lovely, and he had wished for a moment to toss aside his hurt and his absurd jealousy and take her to the ball, just as she had wanted. Then the idiotic part of him had grown angry, imagining she had dressed to enchant other men—and how coldly he had treated her then! How humiliated she must have felt, yet she bore it with such dignity.

The memories began to flow fast and hard, his heart breaking with them. He found himself imagining her thoughts and fears that surely accompanied his heartless actions. Her taking his hand, beseeching him to talk to her, and his cold refusal. His anger and petulance as she tried vainly to please him, in society as well as in their home. Her crying, which he had heard clearly, when he stopped coming to her bed. How torn he had been then, desperately wishing to go to her, but too stupidly angry, too idiotically convinced that she had tried to deceive him. Her fear—yes, he had to admit to the fear in her eyes, fear he had caused, even as he said he wanted her to leave.

He had known for some months now what he truly had done, but he had nevertheless persisted selfishly, wanting her love, wanting her trust, always wanting her to give him something, when he should have been thinking of her. He should have considered what *she* wanted from all of this.

Perhaps nothing. Perhaps she wants to go back to the sea. Perhaps she wants to send me off to Yorkshire.

One thing was certain. He had to ask.

Twenty Seven

When Caroline Bingley heard that Lydia Bennet was marrying at the end of September in London, she surmised correctly that her brother and his wife would likely postpone their removal to Derbyshire. With Jane and Bingley in town for some weeks, it presented her with an opportunity, and she would make of it what she could. What she wanted, Caroline decided, was for Eliza to *go* away and *stay* away. To that end, Eliza should be persuaded she should leave Darcy.

Her brother's wife was having a morning in, and Caroline would attend. Jane, she knew, would not refuse her entry nor would she wish for any sort of scene to be made. So Caroline would go, she would draw Eliza aside, and then she would do her worst.

When she and Louisa arrived, the drawing room contained about ten ladies. As Caroline had predicted, Jane's lips tightened at the sight of her and she shot a glance at Louisa but otherwise did nothing. Eliza sat in the midst of everything, an unlikely queen. Caroline had to admit to some begrudging admiration of her gown—likely it was one that Viscount Saye had chosen.

She did not approach her at first, choosing instead to be demure and quiet beside her elder sister. She was introduced to a Miss Lillian Goddard, who was sweet but stupid and evidently fancied herself an artist but otherwise spoke no more than the barest civilities.

When Eliza rose to go refresh herself, Caroline did likewise, following her to the nearest bedchamber and waiting for her to emerge. When she did, she was startled to see Caroline, rearing back and gasping a moment before saying, "Miss Bingley you frightened me."

"The least of my offences against you I am sure." Caroline tried for her best, most contrite smile. "I know I am not to speak to you, but I hoped I might offer an apology."

Eliza tilted her head, considering. It had the unfortunate effect of also showing off some pearl earbobs that looked very expensive and made Caroline burn with jealousy. Those should be her earbobs!

"Very well," she pronounced at last. "Shall we?" She gestured towards the door to the room she had just quit. Caroline nodded and followed her in.

The door had scarcely closed behind them when Eliza turned. "You do understand I have no power to compel Bingley to leave you in London or admit you to his home."

"I know." Again the contrite smile. "My brother has become quite stiff in his old age."

Eliza did not smile.

"In any case," Caroline hurried on, "I wish to apologise, deeply. I cannot tell you how much I regret the prank that…well, that led to…never mind that, it need not be said. But suffer me to say I am sorry, not only for that but for taking advantage of your absence in the way I did."

"How do you mean?"

Perfect. Caroline tried not to look happy at Eliza's confusion, instead choosing to appear flustered. "Oh…uh, Mr Darcy did not…I assumed he might have said to you…"

"Said what?"

Caroline covered her face with her hands and sighed heavily. Dropping her hands, she said severely, "I should have thought he would be honest with you. Did you not deserve at least that much?"

She shook her head. "Men. They never speak the truth when a lie will do."

Eliza merely studied her curiously.

Caroline licked her lips. "I am sure you knew about our understanding…before. Before he saw you."

Eliza still said nothing.

"He and my brother had spoken, things were…well, not quite settled, but that was the purpose of us being all together in Hertfordshire—to settle things and offer us a time of courtship. Instead, I saw his head turned."

"You blame me that it went off."

"I do. I did. I mean, these things happen, I am sure. The trouble is…" Caroline sighed heavily. "It was more than just convenience and the union of two fine families for me. I loved him. Loved him so much that I had allowed him…"

She looked helplessly at Eliza. Eliza merely nodded coolly. "What has this to do with me?"

"Well, having happened once, it was…well, a short time after you left, it was natural he should seek solace somewhere, and it seems that somewhere was with me. He thought you dead, but he could not quite grieve you as such, and in the meantime, a man does have his needs." This was all said so perfectly earnestly that Caroline almost believed it herself.

"So what you are telling me is that you are ruined? And my husband is to blame." There was no emotion in Eliza's words. Caroline thought she had never been so flat.

"Well…yes. I guess you might say it thus. I do not think myself ruined for we were engaged, after all."

Eliza raised an eyebrow when Caroline called herself engaged but otherwise seemed to believe it. "So what is it that you want? Is there some child lurking about whom Darcy must claim as his? Or is it money you are after?"

"I wanted to apologise, like I said," Caroline replied. "And also…"

"Also?"

"Well, I did wonder whether you thought you would stay this time." Caroline was still sweet but allowed a harder edge to creep in. "I could not remain with a man whose heart was with another, after all, and from what I hear, you had a pretty situation in Weymouth. Quite fashionable. Perhaps it might be happiest for us all if you were there and Darcy—and I—were here."

ELIZABETH CONGRATULATED HERSELF FOR SITTING CALMLY through Miss Bingley's absurd stories. What she wished to do— what she could not do—was lash out violently, scratching her eyes and pulling her hair. But she would not because she was a lady. She listened quietly to Miss Bingley's lies, but when she rose, she permitted herself one small indulgence.

"Has it ever occurred to you," she began in a light, conversational tone, "that if you were not so mean spirited and unkind, he just might have had some designs on you? I suggest you consider some significant improvement of your character, else you are sure to end up alone. No man wants to take a viper to his bosom."

And with that, she quit the room, not caring whether Miss Bingley had any reply.

She could not return to the party, feeling unequal to any sort of conversation. Instead, she wandered in something of a stupor and found herself behind the house in a small courtyard.

Autumn was full upon them, and there was nothing green to comfort her, but she sat and pretended she was looking out on the gardens at Pemberley. She wanted to cry; there was a hard lump of sorrow in her throat that needed relief, but it would not come.

What could she do? She was entrapped in this life where

nasty wenches like Caroline Bingley held power over her. They knew her secrets, and they could come to her at any moment and spew bile on her, and she had to sit there and accept it. She was vastly sick of it all and had deserved none of it.

Something needed to change.

DARCY WAS SITTING WITH HIS COUSINS AT THEIR CLUB WHEN Bingley found them. He immediately insisted on a private room, and Saye, with a short whistle, procured one. Bingley waved off a drink and sat looking grim as he reported the extraordinary falsehood Miss Bingley had told Elizabeth that afternoon.

"She said what?" Darcy felt himself grow cold with anger.

Following some confrontation with Miss Bingley in a bedchamber somewhere, Elizabeth had disappeared. It was Miss Goddard who asked after her—they had been in conversation when Elizabeth had excused herself for a few minutes but did not come back. A search of the house did not locate her until Bingley discovered her in the back courtyard staring at nothing. It took some doing, but Bingley eventually extracted the whole stupid story.

"What on earth does your sister have against Elizabeth," Darcy spat, once the recitation was done, "that she cannot stop herself from trying to upset her?"

"I am sorry. I believed Louisa understood that she was not to enter my home, but Caroline can be persuasive, and she truly believed Caroline would apologise and leave it at that."

Darcy scoffed at the notion. "Has she put these rumours about elsewhere? Is there talk?"

Saye spoke up. "I have not heard so much as a whisper about this, but surely Miss Bingley is not stupid enough to put about her own ruination."

"Therein lies the utter stupidity of it all!" Darcy cried. "In seeking to discredit me, she makes herself disreputable! What of her own marriage prospects?"

Delicately, Bingley said, "Um, I daresay she should vastly prefer being your mistress to someone else's wife."

"Bingley!"

"I do not say I agree with her," Bingley said hastily. "Only that it certainly seems so by her actions."

Darcy cursed. "Just when I had hoped…"

"Hoped what?" Bingley asked.

Darcy shook his head. He would lose Elizabeth because of this, he was sure of it. A sudden vision came to him—returning to the house to find Elizabeth and Bennet gone, back to Weymouth or worse, off to a place he knew not. Panic suddenly clenched him, and he said, "I must go to my wife."

"Now? But Darcy we should—"

Whatever else Saye said, he knew not, for Darcy was gone.

He did not call for his carriage; there was no time, and in any case, it was only a mile to his house. He walked briskly, using the length of his legs to their full advantage, a litany of curses to Miss Bingley interspersed with pleading to Elizabeth running through his mind. All the while, images of an empty bedchamber, an empty parlour ran rampant.

By the time he burst into the front door of his house, he was so wholly persuaded she was gone that it was a shock to hear Mrs Hobbs say, "In the courtyard with Master Bennet," when he asked where she was. He paused a moment, his breath coming in short, quick pants, and said, "You are certain."

"I am indeed, for I left her there not a moment ago. Are you well, sir?"

"Um, yes." Leaving her behind, he strode rapidly towards the back of the house and the door to the courtyard. Moments later, he thrust the door wide, then nearly collapsed with the relief of seeing her, calm and maternal, watching over their boy.

"Pop!" Bennet cried, racing over to show him a rock.

"Oh! Is not that a fine rock!" he said, one eye on his wife. She sat in a bit of dappled shade, a gentle smile on her lips. There was a slight chill in the air, and she wore a shawl about her shoulders that he had given her back when they were engaged. He hoped that was a good sign.

"May I join you?"

"Certainly." She moved aside on the bench to make room for him. Nurse Harriet came outdoors before anything else could be said. It was Bennet's nap time, and she intended to take him inside. Elizabeth rose as well, but Darcy forestalled her.

"Stay with me?"

"Very well," Elizabeth agreed.

When the door closed behind the pair, Darcy's stomach knotted painfully. He could not look at her as he remarked, "I understand Miss Bingley interrupted your visit to your sister this morning and said...and told an absurd lie to you about..."

He knew not what to expect, but what he decidedly did not anticipate was Elizabeth's chuckle. "I begin to think she is mad. What a tale! She should consider writing novels."

"I...I could not stand the thought that she had upset you. I am sure it must have been humiliating..."

Elizabeth rose, smiling down at him on the bench. "No, if anything, I am concerned for Jane. She must see her settled somehow before things get worse."

"Miss Bingley did come here once to see me... I still cannot remember what made me admit her entry. Foolishness I suppose, for clearly she just wished to bestir more trouble."

Elizabeth shrugged as he rose. "Miss Bingley is no friend of mine. I should not be surprised that she sought to take advantage of my absence in whatever way she could. But I can hardly imagine that you would take up with the likes of her. You can hardly stand to be in the same room with her much less take her into your bed."

"While I cannot deny that, it is not Miss Bingley's lack of appeal that should persuade you. The whole of my being was focused on finding you, my beloved wife. The very notion that I should take up with another—"

"I could hardly blame you if you had. Most gentlemen would

have." She said it almost carelessly, her attention ostensibly on a small topiary bush beside them.

He reached out, taking her hand, which she gave him without looking at him. "Will you please look at me?"

From all appearance, she was calm and unconcerned.

"I care not what most gentlemen might have done. I love you, and the very idea of another woman disgusts me."

Her eyes slid from his, and she did not reply.

He dropped her hand. "You do not believe me," he accused.

"I said nothing of the sort."

"Do you believe me?"

"Do I believe Miss Bingley was not your mistress? Of course, I do."

"Do you believe I did not, have not, nor would I ever, ever have a mistress?"

She laughed in a tight, uncomfortable way. "If you say so."

He gasped. "I cannot believe you. You think I had a mistress."

"I do understand that a gentleman has…needs."

Angrily, he retorted, "What I need is you, not the meaningless embrace of some paid vessel."

A flash of anger went into her eyes. "I have never barred you from my bed. In fact, I invited you into it."

"For sleep only!"

"Well, if you want more, take it! Do you expect an invitation?"

"Yes!" He exclaimed. "Yes, I do!"

"Very well," she said, still so damnably placid. "You, Fitzwilliam Darcy, are cordially invited to exert your marital rights—"

"Stop it!" he roared. Why could she not become angry? Where were her tears? Was he really so unimportant to her?

The volume of his voice made her grow stern. "Is all this shouting really necessary?"

"I think it is," he said, still angry but in a low tone. "There is much wrong I have done you, but I cannot sit idly by and allow you to believe—"

The flash of anger was back, and more than a flash, it was a burn. "To believe of you as you believed of me?" she retorted. "Yes, you are an expert at upholding your wedding vows with the exception of the 'to have and to hold from this day forward' portion. That bit only lasted a few months for you. Is it so absurd that I should imagine the rest to be done with so easily as well?"

She advanced on him, and he realised this was it, the true measure of her feelings was about to come forth. Her eyes fairly shot sparks, and her voice, still low, was nothing short of menacing. "Do not dare stand there like some great lumbering hypocrite, indignant that I should think of you just as you thought of me. Yes, I did think you had a mistress, and in my darker hours, I wondered whether it was for her sake that you sent me away."

"I have never wanted any woman, ever, the way I wanted, and still want, you. A mistress? The idea is laughable."

"Except when the laughter stops, and the banishment to Yorkshire begins," she spat back at him.

"I love you. I have from the very first moment I saw you, and you love me too, and we have to—"

"Love is not the problem!" she cried. "Your love did me no good when I was alone and sad, and you would not reply to my letters. You never even read them, did you?"

"Had I the opportunity, it would be done very differently. But to my discredit, no, I did not read many of them. The first one, yes, but many others were sent directly to the fire."

This made her sag, her eyes immediately turned downward. "You did not wish to hear me then, and you cannot blame me for wishing to remain silent now. If you will excuse me, I think I must go lie down."

TWENTY EIGHT

ELIZABETH SCARCELY MADE IT TO HER BEDCHAMBER, SUCH WAS her exhaustion from the events of the day. When she arrived, she went at once to a bag she had owned for some time. In it were the letters she had written to Darcy while at Gunnersdale.

These were the letters written but never sent. Although she had certainly sent an abundance of letters to him, there were wiser days when his continued silence had persuaded her she would do best to cease pestering him with her thoughts. She knew not why she kept them. They had travelled with her through the dark night in Yorkshire, crushed in the bottom of the pack she carried as she walked endlessly to the town where she would find the stage. They stayed with her at Upton Park, buried in the recesses of an old trunk—never looked at, never considered, but never discarded. They moved to the house in Weymouth after Mrs Macy's death, and they travelled to Pemberley and London—always with her, though never opened. They were her reminder of how easily fiery passions could be reduced to cold ash, of how a wife who once believed herself beloved could find herself alone and uncared for on a slag heap in Yorkshire.

She wished now that she had discarded them. She did not think she had the strength to open them and revisit the pain that had guided her hand as she wrote them. She laid them out like a fan around her on the bed but did nothing more than consider them. She had just begun to gather them up again when there was a knock at the door and Darcy entered, some familiar-looking pages dangling from his hand.

"No," she said immediately. "I do not know what you are about with those papers…"

"It is the letters that I kept. Too few, I am ashamed to say. What are these?"

"Letters I wrote to you but did not send. I am going to burn them."

"No! I want to read them."

"No," she protested immediately. "This is not something I want to do."

He sat down on the bed next to her, looking intently at her. "I do not want to do it either, but…but I think we must."

"I cannot."

"Even if, at the end of it, you could be happy? We could be happy?" When she did not reply, he said, "I miss the light in your eyes. I miss your laughter, your teasing."

For a moment, they stared at each other, both refusing to yield. With a trembling hand, Elizabeth reached over, taking one of his pages. She unfolded it, and her eyes fell on one small bit.

"…wish you to know how very sorry I am for the manner in which I have failed you as a wife…"

"Oh! No." Elizabeth shoved the page back towards him. "Why do you insist on doing this?"

"Because if we do not confront this and deal with the pain, we can never be rid of it!"

"We can never be rid of it anyway," she shot back.

"So then, what? We surrender to it all? This is us, forevermore, no trust, no love?"

"I just do not think it necessary to go relive our pain."

"Have we not tried it your way these many months? I have waited, I have tried to be patient, but you remain unhappy, as do I. I made a dreadful, horrific mistake two years ago, and I have tried, truly I have, to pay for it and to change the horrifying person in me who would do such a thing to the woman he loves beyond all reason. However, you will not let me, will you? No, evidently, you would prefer to keep running from me."

Elizabeth shook her head in amazement, two spots of pink brightening her cheeks. "You may have changed your tendency towards resentment, but you are still selfish. It is selfish that you should demand—"

He reached out, grabbing her hand. "Look at me." He waited until she did. "You and I are two parts of a whole, bound together by the love we once shared, and nothing has ever been right for either of us since we separated. I did something horrible to you, and you have suffered, I realise that, but you are still suffering, as am I, and I want to change that."

She shook her head vehemently.

He took both of her hands. "Stop hiding from me. Trust me with your unhappiness, please. Tell me you hate me, hit me, rail at me….anything. Your unhappiness has entombed you, Elizabeth, and I want only to set you—the real you—free from it."

She looked at him for just a moment with the warring of every great emotion reflected in her eyes, until finally, a mask descended. Quietly and firmly, she said, "I am sorry to cause you pain, but I simply cannot do this."

Wrenching her hands from his grasp, she quickly exited her bedchamber.

WHERE SHE WENT, HE KNEW NOT, BUT AFTER AN HOUR HAD GONE by and she had not returned, he concluded that wherever she was, she intended to stay there.

He had spent the time pacing and being miserable at how badly done it had been. He had hoped he could shake her complacency and induce her to begin to express some sort of emotion. He had felt they were nearly there, on the precipice, about to leap forward, but then at the last moment, she had retreated.

Darcy had no notion what to do next, but he knew things could not remain this way. At once, his eyes fell upon the letters that were still strewn across Elizabeth's bed. He regarded them thoughtfully.

She had shared her grief with him after all, had she not? Those letters she had written him, were they not filled with her heart and mind and soul?

He walked over to the bed and slowly gathered them up. An idea had formed in his head, but he knew not whether it was a good one. He would answer the letters. He would sit and read each and every painful line and word, and he would understand her, acknowledge her, and reply to her, beginning with the letter written before she left for Yorkshire.

He went into his room and sat at his writing desk, stacking the letters neatly and in order on the top of it. He prepared his pens and ascertained that he had adequate ink. Finally, he opened the first letter, and sitting back, he read and pondered every last word of it. He allowed the memories to come to him unrestrained, and he imagined, as best he could, all that she must have felt going through such events.

It was not easy, by any means, but he persisted through it with great resolve. He had failed her these many years by not being willing to do this, but he would fail her no more. If nothing else, she would know that all these agonising thoughts she had put to paper had at least been shared by him.

He pulled paper from the desk and picked up his pen.

LONDON! WHY WAS SHE IN LONDON? SHE REQUIRED A LONG ramble amid fields and trees and rivers, not people and carriages and noise! Hoping to commune with nature, she turned and went towards the park, her long, determined strides at direct contrast with the other ladies who minced along prettily.

She was highly vexed by his perceptions and presumptions. How extraordinary, after all he had done to her, that he should now feel it his right to demand more from her! She did the best she could and was giving him all that she could.

But her own reason would ever argue against her—and did so now. *Not quite true,* her heart whispered. *You are, as always, withholding the most tender part.*

It had always been her way, even with dear Jane. It was easy for her to laugh, tease, complain, or share her vexations, but when it came to the things that truly grieved her? These she held close, to share with no one. Indeed, she scarcely liked to think of them herself.

But Darcy wanted to know her pain, for it had begun to consume her. She knew not whether she was strong enough to continue denying him, particularly if they began having regular arguments the like the one that had just transpired.

After all, she did realise that in her current state, she could not have joy. She did not have sorrow but neither was there joy. There was only a medium-sized, neutral sort of...placidity. She was living in a shell that protected her from her memories but that same shell prohibited felicity from touching her as well. Did she intend it to be forever this way?

Her thoughts slowed her footsteps as she returned to the house. It was near time for dinner, and she knew not whether she was equal to it.

Mrs Hobbs greeted her at the door. "The master asked me to tell you he has requested a tray this evening. Shall I do the same for you?"

"Please," Elizabeth agreed. Evidently, Darcy was unequal to seeing her as well.

She went first to the nursery, where Bennet was happily occupied with his own meal, but there was no sign of Darcy. Saye had given Bennet a puppy earlier that week, a small creature like his Florizel, and Bennet was enthralled. She entered just in time to find him lying on the floor with his potatoes, wanting to eat them the way his puppy did. Nurse Harriet was dismayed, but it brought a true laugh to Elizabeth—one that was much needed.

She went then to her own bedchamber, half expecting to find Darcy within. He was not, but sounds from the adjoining room indicated he might be found there. Curious, she silently opened the adjoining door just an inch and saw Darcy in a chair by the fire, using a side table for a writing desk and furiously scribbling away.

She wondered what he was doing and why he did not simply go to his study. With a light shrug, she gently closed the door.

AFTER NUMEROUS REVISIONS AND MARKINGS, DARCY SET DOWN his pen and leaned back in his chair, regarding his letter thoughtfully. It was not perfect of course, and he wished, not for the first time, that he was better able to express his thoughts and feelings. Still, it was a good effort, and he hoped it would be a first step for them. He hoped it would cause her to think better of him, if such a thing were possible.

A quick look at the mantel clock showed it was after ten. The dinner some maid had brought lay cold and untouched nearby. He wondered whether she slept already.

He silently opened her door and peered into the room. She was asleep and did not rouse when he entered. He left his letter on her dressing table and then returned to his own bedchamber.

WHEN ELIZABETH AWOKE THE NEXT MORNING, SHE IMMEDIATELY saw the letter on her dressing table. *So, it was I to whom he wrote with such vigour last night.* Having little time until she was due to see her son, she resolved to save it for later.

Two hours later, she held it in her hand. She felt strangely flattered by the letter, remembering how passionately he had seemed in writing it and the evident zeal with which he had devoted himself to it. She passed her fingertips over her name lightly, thinking of their argument about Caroline Bingley. He had been violently angry and excessively hurt, yet he did not grow cold. He did not remove himself from her. He came to her, and he tried to explain the problem despite all her efforts to resist him.

Nevertheless, she had closed herself off from him and had grown cold to him. Then when that did not work, he wrote a letter to her. Would the letter be an expression of his anger? Somehow she thought not.

She thought of how much she must have pushed him since her return. Always keeping him at arms-length, many times toying with his emotions—not intentionally of course, but she did realise it had happened nevertheless—and refusing to give him what he wanted for months now. He had shown great constancy and forbearance in it all, she acknowledged. As much as it was not easy for her to live with him, neither had it been felicitous for him to live with her.

With a slight tremble in her fingers, she opened her letter, realising at once that it was made even thicker by the inclusion of the dreaded letter she had written before she was sent away. Seeing that caused her to bite her lip with a frisson of nervousness, so she set it aside and began to peruse Darcy's words.

My Dearest Elizabeth,
I know you are not happy, and I see your unhappiness drowning you. I cannot stand by and watch you suffer any longer. I wish to rescue you from a life of misery, as bold as such a claim might sound. I have put it upon you, I cannot deny that, but now I shall do all I can to take it from you, to rescue you from the fear and pain that binds you. If I truly thought you were satisfied in our life here, I

would desist, but you are not, and so I shall not rest until you are joyful once more.

I do not wish to cause you more pain by forcing you to revisit these painful recollections. However, as you left me this evening, I realised those remembrances were yet alive in the form of your letters. I wish admittance to your pain, my love, not for you to relive it, but that I might rid you of it—that in sharing it, we might conquer it together. To begin, I charged myself with the task of reading, in its entirety, the letter you gave to me the day before I sent you away. My hope was that I could read it, not with my eyes, but rather, with yours.

I see now how I have caused you to be afraid of me, how I was so very cold and spiteful to you. I see your loneliness and your uncertainty, put onto you by me, the man who was supposed to protect and cherish you. Although these many years I have long thought on the sin of casting you out, I should have considered likewise how poorly I treated you before that.

I think of how differently this might have been if only just once I had asked you whether the things I believed of you were true. If only I had spoken of it with you, just one of the many times you came to me! My pride and my absurd jealousy stood before me, and I wilfully misunderstood the situation and I am deeply ashamed of it.

An apology is so insufficient and weak for such a grave offence, yet it is all that I am able to offer. I am sorry I did not trust in you, and I am sorry I condemned you when you did not even know you were on trial. I am sorry I believed in the lies I was told, and I am sorry I sent you away. I am sorry you were afraid, sad, and bereft, and I did not see it. I am sorry you were alone and increasing, and that you missed your family and believed you were unloved. Most of all, however, I am sorry I failed to be a man worthy of you. I know there can be no apology sufficient to redress the manner in which I have wronged you, but please know that I shall regret my actions to the end of my days.

Each and every day I see the wall mounted between us. I have tried to take it down myself, but its removal can only be for you to decide. I pray that day will come soon. I long for the return of what we once had, and I do believe we can have it again.

Please entrust me with your heart as you hold mine.

Until then, I remain your adoring husband,
Fitzwilliam

Elizabeth absently dabbed at the tears that had risen into her eyes. Somehow the letter did make her feel…something. Relief? Pleasure? Anxiety? If nothing else, it was surprisingly gratifying to know that he had at least seen and acknowledged the agony she had faced.

But what now? What should she do in reply, if anything?

Slowly, she opened the letter she had written to him. Although she well remembered the sorrow, the fear, and the terror she had experienced knowing she was being sent away, she did not recall precisely what she had written.

Several times, she winced as she read, feeling a particularly sensitive passage that summoned how she had felt as she penned it. Even though she had tried, quite definitely, to avoid thinking of those days, the letter roused those feelings of despair and rejection within her, and she began to weep. The fright of her uncertainty and her shame could still hurt. The tears flowed freely as a seemingly endless well of sorrow emptied itself in her, and it was some time before she could regain her equanimity.

As she sat drying her face and rubbing her head, wishing to ward off a headache, a strange notion came to her. *It can be done.*

It was over, was it not? Those months were over and long gone. Years had passed since that sad, frightened girl had gone off on her husband's order. That girl had become a mother and a person who knew what it was to fear, but she had conquered that fear and carried on. A person who did what needed to be done, whether it was to birth a child, to care for herself in the wilderness, or to run an estate.

This is up to me now. I had no choice but to be sent away. No choice but to return. No choice but to live with him and do as he wanted—but this, this is my choice. I can hold this and remain apart from him. Or...or I can let go. I can forgive, and we can be happy again. It is up to me.

She considered her letter for several long minutes. Taking the pages, she slowly and carefully folded them into their original, well-creased shape. Darcy's letter was left on her table as she rose from her chair and walked towards the fireplace, where a recently stoked fire crackled merrily. She paused for several minutes, staring into the flames, her mind locked on the image of her husband busily writing to her in the middle of the night.

She held out her hand, releasing the papers into the fire, which consumed them rapidly and greedily. She watched as her letter caught fire and began to disintegrate, her gaze unwavering until every last morsel of the paper had been devoured and its ashes mixed with the wood ashes in a manner that was inextricable.

TWENTY NINE

A KNOCK DISTURBED ELIZABETH'S REVERIE OVER THE ASHES. IT was Mrs Hobbs. "Mrs Bingley has called."

"Oh. Yes, of course. Tell her I shall meet her directly."

Elizabeth washed her face and tidied her hair before going to her sister, but Jane immediately cried out over Elizabeth's shocking appearance anyway. "Oh, never mind me." Elizabeth waved off her concern. "All is well, Jane, I assure you."

"Lizzy, I declare you were insensible when Bingley found you yesterday. I had to come see for myself how you were and tell you our plan for Caroline."

"Oh, I could not care two straws for Caroline." Elizabeth rolled her eyes. "What a foolish chit she is though! Who would start gossip about their own ruination?"

"No one will have her now. Louisa is finished, and so are we. Neither is she wanted in Scarborough, so she will need to form her own establishment, somewhere away from all of us."

"As long as she knows she cannot come near me," said Elizabeth. "I care not where she is."

By the time Jane departed, two more letters awaited Elizabeth in her bedchamber. She smiled, thinking it could never be said that her husband lacked industry—once he had set himself to a task, he would finish it.

This time, she chose to first read what she had written to him. He had included two of her letters, ones she had written shortly after arriving in Yorkshire but had never sent. She could see her efforts at good cheer in the first part of the letters, but knew well how thin that disguise had been. She had been miserable, scared, and lonely in those days, and reading her own words brought back much of that feeling.

Approximately halfway through the letter, she had dropped her pretence and had written to him honestly.

My dear husband, although I am making every effort to endure this situation between us and assume you know what is best for our marital felicity, I must put aside my resolve to accept this state for just a few moments and tell you what is truly in my heart. I love you so much, and I beseech you, with all of my heart, to please let me come home to you. I beg you. I cannot live without you, and each day I am without your love, I die a bit more. Please allow me to come back to you, and please allow me to mend whatever has caused this rift between us. I shall do anything you wish, but please, please do not make me stay away from you.

Reading her impassioned plea caused Elizabeth to swallow hard and wipe away a tear from her eye, but it was not sadness that threatened to overcome her—it was rage. How wretched a creature she had been, wishing only to return home! She had not sent this one, it was true, but many others just like it had been sent and disregarded. She had put away all pride and dignity, had thrown herself on his mercy, yet he had had none for her. She trembled with her anger.

Odious, vicious man, how could he do this to me! Am I nothing at all? Could he have not simply answered me? He never had, not any of the letters I wrote, and that was why I stopped sending them!

She had gone to him, still with all the love in her heart, and begged and pleaded for clemency, yet he was unmoved! She was so young—only twenty—and he had sworn to protect and cherish her, yet this was what he did to her.

Shaking with an anger that increased by the moment, she rose and paced, attempting to calm herself, but she simply could not. Her breath came fast and her heart pounded with fury, and she thought that if Darcy had presented himself to her at that moment, she might tear him limb from limb. *How dare he!*

At last, she went to her writing desk. If Darcy wished to hide behind his desk and write, then she would answer in kind. She yanked a piece of paper from her escritoire with a violent force that caused two additional sheets to fly to the ground beneath her.

Fury caused her hand to shake, but she disregarded it, writing fast and pressing hard enough to break her pen. She sometimes pierced the paper with her anger. Ink blotted and blotched haphazardly over her words as she filled three sheets with her venom. She then sanded the sheets carelessly, the fine grit scattering over the desk and onto her skirts and the floor.

When at last it was done, she sat back, feeling spent. There were tears on her face that she irritably wiped with the back of her hand, causing ink, which had blotched on her skin, to smear across her cheek. She did not care.

She looked over the letter, which was nearly incoherent and mostly illegible. It did not matter though, for the gist of it was communicated in nearly every sentence, over and over again: how dare he disregard her. That was all. She simply could not stand the fact that he had chosen to ignore her cries and her pleas. She could not tolerate the fact that her begging and her debasing of herself had gone so entirely unheeded, to the extent that he had not even troubled himself to open the letter.

She had suffered so enormously, and he had…well, she did not know what he had done. In her mind's eye, he had sat silent and haughty, mocking her in her anguish, staring at her with that inscrutable gaze as he had so often in those hated months. She burnt with helpless, unmitigated fury imagining his implacable, disdainful gaze.

At that hapless moment, Darcy chose to knock on her door.

DARCY PERMITTED HIMSELF TO RISE FROM HIS DESK ONCE HE HAD completed his replies to four of Elizabeth's letters. He had to admit, it was not easy going, and he was quite fatigued from the effort. In reading her words, he had often felt as though he might become sick with the unbearable agony of witnessing her suffering. More than once, he had wept, furtive and ashamed of himself, yet wondering at his own embarrassment; after all, a few tears were nothing to what she had endured. Although he had always before felt a vague understanding of her suffering, as he read, he forced himself to truly consider her, imagining her fear and worry and the sadness that must have consumed her.

At several junctures, he had sat back, utterly dispirited and certain that he could do nothing that would ever redeem him in her eyes, nor create in her a desire to love him again. Then he would rally his spirits, thinking of the time they had kissed, when she had caressed his hand, and how she had invited him to sleep with her. In spite of it all, she still loved him, extraordinary as that seemed. Love would triumph over his pride and his foolishness—or so he hoped.

Thus, he continued on, reading and thinking and writing.

He knew she had received the first letter in the morning, as he had placed it there himself. The other two he laid in her room while Elizabeth was with her sister, and the fourth, he decided, he would hand to her in hopes they could speak.

When Elizabeth bid him enter, he found her at the small escritoire on the side of the room. She was silent and still as she looked at him and appeared out of breath.

"Are you well?" he asked. "You seem flushed."

"I am well." Her voice sounded strained and tight.

"Did you read my letters?"

"Just the one so far. I...I thank you for what you are doing. I appreciate the effort."

She looked at her lap, her fingers tightly clutching a sheaf of papers in her hand, papers that seemed to be a letter but were written so untidily he could not fathom who could have sent them. They were as blotted and blotched as the worst of Bingley's had ever been. The tips of Elizabeth's fingers were white from the tight grip she had on the papers, and he noticed she had ink on her face.

He went to a nearby chair and sat. He wanted to talk to her, but the tension and anxiety were so thick in the air, he was paralysed under the weight of them. They did not speak for several agonising moments, and he searched his mind frantically for something to say to break the silence.

Suddenly, she burst out, "You rejected me!" She glared at him fiercely, her eyes on his.

For a moment, he was confused; had he missed something in the conversation? Then he opened his mouth to speak, but she spoke before he could, her voice accusing and relentless.

"How dare you? How. Dare. You?! Did you not see that you were killing me? You did not care! Not at all! You rejected me completely! Look at this!" She waved the pages at him, neither realising nor caring that they were the ones she had just written and not one of her letters from Yorkshire.

"I begged you for relief! Begged! No dignity nor pride was left to me. I threw myself at your feet, begging for a chance to rectify matters, and you rejected me!" Her voice rose to a shriek on 'me' and she leapt to her feet and began to pace before him.

"I know, and I am so—"

"I hardly care what you are! You could not even trouble yourself to read my words—my jagged, horribly painful words— and I was in so…so much pain, and you disregarded me!"

"I—"

"It always must be exactly your way, is that not it? Are my wishes in this matter a concern? Not at all! You said go, and I went, you said come, and here I am. You keep saying you want me to yell and scream and tell you I hate you. Well, get ready, because here it is—I HATE YOU! I hate you, I hate you, I hate you. You neglected me, and you disregarded my pain and my begging and my pleading, and I hate the very sight of you because of it! You are the last man in the world I ever should have married, and I deeply regret the day that I did."

Darcy could not speak, frozen in shock and horror at what she had said. He could only watch her silently.

"Do you have any idea, any idea at all, how terrible it was? That Nelson lady could not even look at me, and I blamed myself, always wondering what was wrong with me. I thought of what I must have done, how greatly I had failed as a wife. I was so ashamed, and I was so very afraid! I could not speak to my family—I was too humiliated by my stupidity, and my father must have known it would be this way all along! I was nothing, throwing myself at your feet and begging for your mercy, yet you looked away from me. You did not care, you just looked away."

"I did—"

"No, you did not! I was terrified! I was so happy to know I was with child, and you rejected him too. You abandoned me, pregnant and alone, and then I walked alone through the darkest night there ever was! I was sure highwaymen or vicious animals would be upon me at any moment, and I shook with the fear of it the entire way! Sixteen miles! Do you know how long that is?"

"Yes and I…" Stupidly, Darcy attempted to reach out to her, and she slapped his arm aside violently.

"Now you want to reach out to me? Do you know how many times, I wished I was dead? If not for Bennet, I would surely have ended my own life. That is how I felt, that is where my wishes were. Bennet saved my life. If not for him, you would be a widower, so how does that strike you? Answer me!"

He opened his mouth to speak, but she did not permit him to do so.

"Do not speak! I do not care to hear you, just as you did not care to hear me, not as I stood before you and not as I wrote to you, letter after letter after letter! And now you have the unmitigated audacity to tell me you love me? Well, go back to university because"—her voice hitched, and she began to cry—"you do not know what that word means!"

Weeping angrily, she began gathering up all the various papers in the room: her letters from Yorkshire, his two still unopened letters, the blotched papers in her hand, some scraps on the floor. Not looking at him, she said, "Do you know how I spent my days?"

She took the papers, which shook in her hands, and walked to the fireplace, tossing them into the flames with a force that caused several of the papers to fly back out. She took the poker and stabbed at them viciously, forcing them into destruction.

"I walked and I cried. That is all I did, walk and cry and cry and walk until I was tired enough to sleep, and then I slept until I woke and walked and cried some more. I never knew such a state of pure despair and utter hopelessness could exist. So of course I left. Why would I not leave? I had nothing more to lose."

Darcy could not speak a word; his chest was tight, and his throat was closed, understanding what pain she had suffered, and knowing with surety that his wife rightly despised him and there was nothing left between them but anger and hatred. He tried to think of something he might say to her, but there was just nothing that could matter. He was condemned to sit in silent agony, wordlessly begging her forgiveness for all the hurt he had known was within her, yet was shocked to witness just the same.

He rose from the chair, intending to at least stand near her, retrieve a handkerchief for her, something... Without looking at him, she held out her hand in a 'stop' motion, so he stopped and instead stood silently watching her.

As the papers burned, her tears stopped, and she seemed to become enshrouded in a terrible, silent calm. Quietly she said, "I offered you everything I had—my heart, my mind, my soul, and my body—and you threw it away like nothing." Her words were accusatory, but her tone was detached.

He opened his mouth to apologise or protest or something, but she saw it and said, "Please do not speak. There is nothing you will say that can make this different."

So he closed his mouth once again and watched with her until all of the pages were nearly entirely consumed, then turning, she said, "Please leave me now. I need to be alone awhile."

Darcy felt like he might be ill. "Elizabeth, please, could we—"

"I need to be alone right now." She enunciated very clearly through what seemed to be gritted teeth. "Just go."

He nodded quickly and rose. She had turned from him and was staring at the rug beneath her feet.

He looked at her for a moment but could think of nothing to say, and so he left.

THIRTY

HE RETURNED TO HIS STUDY FEELING IN COMPLETE SHOCK AT what had just transpired. This seemed a fine notion when he had begun, to go through these letters and revisit the pain of the past, but his goal had been only to begin to heal her existing wounds, not to cause more. He had known the process would be painful, but this was far too much. This was likely doing nothing but more harm. Perhaps she had had the right of it all along. Perhaps if he had only been patient, they might have slowly regained their love and trust for one another.

His movements slow and pained, he went to his desk and sat down. For many minutes, perhaps even an hour, he sat motionless and stunned at what had happened, his mind determined to replay it over and over.

The remainder of her letters sat piled neatly on his desk; the one he had read most recently but not yet replied to was open squarely in the centre of his blotter. He picked it up, glancing over it and intending to compose his response, but the words before him were meaningless. Indeed, at this moment, this entire exercise felt meaningless, just another way in which he had erred.

He decided to mend his pens instead, feeling a sort of satisfaction in taking the blade and using it to create a sharp, exacting point. When that task was complete, he picked up a fresh sheet of paper and began to write, but nothing of any sense would come forward.

When five pages had been wasted on senseless letters started and left incomplete, Mrs Hobbs entered.

"Sir, Blake tells me that Mrs Darcy sleeps in her bedchamber. She thinks she must have taken ill as her sleep is quite restless, and thus, she does not wish to wake her. Would you wish her woken?"

Darcy's mouth was dry, and his thoughts were jumbled, but he managed to say, "Uh, no, she might be ill, so true. Blake should sleep...um, I meant...rather allow Eliz-...that is, Mrs Darcy to sleep."

"Shall we hold dinner, then?"

"Dinner?" Darcy looked at her. *Dinner.* It was astonishing how a man's life might be crumbling around him, yet the inexorable needs of life continued on. A war might rage, a loved one might die, and a marriage bond might disintegrate, yet dinner must be eaten, sleep was needed, and the chest would rise and fall with breath. It was inescapable.

Slowly, he shook his head. For himself, at least, the war must take precedence. "I am very sorry, but I shall not require dinner tonight."

WHEN DARCY HAD AT LAST LEFT HER, ELIZABETH WEPT. EVEN as she sobbed, she had to think, in some part of her mind, of how very tired she was of weeping. Truly, she only wanted to feel happy, yet it seemed more and more that it was her lot in life to be maudlin.

An intense crying spell, coming so hard on the heels of her fit of anger, was exhausting, and although she knew it was close to dinner time, she found she could not face it. She decided she would lie down on her bed for just a few minutes, to rest her eyes with a cold cloth and try to revive herself.

When she awoke, it was past midnight, and the room was nearly dark save for the light of the fire. Her head ached, and it felt as though there was sand embedded under her eyelids. The cool cloth that had been on her eyes had long since fallen to the side, creating an unpleasant, damp spot on her pillow. She rose to take the cloth over to the washstand, and as she walked, she espied a letter that lay near where Darcy had sat earlier. She picked it up and looked at it for a moment, then sat in front of the fire in the chair in which he had sat several hours ago.

She recalled then that he had carried a letter in his hand as he entered the room but had not yet given it to her at the time she had erupted. Likely it had fallen at some time during her tirade.

She relived all she had said to him earlier, feeling a great sense of relief for having said it, yet guilty for it too—the remembrance of the expression on his face was painful. She had not meant to cause him so much anguish, but the words would not be denied, pouring out of her like a tidal wave of black, bilious disgorgement.

It was an apt metaphor, for the way she felt now was exactly how she felt when she was sick to her stomach. Vomiting was dreadful and one never wanted to do it, but once it happened, you felt better. Weak, but overall relieved.

Of course, it was quite another matter that, in so doing, she had vomited hatred all over her husband, who had undertaken this entire exercise in an attempt to resolve the problems between them. Likely he had never imagined that such bitter, unmitigated ire and sorrow might result. He had certainly not yearned for such abominable abuse.

Gently, she opened the letter, which was fairly short but still almost unbearably sweet, particularly given the fact that soon after writing it, he was destined to come to her room and be lambasted by her venomous words.

Elizabeth,

I have only just read your fourth letter to me from York-shire, and I must be honest with you. You are far, far better than I to have been put through such misery by my hand yet have the fortitude to return to our home, to raise our son as you have done, and to treat me with such unfailing kindness and solicitude.

What I cannot comprehend is how it was that you did not write me letters filled with vitriol and spite. I imagine you in these dire circumstances, yet you were still able to write sweet and loving letters to me when I deserved only your cruellest invective.

In your letter, you asked me, again, to tell you what you had done that you might remedy our marriage. In my mind, I imagined what I should have said to you then. I should have learned the truth, and I should have written back to you saying you need do nothing, that I would be on my horse in the next minutes to come and get you and throw myself at your feet to beg your forgiveness for my callous stupidity.

You spoke of your hope for our reconciliation and vowed again to do whatever was needed to put things to rights between us. Does it mean anything at all if I should tell you now that I pledge the same to you? I do not pretend to know what I must do. I want to anticipate your needs, and I want to understand your fears and sorrows, but I am greatly deficient in these areas. Please just know that I shall hear any tales, as much as you should choose to tell me, and I shall reassure you a thousand times of the steadfastness of my love and that you may trust in me. I shall bear your anger, your pain, and your sorrow, and I shall return it with patience, forbearance, and love for as long as you will it.

I love you so much, my dearest, loveliest Elizabeth. You are truly the most worthy and honourable person I have ever met, and I bless the day I first knew you. I thought, today, of the first sight of you I had that day in Weymouth. I was so terrified that somehow it was not true, that it was not really you or you had already gone away or even would refuse to see me. Then you came, and I was nearly overcome with my joy. You looked as beautiful as anything or anyone I had ever seen, and it required every ounce of my strength not to gather you into my arms, hold you tight, and never let you go.

The vision of you that day has always stayed in me. So many times, my eyes have rested on you, and I am made glad simply that you have deigned to grace me with your presence. You are truly everything to me, my dearest, sweetest wife.

I beg and plead with you for just one more chance to love you. I promise to do a better job of it this time.

F. D.

She closed her eyes and winced a moment, thinking of all she had said to him. Such cruelty and unflinching fury and meanness —how many times had she said she hated him? She could not even remember but knew it had been many. He must despise her now.

What good could there be when people allowed their fury free rein and hurled insult and anger upon one another? Was it not much, much better to maintain peace and decorum? Where could they even go from here?

What sort of person did it make her that she now felt better, having made her husband feel so much worse? She had taken her pain and dumped it onto him, and he had absorbed it all, unflinching, save for the time she had slapped his hand away.

Given the hour and the silence from his bedchamber, she was certain he slept but decided to look just in case. She went to his door and very quietly knocked. She heard no response, so she silently eased it open.

It appeared as though the fire had burnt out. With the curtains not drawn around the bed, which remained undisturbed, she could quickly see he was not within. She wondered where he was and decided to look for him.

After briefly straightening her hair and clothing, she went to his study. In contrast to his bedchamber, the fire burnt warmly and the candles remained lit. Darcy was there but deeply asleep, half lying and half sitting on a small chaise lounge close to the fire.

The chaise was hers—she brought it from Longbourn and had it placed here so she might sit with him and read while he worked. She had only done that once, in early days, and had only read a page or two before he came to kiss her, and she leant back to caress him and…well, it was a pleasurable remembrance. She smiled thinking of it.

But it was nowise large enough to ensure his comfort. She looked at him for just a moment, then went to a chest in the room to retrieve a blanket. She put it on him, smoothing it with a nearly imperceptible touch over his chest and shoulders. Quietly, she whispered, "I would not hate you nearly so much if I did not love you so."

The problem was, and always had been, that she loved and needed him far too much. The only way she had survived those years without him was by trying to forget that need, as a starving man would avoid thinking of food. She had tossed herself into her marriage with her heart wide open, holding nothing back from him. Her entire being had been dependent on him, and he had failed her. She was terrified of making the same mistake again.

Promises were in vain. The promise had already been made before any of this had ever happened—a solemn promise, a vow before God and family—and that had been set aside and discarded like it was a mere nothing. How could another promise ever matter when such a thing had happened under that vow?

Yet one could not deny that his more recent actions had proven his constancy. She had run from him, she had hidden from him both in deed and in thought, yet he had pursued her. In every particular, he had proven that he wished to repair their marriage even though she had rebuffed him constantly. Still, he had not faltered. He had been true to her.

Rising, she went to his desk, seeing on it many papers, some with only a single line written on them, lying discarded and useless. She read them all, wondering whether it was wrong to do so but unable to resist nevertheless.

There was one particular page that struck her. It could not be called a letter for it was only a few sentences written in the middle of the paper and then crossed over with one firm line that did not prevent her from reading them.

Elizabeth, you were correct. I should not have forced this from you but, instead, allowed you to maintain this farce of contentment that you have upheld thus far. Perhaps in time, it might have become our reality. I am sorry.

Did she regret that he had forced his way past her barriers and extracted these violent emotions from her? In truth, no, she did not.

She could see now that she had been hiding. She hid from their love, hid from her grief and her anger, but in her defence, hiding was all she had been able to do at that time. It was what she needed to do to keep herself from being overwhelmed by her sadness and fear. Yet now, she felt differently. She felt as though she might be able to come out of hiding and at last accept some of these things before her.

The choice was clear: to take a chance and risk another failure for the opportunity for love and true happiness or to continue on in dispassionate, sedate amiability, never again to know the fire of life and love and passion.

The disagreement and discussion for which he had pressed her, although painful and sad, was having some effect. She was spent from her tears and her screaming, but now with it behind her, she felt better. Something akin to true forgiveness was awakening in her, though with all she had said and done to him, she would not be surprised if Darcy no longer wished to go forth in this manner. He had surely not wished to suffer such abuse, and it was selfish of her to wish to inflict it upon him.

Looking at the papers, she decided she would write him another letter—not the angry ramblings she had penned before, but a letter of truth. She would explain how she felt and why she so often would vacillate between tenderness and feigned indifference towards him. Then she would tell him that she was willing to try to discuss in an amicable way all that had happened in the past two years.

She looked over at him, sleeping so deeply on the chaise.

For a moment, she sat, musing on the issue of the mistrust between them. She could not trust him, she simply could not, nor could she imagine that he would trust her. She knew he still feared she might leave him, but she would not.

She had often, in the time since they had reunited, reflected on how different things might have been if she had remained in Yorkshire. He would have come to retrieve her, and he would have then admitted his mistake. They might have argued, but it would not have lasted for two years. Her son would have been born at Pemberley. She had not given any of them that chance. Darcy had started this, she knew that, but it was she who had continued it.

In many ways, they were equal. Darcy had doubted her just

as she now doubted him. He had borne her absence and the fact that she had run away from him just as she had borne his rejection and dismissal over two years ago. Now, Darcy believed they could love again and hoped for the restoration of their marriage. Did she?

She realised that a choice must be made: a civil marriage or a loving one. In Weymouth when she had agreed to go back to Pemberley with Darcy, she had determined that civility was the most she could offer. Loving him was too frightening.

Now she knew it was impossible. Whether she wished to or not, she loved him. Each and every day, a bit more of her heart was given over to him no matter how she tried to resist it. Her 'farce of contentment' as he had termed it, was not the sum total of her hopes. Her hopes were for the love they shared before, but that hope had been obscured by her fear of him.

Could she believe in him enough to risk being wrong again?

She decided to stop this endless debate in her mind. Moving quickly, she wrote and sealed the letter and placed it on the desk where she hoped he would find it among the other papers.

The fire had died down when she was set to leave, so she went to it, adding some wood and building it up a bit. With one last look at him, she departed.

THIRTY ONE

DARCY AWOKE WITH A SHARP PAIN THAT RADIATED DOWN HIS neck and into his back from lying on the uncomfortable chaise all night. The pale, weak rays of a November dawn were just beginning to illuminate the dusky sky as he opened his eyes.

He adjusted himself to more of a seated position, rubbed his eyes, and felt a sinking sensation as he was reminded of all that had occurred in the past days.

He supposed he should not be so entirely shaken by her rage. He had suspected vicious anger and bitterness all along. She certainly had cause. To some extent he had begun to accept her guise of contentedness, and now, the reality of her sensibilities was shocking.

It was not the fact that she had said she hated him that bothered him so. Hate was preferable to indifference at least. No, what had bothered him the most was how ardently she had expressed herself. The rage had nearly boiled over from her, and it was obviously deep and well rooted. How could such anger ever be mollified?

He would go to her and apologise, he decided. He would tell her he regretted this stupid idea of his and would cease to trouble her to relive the past and to discuss their sorrows. He would read and answer her letters for his own understanding and for the regard of her, but he would not force her to do it as well. Then he would have to hope that they could return to the state of cordiality they had lived in these past months and pray that in time it might grow to more

Darcy went to his desk, intending to gather up the letters and papers and put all of them away in a locked drawer somewhere. When he did, his eyes fell on a letter, sitting in the centre of the blotter and addressed to him. When was it written? From whence had it come?

He lifted it, not without some anxiety. Surely nothing good could be said therein? For a brief moment, he imagined it containing word that she was once again gone, fled to who knows where. His mind dismissed that immediately, but his heart would not surrender the fear.

Fitzwilliam,

I cannot imagine what you might feel towards me at this time. It cannot be denied that I allowed all the emotion that has been building over these many months full and unbridled leave last night, and you no doubt received far more than you ever imagined was within me. I would think you might despise me, but perhaps you will afford me a bit of pity as well. I hope you will, for there is much I need to say to you and a spiteful heart will not hear it so well.

When I returned to our home, I had but one goal, which was a civil marriage. I guarded myself carefully against my feelings for you, but I know at times I confused you with the occasional glimpse of what was truly in me: caring, tenderness, but also great anger and sadness. I knew you wished for more, and in some ways, I must own that I deceived you in allowing you to hope for that which I never intended to give.

It is difficult to be around someone who holds the power to destroy you. Someone who you try not to love because you know that your love for them could be your undoing, yet you cannot stop yourself. I have been clinging on to a precipice, knowing each day that my strength was failing me. It is frightening, and even more so in this instance, because you very nearly did destroy me.

You came to me, a young naive girl from the country who had never known anything of men or marriage or love, and you took me away from everything and everyone that I knew, and then you turned your back on me. You made me feel too ashamed to even speak to my family. I felt less than nothing, a shamed and despised woman, cast out and left behind, with nothing in the world for solace, and in truth, the girl who I once was, crumbled and fell away. I had always believed Elizabeth Bennet was a strong and courageous person, but in this, I learned that like anyone, without the loving arms of my family around me, I was as delicate in constitution as any.

I cannot say what might have happened had I not found such a person as I did to love me and to make me feel my worth once again. Through Amelia, I grew truly strong, but I cannot deny that the person who emerged from her care is much altered from the girl I once was. Then there was Bennet, and he too changed me, in ways both good and bad. Through him, I realised a greater purpose and a meaning of myself beyond just me.

I persuaded myself that the new, stronger person I was

would be well able to live with you yet abstain from loving you, but it was not so. Each day that has passed has seen my struggle grow more difficult and my heart grown more soft.

It is for that reason that I have so ferociously guarded myself against you. I could not bear to risk again that which had so nearly destroyed me before. I know not how I survived the time when first, you took your love from me and then, sent me away. If it were not for Bennet, I might not have survived it. For him, I forced myself to put my feelings aside and go on. For him, I lived. I know not whether I could ever do it again—it was so terribly diffi-cult and required every brave part of me.

Still, although I am so very afraid, I must admit I did not fully apprehend how very much these pains and miseries I have carried with me have affected me. I have been walking about with a heavy burden on myself with which I stupidly refused your assistance. Only now, when you have forced me to relinquish a bit of it, do I realise how much it has been there, pressing upon me and weighing me down. In opening the door to a scant bit of light, I have at last seen that I have been living in darkness, and I do not want to do that.

What I am trying to tell you is that although I love you and have never ceased loving you, I am terrified of you. You had everything of me that mattered—my heart, my mind, and my soul—and you tossed it away as though it was nothing. As though I was nothing. You became a heartless and cruel man who I knew not. A man who I despised and feared—and who I still fear—who haunts my worst dreams and shakes my belief in the love I thought I once knew.

When I returned to live with you, I did so because I had no choice. I did it for Bennet and because I was required to by the letter of the law and the vow I had made to you. I said that I would obey you, and so I did. But make no mistake, I did not want to come back. Even when I did, I vowed that I would give you only that which was needful and required. I vowed to myself that I would never, ever turn myself over to you as once I had. I did not want love from you, and I did not wish to return it to you. I wanted only civility and respectability and believed it would be enough to make me happy.

I cannot say at what point or spot that changed, but it has changed. I no longer want to hold myself apart, though the thought of being together terrifies me still.

I know not where we might go from here, but I believe I now wish to make an attempt to regain some of what we have lost. I realise I have hidden from this and made every effort to avoid it—it was my fear that compelled me thus. However now, I do wish to understand what happened, and in so doing, perhaps allow myself to finally, truly put it away. I do not believe we can go back. I think there are things between us that can never be altered, and perhaps we would not wish them to be. I believe we must attempt to build something new, something to take the place of these grievances and the hurts that hinder us.

I realised last night that I do at last have both a hope and a desire for something more between us than a civil union. I am not yet prepared to emerge fully, but I am ready to stop hiding in the dark behind a locked door.

I await you, should you still wish to speak to me.

Your wife

Darcy read the letter thrice, hoping his eyes did not deceive him. He wondered how it could be that he had fallen asleep late into the night believing that his wife hated him and the situation was irremediable, and now she wished to talk to him.

He cautioned himself against too much hope. In the past, she often had been clear that she did not wish to remember all the pain of the past. Perhaps when they began to discuss it, she would want to stop. Possibly she regretted writing this note or did not recall that she had agreed to talk to him.

He debated sending her another note, but he wished more so to talk to her and set off to find her.

It was still early, just after half past seven, so he began with her bedchamber. He went to the door that connected to his bedchamber and knocked softly, relieved when she bid him to come in. He entered with his heart in his throat.

She offered him a tentative smile, seeming quite nervous herself. He said nothing but walked towards where she was curled in the window seat. She straightened her legs, creating a space next to her, which he accepted for the invitation it was. For a minute, possibly two, neither one spoke.

"It would seem"—Elizabeth's voice came out a bit hoarsely, likely due to the lack of sleep she had had in the two nights past —"that I am a great deal more angry than I had previously suspected. I am sorry if that realisation came to me at the cost of wounding your feelings with the things I said."

Darcy shifted slightly and took her hand. "I could endure any amount of grief or vexation if I might have a hope that we could one day be well again."

Elizabeth looked down at their intertwined hands on the window seat. Slowly, she pulled them both into her lap and began tracing a light pattern on the back of his hand with her fingertip. "I do not like hurting you, but as you have said, we cannot go on until we deal with all of this. I can only hope I am not too late."

"Of course not." Darcy dared to lay his free hand against her face. "I want very much to hear anything and everything you have to say."

"Thank you." Ever so slowly, she edged closer until her leg touched his. "But what if..."

"What if...?"

"What if we bring up all this suffering, relive it all again, and it does not work? What if it makes no difference?"

"Please look at me." She tilted her chin up to look at his face. "We love each other—I know that is true. And whatever comes from our conversations, let us not forget that."

She nodded. "But we must realise things will never be as they were, nor will they ever be what they might have become. What we had before was a mere infatuation. It was passion and romance, but there was not the trust and honesty a marriage needs. We had not the foundation needed to withstand a trial, and it has led us to where we are this day."

"I know," he agreed softly. "That I do know."

"But I do want things to be better. I want to trust you again, much as it frightens me."

"I know you are frightened. Indeed, if one looks at this in a reasonable manner, there should be no inducement for you to ever trust or love me again. So I must appeal not to your reason but to your heart and plead with you to grant me the gift of your trust. Try me, that I might prove myself to you. I have changed, Elizabeth. I have grown and altered and banished the hard man within me who inflicted such pain upon you. Allow me to prove it to you."

She took his hand, pulling it to her lips for a kiss, then looked into his eyes. "Let us get to it, then."

THIRTY TWO

BEFORE BEGINNING WHAT WAS LIKELY TO BE A PROTRACTED AND emotion-filled discussion, Elizabeth and Darcy decided to dress and join their son for breakfast. It had become a daily ritual that Darcy said he would not forgo for anything. When they had finished eating, he quickly met with his steward to tell the man he would be not be at his disposal for the remainder of the day. Elizabeth told Mrs Reynolds and Nurse Harriet that, barring emergency, she and Darcy were occupied with important matters.

They settled in the sitting room adjoining their bedchambers, and for a moment, neither knew how to begin. Darcy spoke first.

"In this letter"—he gestured towards the one she had left for him the previous night—"you said that I tossed you away as though you were nothing. Before anything else, I must tell you, never were you nothing. You were, and still are, everything. It was only my exceedingly great agony over what I feared was happening that led me to wish for a brief separation from you."

"So you planned to send me away for just a short time?" Elizabeth asked carefully. It still caused her a stab of pain to refer to that time. Even speaking the phrase 'send me away' was extra-ordinarily hurtful, but she forced herself through it.

"Such was my despair at the time, it is difficult to recall my precise thoughts and plans. When I reached the decision to send you to Yorkshire, it was born from the notion that I could not think on our situation with reason when I was seeing you day in and day out. I believe I thought that I would find out the truth from Wickham—which I did, though not in the way I expected—and then you and I would resolve the problem between us. I also thought if you were with child, then we would be better able to hide it."

"Hide it... Except it was your own child."

"Yes."

Elizabeth felt a pulse of anger that she strove to maintain control over. "Did it ever occur to you—ever, even once—that you should ask me? You waved handkerchiefs at me and acted as though I should know things, but I had no notion of who George Wickham was!"

"I did not wish to ask you because...because I assumed you would lie. In any case, it all seemed so...so plausible."

"Your sister lied. Caroline Bingley lied. You had no reason to assume I would lie." Elizabeth's hands began to shake, and she struggled to remain calm. "And plausible? How did you think it plausible?"

"No! I...I was very confused and distressed, and I was not thinking clearly."

"How was it plausible that I, who had never corresponded with a man, kissed a man, allowed a man to touch my bare hands...how was it suddenly plausible that I might have had this illicit love affair?"

Darcy raked his hands through his hair. "I only meant it seemed plausible because we had not known each other very long. I knew hardly anything of you or your past."

"My past?" Elizabeth cried. She stopped herself a moment and breathed deeply, trying to gain control. "How is it plausible that you believed you had married a scheming, adulterous trollop? That I shall insist on knowing."

"This is coming out wrong," Darcy muttered. "I only meant plausible in the sense of me not knowing you and imagining you could be a different person than I had thought you were when I married you. Back then, I could only think that perhaps I had been deceived."

"What about my father's reluctance to allow us to marry? If I, and my parents with me, had schemed to trap you into marriage, would you not suppose he would have eagerly granted his consent?"

"That is very true, but alas, I did not think of it," Darcy admitted. "Not at that time. I did think of it later, after I knew the truth, and it was yet another thing I felt stupid for."

Elizabeth rose from her seat, feeling the need to pace a bit. "What if you had never learned the truth? What if it had been years? Would you have left me in Yorkshire forever?"

"I do not know," Darcy said, looking miserable. "I had no clear sense at that time what I was doing. There was no plan, I was only reacting. Please, darling, just think of it this way: when I began acting as I did, did you not have moments of doubt? Did you ever think I was a different person than the one you married and wonder whether you perhaps had been deceived?"

That did give her pause. As much as she was angry and upset, she wished to be fair and consider the situation from every perspective, including his. Yes, she had to admit that she had believed he was a different person—a worse person. She remembered worrying that she had made a dreadful mistake in marrying a man she scarcely knew, and she had those twinges of conscience where she thought her father had been correct.

"I did, several times, when I saw you acting so very differently from the man with whom I had fallen in love. But Fitzwilliam, that was based on your actions, not on falsehoods and stories from others. It was based on you."

"I know." Darcy lowered his head, his gaze on the rug at his feet. "My entire life I have feared that those around me would seek my friendship for only their own gain. In you, I believed I had found someone who truly loved me for me alone. To hear it was not so, shattered me and very quickly caused all my old fears to take control of my mind. It is so difficult, when we believe we see our greatest fears coming true, to put emotion aside and think rationally and sensibly. I was in agony, and I could hardly think for all that I felt."

Elizabeth considered his words for a moment. Of course, everyone had those deep-seated fears and worries. For herself, it was what her mother had always said—that she was neither so beautiful nor so good tempered as Jane. Although outwardly, she dismissed those words, inside, it did always trouble her just a bit. What if someone she trusted had come to her and told her Darcy was secretly in love with Jane, perhaps had even betrayed her with Jane? Could she have behaved rationally if faced with that?

She put such thoughts aside for later consideration. "But how could it be that you said you loved me yet thought so poorly of me? So very poorly, that to even question such lies was not considered. How could you believe such nonsense without the least attempt at verification?"

Darcy was silent for a moment, looking pensive, before finally admitting. "Mostly because I was too afraid to hear you say it was true."

HOW IRONIC IT WAS, THAT WHEN AT LAST ELIZABETH WISHED FOR these answers, he felt so inadequate in giving them to her. *Her.* It was never about her, was it? It was him and George Wickham and the tangled, dark web that had always been around them.

He began slowly, wanting to get it just right. "George Wickham and I share a complicated and difficult history, full of betrayal and me being taken advantage of for my wealth and station."

"But I am your wife. Surely my character should have accounted for more than history with a childhood friend."

"Yes," he agreed. "Except that in this case, you were the

young woman I had married but scarcely had taken the time to know, and he was the reprobate whose cruelty I had known most of my life.

"Wickham's father came to Pemberley to serve as steward when I was ten and George was nine. He was younger, but he seemed older somehow. He was adept at skipping rocks, he could jump on a horse, and he was permitted quite a bit of freedom—all very exemplary qualifications for a friend when you are a young boy, particularly a boy like me."

She asked, "What sort of boy were you?"

"I was shy. I never had an easy time making friends and preferred the company of my father above anyone my own age. I was eager to call George my friend, even with his frequent instances of unkindness. He was my confidante on one hand, but on the other, he would meanly tease me, blame me for his misdeeds, play pranks on me, and engage in unduly rough play, that sort of thing. But I cared not. I was just glad to be included even if it meant withstanding his abuse."

"Your parents did not see the truth of it?"

"My parents pitied him, and his father too. His mother was a horrid, vulgar woman, who abused George abominably in both word and deed. She often told him he was stupid and useless, she chastised him endlessly, and I had never heard a kind word from her directed at her son—or anyone else for that matter. George had had an older brother who had died when he was five, and she would frequently tell George she wished it had been him instead."

Elizabeth gasped. "How awful!"

"She beat him for anything and everything—I once saw her hold his head underwater in the horse's trough, screaming that she meant to kill him. I learned later it was for the offence of not finishing his dinner. He once tore a new pair of breeches, and she told him that if he meant to act like a wild animal, she would treat him as such. Then she tied him outside in the pen with an old, mean sow and left him to fend for himself overnight. My father learned of it from one of the stable hands and went out and untied him, then brought him into the house to spend the night. In the morning, he sent a note to Mr Wickham to retrieve him. All of this was only what I was witness to. George never spoke of it, and my parents and I never discussed it. I was too young.

"Soon it came time for me to go away to school, and I was distressed—I did not want to go. I begged my parents to send George with me, and so they did. Looking back, I believe they might have also wished to remove him from his home situation, but it was mostly at my instigation.

"Off we went to Eton, and it was there that George's schoolboy pranks took a more serious turn. He began to cheat on examinations, steal from the other boys, and as we grew older, dally with the serving girls and the maids from the village. I covered for him many, many times to keep him from trouble and from being expelled."

"Why?"

Darcy grimaced before replying. "I wanted him to like me. I wanted to be indispensable to him. Everyone liked him, and my connexion to him brought me some measure of acceptance at school. Although other boys would be friendly towards me, it was mainly because their parents told them to seek the connexion. They did not truly like me. I was serious and shy, and most of them thought I was arrogant and proud because of it. But if George was invited to be one of a party, then I would be too."

"And your father never knew?"

"I do not know," Darcy replied. "I think he might have had some notion, but his sympathy for George outweighed such concerns. And my father believed I needed him."

"What changed things between you?"

"Things changed for me at university. I made some other friends, gentlemen more like myself, and that opened my eyes to the fact that Wickham had really become quite dissolute. The true break came when my father died. I believe I have already told you of that."

"The issue with his legacy?"

Darcy nodded. "He was paid a fair sum as an equivalence for the living my father had set aside for him—three thousand pounds in addition to one thousand from my father's will. When that was run out, he wanted the living anyway and expected me to hand it over without question. My refusal was a shock to him, but I knew his true character then and did not yield, no matter how much abuse he heaped upon me. He vowed he would get his revenge.

"His first strike at me came in the spring before I met you, in '11. There was a young lady involved...I might have told you this story before?"

"A romantic attachment?" Elizabeth asked, in a gentle tease.

Darcy shrugged, feeling himself flush. "I liked her, but it had not gone beyond a few dances here or there. In any case, Wickham seduced her. Ruined her, in fact."

Elizabeth inhaled sharply. "Poor girl. I do remember you telling me this but not how it turned out."

Darcy nodded. "Her future was finished for one night with a handsome liar. She was sent to live in an aunt somewhere—in truth I know not what came of her since. But I did not love her, not nearly. I had never really loved anyone before, not until one night in an assembly room in a little village in Hertfordshire."

Elizabeth blushed and looked down at her lap.

"I had never felt anything as I felt that night, and truthfully, it frightened me how much I needed and desired you. I had never before considered myself a man who acted on impulse, yet I could not help myself. I was madly in love and exhilarated and scared because of it. I shall admit, there was part of me that believed I should marry you as quickly as possible before *he* found out about you, but mostly I just thought about how much I truly loved you."

Elizabeth sat quietly absorbing it all. "Given such a history, I suppose I can see why this tale that was concocted of Wickham being my lover...well, it does seem to fit into his pattern, does it not?"

"It did," Darcy acknowledged. "And the pain of it obscured my rational thought. I was angry with myself, him, you... My mind was filled with images of you and him conspiring against me."

"I should have thought it was quite clear on our wedding night that I was a maiden. Did you not think of that?"

Darcy looked to the side, fiddling with his watch fob. "George often said that he knew of things...ways for a lady to remain a maiden yet...not."

Elizabeth seemed to ponder that for moment before her mouth wrinkled into a frown of distaste. "I am not sure I can imagine what he must mean, but likely, I am better off not knowing. I begin to see why you grew so cold, so disdainful of me."

Darcy had lowered his head to gaze at the carpet beneath him. "There can be no just cause for the way I treated you. But every time I saw you, it was as if a hot brand went into my heart. I was in constant agony—you must not mistake what you saw for what I truly felt. I was in turmoil, every minute of every day."

Given his study of the rug, it was a surprise to feel her lean close. Still more shocking was the kiss she placed on the side of his mouth. He restrained himself as much as he could but then turned to her, placing one hand behind her head as he deepened their kiss.

ELIZABETH COULD NOT HAVE ACCOUNTED FOR THE IMPULSE THAT drove her to kiss him. It was not mere compassion, though that was surely part of it. His story stirred within her the love she had for him, then and now.

It felt good and right to be on his lap, to feel connected with him in this chaste, fully-clothed way, but she recognised too soon how much more she wanted from him. The thought made her pull back. She was not yet ready to abandon her quest for information.

With a final quick kiss, she slid away from him and asked, "Why did you not help me into the carriage?"

Darcy appeared dazed for a moment, then sat up straight and ran his hand though his hair. "Uh...help you into the carriage?"

"That scene has tormented me," she admitted. "On the day I left for Yorkshire, you just stood there staring at me while the footman assisted me into the carriage."

"Oh. Yes." Darcy sighed. "I knew that had I touched you, even briefly, I would grab hold of you and pull you tight. I knew I could never let you go. You were so dignified. Part of me almost wished you would kick and scream and refuse to go so I could keep you."

"When I was gone, were you relieved?"

"No, it was much worse. I ached with your absence, and the house seemed doused in sorrow. I hardly knew what day it was, what time...it was madness."

He went on to tell her more about the time she was gone, about learning the truth from Wickham, and his horror when he comprehended that Georgiana had lied and Miss Bingley had played her cruel trick. She had already seen his investigative efforts, so her next question was simply, "Did you believe I died?"

"No," he said firmly. "Perhaps it was fanciful, but I always thought I would feel it if you had died, as if a part of myself would go dead as well."

They sat for a moment in silence, contemplating all that had been said. At length, he asked, "And you? Will you tell me about your side of it all?"

With a smile, Elizabeth said, "Yes, I think I can if..."

"If...?"

"Will you kiss me again before I do?"

THIRTY THREE

HE LEANED TOWARDS HER, GENTLY CRADLING HER FACE IN HIS hands and teasing her mouth with his before deepening the kiss. She had forgotten how affected she was by him. Every sense swirled within her—the scent, the feel, even the sound of him kissing her in this way. She knew that in some ways she was likely torturing him; indeed, it was a torture for her too.

He pulled back and closed his eyes for a moment before asking, at last, "Is this a part of my punishment?"

She giggled. "It is. I am going to make you kiss me ardently at least ten times a day."

"That is hardly a punishment, though the unrelieved effect on me perhaps will be. But let us speak of you, please."

Elizabeth started by telling him much of what was in the remainder of the letters from Yorkshire: how she had tried valiantly to be of good cheer, believing in the advice of her aunt that if she could only sound accepting and not vex him, he would eventually wish to reconcile with her.

He rubbed his hand across his eyes. "Mrs Gardiner meant well, I suppose."

"She did." Elizabeth nodded sadly, then went on to tell him

of her dark days in Yorkshire. "Weeping and walking and sleeping. Then, when I realised I might be increasing and decided to leave, I became focused on that. With rare exception, I did not cry after that."

"Did you think long on your decision to depart?"

"No, I gave it hardly any thought at all. I could not subject my child to the life there. I was more afraid to imagine what might happen if I did not survive the birth. Would Mrs Nelson have cared for him? You were not responding to my letters, so I could not know what you thought or would do with him. I had many dreams in which I saw Mrs Nelson taking my baby to the foundling hospital."

With an unmoving gaze on her husband, she asked, "Did you know how it was in Yorkshire before you went there yourself?"

"I had no idea," Darcy admitted. "It belongs to a friend of Fitzwilliam, but that is no excuse. I should have asked more about it."

"I am sure, thinking of me as you did, that my comfort was not much of a concern to you."

"I could only really think of how much I wished you separate from your lover. I did not want him to be able to find you."

Seemingly from nowhere, a tear fell from his eye. Elizabeth was shocked by it but reached over and dabbed it away.

"Forgive me," he said. "I had a sudden vision of you there, so very alone—it really does grieve me. I am so sorry for what you suffered."

"It is in the past," she said gently, and for the first time, she meant it.

Darcy swallowed hard. "I want you to be happy. I know you have been unhappy, and afraid and sad, and I want you to know that if you cannot live with me, if our situation is unfixable, I could...I am willing to...go elsewhere. If you will it, I could live most of my time in Pemberley while you remained in London with Bennet, or vice versa. I shall tell you that although I would hate it, if it would bring you more true happiness, I would do that for you."

This made Elizabeth laugh. "Now you wish to know whether I would like to send you off? Goodness, what is to become of this family if all we do when we are sad or angry is send each other off?"

"I only wish for your peace and joy. I am willing to do anything for that."

Elizabeth studied him carefully. "No, I do not want you to live apart from us. Is that not why we have undertaken this discussion? So that we might improve things between us?"

"I did not mean it when I said I hated you. I was angry, very angry, and I wanted to lash out. In truth, I have at times hated myself for being so weak and allowing my love for you to overwhelm my need to exercise prudence and caution for the sake of my heart.

"I shall prove myself to you," Darcy promised. "I shall earn your trust, if you will permit me to."

Elizabeth smiled but could say nothing to this assertion; so much had been said already that needed evaluation and further consideration. She dearly wanted to believe him, and believe *in* him, but her fears could not be so easily dismissed.

With a deep sigh, Elizabeth said, "I find I am quite weary of this room and, indeed, of everything within-doors. What say you to a brief stroll of the garden? I need fresh air." Darcy agreed, and they parted briefly to prepare.

IN HER BEDCHAMBER, ELIZABETH PAUSED FOR A MOMENT, pulling from a drawer the first letter Darcy wrote, the one that initiated all of this. Her eyes fell upon a passage she had particularly appreciated when first she had read it:

I love you today even more ardently than the day I asked you to be forever mine, and even more passionately than

*the day you vowed that you would. I would give anything
I own to have your love once more.*

Her finger gently traced his words as she tentatively explored the feelings in her. *What is it that I want here? Is it recompense? Retribution? Those things cannot make me happy. They cannot make our marriage alive again, nor can they remove the sorrow in him—or in me. If I am ready to let go of this, it will be our love that soothes us while our trust and faith can grow.*

I want to have hope and trust and faith in him, and in our marriage again. I wish for us to be in love as we once were. I wish for us to have true happiness between us. It is a risk, and it is terribly frightening, but I believe I am prepared to face it.

To build trust, you have to start with trust. If your heart is closed, you cannot begin. I suppose it is the faith and love you have in one another that allows you to open your heart to another.

Darcy knocked at her door, and she bid him come in. Pulling his gloves on, he remarked, "Perhaps we should see how Bennet is occupied; he might wish for a bit of outdoor time."

She looked at him, and she realised that she could no longer deny how much she loved him and wanted him. In her, there was a sense, almost palpable, of release from the fears and sorrows that had bound her for so long, and in their place, was simple love and the beginnings of a desire to place her faith and trust in him once more.

"Come here," she said.

Uncertainly, he walked closer to her. She took his hand, tugging off the gloves he had just put on, then reached for his cravat, untying and undoing it before tossing it towards a nearby chair. She then slid her hands beneath his coat, easing it off his shoulders and dropping it behind her.

"What…what are you…"

"Has it been so long that you forgot?" She smiled up at him, feeling still a little unsure but hopeful.

"No," he said in a voice suddenly deeper and husky. "No, I could never forget. But do you want—"

"You?" She smiled at him. "I do. If you want me too, that is."

"Of course I do." Tentatively, he raised his hand to her hair, smoothing back her curls. "Is this…can I do this?"

"Yes," she whispered, and he reached into her hair, sliding out the pins that held it up. The heavy mass fell, her curls springing about wildly.

"So beautiful," he murmured, then leant in, kissing her with an ardency that grew quickly.

Although she understood her need for him, she could not have anticipated the depth of her longing. When he kissed her, she wanted to revel in the taste of his mouth, and when they had removed their clothes and lay side by side, she pressed towards him, wanting them to join.

"You are certain?" he whispered.

"Yes. Quite certain."

It seemed as though their coupling encompassed every bit of her, and when he moved within her, she grasped on to him, wanting him deeper. There was so much emotion and love for him within her, it was nigh on unbearable, and the depth of pleasure he gave her was sweetly agonising.

When it was over, they lay still, her head resting on his chest while his hand played idly with her hair.

"It is not so many weeks until we are married three years."

Elizabeth laughed lightly. "Strange as that may seem."

"I wish I could do it again."

"Which part of it?"

"All of it," he replied. "Ask for your hand, ask for your father's consent, and then stand in a church and tell you and God and our witnesses all over again how much I love you, and how I vow to care for you and protect you forever. Do it all properly this time, with no haste, no selfishness, and no resentful temper to mar us."

Elizabeth tilted her head and looked up into his eyes. "Well then: Will you love me, comfort me, keep me in sickness and in health, and forsake all others?"

He gazed at her seriously. "I shall love you beyond reason and provide you comfort to the utmost of my ability. I shall keep you always, and if you are sick, I shall stay by your side until you are well again. As far as forsaking all others—there are no others. There is only you, Elizabeth. Always and forever, only you."

"Will you have me and hold me from this day forward? Love me and cherish me until death do us part?"

He gently kissed the tip of her nose. "I shall have you and hold you and never let you go. I do love you…with my heart and my soul and my entire being. I cherish the day I met you, and still more, I shall cherish this day, when you have allowed me to dedicate myself to you anew. You are more to me than my own life, my dearest wife. There is nothing on this earth I would not give to you or do for you."

"That is quite a vow," she said softly.

"Yet there is more, for I shall also pledge to you honesty and faith and my belief in your good character, your wisdom, and your strength. I promise that I shall never fail you again, that I shall protect you from all harm and all sorrow forevermore. I shall be a man worthy of your love."

She could not answer this. Happy tears clouded her eyes, and felicity choked her such that she could only squeak out, "Thank you. That makes me so happy."

Darcy tightened his hold on her, kissing her gently. She felt a dampness against her cheek, telling her that he cried too, and it released her, sobbing with the freedom of at last loving him as she had wished to all along. She had felt so very alone for what seemed to be an eternity, that to be held and comforted so was exquisite.

Elizabeth felt herself slipping under the tide of her emotions as his tears mingle with hers, and she enjoyed the sweet sensation of resting in his embrace. Somewhat incoherently, she said, "I know I have not been truly willing to try and make our life happy…I was afraid…I am still a little afraid, but not really…"

Darcy, too, was a bit insensible, and he began to kiss her tears away. "I shall make you happy, I shall earn your trust, I promise you that. You will never have cause to fear me again. I shall do all I can to fix what I have broken between us. I have changed…"

"I know," Elizabeth said. "I believe you, truly I do."

It was unsurprising, given the nights of lost sleep and the turmoil of their emotions, that Darcy and Elizabeth both retired early on the day of their tentative reconciliation.

Although exhausted, Darcy could not forgo the opportunity to again kiss and hold her. After some time, she snuggled against him, wrapping her leg around his and throwing her arm across his waist. Her head lay on his chest, and he reached for her plait, loosening the tie around it and allowing her hair to flow freely over him.

She giggled. "You never have believed what I say about my hair. There will be tenfold more of it in the morning, and you will be inhaling it in your sleep."

"I shall gladly inhale it all night long, but if you wish it plaited, I can do that. I would not wish you to suffer tangles."

"You know how to plait hair?"

He paused a moment in the darkened room, then admitted, "I used to."

"Did you? But why?"

He shrugged. "I was guardian to a young girl. At times, there was no one else around, and her hair required plaiting."

"Now this I must see." She sat up and turned her back to him, pushing her hair behind her. "I must warn you though, curly hair such as mine can be more difficult to plait than straighter hair like Georgiana's."

"Is this a challenge? I shall have this plaited so quickly, you will be amazed."

He sat behind her, gathering her hair and attempting to divide it into parts. He soon realised what the problem was—curls sprung free, seemingly with a life of their own, and her hair appeared to grow as he worked on it. The strands of hair seemed to work themselves into knots as well as between his fingers. Just when he believed he had a semblance of a good plait, he then discovered half of the side had worked itself loose. He tried not to curse in frustration; instead, chuckling lightly, he combed through it with his fingers and then informed her, "Wait here, I shall summon Blake."

She laughed. "No, I can fix this. I have enjoyed your efforts however."

While she busied herself with tidying her hair, he excused himself for a moment. When he returned, he extended to her a small box. "I have something for you."

"What is it?" She smiled as she took it from him.

He gently caressed her cheek with the back of his hand then urged her to open it.

The box contained a beautiful ring, with several rose cut diamonds and emeralds. The band bore the inscription *de m'amour soiez sure*—of my love be sure.

Darcy took the ring from the box and slid it onto her finger, atop her wedding band. The two fit together nicely, as he had hoped they would when he had commissioned it from the jeweller's. He took her hand and gently kissed each knuckle.

"It is so beautiful," she said. "I shall wear it always."

THIRTY FOUR

BEING CAST OUT BY HER FAMILY TROUBLED CAROLINE BINGLEY not a bit. To think that they should all side with the horrid Eliza Bennet over their own blood was insupportable—and revealed they were all of weak character anyway! In his last act of brotherly concern, Charles had assisted her in finding her own place to live, and she found that much more agreeable. Decorating it in the most elegant style proved ever so diverting, and she made only the most fashionable, most costly selections. The result was far superior to anything Eliza Bennet might achieve, to be sure!

Then the bills came due, and she recognised she might have stretched herself a bit. Then more bills came, and she realised she had stretched herself a lot. A few bills more, and she was positively frantic.

For several days, she could not eat, scared from the effects of her mad shopping sprees. She kept adding the amounts, hoping there was some mistake, but there never was.

For a brief, mad moment she wondered whether Darcy actually would consent to keeping her. But no… Perhaps she could find someone to marry her?

She sat back, chewing on her nails and thinking about it.

Her friend Miss Grantley, rapidly consulted, had an immediate solution. "William Redmond-Creigh is said to be seeking a wife."

"Redmond-Creigh?"

"Very old family from Waterford," said Miss Grantley with certainty.

"Waterford?" Caroline asked dubiously.

"In Hertfordshire. You must know of it."

Caroline sniffed. "One cannot know too little about Hertfordshire, though it is close to London. How is it I have not heard of them in town before?"

"The son is here now and simply must marry. His father is reportedly very ill."

"How old and how ugly is he?"

Miss Grantley shrugged and picked up the large pile of bills that sat on her friend's writing desk. "Better looking than these are."

As it stood, Mr Redmond-Creigh was forty-seven but not so very objectionable. Old family and presumably the money that went with it… Caroline decided she could do that and then some. Someone had said he must surely live in a castle, and she rather liked the notion of herself as mistress of a grand castle.

She got herself invited to a dinner where he was present and, with a few words to the host, sat next to him at dinner. Desperation made her throw caution to the side, with any and all arts and allurements employed to her cause.

Her family might have been scandalised except they were not speaking to her, so any embarrassment was of their own doing. When Mr Redmond-Creigh found himself alone in a dark spot after dinner, she left him in no doubt of her intentions, and he, being honourable, thought himself quite in love.

When their hosts had grown alarmed by their absence, Lady Pugh-Dibley, who turned out to be cousin to Mr Redmond-

Creigh, did not want scandal in her house and sought them out herself. She found them in a lover's tangle in the servants' hall, and with a frown, told her cousin what he needed do.

"Gladly," the man said warmly.

"AND IT WAS AS EASY AS THAT," CAROLINE TOLD MISS Grantley a few days later. "I need no one's permission, thank you very much, and soon, I shall be mistress of a grand castle in Hertfordshire."

"Hertfordshire?" Miss Grantley asked.

Caroline rolled her eyes. "Yes! Waterford. Did we not have this conversation just a few days ago?"

"Oh...yes, I daresay we did. Did he say he was from Hertfordshire?"

Caroline paused a moment. "Well...not exactly. He told me about the castle, of course, and the sea..."

"The sea?" Miss Grantley giggled. "What sea is that? I was terrible at my lessons, as you well know, but even I know there is not a sea in Hertfordshire."

And so when Mr Redmond-Creigh came to call later that day, bearing the licence and other matters needed for the nuptials, he was asked immediately as to the precise location of his family home.

"Why, Waterford my dear. Did we not talk of this just last night?"

"Yes, of course, of course...and Waterford is in, um...?"

"Munster," he said. "I suppose you could say it is between Dublin and Cork."

Panic began to flutter in Caroline's breast. Although she was not certain, none of the names he said sounded like they were in Hertfordshire. Speaking carefully, she asked, "What part of England is that, exactly?"

With a laugh, he chucked her under her chin. "The Irish part, my love. Hope you do not mind a bit of rain!"

As December arrived, Elizabeth found herself increasingly easy when in the company of her husband. There had been more discussion of their time apart and painful remembrances would occasionally intrude; there were still tears and anger to be dealt with. But the sorrows did wane, and Elizabeth had no doubt that they would soon be gone for good. Not forgotten, by any means, but no longer the source of acute misery they once were.

Darcy continued to reply to Elizabeth's unsent letters, and she continued to read them. She had observed that, with each one, her emotions seemed less engaged, almost as if she were reading about something that happened to someone else a very long time ago.

"Have you read and replied to them all now?" she asked one evening while she got ready for bed. "It seems as though you must have."

"Most of them several times over. And you? Have you read all my replies?"

"I have." With a quick smile, she added, "Thank you for doing it."

"Have you a wish to speak of them?"

"Oh, I do not think so. We have said what needs to be said. Do you agree?"

Darcy considered it a moment. "I think most everything has been said many times over."

She walked over to where he lounged against her headboard. "So let us burn the lot, shall we?"

Darcy simply looked at her agape.

"We are almost at a new year," she explained. "The start of our fourth year of marriage, 1815, the hibernal solstice...let us put it all behind us. Knowing those letters remained has weighed on me. I wish them gone for good."

He gently traced her arm with his hand. "Then let us gather them up in the morning and—"

She gave him a quick kiss. "What if we did it now?"

After a short delay, in which Elizabeth gathered up those letters in her possession and Darcy found those in his, they settled themselves in front of the fire. Elizabeth tossed them in one by one, enjoying the burst of flame each one engendered. At last she was down to the end, a single sheet that she did not throw into the fire.

Darcy had risen and extended his arm to help her. "Will you not throw that away too?"

"This one? No, this I think I should like to keep."

Elizabeth watched as comprehension dawned on her very dignified husband's face. "Wha—oh...no. That is not...is that...I meant to get rid of that."

Elizabeth bit her lips to stifle a giggle. "I love it."

"I was trying to, um...it's terrible, I know."

"No, no," she said immediately. "It is charming, truly delightful." She could hold back no more, and gales of uncontrollable laughter burst from her. Darcy looked at her in absolute chagrin, then put his hands over his face in mock despair.

"I am certainly no poet. I cannot think what possessed me to attempt a sonnet. I only wished to somehow express to you how much I do love you. My letters seemed so dull and repetitive."

Elizabeth could not stop her gales of laughter and used her sleeve to dab the mirthful tears from her eyes. "Why be dull? Really, it is truly wonderful. Do not think I laugh because it is poorly done, not at all. I can tell you really love me by the way you compared my eyes to—"

Darcy tried to grab the page from her. "Very well then, enough of that."

Elizabeth scampered aside quickly, keeping the paper out of her husband's reach. "My mother has gone on for years about some former suitor of Jane's who wrote a few verses on her. Just wait until she learns of this ode to me and my eyes! How pleased she will be."

"Pray, tell no one of this, particularly not your mother!"

"Come now!" Elizabeth pulled herself out from his almost-grasp. "Poetry is the food of love, after all. I am quite flattered and thrilled to have one dedicated to me."

Darcy groaned. "The pointless nonsense of a non-poet is more likely to starve the love away." He lunged for her and caught her, picking her up and tossing her on the bed, then diving nearly on top of her. She attempted to raise the paper above her head, but his arms were so much longer that it was useless to try to avoid him.

She suddenly stopped laughing and looked at him in the eyes quite seriously. "Please let me have it."

"I can deny you nothing." Darcy rolled his eyes with a heavy sigh. "I cannot think why you would wish to keep it. It looks to be the work of a raving madman. For as much as I do enjoy reading poetry, composing it is another matter entirely. I am humiliated by such a poor effort."

"Perhaps the result is not what you wished it to be, but I do love it."

"Because it makes you laugh?"

"No. Well...perhaps a little. I like that you tried to do it for me most of all. I like that it is not—"

"Not poetic? Not interesting or coherent or in any way good?" Darcy rolled off her and lay on his back next to her, covering his face with his arm. "I beg you to please not show it to anyone. Would you wish the world to know you have married a simpleton?"

Elizabeth turned so she was over him. Looking at him, she leaned in and kissed him. "It is because it is embarrassing to you that I like it the most. This poem shows me you are willing to make a fool of yourself for me."

She kissed him again, more lingeringly, and then whispered,

"Every woman wishes for a man who is willing to be a fool in love for her."

Darcy insisted that they spend Christmas in Derbyshire despite the excess of travel involved. Elizabeth did not mind particularly as she was hopeful that snow, similar to that which was seen the year they married, might grace them—she was certain Bennet would love that.

So to Pemberley they went, and her hope was rewarded on the day before Christmas, though not in the quantity she might have liked. Still, they dressed Bennet as warmly as they could and took him out on a walk with his puppy bounding alongside him.

"What did you do last year on Christmas Day?"

He shrugged. "The Gardiners and Matlocks came to Pemberley. I believe I drank too much and wished for you. What did you do?"

She smiled a bit wistfully. "Amelia was very close to dying then, so I believe I thought on it but little. No one in the house was of a mood to celebrate in even the slightest way, and Bennet was too young to know it was any different than any other day. I believe we did have a special pudding with dinner—Cook insisted on it."

"Perhaps that is why I am quite eager for this Christmas to be perfect. As I recall my thoughts at the same time last year, I quite despaired of ever having you with me again, and now you are here, and I have a son whom I love beyond anything. If someone had told me last year that this time it would be so, I would have declared them quite mad."

"When seen in that light, I must agree with you," Elizabeth said. "That you found me, that we are where we are, is nothing short of miraculous." She tilted her head up to receive the kiss she wanted him to offer her.

"It is a miracle indeed," Darcy murmured, immediately

bending to kiss her. "And like most miracles, it is not deserved but hailed with great thanks."

ALTHOUGH THEY HAD GIVEN ONE ANOTHER GIFTS ON THE FIRST year of their marriage, it was not a practice they intended to keep. Nevertheless, Elizabeth had something for her husband—not really a present, but something she thought he would truly appreciate.

Darcy never tired of hearing stories about his son as a baby. Her sense of guilt for what she had denied him sometimes tore at her. He had missed eighteen glorious months in which Bennet had been born, learned to walk, waved his pudgy hands, crowed his little sounds… So much joy, and he had missed it all. To this, he offered no reproach, but still, Elizabeth knew she had denied him treasures.

She could not give them back to him, these small pleasures, but she did have one thing she wished him to have.

Although Amelia had not always been in her right mind, when she was, she was an excellent drawer and painter. As such, once Bennet was born, she delighted in making his likeness, and Elizabeth had a particular favourite from when he was only a few months old. He had lain sleeping on the grass, and Amelia had worked quickly and confidently, producing what was, in Elizabeth's mind, a masterpiece, from the curl of his hair to the flush on his cheek. Looking at it, one almost felt you could kiss that image and feel his precious warmth and smell his sweet baby smell. At the time the painting was done, Elizabeth had carefully and discreetly clipped one of his curls to put with it, tucking it behind the frame.

She carried the painting to the library where Darcy was reading, concealing it behind her back.

He rose when she entered, smiling to see her. She smiled back. "I have a small something for you."

"But we said no presents!"

"No, it is not really a present." She pulled the painting from behind her, handing it to him.

"Bennet," she said simply. "About three or four months old."

Darcy's eyes lit. "This is wonderful! Did you do this?"

She laughed. "No, Amelia did, before she became so very ill. You have seen my efforts—I could never produce anything so true."

"I thought perhaps you had grown far more proficient in our time apart." He then grew serious, sitting down to gaze on the image. "This is wonderful. I shall treasure it."

"There is this too." Taking it away for a moment, she showed him where the small curl was concealed. He took the lock of baby hair and gently traced it over his hand as he looked at the image, hardly able to tear his eyes away.

After a few minutes, she kissed his cheek. "Happy Christmas." She left him there, still looking at his infant son intently.

HAVING MISSED BOTH THE ACTUAL DAY OF HIS SON'S BIRTH AS well as the time he turned one, Darcy awaited eagerly Bennet's second birthday. The night prior, Darcy went to the nursery just as his son was being prepared for sleep. He had purchased a small pony, which even now was happily frisking about in the stable. Darcy found himself quite at sixes and sevens with his own anticipation of his son's joy in the animal. Bennet was quite sleepy, but still enjoyed having his Papa put him securely into his bed.

"Bennet, I am eager to celebrate your birthday. Two years old! Quite a young gentleman."

"Mama says cake," Bennet replied.

"Ah, yes. A special cake for a most wonderful son." Darcy stroked his boy's soft, rounded cheek. He could not help himself, and asked, "So tell me, is there anything you would especially wish for your birthday? A toy or…perhaps—"

"Butter," Bennet replied sleepily.

"Butter?"

"Butter," Bennet confirmed. "No sisters, just butters."

Darcy sat back, surprised by the request. Bennet had never seemed particularly impressed by his interactions with other children, but it seemed that might be changing.

"Well, brothers do take time to arrive, my darling. I do not think I can procure one for you by tomorrow."

Bennet mumbled something, having already succumbed to sleep. Darcy watched him for a few pleasant moments before going to the drawing room. Elizabeth was therein, playing some Christmas carols on the pianoforte. He joined her, always loving it when she sang to him.

When she paused, he informed her, "Our son would like a brother for his birthday."

She laughed. "Is that all? Let me see whether I have one in a closet somewhere."

He chuckled, his hand tracing her spine. After a short pause, he asked, "Bennet was...well, it was an easy birth, was it not? I believe you said it was."

"Oh yes. Nothing to it at all."

"So you would like more children or..."

She turned towards him then, giving him her attention in full. "I would love more children."

"Is that so?" He leaned in to give her a series of light kisses on her mouth. "How many?"

"A lot. Ten, twelve. So many that we would run out of names for them all."

"Seems we had better get started, then." He rose and quickly swooped her into his arms, ready to take her up to their bed, but her next words stopped him.

"If memory serves," she said with a little wink, "that fainting couch over there does very nicely."

Thus, the Darcys spent Bennet's birthday bleary-eyed, tired, and more in love with one another than ever. As Bennet stood in the stable shrieking with delight at his pony (who he named Horse, after being discouraged from naming it Pop), Elizabeth remarked, "This feels very much like the first days we were married, this feeling of…happy lethargy."

She gave her husband a smile that seemed innocent, but there was a naughty twinkle in her eyes.

"I like that," Darcy mused, and after seeing that the stable boy and Bennet were occupied with Horse, pulled her closer. "A felicitous fatigue, you might call it."

Elizabeth laughed just a bit, then with an arch look said, "A satisfied sleepiness perhaps?"

Darcy shook his head instantly. "Oh no, Mrs Darcy, not at all. I have missed you a very, very long time. Last night, delightful as it was, was not nearly satisfactory."

Elizabeth blushed and looked at him, murmuring, "I have missed you as well."

Spying the stable hand coming towards them, Darcy quickly said, "I adore you."

"As do I, you," she said with a tender look that nearly melted him.

THIRTY FIVE

January 1815

ALMOST AS SOON AS THEY HAD ARRIVED AT PEMBERLEY, Elizabeth received word from her mother that she was needed urgently at Longbourn immediately after the New Year.

"What now?" Elizabeth rolled her eyes. "She knows we are in Derbyshire. I think she wishes to see whether she can make me run to her."

"What if it is your father?" Darcy asked.

"If it were my father, she would already be asking how much she could spend redecorating the dower house here," Elizabeth replied. "Trust me, this is nothing. Do not think of it."

But strangely, Darcy insisted that she should go. "I really think it necessary," he said. "She would not summon you otherwise."

"Yes," Elizabeth said, "she positively would."

Darcy also claimed he could not attend her the entire way to Longbourn. "I shall set you as far as Harpenden and hire a coach for the last leg to London. I have some business that will not wait. You spend your time with your family and follow behind me."

"Your business cannot wait a few days? It is the festive season, no one in London is doing anything of consequence."

"Forgive me, darling, I must insist we abide by the plan."

She believed she knew what it was about. Relations remained strained between the Bennets and her husband. Darcy had done all he could to heal the breach, but her father responded to him but rarely, and her mother considered herself too busy to write letters.

Elizabeth fought the impulse to cry as she watched her husband board his arranged carriage at the small station nearest Meryton. She and Bennet continued on to Longbourn.

Why her mother had summoned her remained a mystery. Mr and Mrs Bennet had no true interest in their grandson, no one was ill, no one was getting engaged, and if anything, her mother seemed vexed to have her least favourite daughter lingering about. Her father was more amenable to her presence, though not so much that he was bestirred from his book room.

On the eve of her departure, Mrs Bennet said, "There is a gown upstairs you will need to take for Kitty."

"A gown for Kitty? But Kitty is yet with Lydia and Mr Rollings."

Elizabeth caught her father sending her mother a stern look that sent Mrs Bennet into querulous rambling about how, in her day, a young lady did not go here and there and all about the countryside such that their relations had no notion of where they were. In the midst of her effusions, another declaration was made —she would attend Lizzy to London.

"Well, if you will go, then I shall too," said Mr Bennet, to Elizabeth's utter shock.

"What? But, Papa, you despise London."

"Oh, not all of it. January is a dreadfully dull place in the country. A man needs a change of scene and society."

Before she knew it, she, her parents, and her son were in the

Darcy carriage, headed back to London. Her parents refused to stay in Darcy House, preferring the Gardiners' home. She thought it odd, when leaving her parents with her aunt and uncle, how unsurprised the Gardiners appeared to see them.

Darcy House was deathly quiet and nearly deserted when she arrived, with Mrs Hobbs seeming rushed and perfunctory in her duties to her mistress. When Elizabeth asked after Darcy, Mrs Hobbs flushed, saying, "I believe he has gone out, madam." Elizabeth frowned, wondering why he had not made the effort to be there to see her.

She went immediately to her bedchamber, trying to be unconcerned. Blake had already prepared her bath and had laid out a brand-new light blue gown that was more suited for a soiree at St James than a simple dinner with her husband. "Well, this turned out very well, but I think it is a bit much for dinner at home."

Blake blushed. "Beg your pardon, ma'am, but the master had instructed me specifically."

"Darcy told you what I should wear?"

"He did." Blake smiled ruefully. "Let us get you bathed, shall we?"

Elizabeth entered her bath more than a little annoyed. Darcy could not be bothered to greet her yet had chosen her gown for dinner? How absurd! She resolved that when she saw him, she immediately would demand an explanation for this behaviour.

She was silent as her hair was arranged, the coiffure an elaborate one. When she was finished, Elizabeth looked as pretty as ever she had. She complimented her maid's efforts, though she had to remark with more than a hint of sarcasm, "I am surprised Mr Darcy has not selected jewellery for me as well."

"I believe he has, in fact." At the sound of her husband's voice, Elizabeth looked up in surprise, seeing him leaning against the door frame. He looked so handsome, her breath caught despite her vexation with him and the worry he was causing her.

Darcy entered Elizabeth's bedchamber, pulling her from her seat at the table and into his arms for a passionate kiss. "I apologise for not greeting you when you arrived. I had some urgent matters of business that kept me occupied."

Elizabeth returned his kiss, feeling somewhat relieved though still vexed. Before she could speak, however, he handed her a box.

"You must allow me to tell you how ardently I admire and love you," he said. "And how grateful I am to you for marrying me, for giving me a son, and most of all, for allowing me your heart. You are too good for me, my darling."

With that, he opened the box, revealing an exquisite and enormous necklace and bracelet set with sapphires and diamonds. Her eyes went wide, and she gasped, seeing they were certainly the most expensive pieces of jewellery in her collection, which included the Darcy heirlooms.

"Oh! But surely I cannot—"

He stopped her, reaching around her and placing the necklace on her neck and the bracelet on her wrist. "Will they do? I believe they are rather nice with this gown, though I cannot deny I had the assistance of both Jane and Saye in the matter."

She was breathless with shock and amazement. "I…yes, they are perfect, but surely, just for dinner we need not—"

"Too true." He looked into her eyes a moment. "As beautiful as you are this night, it is almost as though there should be a ball in your honour."

So saying, he placed her hand on his arm, using his other hand to cover it, and then he began to stride rapidly out from their chambers and headed towards the front of the house.

"Where are we going?" As she was a good deal shorter than her husband, the effort of remaining at his side when he walked so quickly was not inconsiderable.

"Were you not listening? A ball!"

"Whose ball?" Then she heard it—strains of music in the air. "Here? We are having a ball?"

"I am having a ball," Darcy said. "In honour of you. I wanted to surprise you, so you would have none of the work and all of the enjoyment."

Elizabeth was filled with delight. The idea of a ball in and of itself was wonderful, and she was already anticipating an evening laden with enjoyments, not the least of which would be waltzing with her husband. More so than the ball itself, however, was the notion that Darcy had done all of this for her. He had planned and schemed and done so much, all for her benefit.

The ball was an undisputed crush. Elizabeth continually resisted the impulse to pinch herself to see whether she was dreaming as person after person came through the receiving line. Jane and Bingley were there, as were the Gardiners, Lord and Lady Matlock, Colonel Fitzwilliam and his wife, and Viscount Saye, of course. Lydia and Jolly had returned from their wedding trip, and they, with Georgiana and Kitty, were delighted to be among the group. Even Mr and Mrs Collins, though they carried with them the air of disapproval for such frivolity, had come to London to attend. Darcy House was filled to overflowing, and Elizabeth delighted in it.

Darcy and Elizabeth danced the first together, and from then, she was kept occupied by the gentlemen in her family: Saye, Jolly, Colonel Fitzwilliam, Bingley, Mr Gardiner—and her father even emerged from the card room to dance with his daughter. However, by the supper dance, Darcy had once again claimed his bride, and they enjoyed a waltz together.

The supper was...different. The entire meal was planned around Elizabeth's preferences. This was most evident when the desserts came, for such a profusion of sweets had never been seen in one place altogether. When she remarked on it to Darcy, he laughed, saying, "All of your favourites, my love. What else for an evening in your honour?"

ALTHOUGH MRS DARCY'S ILLNESS WAS NO LONGER SPOKEN OF, there were still some who, at times, wondered at the sudden emergence of Darcy's heir.

Viscount Saye found himself engaged in one such conversation. Being the gregarious person he always was, he found himself holding court in a large circle that included many noted gossips as well as Lord and Lady Carlisle. Lord Carlisle, a genial and none-too-witty gentleman, mentioned he thought it odd that although Mrs Darcy's illness had been reported, he had not heard word of Darcy's son.

Saye raised an eyebrow, a deeper shade of hauteur coming over his face. "Never? That is peculiar."

Carlisle looked unsure. "Tonight is the first I heard of the child, and he is already above two years old."

With just the faintest touch of pity, Saye replied, "You see, that is why I do not like to stay off in the country too long. You miss all the news! And then, when you do come back to town, you must spend half your time learning what everyone else already knows."

He watched Lady Carlisle flush. There was nothing worse than the suggestion that one did not know the town gossip. It implied a lack of friendship—or a general sense of exclusion. One had to exercise utmost caution in expressing what was known and not known, else appear to be out of the inner circle.

"Oh, my dearest, how silly you are!" she said to her husband with a maniacal titter. "Of course we knew. Why, dear Mrs Darcy is among my most intimate circle! I was distressed by the difficulties she had and so very, very worried for her sweet little boy...Bennet! Such a fine, strong-sounding name, Bennet! I saw him just the other day, and he is certainly the image of his father."

The tide of the conversation turned from there. No one would be fool enough to admit that they were on the outs of Mrs Darcy's circle, a circle that had been circumscribed by Lady

Matlock. All wished to appear that they had been fully aware of Darcy's heir almost from the moment he quickened.

"I SHALL NEVER UNDERSTAND YOU," SAYE ANNOUNCED, arriving at the side of Miss Lillian Goddard. "You are violently in love with me, yet when I see you at parties, you pay me no heed."

Despite herself, Miss Goddard blushed. She could not say exactly what it was about the viscount that endeared him to her. Yes, he was handsome, and yes, he was wealthy and titled. But that he was obviously aware of those facts far outweighed any attraction engendered by them.

"Violently in love? Sir, you have mistaken me for Lady Charlotte—she is across the room. Both of us so blonde, I can understand how it confuses you."

"Minx," he drawled comfortably. "Come, let us go into the courtyard and make your chaperon earn her keep."

She laughed. "Never."

"What do you fear more?" he asked. "What you might find? Or how much you might like it?"

She reached out with her fan, using the tip to give him a little shove in the chest. "Insufferable man."

"Insufferable perhaps, yet you suffer me gladly," he retorted. "Come now, Lilly, one kiss. Would it truly pain you?"

"I am not going to sneak off into the garden and kiss a rake!" she said, half-scandalised and more than a little captivated. The boldness of this man to simply request such liberties!

"A rake is only as rakish as his last rakism," Saye proclaimed.

"Rakism?"

"The act of being a rake," Saye replied blithely. "That is in the Bible you know." He took her arm and began leading her towards the back of the room.

"What Bible are you reading?"

"Oh, the one about forgiveness and so forth. My point is that I am keen to change myself for you, while at the same time, I am willing to permit this odd occupation of drawing fashion illustrations to continue. And still, you reject me! Why, I begin to think I must be mad to pursue you as I do."

Lilly was so astonished that she kept going along with him, somehow finding herself in the back of the house and then slipping out a side entrance into the courtyard. "Yes, you must be, for I have certainly given you no encouragement."

"That is just it, after all," he said, drawing her into a darkened area away from the line of sight of the door. "You are certainly quite spoilt and have given me very little consideration. Half of the time I call on you, I wonder whether you wish yourself elsewhere."

"I am not spoilt."

"You are. But not half as much as I should like to spoil you."

Looking up into his face, Lilly felt a strange pounding of her heart. She cursed it. She did not wish to have feelings for Saye. Every rational part of her protested against it. Yet he looked rather dear standing there looking down at her. Arrogant as ever, of course, but in his eyes shone a strangely vulnerable light.

"I like when you call on me," she whispered. "There have even been a few times when you did not, and I...I wished you had."

"Ha!" he crowed. "I knew it! You are obsessed with me."

That made her laugh, and she covered her mouth, hoping she had not been heard by the person—blast them!—who had just opened the door from the inside. It seemed they had been found. Lilly heard her aunt calling into the courtyard. "Lillian, is that you out there? Come back to the ballroom at once!"

"Last chance," Saye whispered. "If you want to kiss me, do it. A simple peck on the cheek will do; however, should you like to marry me...well, then only *un baiser amoureux* will do."

"Lillian?" It sounded like her aunt was advancing into the courtyard.

Auntie be hanged. Obeying an impulse she did not fully understand, Lilly leant in and kissed Saye directly on the mouth.

ELIZABETH'S BALL WENT ON WELL INTO THE WEE HOURS OF THE morning. Relieved of the usual duties that would have fallen to her as the host, she was free to dance the night away, which she did with relish.

Her husband claimed three dances, with a look on his face that dared anyone to object to such a social faux pas. "Whoever does not like it may leave," he informed his wife. "I make the rules here."

When the last guest had gone, it was very nearly dawn. By the time Elizabeth and Darcy at last fell into bed, it was past six in the morning. Elizabeth was asleep almost as soon as her head hit her pillow, her slumber filled with pleasant dreams. Indeed, when her husband began to trail kisses over her neck and bosom, she believed herself still in one of those dreams.

She groaned into her pillow. "I feel as though we only just lay down."

"Sleep as long as you like."

She opened her eyes and snuggled into him, noting that the clock on the mantel declared it was nearly eleven in the morning. "I had such a wonderful time last night. Thank you again." She laughed a moment, then teased him, "I still cannot believe you kept it so secret from me. As my sister Lydia would say, what a fine joke!"

THIRTY SIX

THE DARCYS' BALL HAD SERVED AS AN EXCELLENT reintroduction for Elizabeth into London society. Most everyone found it quite charming that Mr Darcy had planned it as a surprise for her, and several commented on how very much in love the Darcys were, and in particular, how sweet it was that Mr Darcy was so entirely besotted with her that, after three years of marriage, they seemed as though they were newly wed.

It was a relief to have her sisters back with her as well. Kitty elected to remain at Lydia's house, and Elizabeth did not wonder why. Lydia was determined, in a manner almost scandalous, to see Kitty wed, and the parties and balls were nearly continuous. The Darcys were far too sedate for such goings-on. Georgiana had returned to live with them in London but, unlike Kitty, showed little interest in the social whirl.

In April of 1815, Elizabeth began to feel unwell. She was often headachy and felt nauseated at strange times in strange places. Foods she had always generally liked might suddenly overwhelm her with their sight or smell, and fish was in no way tolerable.

One day towards the end of April, Elizabeth woke late,

feeling unaccountably muddle-headed. Darcy was in the room and teased her for her lassitude. She rose, a teasing reply on her lips, but suddenly, the room began to spin and Darcy's voice seemed far, far away. Her stomach churned, and she would have stumbled back had she not been close to the bed. Her hand reached out blindly, grasping her husband's shirt to steady herself, but it was of no use. She moaned, feeling a wave of nausea rise in her, and she gathered all of her strength to rush towards the water closet, praying she would make it in time.

Darcy was hard on her heels as she sank to her knees, nausea crashing over her in waves, and a light sweat forming on her brow. Her hands shook as she prepared herself to heave, knowing it would be unpleasant but welcoming the relief it would give her.

But nothing happened beyond that. The nausea subsided, leaving a faint, metallic taste in her mouth. She breathed heavily, willing her stomach to settle. Her husband knelt beside her, gathering her into his arms, smoothing back the curls around her face. "Let us get you back into bed. I shall call Blake, for you are clearly unwell."

She shook her head, already feeling immeasurably better with the clutch of nausea abated. "No, that is not necessary." She smiled at him, inhaling a deep, calming breath. "I am well enough now."

He stared at her in surprise. "You are ill."

She rose to her feet unsteadily, Darcy reaching out his hand to assist her to her feet. "I shall be perfectly well."

"You are certain?"

"Quite." She smiled up at him. "Nothing some toast will not remedy!"

She felt healthy for the remainder of the day, albeit a bit absent-minded as thoughts and dreams danced in her mind.

THE NEXT DAY, DARCY HAD BUSINESS WITH HIS SOLICITOR THAT required his attention for a good bit of the morning and early afternoon. At two, he at last returned home, inquiring immediately of Mrs Hobbs as to the location of his wife.

Mrs Hobbs assisted him in removing his hat and replied, "Mrs Darcy is asleep in her bedchamber, sir."

"Asleep! At two in the afternoon?"

Mrs Hobbs nodded. "Yes, sir. I believe the late nights you have kept recently have taken their toll on her."

"Of course. I shall be in the study when she wakes."

Darcy had a good bit of work awaiting him, and it engaged his attention in full, so much so that he was shocked to see the time was nearly five o'clock when he remembered to look for his wife. *Mrs Hobbs has clearly forgotten my summons.*

She was not sitting with Georgiana, and his sister denied having seen her at any time that day. The library was empty, and the parlour was bare. Darcy went to their chambers; seeing an empty sitting room, he went directly into Elizabeth's bedchamber. He was very surprised to see her still in bed, though she had evidently begun to stir. He went to dress for dinner before going to her, thinking that when he returned, she would have wakened completely.

She was awake although she remained in bed. He sat next to her on the bed and reached out his hand to feel her head, which was cool.

"I am worried about you."

She stretched. "No doubt it is our late nights that have fatigued me."

He frowned slightly. "Then we must curtail our engagements. I cannot have your health ruined by blasted parties and balls."

She gave him a sleepy smile.

AS DARCY SMILED BACK AT HER, SHE GAVE HIM AN APPRAISING glance. His shoulders looked so broad and manly beneath his coat, and he had clearly been running his hands through his hair as he worked as it had a fetching, tousled appearance. She felt her heart rate gain speed as she allowed her eyes to travel downwards over his muscular chest and tight thighs. Goodness, but Darcy was a handsome man! How very long it felt until they could decently retire.

Darcy stood. "I would imagine you would like to dress for dinner then." He leaned over and kissed her.

Quickly, she placed her hand on the back of his head, rising up on her knees to press her body to his. She had had the foresight when she lay down to put on a night-shift, knowing her nap would be long; thus, there now was little between them but his clothing and her thin linen gown. The heat of his body enflamed her, and she ran her hands underneath his coat to pull his hips closer.

"Elizabeth? Are you...do you want...?"

"I do want," she said with an impish grin. "Do you?"

Darcy appeared to be gaining favour for the idea but seemed a bit baffled by the unexpected turn of events. "But dinner with the Smythe's..."

"We shall be quick about it."

A LITTLE MORE THAN AN HOUR LATER, AS THEY ENTERED THE carriage that would convey them to their dinner engagement, Darcy looked at his wife with great contentment.

It had been just under six months since what Darcy considered their true reconciliation had occurred, after days of fighting and despair that had been painful but led to some true healing for both of them. With each day that had passed since, he felt more sure of her happiness and more secure in his own.

He looked over at her, so beautiful in the sunlight beaming in through the carriage window. He wondered whether she had any idea of the power she held over him. Power that he gave her gladly, pleased beyond measure to be held in the palm of her hand, knowing it was only through her mercy and goodness that he was permitted to dwell there.

The dinner they attended was pleasant. Their hosts, the Smythes of Warwickshire, were genial, and Mrs Smythe set a bountiful table and was known for her ability to arrange her guests in a manner ideal for stimulating conversation. This night was no different.

Elizabeth was seated next to a former acquaintance, Captain Norman Bolton, and Darcy could not help but glance at them as they spoke. The conversation had begun in an animated fashion, but now Elizabeth seemed more intent and sympathetic.

Darcy wondered for a moment whether he were jealous, but then realised he was not; Elizabeth was a beautiful, vivacious woman who spoke to a man's interest, and he must have become accustomed to that. She had tolerated much from him, then gave him and their marriage a second chance and continued to love him despite all that had happened. There could be no more grievous insult to her than to grow jealous because she spoke to a man at dinner.

After dinner, once the ladies had withdrawn, Darcy found himself approached by Mr Thomas Haverhill. Haverhill was a widower who lived near Lady Catherine in Kent, and Darcy had known him for years.

"Darcy! May I join you? Darcy agreed and the man sat down next to him.

"I had the very great felicity of seeing Miss Bennet and Miss Darcy at the opera last week with their companion."

"Was the performance to your liking? My sisters felt it sublime."

"It was wonderful, though I own I was more interested in seeing Miss Darcy than I was the show. That is why I seek you out this evening. I would like your permission to call on her."

Darcy nodded slowly, considering it. "I shall speak to my wife and tell her to expect you."

WITH ALL THE PERVERSENESS OF FATE, ELIZABETH APPROACHED Mr Haverhill when the men re-joined the ladies in the drawing room after dinner.

Elizabeth had met Miss Jenny Haverhill, Mr Haverhill's sister, at a card party in Weymouth in the summer of 1813. Although the acquaintance had been necessarily constrained by the secrets of Elizabeth's situation, they had met again in London and became fast friends. She was a lovely girl, with excellent manners, good accomplishments, and a handsome countenance, but she was yet unwed at the age of three and twenty. Elizabeth suspected that her failure to secure a husband was likely due to the inability of many gentlemen to appreciate a woman with a quicker wit than most.

However, as she conversed with Captain Bolton at dinner, an idea had been born, and she quickly approached Mr Haverhill for his thoughts on an introduction. Darcy almost laughed aloud at the expression on Haverhill's face as the man stammered about. "Ah, well, naturally any friend of so regarded a person as you, Mrs Darcy, would be...I suppose Jenny might...she is above one and twenty, so my influence..."

Laughing, Elizabeth laid her hand on his arm. "Mr Darcy and I shall host a small gathering in the next weeks, just a few people, and perhaps contrive to see them together in that company. The rest we shall leave to them."

Haverhill acceded reluctantly but only after Darcy cleared his throat and asked his wife (with a bit of a pointed glance at Haverhill) what day she might like to receive the man. Elizabeth named the day, and Haverhill agreed. "It is a bit tricky, this business of sisters, is it not, Darcy?"

Darcy grinned and replied, "You will find no sympathy here, Haverhill. You have one, and I have five. And by the time they are all settled, I shall likely have daughters to consider."

Haverhill laughed as Elizabeth blushed, with a sweet glance up at her husband.

ANXIETY FOR HIS WIFE'S HEALTH LED DARCY TO PERSUADE Elizabeth to be among the first to depart the party. As she entered the carriage, Elizabeth remarked, "Were not Richard and Marianne meant to be there tonight? I was surprised not to see them."

"I believe Marianne was indisposed."

"I do hope it is nothing serious."

"Richard says little of it, but from what he has said, I fear it weighs heavily on her that she is not yet with child. You might not realise this, but she was with child when they married and then lost it."

"Oh no!"

"Indeed." Darcy offered a wry smile. "I think she believed it would have happened many times over by now."

"What are Richard's feelings about it?"

"He was eager to become a father. We spoke of it one day when they were only just engaged, and he was quite pleased. I am sure it is disappointing to him, but Marianne is full young. There is time for her."

Elizabeth nodded and did not say anything more. Sorrow had suddenly overwhelmed her, though she knew it was excessive. When she could abstain no more, she pulled her handkerchief to her face and tried her best to sob silently.

"Elizabeth!" Darcy immediately moved closer, pulling her into his embrace. "What is wrong?"

She allowed herself to weep more fervently. "It is just so sad! Oh, the poor, poor things! Dear, sweet, Marianne, so bereft! And, Richard, his disappointed hopes! Oh, it breaks my heart, truly, it does."

"Well...I think they both know children sometimes take years to come. I do not doubt that they will be blessed shortly."

"I know," Elizabeth said with a sigh. "Still to imagine life without Bennet—terrible indeed. I only want everyone to know such happiness." Unable to stop herself, she allowed a few more tears to escape but soon regained her composure.

THE DINNER PARTY HELD A WEEK LATER WAS AN ENORMOUS success. Georgiana was taken with Mr Haverhill, and Captain Bolton and Miss Haverhill got along famously. The only part that was not a success was Elizabeth, who found herself drooping into her tea after dinner.

"Georgiana," she whispered to her sister at an opportune moment. "I need you to act in my stead for the remainder of the evening."

"What?" Georgiana asked in shock.

"I cannot stay awake," Elizabeth replied ruefully. "I want to, but I simply cannot. Make an excuse for me." She rose and began to leave, but in terror, Georgiana grabbed her arm.

"Lizzy, no! I could not, I promise you!"

"You can and you must," Elizabeth insisted gently. "Tell them I took ill."

"I cannot, oh Lizzy, please, please do not make me."

"Georgiana," Elizabeth said sternly. "Did I not forgive you what you did? Have I not done what I could to help you move past your errors?"

"You have," the girl admitted.

"Yes, I have," Elizabeth replied. "And have scarce asked a thing in return. But now I do ask—nay insist—and you will oblige me."

With that, she left her own party into Georgiana's hands.

June 1815

ALTHOUGH NO ONE COULD FAULT HER—INDEED, MOST BELIEVED they understood the likely nature of Mrs Darcy's malady but were happy to await an announcement—Elizabeth's abandonment of her dinner party made Darcy adamant that they leave London. They departed in early June for Pemberley with Georgiana alongside them.

He was relieved to see that, almost immediately, Elizabeth

seemed to recover her energy and her appetite. She was even able to resume her walks, and soon after their arrival, he found her sitting on the bank by the pond. Her book lay beside her as she looked over the water, a light breeze causing her curls to dance around her. As he approached, she gave him a welcoming smile. He sat next to her, and she leaned towards him.

"I am grateful you are feeling better."

"I am, thank you," she said. "Though when you learn the source of my ailment, you might understand it was all for the best."

"The source of your ailment?"

She took his hands then, pulling them to lay atop her stomach.

"Another child, my beloved husband. We are expecting a blessing."

He felt joy suffuse him in a rush. "A child! Another child!" He burst out laughing. "When?"

She laughed. "November or December, I think."

"Do you think it is a girl or a boy?"

"I have no idea," she said with another laugh. "Our son wishes for a brother."

"I wish for a girl, one just like you."

"What exactly is a girl like me? Limited in stature with a bent towards being impertinent?"

Darcy teased, "That about sums it—but also good, kind, and loving, a lady who brings joy to all she meets."

"You are a wonderful father, and I am so eager for our child to know you."

"You are the finest mother anyone could ever hope for," Darcy replied. "Indeed, I almost hope there is more than one child in there, for as good as you are, there should be many who benefit from it."

November 1815

As Darcy stood at the window of his study at Pemberley, he thought that never had a day passed so agonisingly slowly as the one in which he was currently mired. Then he chastised himself for such a cowardly thought, for it was Elizabeth who suffered and underwent travail. All he needed to do was stand here and await the appearance of his child. It was she who made the real effort. Still, waiting was difficult, particularly when nothing could gain his interest.

Elizabeth's pains had begun early in the morning. When he had awoken, the dawn was just beginning to emerge, and Elizabeth already was pacing the room, clearly in misery. Darcy leapt from his bed, "Has Nurse Harriet been summoned? I shall fetch her. Where is Mrs Reynolds? What shall I do? Do you require my assistance? Please, darling, sit. Or do you prefer to stand? I shall stand with you, then."

Incredibly, Elizabeth had laughed, though she ended it with a grimace. "We have only just begun, my dear, you must stay calm."

He ran his hands through his hair, which was already a bit unkempt from sleep. "Impossible! I must do something."

"Darling, your part in this is long ago done. 'Tis the business of ladies from here on. Go and get dressed, have your ride, and enjoy your breakfast. I assure you, I shall still be much the same when you are through."

He immediately declined doing any such thing, but she insisted. He did not ride but dressed quickly and then went to his son for a brief breakfast. Georgiana was already there, having received the news through her maid. They both greeted Darcy happily, and their cheer was reassuring.

"I have just been telling Bennet that by the time he goes to bed tonight, it is quite likely he will have a new brother or sister. Is that not right, my darling?"

Bennet replied firmly, "Just a brother."

"Alas, Mama cannot take requests in this matter. I was an

older brother to a younger sister, and it was quite agreeable, I assure you."

Georgiana smiled with a light blush. "Brother, worry nothing for Bennet today. I told him that his mama needs Nurse Harriet, but I shall play with him all day."

"Good." Darcy might have said more but he heard Mrs Reynolds bustle by in the hall, and his heart leapt. He rushed out of the room. "Any news? Am I needed?"

Mrs Reynolds smiled, and he could see clearly how exhilarated she was, a pink in her cheeks and a sparkle in her eyes. "Do not worry for even a moment, sir. Nurse and I shall take good care of your wife and baby. She is doing very well, but these things do take time."

"Of course," he responded dully, then returned to Georgiana and Bennet. They had finished eating, and Georgiana was selecting clothing for Bennet to take him outdoors.

Georgiana shooed him away. "You just attend to Elizabeth. I shall take care of your son."

Darcy nodded slowly. It seemed everyone wished to remove from him all source of occupation so that he could focus on his wife, which was kind but, alas, left his mind nothing to do but fret. Slowly, he walked towards his study.

His alarm was heightened because it seemed she was earlier than had been foretold. They had anticipated the end of November or the beginning of December, but it was scarcely November. Her sister had wished to attend her but naturally had not yet arrived, and to that end, Mrs Reynolds had sent a stable hand to Hopton to inform them of the proceedings, urging the man to ride with haste.

Bingley was announced in his study just before the noon hour. Darcy had spent the intervening time standing before his window, feeling a pain in his gut and a sweat on his brow. Mrs Reynolds periodically came into the room to assure him all was proceeding according to plan, but he could not so easily dismiss the feeling of foreboding that was upon him.

"Darcy! Old man, you are looking quite unwell! Chin up, there, we have a long day ahead of us." Bingley grinned even as he clapped Darcy on the back and handed him a bottle of brandy. "Brought that special for you. Let us drink to your son or daughter!"

"It is scarcely noon."

"Just a bit to relax." Bingley grinned. "You look terrible."

Darcy took a small swallow. "Thank you. Jane is gone to her then?"

"I could hardly keep her back. I thought she might climb on top of the carriage and take over the driving herself if those men of mine had not hurried things along as they did." Bingley laughed but then took on a reassuring tone. "It is a frightening thing, I know, but there is little you or I can do for it. It is all up to Elizabeth and the child now."

Darcy rubbed his hand across his forehead, "It is so early, that is all." He sank into a chair next to his friend.

"Ahh, early. Well, they never really know precisely, do they? It is all just a guess, so they were off some weeks for her. In any case, I have been through this twice now, and believe me, the best is for us to occupy our minds with something else. Now, do you remember Mr Robert Archer? He would have been two years behind you at Cambridge, and he married a Miss Cantwell, who was from…"

With that, Bingley was off and running, keeping up a steady monologue of pointless *on dits* and twaddle, told for the sole purpose of attempting to remove Darcy's mind from the agonising pain his wife was in and the possibility that she might be, even at that moment, facing death. Darcy was grateful to him for it; it did not work, of course, but it did serve the purpose of passing time.

It was not until later in the evening that things became truly difficult.

Bingley, Darcy, and Georgiana had dined together, or rather, Bingley and Georgiana had dined, while Darcy pushed food around on his plate and wondered why gentlemen could not be permitted to attend their wives during the birth of their own children. Mrs Reynolds had faithfully reported to him nearly hourly, but it would seem that the progress had stalled, and the ladies anticipated a difficult night.

After dinner, Darcy had gone to the nursery, where Georgiana was assisting Bennet in preparing for bed. Not wishing to disturb his son's nightly routine, he settled in to read to him.

When Mrs Reynolds appeared at the door, he knew instantly something had gone wrong. Her face had lost its eagerness, which was replaced by concern and fear. He was up and out of the room almost before he knew he was in motion.

"Mr Bingley has already gone for the doctor." She matched his rapid stride down the hall to the room wherein Elizabeth lay. "You must not worry. There is just a little difficulty, but it will be well. Things have stopped moving along, and Mrs Darcy...Mr Darcy, sir, you must not go in. A birthing room is no place for a gentleman."

Darcy cared nothing for that. Having reached the door, he knocked and began to push it open simultaneously. Jane met him, looking surprisingly stern. "Everything will be well, Darcy. Her pains are exhausting her, and the baby is not moving. It is very common."

"Please let me see her?"

Jane was shockingly firm, putting her hand on his arm and pushing gently to remove him from his wife's room. "If you are here, then she must worry about you too. At the moment she needs to focus on herself and your child."

He spoke vehemently, "If something were to happen to her, I would wish her to know how very loved she is. Please, Jane, just five minutes. You must permit it."

"Jane?" It was Elizabeth's voice but very weak. "A few minutes cannot hurt."

His first thought as he approached the bed where she lay was of how very wretched she looked. Her hair was laden with sweat, her face was pale, and her eyes were bloodshot. His heart ached to see her so, even as fear pulsed through him. He sat next to her on the bed, and a tear fell from his eye as he took her hand, using the other to smooth away the sweat-drenched curls. "I would do anything to take this from you."

What she might have replied was lost as a pain hit her at that moment. Nurse Harriet said hurriedly, "Sir, you will want to—"

But it was too late. On the crest of birthing pain, Elizabeth clenched his hand. Darcy very nearly emitted a shriek as she gripped his hand with such a ferocity that it felt as though she broke it. Her grasp tightened as she pressed her face into his chest, tears flowing freely down her face, and rode the pain to its completion. Darcy disregarded the pain in his hand, welcoming it and wishing it could somehow lessen that which Elizabeth experienced, though he knew it did not.

When her pain eased, she released his hand and leaned back into her pillow, her eyes closed and her face sweating. "I am so, so tired. I just need a little rest."

Leaning down, he kissed her face, taking a nearby cool cloth and wiping her brow. He smoothed her curls back, and whispered, "You can, my darling, you can do this. Look at all you have done. You are a wonderful, remarkable woman." He gently kissed her brow. "I love you so very much."

"Bennet did not prepare me for this. This is much, much worse than before, I must admit it." She laughed weakly. "You see, I told you that he was so easy, our next would be a terror. It begins already, just as I said it would."

He chuckled lightly but quickly sobered. Speaking in a low voice, he said, "Promise you will not leave me. I must have your word on this. You are tired, I know, but you cannot give into it, please. Have strength, love, please."

She looked into his eyes, hearing the voice of the doctor outside the door. "I promise you," she whispered. "I said I would not leave again, and I shall not."

With one last kiss, he allowed Jane to shoo him from the room.

Despite every effort of the doctor and Nurse Harriet, the baby, Arthur George Darcy, was not born until the wee small hours of the next day. Darcy was drinking his third pot of coffee, and Bingley was snoring peacefully on the chaise lounge in his study when Mrs Reynolds came to tell him the news.

"However, you will not go to her just yet, sir. Mr Blackmore believes there is another."

His own fatigue rendered him witless for a moment. "Another what?"

Mrs Reynolds laughed. "Another baby."

"Another baby? Can she manage it? Is she well?"

Mrs Reynolds grew sober. "I cannot lie. She is very weak, but I think she can do it, sir. She is staying strong."

It was not more than an hour later when Amelia Jane Darcy chose to make her entrance into the world. Mr Blackmore went to Darcy in his study while Nurse Harriet finished attending Elizabeth.

Darcy felt as thankful as he ever had in response to the man's news that Elizabeth, although exhausted and in a great deal of pain, was alive and as well as could be expected. "Mr Blackmore, I am very grateful to you."

"It was not an easy birth and having twins is always complicated for the lady. I would not be surprised if there were no more after this. But they are strong and healthy children, and you have much to be thankful for."

Darcy smiled with relief, bidding the doctor adieu and nearly running to his wife's room.

Nurse Harriet had left the door ajar as she left to dispose of some of the linens, and he pushed it open gently. Elizabeth was sound asleep on the bed, the babies asleep beside her.

Silently, he joined them, gazing down at his precious family, feeling all of the rapture of the moment fill him. He pulled his babies into his arms, looking at them and thinking of nothing more but how very impossible it seemed to love someone so ardently who you had only just met.

He knew not how long he sat there, but seemingly at once, it was morning, and there was a gentle knock at the door. Georgiana had brought Bennet to greet his brother and sister, and his cries even managed to rouse his mother.

Darcy settled the twins carefully in their mother's arms and pulled Bennet onto his lap. He smiled. "You kept your promise."

"Always," she vowed.

Bennet was disappointed to learn that Arthur was not going to be able to play with him that day or, in fact, for many days. It would seem he had expected a baby of Thomas Bingley's size to be born, but Darcy told him he must be patient, that it would not be so long until Arthur would play right alongside his older brother.

Bennet then set his eyes on his sister. "She is pretty, like Mama."

"Yes, she is," Darcy agreed.

"Will she play with Arthur and me?"

"It will take her some time as well, but soon enough, you will have two friends in the nursery to enjoy games and schemes with."

Bennet studied his sister carefully. "I do not wish her to be a dull girl like Liza," he pronounced, referring to young Elizabeth Bingley.

Elizabeth laughed at him. "Your cousin is a sweet girl. She simply enjoys playing indoors and doing ladylike sorts of things."

Bennet shrugged. "All she does is smile."

He shifted his seat to look at his new sister a bit more closely. Amelia opened her eyes and looked at him, so he spoke to her directly. "Amelia, you will not scream at bugs or be afraid to get dirty."

Darcy laughed. "Yes, well, if she is anything like her mother, then I believe you may depend upon it."

Bennet wanted to touch his brother and sister then, and Elizabeth asked for some assistance in moving herself up on the bed to make room for Bennet. Soon they were situated, a beautiful mother and her three children, and Darcy was overwhelmed by his happiness at the sight of them.

Elizabeth smiled up at him inquiringly as Bennet gently patted his new brother and sister.

"You have given me treasure beyond compare, my wife." He bent and kissed her. "Never misunderstand how much I love you."

EPILOGUE

London, 1817

"Miss Bingley is with child?" Darcy's voice rang out with shock, shattering the peaceful dark of their bedchamber. "How did that happen?"

"Oh, the usual way I suppose," Elizabeth teased gently. "Cast your mind back about fifteen minutes if your memory requires refreshing."

Darcy groaned. "I shall thank you not to put such notions in my head when the name of Miss Bingley yet hangs in the air. But who is her...? Surely not...?"

"Mr Frederick Fitzwilliam," Elizabeth confirmed.

"Who has just married."

"And who does not believe the child is his."

Elizabeth felt his head shaking. "Does he have cause to think thus?"

"I cannot say. To be sure, Miss Bingley has not...maintained her good character."

Miss Caroline Bingley had scandalized the *ton* some years past by ending her engagement to a very kindly Irish gentleman,

Mr Redmond-Creigh. Since breaking the poor man's heart, she had grown increasingly forward and desperate in her attempts to secure a husband. Most had come to see her as nothing more than an embarrassing fortune hunter.

"Jane tells me that she has vastly overspent her income. They think she has been gambling."

"Bingley will not consent to taking her in."

"Nor will my sister plead her cause."

Jane could not and would not forgive her sister-in-law Caroline for the acts she had perpetrated against Elizabeth. Elizabeth was alternately gratified and embarrassed at her sister's fierce loyalty, but as Jane often said, no consideration would tempt her to accept a woman back into her house who had so injured a most beloved sister.

Mr and Mrs Hurst had all but turned their backs on her as well. Caroline's acceptance among the ladies of fashion had always been tenuous at best.

Alone and bereft of the guidance of her elder brother and sister, Miss Bingley had gone from one poor choice to the next. Her only goal seemed to be to entrap a wealthy man, and her methods grew increasingly desperate as the years went on.

"How many know?" Darcy asked. "Is it all over London?"

"I do not think so," Elizabeth replied. "Lydia and Kitty called today and neither said anything about it, and you know how they love to gossip. It was not until I was alone with Jane that she told me what happened."

Miss Bingley had gone to her sister-in-law in desperation. Having found herself short on funds, she had taken a position—though she never referred to it as such—as friend-in-residence to Mrs Charles Fitzwilliam, cousin of Lord Matlock. It was shortly thereafter that she became dear—and rather too near—to the widow's thirty-three year old son, Mr Frederick Fitzwilliam.

"Were it anyone else," Darcy opined, "I might believe she fancied herself in love. Freddie does have a certain charm. But knowing Miss Bingley as I do, one cannot know whether she was the predator or the prey."

"In any event, Mr Fitzwilliam got married, and Miss Bingley got...something she does not wish for." After a short pause, Elizabeth said, "I am thinking of Richard and Marianne."

"Thinking *what* about Richard and Marianne?"

"That they should adopt the child."

Elizabeth knew she was not the only one who had seen the grief of Richard and Marianne Fitzwilliam. The years of their marriage had yielded nothing but disappointed hopes. Though she was yet young, Marianne had confided to Elizabeth that she knew not how much more she could take of the endless cycles of promise and despair.

Darcy sighed. "The child will have Fitzwilliam blood, assuming Miss Bingley is being truthful. But is this the way it will be now? Having successfully made matches amongst all your acquaintance, you will move on to procuring babies for them?"

"A matchmaker? Fitzwilliam..." Elizabeth chided gently. "Surely you do not accuse me of that?"

"Well, my beloved, what do you call it?"

"I introduce people who I think might be well suited, nothing more!"

"And should the need arise, host balls, dinners, theatre evenings, and walking parties to continue the introduction right into matrimonial bliss."

Elizabeth laughed. "Have I been truly so dreadful?"

"Dreadful?" He shifted in the bed, drawing her closer. "I daresay that Georgiana would not think it so, particularly as she is so happy with Mr Haverhill."

"And Captain and Mrs Bolton as well," Elizabeth replied with a little sigh. "Ah, but I am quite fond of Jenny. She is a dear, sweet girl. I suppose you will accuse me of making Kitty's match next, but she is so very shy—"

"Shy? Kitty?"

"—she absolutely required my assistance, and in any case, I think she will be very happy as mistress of the parsonage in Kympton."

"Such bleak times! No more Bennet sisters left to settle, and all our acquaintances wed, or nearly so."

"And all the daughters too young to think of just yet. Yes, these are dark days indeed." Her giggle belied her words.

"But what of Miss Bingley?" Darcy asked. "I do not think it will surprise you when I say I dislike the idea of being involved in any business of such a woman. It is nothing less than taking a viper to our family bosom."

What Elizabeth could not—and would not—say was that she had all too many reasons to sympathise with Miss Bingley. Alone, facing her lover's abandonment, carrying a child, and unsure of her future—it was a position she knew and would not wish on anyone, not even this woman. For Elizabeth, such feelings were long in the past, but it did not mean she could not feel for another. Such a fragile position women occupied! Mr Frederick Fitzwilliam could, by choice, walk away from his misdeeds, but Miss Bingley, alas, could not.

"Will you consent," she asked softly, "to a mere visit? The four of us, perhaps? Or Marianne and I alone?"

She felt his gaze upon her, though with the curtains drawn and the room mostly dark, they could not see one another. She heard him sigh. "You have never left anyone to the fate they deserve, including me, so of course, I cannot deny you this."

Miss Bingley received Elizabeth and Marianne in the parlour of the Widow Fitzwilliam's house in town. Elizabeth had not seen her for some years and found her much the same as she ever was. She had always been a beautiful woman, her features marred only by the spite of her character; now, those same features were creased and wrinkled by worry.

She did not send for tea.

"Your relation is from home," she said by way of greeting. "You find me alone this morning."

"We know that," said Elizabeth. "We wanted to speak to you, only you."

"Oh?" Miss Bingley glanced at the calling cards the footman had brought her as if they might have some clue as to what the two ladies wanted. "Why?"

Elizabeth could feel Marianne tense beside her. She had confided her anxiety in the carriage ride over, and she now sat as if she expected a blow or might cry. Elizabeth laid her hand over Marianne's to steady her. To engender a short delay, she said, "It has been a long time since we last met. I wished to see how you were."

Miss Bingley narrowed her eyes and stared at Elizabeth. "Come now, Eliza, you hate me."

"I do not."

"Well, you should."

"I choose not to. Why should I let hate corrupt my felicity?"

Miss Bingley scoffed and rolled her eyes. "Is that why you are here? To show that no matter what I have done, you still have him and he is still besotted with you? And that your life—the life that *should* have been *mine*—is perfect?"

"That is not why we are here."

But Marianne, her tension coiled within her like a spring, burst out, "*My* life is not perfect. Far from it."

Miss Bingley shot her a mean look. "You are daughter to an earl and have everything you should wish for."

Elizabeth patted Marianne's hand. "No, she does not, Miss Bingley, and do not presume that money and position can satisfy everyone. She wishes for something that you have and she does not. And that, my dear, is why we are here."

Miss Bingley's back stiffened almost imperceptibly. "I do not know what you mean."

Elizabeth nodded. "I daresay that you do."

A vast array of emotions washed across Miss Bingley's countenance. Fear, loathing, relief, sorrow, delight—too many to comprehend or identify—there and gone in a trice. She lowered her face too quickly. "Jane is a gossip."

"Not at all," Elizabeth assured her. "She came to me, and me alone."

"So there you have it," said Miss Bingley bitterly. "Ruination, just as I deserve. You must be thrilled to see me so low. Mrs Fitzwilliam does not know yet, but I shall be out as soon as she does, and then what is left for me? I shall never be received anywhere ever again, my sister and brother will disown me even more than they already have, I—"

Elizabeth had risen and gone to her side. Pushing herself into the narrow space beside her on her sofa, Elizabeth took Miss Bingley's hands in hers. Marianne watched with wide-eyed hope and fear commingled.

"Yes, that is all very likely—unless you allow me to help you."

Although her face looked as mean as ever, tears began to wend their way down Miss Bingley's cheeks.

Marianne found her voice, thin and high though it was. "I cannot have a child. Your child is of Fitzwilliam blood. I could… it would…"

Pressing her lips together tightly, Miss Bingley nodded. "You would adopt him or her."

Elizabeth nodded. "Yes. It would be their child. You would be—"

"Nothing," said Miss Bingley quickly. "I would be nothing."

There was a short pause among the ladies. Elizabeth broke the silence after some minutes. "You would live at Richard and Marianne's home, unseen, until the child is born…"

"No one would be the wiser," Marianne finished. "Everyone knows the troubles I have had. It would not be surprising that I should retire to the country for the sake of the child."

"But that I should go with you?"

"You were dearest friends at school," Elizabeth said firmly.

"And wanted to provide companionship during this difficult time."

For a long time, Miss Bingley sat in contemplation of the notion. Elizabeth did not think Marianne breathed a single breath throughout. At last, she said, "Afterwards, I think I should like to go to the Continent. People there have a broader view of things."

"Italy," Elizabeth suggested. "Or Barcelona. Our musical friends, the Esparzas, might have some suggestions for you or know who could help."

"Everything would be arranged," Marianne promised breathlessly. "You would not have to fear for anything."

THE DIFFICULTIES SHE HAD DURING THE BIRTH OF HER TWINS HAD left Elizabeth thinking she was likely unable to conceive another child. It left her rather wistful—Bennet's infancy had been fraught by so much anxiety in so many different ways, while the twins left her ill for a time and exhausted for an even longer period. She always thought, privately, that it would be nice to have just one more child. Girl or boy, it did not signify, but her heart felt there was one more to be had.

Alexandra Fitzwilliam was born on a fair day in April 1818. She was a gentle, sweet baby whose looks bespoke her Fitzwilliam heritage. When they joined the new family at their country seat, Elizabeth fell instantly in love with her, as did Lillian and Saye, who had themselves managed only two boys to that point.

"An heir and a spare," said Lillian with a cheeky smile at her husband. "Now I need someone to keep me company in the drawing room."

"I shall take you upstairs right now," Saye promised with a grin. "Richard, which room should you like us in?"

"None," said Richard. "And pray do not tease so when my daughter's ears can hear you."

Miss Bingley had refused to hold her, would not even look at her. "I cannot do this otherwise," she said, with a slight tinge of apology in her words. "Eliza, you will understand me."

And strangely, Elizabeth did. She knew not how her former adversary did it, but Miss Bingley left her bed mere days after the delivery and was on her journey to Italy in only a week or two. Jane and Bingley received a letter from her some years later, telling them she was married to an Italian nobleman and had a son and two daughters. They replied to her but heard nothing thereafter.

With all the perverseness of fate, Marianne found herself increasing shortly after Alexandra's birth. "It will go the way of the others, I am sure," she told Elizabeth and Lillian. "I just wish I could hurry it up—I am too busy with dear Alexandra to be laid up forever."

Oddly enough, it did not. One of the midwives Marianne consulted told her that with all her anxiety gone, it likely made her womb more hospitable to the child. Thus it was that Marianne found herself with a son in 1819 and another in 1821. A third son was born in 1825.

Jane and Bingley had five children, as did Lydia. Kitty had only two before childbed fever nearly killed her. After that, there were no more for Kitty, though she was content. Mrs Collins, as she liked to be called, had one well-behaved son and one prim daughter to her credit. Elizabeth hoped for Mary's sake that she had barred her husband from her bed.

But for Elizabeth, the elusive child, the one she felt would make them complete, did not come. Years passed, and her fortieth birthday soon loomed.

"Forty!" She exclaimed one day to her husband. "How is it possible?"

She was sitting at her dressing table, staring at a dreadful array of grey hair amongst the arrangement of her curls.

"And still as beautiful as ever," Darcy proclaimed, bending to kiss her.

"That is always easy for men to say. They do look handsome

with some grey at their temples—quite distinguished. Ladies just look...older."

She supposed she must be glad for, no matter that her waist was thicker and when she smiled, her eyes crinkled too much, Darcy's ardour had not dimmed a bit. They often embarrassed their children, particularly Amelia, who at sixteen, found her parents' delight in one another unseemly. "I suppose all children are disgusted by imagining their parents in the activity that they know was needed to create them," said Darcy.

For Elizabeth, it was a peculiar time. Mr and Mrs Bennet had recently passed away within days of one another, and her children needed her less and less. Bennet was at university, surrounded by dozens of friends, and was in and out of the house like a whirlwind—when he came home at all. Amelia and Arthur would soon be out. Amelia was already a noted beauty, and with her fortune, Elizabeth was sure she would marry quickly.

With a sigh, she told her mirror, "I daresay, then I just wait for grandchildren."

As soon as she said it, the odd gassy feeling she lately had been experiencing hit her again. A strange burble, deep within her—she suspected it was due to eating too much cheese, or perhaps coffee? She knew not. Rising from her dressing table, the feeling grew stronger, almost as a...well, it felt very much as it did when she was increasing with the children.

"You know," she said to her husband as they walked through town later that day. "I have had the most peculiar sensations in my stomach. Almost as though..."

"As though what?"

"Well, it is nothing of course. What could be more unusual than a woman of my years, with three children nearly grown...?"

"What is it you are saying?"

"Nothing. I am saying nothing." She smiled up at him. "Forget I mentioned it."

But Darcy would not forget it. He asked about 'the burble,' as they called it, over the next few weeks, at last insisting that a midwife be sent for.

"You should not be the first," the midwife said, tossing a scornful look at Darcy. "Some men never do outgrow their boyhood appetites."

"Never," Darcy mouthed silently at Elizabeth, "until I am dead."

"I do not think I need to tell you what danger comes with a woman of your years having a child." The midwife then rattled off every possible disagreeable effect of the pregnancy, from fainting spells to death, and stomped away promising to look in on her in a month.

"A baby," Elizabeth said with no little wonder in her voice.

"A baby," Darcy confirmed. "But we must keep you healthy. No bulbous veins or unseemly fits for you, my love."

Besides the unexpected nature of it, Elizabeth's pregnancy caused her little to complain about. There were raised eyebrows amongst the *ton* and much slapping of his back from Darcy's friends, but on the whole, most were happy for them.

Although it had been over sixteen years, when her time came, Elizabeth's body remembered exactly what to do. The large, squalling girl who arrived—Violette, they decided—was not her easiest delivery, but it was easy enough.

They presented her to her older brothers and sister when Elizabeth felt well enough for everyone to join them in the drawing room upstairs. Bennet was amazed by her, Amelia was entranced, and Arthur thought she was the prettiest of all of them.

Elizabeth was at last contented, looking around her at the handsome, tall people who were kind and of good character. She smiled at her husband, who was telling them all that they needed a family portrait done, and she had but one thought in her mind.

We are at last complete.

A Fine Joke

What would you do, knowing you had only weeks to live?

Such is the question Fitzwilliam Darcy faces shortly after his visit to Kent in 1812. A gentleman of honour, he decides he will go to his end having done his best to discharge the duty of providing an heir for Pemberley. A gentleman of passion, he decides it will be with a bride who suits his own fancy. Going immediately to Hertfordshire, he meets with Miss Elizabeth Bennet and asks her, a second time, to marry him, with the knowledge that the marriage will be short and that she will be soon left a wealthy widow.

Elizabeth agrees to be Darcy's bride feeling all the compassion of a woman granting a man's dying wish. However, soon she suspects the truth, that Darcy is not, in fact, dying. She begins to question what exactly happened between the time that Darcy proposed to her the first time and when he was given his dreadful diagnosis—and if, in fact, any of it is indeed true.

The Mysteries of Pemberley

Elizabeth Bennet made her sister a promise on her deathbed: to love and care for her son, young Charles Bingley, like her very own child. And so she did, for four years, until the boy's guardian, Fitzwilliam Darcy showed up in Meryton, insisting on removing the boy from his aunt, his life and everything he knew, to be raised at Pemberley.

Elizabeth, determined to honor Jane, insists on going with them, soon finding herself installed at Pemberley as an unwanted guest of Mr Darcy and his aunt, Lady Catherine de Bourgh. It is 1816, the year without a summer, and Pemberley is austere and ghostly, with shadows and secrets lurking in every corner. With too much time to herself, Elizabeth soon finds herself wondering about Mr Darcy's past, and the identity of a young lady who she reads about in the lady's journal.

She soon thinks she has a faithful sketch of Mr Darcy's character until one key truth emerges which shatters all her prepossessions. Bit by bit the mysteries of Pemberley unravel—but what will she find at the end of it?

A Lady's Reputation

"Mr Darcy, I am eager to hear your explanation for the fact that quite a few people believe we are engaged."

It starts with a bit of well-meant advice. Colonel Fitzwilliam suggests to his cousin Darcy that, before he proposes to Elizabeth Bennet in Kent, perhaps he ought to discuss his plans with their families first.

What neither man could have predicted however was that Lord Matlock would write the news to his sister, or that Viscount Saye would overhear and tell his friends, or that his friends might slip a little and let their friends know as well. The news spreads just as quickly through Hertfordshire once Mrs Bennet opens the express Mr Bennet receives from Mr Darcy, and in a matter of days, it seems like everyone knows that Mr Darcy has proposed marriage to Elizabeth Bennet.

Everyone, that is, except Elizabeth herself.

Her refusal is quick and definite—until matters of reputation, hers as well as Jane's, are considered. Then Mr Darcy makes another offer: summer at Pemberley so that Jane can be reunited with Mr Bingley and so that he can prove to Elizabeth he is not what she thinks of him. Falling in love with him is naturally impossible…but once she knows the man he truly is, will she be able to help herself?

A Short Period of Exquisite Felicity

Is not the very meaning of love that it surpasses every objection against it?

Jilted. Never did Mr Darcy imagine it could happen to him.

But it has, and by Elizabeth Bennet, the woman who first hated and rejected him but then came to love him—he believed—and agree to be his wife. Alas, it is a short-lived, ill-fated romance that ends nearly as soon as it has begun. No reason is given.

More than a year since he last saw her—a year of anger, confusion, and despair—he receives an invitation from the Bingleys to a house party at Netherfield. Darcy is first tempted to refuse, but with the understanding that Elizabeth will not attend, he decides to accept.

When a letter arrives, confirming Elizabeth's intention to join them, Darcy resolves to meet her with indifference. He is determined that he will not demand answers to the questions that plague him. Elizabeth is also resolved to remain silent and hold fast to the secret behind her refusal. Once they are together, however, it proves difficult to deny the intense passion that still exists. Fury, grief, and profound love prove to be a combustible mixture. But will the secrets between them be their undoing?

The Best Part of Love

Avoiding the truth does not change the truth.

When Fitzwilliam Darcy meets Miss Elizabeth Bennet, his heart is almost immediately engaged. Seeing the pretty lady before him, a lady of no consequence or fortune, he believes he should not form an attachment to her, unsuitable as such a woman is to be his wife.

What he cannot see, however, is the truth, that the simple country girl harbours a secret. Before she meets Darcy, Elizabeth has spent two years hiding from the men who killed her beloved first husband. Feeling herself destroyed by love, Elizabeth is certain she will never love again, certainly not the arrogant man who has offended her from the first moment of their acquaintance.

In time, Elizabeth surprises herself by finding in Darcy a friend; even greater is her surprise to find herself gradually coming to love him and even accepting an offer of marriage from him. As the newly married couple is beginning to settle into their happily-ever-after, a condemned man on his way to the gallows divulges a shattering truth, a secret that contradicts everything Elizabeth thought she knew about the tragic circumstances of her first marriage. Against the advice of everyone who loves her—including Darcy—Elizabeth begins to seek the truth, knowing she must have it even if it may destroy her newfound happiness with Darcy.

ABOUT THE AUTHOR

Amy D'Orazio is a long time devotee of Jane Austen and fiction related to her characters. She began writing her own little stories to amuse herself during hours spent at sports practices and the like and soon discovered a passion for it. By far, however, the thing she loves most is the connections she has made with readers and other writers of Austenesque fiction.

Amy currently lives in Pittsburgh with her husband and daughters, as well as three Jack Russell terriers who often make appearances (in a human form) in her book.

A Wilful Misunderstanding is Amy's sixth book.

ACKNOWLEDGMENTS

My deepest appreciation goes to all who contributed to the publication of this book. Many thanks to my beta readers and the commenters at A Happy Assembly (AHA) for their valued support during the initial stages and to my editors Gail, Julie, and Jan who took it from the head-hopping, heavily anachronistic, borderline sadistic mess that it was into something fit for publication.

Special acknowledgement goes to Meredith Esparza who is an adored and much-respected member of the JAFF community for her support of our authors. Meredith made a special donation to the Jane Austen Variations fundraiser for hurricane relief back in 2018 to have a cameo in this book—I hope she and her own dear husband have enjoyed the roles I gave them!

Lastly to Tom, Allie & Lexi—I love you all.

56151991R00234